Praise for *Pure Blood*

'*Pure Blood* pounds along hard on the heels of *Night Life*, and is every bit as much fun as the first in the series. With a gutsy, likable protagonist and a well-made fantasy world, *Pure Blood* is real enough to make you think twice about locking your doors at night. A swiftly paced plot, a growing cast of solid supporting characters, and a lead character you can actually care about – Kittredge is a winner'

New York Times bestselling author Jim Butcher

Praise for Caitlin Kittredge's *Night Life*:

'I loved the mystery and the smart, gutsy heroine'
New York Times bestselling author Karen Chance

'Don't go to bed with this book – it will keep you up all night. It's that good'
National bestselling author Lilith Saintcrow

'Luna is tough, smart, and fierce, hiding a conflicted and insecure nature behind her drive for justice and independence, without falling into cliché. It's also just a lot of fun to read'
National bestselling author Kat Richardson

'Fast- paced, sexy, and witty with many more interesting characters than I have time to mention'
Fresh Fiction

'The last time I reacted to a book this way, it was the first Mercy Thompson book by Patricia Briggs'
Night Owl Reviews

'A tense, gritty urban fantas
from the
Mystery C

D1386933

Also by Caitlin Kittredge:

Night Life

Pure Blood

Second Skin

A NOCTURNE CITY NOVEL

PURE BLOOD

CAITLIN KITTREDGE

First published in Great Britain in 2010 by
Gollancz
An imprint of the Orion Publishing Group
Orion House, 5 Upper St Martin's Lane, London WC2H 9EA
An Hachette UK Company

1 3 5 7 9 10 8 6 4 2

A CIP catalogue record for this book is available
from the British Library

ISBN 978 0 575 09373 7

Printed in Great Britain by Clays Ltd, St Ives plc

www.caitlinkittredge.com

www.orionbooks.co.uk

The Orion Publishing Group's policy is to use papers that are
natural, renewable and recyclable products and made from wood
grown in sustainable forests. The logging and manufacturing
processes are expected to conform to the environmental regulations
of the country of origin.

For Richelle and Jackie,
truly the best friends anyone could ask for.

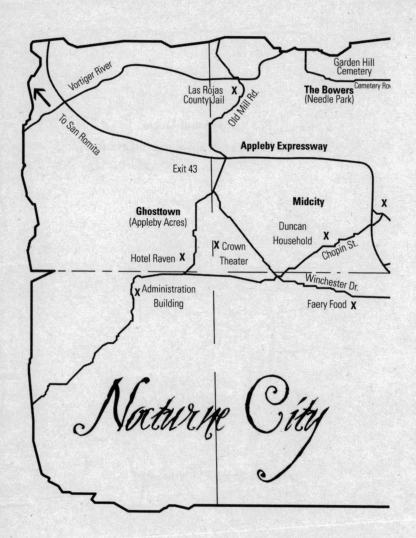

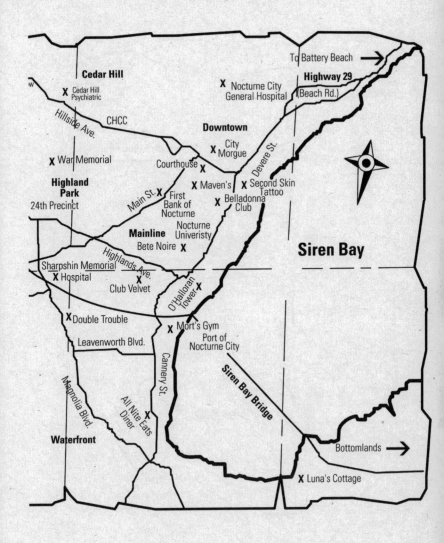

CHAPTER 1

I'm not a patient person under the best of circumstances. Standing next to a dead man on a cold city
sidewalk is not one of them. Add in the fact that I was
the only homicide detective on the scene, and had been
standing around stamping my feet and rubbing my hands
together for almost half an hour, and you could kiss
any patience I started the night with goodbye.

I grabbed Officer Martinez by the elbow as he walked
past, headed to his patrol car.

"Where in seven hells is CSU?"

He shrugged. "Sorry, Detective Wilder. There was a
drive-by shooting on Archer Avenue. Could be another
forty minutes. We're low priority tonight."

I looked back at the dead man. Under the flickering
sodium light his cheeks were gray hollows and his eyes
receded until there was only black. He was thin, with
grayish skin that puddled around his neck and wrists. A
tan uniform shirt did nothing to cover the track marks
on his forearms, between his fingers, in the fold of his
elbow . . . everywhere. If I took off his shoes I'd find
them in his ankles, his toes, and anywhere else a vein
might be hiding.

A simple OD doesn't usually warrant a homicide detective, but I had been driving to work and picked up the call. It was a block away, so I swung by. By the way the dead guy smelled, I was wishing I hadn't. He was stale—stale skin, stale sweat. The tang of cooked heroin burned the back of my mouth as I inhaled.

"CSU is on the way, Detective!" Martinez called from his patrol car. I rolled my shoulders. Thank the gods. I was in a bad neighborhood with limited backup, and someone in the dark row houses that lined the street was probably itching to shoot me right this second.

"You want a cup of coffee, Detective? I got a thermos in the prowler."

I shook my head at Martinez, who looked sweetly disappointed. He was baby-faced, stocky and short, but had blazing black eyes and big hands that could probably snap a suspect in half.

"I don't drink the stuff."

"Something a little stronger?" He pulled his blue satin jacket aside to show me an engraved silver flask. My mouth quirked.

"Your captain know you have that?"

"Don't ask about the captain's late-night lady visitors, he won't ask about what you do on patrol." Martinez grinned back at me. "Hey, don't take this as a come-on or nothin', but you look familiar. You didn't just transfer in, did you?"

I sighed. It had to happen sooner or later. Savvy editors had slapped my headshot from the police academy on the front page of every major newspaper in Nocturne City. Above the fold. "I've been on medical leave for three months. Just got back today."

"Three months . . ." Martinez's gears ground for a second and then he blurted out, "Hex! You're that cop that killed the DA!"

"*Former* DA," I growled, "and it's not like he didn't try to kill me—*and* call a daemon—before I did something about it."

"Holy shit," said Martinez, slapping his leg. "We got all your clippings up in the locker room at the precinct house. There was a pool whether they'd let you back on the force or Section-8 you."

I had an unpleasant flash of Dr. Merriman, my department-appointed psychiatrist, and beat it back. "Can I assume you bet against me?"

"Hell, no," said Martinez. "You're a tough bi—er, lady. I knew you'd be back."

"Your confidence is touching," I told him, and turned back to the body. Suddenly, the company of a dead junkie didn't seem so bad. At least he couldn't point and whisper.

I was going through the black messenger bag emblazoned with a fancy winged-foot logo and the legend MESSENGER OF THE GODS when the CSU van pulled up.

A black Lincoln with the seal of the city medical examiner parked behind the van, and Bart Kronen exited after a fight with his seat belt. He brought a canvas tote bag holding the tools of his trade and waved to me with his free hand.

"Good to have you back, Detective! What present have you got for me this evening?"

"Nothing exciting, I'm afraid," I said as a CSU camera clicked and lit the scene to blinding daylight with a flash. "Just your standard street OD." I gestured to the one lit row house a block away. "I figured he came out of that shooting gallery and dropped dead before he realized he'd gone past the point of no return."

Kronen checked the man's pulse perfunctorily and then wiggled the arm. It moved like a store mannequin, all stiff joints. "Rigor is fixed, skin is close to ambient temperature . . . dead less than six hours. Can't be more specific, I'm afraid."

I shrugged. "Makes no difference to me, unless someone jabbed him with that needle against his will."

Kronen flashed his light over the man's hands and fingernails. "No trace evidence that I can see." He lifted the lids of the staring eyes and examined them. The dead man had had green eyes, a bright grassy color that was already fading.

The pain caught my gut, a physical sensation to go with a memory of dark green eyes and shaggy auburn hair falling across them like autumn leaves on a deep pond. *Hex you, Dmitri. Hex you and the ground you walk on.*

"Now this is interesting, Detective. Detective?"

As quickly as he'd come, he was gone, fading into a cloud of clove smoke and gravelly laughter.

I crouched next to Kronen, trying not to wince when he poked the dead junkie's eyeball with a rubber-tipped finger.

"See this here?" He indicated spidery columns of red drifting across the white.

"Little late for drops," I said. Kronen's mouth curled in displeasure. I stopped smiling.

"This is petichial hemorrhaging," he said. "A bursting of miniature blood vessels on the surface of the eye."

"So?" I said.

Kronen snapped off his light and stood, fixing his tie and expansive waistband. "This is not consistent with a heroin overdose. Petichia usually occur when the brain is deprived of oxygen."

"He wasn't strangled," I said defensively. "He's just dead." I was competent, dammit. I didn't need to be walked through my own crime scene like a first-year patrol officer. I'd know if someone was strangled, thank you.

Kronen went about tucking all of his accoutrements back into their case, and he pulled out a clipboard, initialed a report of a white male, dead on the scene, and handed it to me to sign as the ranking responding officer.

"I have no idea what could have happened to him," he said. "But once I do the post I'm sure all will be revealed. In the meantime, do you . . . detect . . . anything?"

My pen froze mid-signature. "Exactly what's that supposed to mean, Bart?"

He spread his hands. "Well, after the incident with Alistair Duncan certain . . . rumors have been flying heavily. If you can put your abilities to good use, it might speed a cause-of-death determination along."

I flung the pen down and shoved the clipboard back at him. "I don't know what you think you know, Bart, but you're barking up the wrong damn tree." He looked like a perturbed owl, eyes wide, as I snarled, "I'm not a trick dog," and stormed away up the street.

My hands were shaking and I compensated by stomping my motorcycle boots on the pavement. I'm a werewolf, and thanks to the debacle with Alistair Duncan, anyone who read the *Nocturne Inquirer* knew it, which included most of the department.

Kronen probably had no idea he was being insensitive, and I was a bitch for snarling at him, but since the Hex Riots, weres and witches don't enjoy the best reputation. Or any kind, except as the thing under your bed that you pretend doesn't exist.

And Hex it, I *wasn't* a hound dog that could sniff clues on cue. Being were didn't mean a shiny package of heightened senses that made my job easier. It was that, and uncontrollable rage and strength that could separate someone's head from their neck if I ever let myself off lockdown.

I'd only met one person who knew what that felt like, and he was somewhere on the other side of the world.

I breathed in, out, and willed myself to turn around and go back to the scene, knowing that everyone currently clustered around the body was talking about me.

Down the street, light spilled out of the condemned row house as a door opened and another scarecrow started up the walk toward me. He saw the patrol car, Martinez, and the CSU techs. He used what was left of his brain and ran.

"Better and better," I muttered, taking off after the live junkie. I figured if he was sprinting he probably knew something about the dead one. I caught up with him after a block and used my arm like a battering ram to drive him into the iron fences marching up the sidewalk.

"Get off!" he yelled, shoving back and making me stumble off the curb. I windmilled and caught myself on a rusted-out Ford, panting in surprise. Not many plain humans can stand up to were strength.

He was fumbling in his coat for something undoubtedly hazardous to my health when I brought my service weapon to bear between his eyes. Just a Glock nine-millimeter, nothing special, but it does the job. The junkie froze, hollow chest fluttering from the exertion.

"Police officer," I said. "Show me your hands."

A shiver ran through him. "Don't shoot."

"Give me one reason not to, good or bad," I said, thumbing the safety off. His hand was still inside his jacket. His eyes held entirely too much panic for me to be comfortable.

"Please don't shoot."

"Get your hands behind your head!"

He didn't move, just watched me, unblinking.

"Show them to me!" I ordered again.

"It will be all right," he said in a low singsong voice. "Just calm down. We're fine." In the low light, my were eyes saw his arm tense as he gripped whatever was inside his jacket.

Hex it.

"Please don't kill me, Officer," he begged as I saw his hand come out of his pocket in gut-twisting slow motion.

I should have pulled the trigger. It would have been a good shooting, because unless the guy was the most idiotic plain human in existence he was armed and he was going to kill me.

My finger dropped to the trigger, everything happening in two clock ticks but seeming to draw out forever as my blood buzzed in my ears. The were instincts living in my hindbrain screamed *Shoot!*

"Please," he hissed again.

I didn't shoot. I froze, like my limbs were encased in glass. What if he was just high? If he wasn't armed I'd be a murderer. I was already a murderer . . .

The curved knife came at me in a blur. My better reflexes threw me sideways and I landed on my gun with a hot pain in my ribs. The junkie was on me, face wild, knife like a silver claw poised above my eyeball. I braced and kicked out, rolling us over so I was on top. I hit him one sharp blow to the side of the temple and he went limp, fingers relaxing his grip on the weapon.

Martinez came pounding up with one of the CSU techs. "You okay?" he asked me, training his service weapon on the unconscious man.

I stood and brushed myself off. I didn't smell any blood, but I'd have to check myself under better light. A ragged piece of black hair brushed my face, and I reached up to feel a chunk lopped off. The knife had come within millimeters of my left eye.

"Hex me," I muttered. "Cuff this piece of crap," I said to Martinez. "You can run him over to the Twenty-fourth Precinct. I'll meet you there."

I pulled my leather jacket around me tightly as I walked away, so they wouldn't see I was shaking.

CHAPTER 2

For the first time since I'd been put on extended medical leave three months ago, I pulled into the parking lot of the Twenty-fourth Precinct. Serving Highland Park and the Waterfront district, the Twenty-fourth was tucked into a converted firehouse that had seen better days, although the neighborhood around it was slowly but surely yuppifying. I counted four shiny Hex-the-environment SUVs parked across the street in front of newly refurbished brick town houses.

I pulled my '69 Ford Fairlane into my assigned space and went up the wide stone steps of the Twenty-fourth. Just before I pushed open the doors I paused, breathing in the stink of old linoleum and sweat and bad coffee. It smelled homey, but foreign, like going back to your childhood bedroom after you've moved out. I steeled myself for whatever stares and mutters I might meet on the other side, and shoved the door open. It banged loudly on old springs. Way to go, Luna. If *everyone* didn't know you were coming back on duty tonight, they do now.

Rick, the night desk sergeant, looked up abruptly when I barged in. His mouth parted in a grin. "Good to see you, Detective!" He left his high judicial-style desk and came to shake my hand.

Relief washed through me. "Good to see you too, Rick. How's your son?"

"Teddy? Fine, started grade school a few weeks ago." Rick beamed. "And how's your cousin?"

My good mood washed away like a shack in a flash flood. "She moved out. She's living up on Battery Beach."

Rick whistled. "That's a long drive."

It was a long drive, long enough so that my cousin Sunny only made it every few weeks. I'm sure the fact I'd barely spoken to her for the entire summer pleased our grandmother, Rhoda, no end. Rhoda had thrown me out at fifteen, and the only time she'd ever helped me since, I'd had to agree to let her move Sunny back into her house, far away from my bad-nasty-corrupting were influence. Evil old witch.

I excused myself from Rick and walked down the narrow fluorescent-lit hallway to the squad room, pretending the roiling in my stomach was from those two bacon cheeseburgers I'd consumed for dinner.

Not that I could really blame Sunny for moving out. In the course of the Duncan investigation, our cottage had been broken into by a witch sent to kill me, I'd gotten myself shot, and Sunny had been arrested by the Nocturne City SWAT team. A stable life, it was not. And it still twisted my heart every time I unlocked what used to be our front door and found myself alone in the cottage.

My desk still sat in the back corner of the squad room, dusty with disuse. Someone had scrawled the words BITE ME into the layer of grime on my computer monitor.

I spun quickly and scanned the half-empty room. No one was bent over snickering, or looking embarrassed. A couple of rookies from Traffic stared at me with their mouths slightly open.

"Take a picture or cut it out," I snapped. My heart was pounding and I reached out and smeared the slur away, leaving fingerprints in its place. At least one person in the Twenty-fourth wasn't happy I was back. If it was just the one I'd be lucky, truth be told.

"Jesus, you look like someone just pissed on your grave." Lieutenant McAllister came to the edge of my desk and looked at me with the little crease between his eyebrows that telegraphed immense concern.

I brushed the dust off my jeans and collected myself. "It's been a busy night, Mac."

"I heard," he said. "Some tweaker tried to give you a brow lift?"

"Yeah, too bad he missed," I said. "I would have gotten one of those sexy little eye patches."

Mac clasped my shoulder and looked into my eyes. "I'm glad you're back, Wilder, don't get me wrong . . . lot of shuffling around after the Duncan thing, and we're short-staffed."

"Yeah, I miss Bryson's stinky cologne," I said, jerking my chin at the desk across the aisle from me, where Dave Bryson used to sit. His obnoxious souvenir footballs had been replaced with pictures of some guy's kids.

"Wilder," said Mac, "if you'd let me finish, I'm saying you don't look okay. At all."

And I didn't feel okay. At all. But if I had to spend one more minute in my silent, haunted cottage I was going to go insane. So I moved Mac's hand off my shoulder and lied.

"I'm good, Mac. Just a little shaky because of that guy jumping me." And because everyone knew I was a were, and Dmitri was gone, and I was so, so not ready to be back here with all of the memories of him and me . . .

"I hope you're not bullshitting me," he said. "Because the captain wanted to speak with you as soon as you came in."

It took me a minute to realize he couldn't be talking about Wilbur Roenberg, the former captain of the Twenty-fourth. *That* captain was doing twenty-five-to-life in Los Altos for conspiracy to conceal multiple murders. Although, with the shift I'd had so far, it would be conceivable he might show up.

"What does he want to talk to me about?"

"She," said Mac. "And I have no idea. She's not very chatty."

Well, that was a new wrinkle. There were only fifteen or twenty female detectives out of two hundred in the city, and a handful of lieutenants. No captains I knew of.

"Who is she? Where'd she come from?"

"Hex me, Wilder, I don't know the woman's life story. She was a shift commander in the Forty-third and she transferred to the detectives' bureau. Her name's Matilda Morgan and from what I've seen she gets pissy when people are late. Move your behind." He spun on his heel and went back into his office. I winced as his door slammed. Mac was unflappable as a rock in a stormy sea. Captain Morgan must be a grade-A tightass if she had him that riled. *Great, can't wait to be grilled by her.*

I went down the hall to the captain's office and knocked.

The first thing I noticed was that Roenberg's name had been scraped off the wavy glass door and fresh letters that still smelled like paint spelled out MATILDA MORGAN — CAPTAIN.

"Enter!" Her voice was sharp and had bite behind it, like a drill sergeant or a Catholic schoolteacher.

I turned the knob, not liking it that my palm was sweating just from her talking. "Captain Morgan . . ." I bit back a giggle as the image of the petite blond-haired woman in front of me decked out in a wig and pirate garb sprang to mind. *Oh gods, Luna. Not now.*

Morgan looked at me over the top of a pair of half-moon glasses, case file held at half-mast. "Yes? What is it, Detective?"

"Captain Morgan," I tried again, a little more successfully this time. "I'm Luna Wilder. You wanted to see me?"

Recognition dawned in her eyes and she set the file down with a *thwap*. "Of course. I should have remembered you from the copious press coverage of your last case. Shut the door and sit down."

I closed the door with a meek click and sat in the new chair across from Morgan's new desk. All of Roenberg's masculine wood and musty old chairs had been stripped out and the captain sat behind a blond-wood-and-chrome desk set with two aerodynamic plastic chairs facing her. I squirmed as she bored into me with her sea-blue gaze, which I'm sure was the effect her office was calculated for.

Then again, I could be reading too much into this. Morgan was a high-ranking woman, she probably had to take a lot of shit. Her ice-bitch façade could be just that.

"Detective Wilder, let me state right off that I was not in favor of allowing you to return to the force."

Or it could be she really was an ice bitch.

I swallowed and managed to remain polite by gripping the seat of the plastic chair until I felt shavings curl under my fingernails. "Why's that, ma'am?"

"If you have to ask, you're even less of a detective than I've been led to believe."

I felt my cheeks go red-hot as Morgan continued, "I run a tight squad, Detective. I have no place for grandstanding, disregarding orders, and especially"—she removed her glasses and looked me up and down, as if she were Anubis, weighing my sins—"weres who have no control over their impulses and endanger the *human* members of my squad. If you so much as ruffle one of my hairs out of place, I will have you removed."

Anger jetted through me and my better impulses went the way of good scotch at a policemen's ball. "What the Hex are you insinuating?" I demanded roughly.

Morgan smiled with closed lips, her eyes hard as cut sapphires. "There's that famous were temper," she purred. "I was wondering how long you could keep it in check." She turned her head to examine her chrome wall clock. "Not very long at all."

She closed the file and pushed it across the desk to me. I saw my name on the tab and realized it contained my disciplinary reports. There were more than a few yellow administrative memos inside the brown cover. "If you want to keep your job here, Ms. Wilder, I suggest that you chain yourself to a desk and stick to work befitting someone with limited interpersonal skills. The OD case you pulled earlier will do nicely for now."

Gods, how I wanted to hurt her. I ached to clear the ugly modern desk and wring her neck, tear it, spread her blood all over her pristine furniture.

I stood up, my hands vibrating, because I had to move somehow. If I let the were become trapped, I would lash out and someone would be hurt. Much as Morgan had endeared herself to me, I would not kill the bitch. She wasn't worth the Hexed effort.

"Will that be all, ma'am?" I whispered. Morgan thought for a moment and then nodded.

"For now." She handed me my folder. "Please file this on the way back to your desk."

I don't know how I kept from ripping her hand off. Years of self-control and reining in and teaching myself to keep the were inside washed away under her smirk and her quiet blandishments. If this was what I came back to, who wanted the Hexed job anyway?

No. Matilda Morgan would not make me quit. Dead junkies and knife attacks would not force me out. Not even desk work would get rid of me. I was a good Hexed cop, and I was staying that way. Sunny wouldn't have to hear how I got fired—again. And Dmitri, if he ever came back, wouldn't see how much his leaving had wounded me.

I didn't even slam the door when I left Morgan's office, and I didn't let anyone in the hall see the tears pricking my eyes until I got to the empty file room and let myself cry.

Rick caught me as I came out, scrubbing my eyes against the back of my hand. "That guy who tried to stab you just rolled in. We put him in Interrogation Three."

I smiled perfunctorily, my Nothing-to-See-Here smile. "I'll be right there."

Rick cocked his head at me. "You okay?"

"Will everyone stop asking me that?" I demanded loudly. "If I wasn't okay, I wouldn't be back on the damn job."

"Hex me," Rick said, stepping back. "I'm sorry. Bring the guy to the front when you want him booked." He turned and shuffled back to his desk. I immediately felt like an even bigger witch than Morgan for snarling at him. I needed to get out of here in the worst way. I shouldn't have come back yet. I could have taken that last month of paid leave to get my head together.

I stopped myself as I pushed open the door to Interrogation Three. Another month to sit around the house wouldn't have improved my outlook any. My life rotating around a clock ticking down the seconds until the phase, knowing I would be alone when it happened. At least going back to work would keep my mind off that.

The junkie was handcuffed, his head nodding against his chest. I kicked the leg of his chair. "Wake up, jackass."

I smelled a faint wave of body odor and perfume from behind the observation mirrors and felt my neck prickle. Was Morgan out there, watching me? I pulled the curtain across the mirror with a grim smile of satisfaction for whoever was on the other side and turned back to the junkie.

"What's your name?"

"Edward," he said sullenly.

"You've been advised of your rights, Edward?"

His burning brown eyes raked over me, settling on my face, and he grinned with cracking lips. "Nice haircut, Officer."

He just had to push my buttons, didn't he? I was on him in a second, hand around his throat, taking him back to the wall and slamming his head into it with an impact that made his yellow teeth snap together. The back legs of his chair left skid marks on the linoleum floor. Were strength definitely has its perks.

"You listen to me, you strung-out asshole," I growled in his ear. "Assaulting a cop is a felony, and I doubt any judge is going to suggest a cushy rehab for your junkie butt."

He choked and struggled a bit, more dramatics than anything because I wasn't holding his throat tightly enough to cut off his airflow. Not that it wasn't a tempting idea.

"Who's your dead friend?" I demanded. "Tell me and I might look into getting the charges reduced to misdemeanor assault." Which was all Hexed talk, of course. I had less than no relationship with the DA's office after what I'd done to their boss.

"You can't help me," Edward rasped. "Bitten bitch!"

I let go of him, startled that he'd made me as a were. He grinned again, eyes rolling around the room before resting on his lap. "He felt the poison in his veins," he said abruptly. "He saw with the empty eyes."

I stifled a sigh and rubbed my eyes. Crazy ramblings were just what I ordered for my first interrogation. "What are you talking about, Edward?"

His head was down on his chest again and he was

mumbling. "Empty eyes . . . every one of us. He sees every one of us."

Well, this was going just wonderfully. Maybe if I got lucky he'd start chanting "Redrum!" and drawing on the walls.

"He sees every one of us!" Edward moaned again. I reached for him to take him to a holding cell and abruptly his head snapped up and he locked eyes with me, lucid as a sober judge. "He sees you too, Detective."

I gripped his arm and hauled him up. "Yeah, okay. Move it along."

Edward let me lead him to Rick's desk, where he refused to say a word as Rick booked him. I handed him off to a uniform, unable to take the proximity of insanity any longer, and leaned on the outside of the metal detector. "Remind me again why I took this job."

Rick wordlessly offered me a toffee from the dish he kept on his desk and I popped it and chewed vigorously. "Maybe I can eat enough of these to go into shock and not have to come back tomorrow."

Down the hall, Captain Morgan came out of her office and locked the door. She wore a gray pantsuit that flattered her stubby frame and a pair of truly exceptional Marc Jacobs boots that I hadn't noticed when she was reaming me.

"Hex the gods," I muttered, making a beeline for the squad room. Morgan stopped and looked at me for a few long seconds as we drew even. "Don't you have a desk, Detective?"

"I do, Captain," I said tightly. She sniffed.

"Then I'll assume this lounging around the booking area is the result of some thyroid issue unique to weres that renders you unable to sit still. Return to your work." She clopped across the lobby in her boots that cost more than my monthly salary and let the outside door swing shut behind her without so much as a glance at Rick. I wanted to follow her and hit her over the head with her own boot.

Instead, I grabbed another handful of toffees, clocked out, and went home early.

CHAPTER 3

At 2 A.M. I could hear the ocean but not see it when I parked the Fairlane in front of my cottage. The ghostly shape of driftwood steps disappeared down the dunes to the water, and the waxing moon sat high in a sky of crisp autumn stars.

The cottage, a one-and-a-half-story clapboard wreck that was covered in climbing roses and rented cheap, was dark. Leaving lights on never deterred a burglar that I'd seen, and it wasn't like I could shell out to Greater Pacific Power & Light every month like when Sunny was around.

I stopped at the threshold, making my body absolutely still, listening. Nothing came to me except the measured *hush-hush* of the waves, and no smells except dead roses and fresh salt made themselves known. I shut the door behind me and reached for the light switch immediately, my spine giving a frisson of memory just before the bulb flickered on.

Not too long ago, I'd been attacked by a witch on the same spot where I stood to take off my jacket and shoulder rig. I still had nightmares, and bad moments when I was sure someone was behind me, waiting as I stood in the dark.

But the sitting room was the same, a new carpet over the spot where I'd shot Regan Lockhart. I hung my motocross jacket on the coat tree and slid my Glock into the drawer of the desk that served as my entryway table. I used to lock the drawer. Now, I left it unlocked and slightly open, where I could reach the Glock in under a second.

A lot had changed since I'd stopped Asmodeus. I no longer slept through the night. I kept a hunting knife taped to the underside of my bed frame and a gun readily available. Tiny parts of my brain whispered that I was paranoid, one of those cops who sat alone watching old movies and holding their guns while they thought about how they'd die.

Okay, maybe not that bad, but I was more paranoid now than I'd ever thought I'd be. Dr. Merriman had vetted me for post-traumatic stress, but what she didn't know was how Asmodeus had talked to me, just before I killed Duncan and released him. I *released* him, let something horrible and ancient roam free. And I had killed, as a were, and it wasn't clean like when I had been forced to shoot a murder suspect my first year in Homicide. I had given in to the were and I'd killed.

And it wasn't the first time.

"Why do you think you keep coming back to that moment?" Dr. Merriman had asked me, crossing her legs at the ankle and twisting a fountain pen cap slowly between her fingers.

I focused on the spot over her left shoulder, reading the titles of the books she kept on her shelves for show.

Merriman dealt with bad shootings, suicidal thoughts, cop divorces. She didn't do weres. I smelled the sweat stippling her blouse every time we were in her office together.

"Do you feel guilty about what happened to Mr. Duncan?"

"Hex me, no," I snorted, giving her a grim corpsey smile to show what a badass I was. Merriman was a lousy shrink, but even she could see through that.

"Then why do you keep dwelling on his death, Luna? Why do you feel the need to relentlessly pursue these situations, when you know they are destructive?"

And just like she and everyone else expected me to, I exploded. *"What the fuck do you want me to say, Dr. Merriman? You want me to sigh and look at my feet and admit that I'm an adrenaline junkie and I thrive on chaos, and on those images of death that I carry around in my head? You think I* don't *know that I'm self-destructive?"*

Merriman smiled, and jotted on her pad, because she had something she could rat me out about finally, after three months of sessions where I'd given pat responses that cops involved in case-related deaths are supposed to give. *"Honestly, Luna? I think you won't be satisfied until everything around you is in flames."*

I walked out of her office at Cedar Hill Psych, and even though we had two more appointments I didn't go back. Too many people had seen through me, but Merriman was going to be the latest to think she had something to hold over my head.

After I made it upstairs with the echoes of memories I'd rather not have, I stood under my shower until my fingers started to crimp at the ends, then I towelled off and put on sweats that had already seen more than one wearing. I shut off my lights and watched the moonlight play through the trellises outside my window. I thought about golden daemon eyes and the screams of Alistair Duncan. Sleep, when it finally came, was drenched in bloody dreams.

At exactly 4 A.M. I woke with the certain knowledge that someone was inside my house. I heard the screen door slap shut and then the inner door gently close, and a muffled curse as whoever-it-was caught themselves on my furniture.

I was out of bed and had the knife in one motion, keeping low as I crouch-ran to the top of the stairs. I reached up for the switch and stood, screaming, "Police! Freeze!"

"Hex me!" The figure below threw up his arms and dropped the pair of white bakery bags he was holding. Hot coffee sloshed out of one and across my new rug. "Shit!" he exclaimed, grabbing a grungy bandanna out of his back pocket and mopping at the stain. "Luna, you scared the crap out of me!"

Still poised with the knife on the stairs, I let out a long sigh. "Trevor, what the hell are you doing here?"

Trevor Wick gave me a look that was equal parts sheepish and pissed. "My last set ended early. I brought you breakfast in bed . . . or tried."

I dropped the knife to my side and came down to help him pick up the bags and blot at the coffee. "How did you get in?"

Trevor sat back on his heels. "You gave me a key, remember?" He cocked an eyebrow at the hunting knife. "Babe, what are you doing with that?"

I set it on the arm of the sofa. "I don't like having a gun in my bedroom." Admitting it to someone else in a lit room, I felt ridiculous and more than a little crazy. Trevor kissed me on the cheek.

"You're one scary chick. I love it." He took the bag from me. "I'm gonna go toast the remains of my surprise. Cream cheese or lox?"

"Cream cheese," I said, still crouched, not able to meet his eyes. Yeah, we hadn't been dating for that long, but how much more of a freak could I look like?

Trevor brushed the side of my breast with his knuckles as he stood. "Don't keep me waiting too long, sexy." He disappeared into the kitchen. I stared down at the brown stain on my rug and felt like an idiot.

I got orange juice and plates while Trevor spread cream cheese on my bagel. Seeing him standing in my kitchen, easily finding knives and spoons and a plate for the lox, was weird. In a big way.

Trevor sensed me looking at him and cocked an eyebrow. "What's on your mind, babe?"

I swallowed. He had only been in my house once before, but he'd stayed long enough to make me breakfast the following morning, and in what was obviously a fit of insanity I had given him my spare key. Had I somehow telegraphed that it was okay for him to barge in whenever he liked?

"Nothing. Last night was my first shift back at work."

Trevor licked the knife and tossed it into the sink. "Cool. You bust any bad guys?"

Did crazed junkies trying to stab my face count? "Only one."

He shoved half a bagel slice in his mouth and chuckled, swallowing before speaking. I took a token bite of mine, even though I was too nervous with him sitting across from me to be hungry.

"You know," Trevor said, "I can't get over the fact that I'm shacked up with a cop. I mean, do you know how many times I've been busted?"

Twice. Both misdemeanor charges that were cleared with a fine. I also knew that Trevor was five-ten instead of six feet like he always claimed and that he wore blue contacts. What, I was supposed to sleep with someone who, for all I knew, could be a chain-saw sex killer? How did normal women date like that?

I said, "Yeah, that's funny," in a tone that sounded dolorous even to me.

Trevor reached across the table with fishy-smelling fingers and brushed my hair behind my ear. "You okay, babe? You seem really spacey." There was genuine concern sitting in his eyes and I breathed in before answering, to fill my nostrils with the scent of the here and now and dispel the clove-tinged past.

"Fine. Sweetheart." That came out easy enough. I tried again. "Thanks for coming over. It was . . . nice."

Trevor snorted. "Nice? I'm not nice. But I like you." He winked, dropping his plate into the sink and going to my shiny new stainless refrigerator. The old Frigidaire had been scrapped due to damage from large-caliber bullet holes. "You got any beer?"

"No." I had drunk enough of it in my teens to last for a while, possibly the rest of my life. And what the Hex did Trevor think he was doing, anyway? Was there a set of relationship semaphores I wasn't privy to that said, *Hey, invade my privacy and drink all of my beer, if I have it?* The one nice thing about life with Dmitri had been the lack of bullshit. He wanted me, and one time I had wanted him, and it happened, and afterward he made it okay with an easy smile and a touch against my cheek. Weres are creatures of instinct, and you know where you stand, even if the only slots to stand in are "prey" and "mate."

Trevor came behind me and massaged my shoulders. "You're tense, darlin'," he murmured in my ear, lips grazing the top. "Let's forget the beer and go upstairs. See what I can do about that."

My fight-or-flight instinct kicked in with a vengeance, the memory of Dmitri's hands where Trevor's sat now twisting my stomach. I twitched under Trevor's touch, and he noticed, stepping back with a sigh.

"It's him again?"

I turned with what I hoped was a convincingly perky smile. "Who? Babe." Hex me, I was awful at platitudes. Probably why I never made it as a cocktail waitress.

Trevor leaned against a counter and pushed a hand through the green-streaked black hair that fell in front of his eyes. "Your mysterious ex that you won't talk about. Luna, you know I think you're the hottest woman I've ever been with, but this existential crisis shit has gotta go."

I looked down at the braided rug, shamed. Just how much I didn't talk about, Trevor had no idea. And it was unfair. Dmitri was gone. I had met Trevor *because* he was gone. Hadn't I gone out determined to rejoin the population at large, and forget him? Now I had Trevor, and cutting him off would be cruel and brand me a truly dysfunctional individual for life.

He looked at me again when I came and slid my

arms around his waist, pressing our bodies together. I made sure he could feel I wasn't wearing a bra, and his eyes darkened a bit, a smile creeping to the corners of his mouth. I kissed him and paid special attention to sliding my tongue between his lips. Pressure against my groin through his jeans told me that we were well on the way to making up.

"Upstairs, you said?" I purred, pulling back. Trevor nodded, his breath coming out in little puppy pants. I could smell his plain human pheromones, cloyingly sweet like a narcissus flower.

"Upstairs," he agreed, grabbing me by the arm and pulling me after him.

The sun had set again by the time I woke up, showered, and made my way downstairs to my office to check e-mail. Trevor was still snoring and tangled in my sheets, and I was inclined to leave him there. I made sure to put some antiseptic and a box of bandages on the nightstand, embarrassed at the deep welts my nails had left on his shoulder blades.

At least I could explain it away as his driving me to heights of heretofore unimagined, romance-novelesque passion. A little white lie was far better than blurting out I was a were.

I should have told him the first night we met, at the club where his band was playing. Definitely after the first time I slept with him. I checked the lunar calendar on the wall of the office and saw that the full moon was sixteen days away—too early for any signs of the phase to be showing, thank the gods. How I would explain this one away, I didn't know.

My e-mail in-box lit up with a few pieces of spam.

Not surprising. Who would want to talk to me in the mopey state I was in?

The last remaining e-mail in the box caught my eye, and I vowed I would be strong, I would not click on it. Would not, would not . . .

I moved the mouse and clicked with the same compulsion as when I bid on vintage pumps and purses at auction, and the resulting emotional gut punch was the same.

From: dsandovsky31@netmail.ru.com
To: wilderlu@nocturne.pd.gov

Subject: Don't worry about me . . .

Dear Luna,
    Don't worry about me, darlin'. I can't talk long but I'm in the Ukraine and I'm okay. Don't talk to anyone about me, or you, or us. Please. Can't say exactly what will happen if you do, but things could get serious.

I'll try to protect you. Don't know if I can . . .
—Dmitri

Dated almost a month ago, the last I'd heard from Sandovsky. That night, I had gone out and met Trevor. The last line of the message haunted me, in the times when I was halfway between waking and dreaming. *I'll try to protect you.*

"Well, Dmitri, you've done a great gods-damned job so far," I muttered. Footsteps thudded above me and Trevor called down the stairs.

"Babe, you down there? Got any breakfast for me?"

I stabbed at the monitor's power button and hustled

out of the office. "There should be cereal in the kitchen. I'm late for work—I have to go." How old the cereal was, I wouldn't testify to. I wasn't late, either, but looking at Trevor in the aftermath sent a flush of guilt through me. I should enjoy him more—or less. Or what the Hex was wrong with me? Since when had I become a whiny urbanite whose biggest concern was boinking?

Trevor hurried down to stop me, grabbing me by the elbow in his way. I fought the instinct to growl at what the were perceived as an attempt to dominate.

"Do you really have to run off?"

I kissed him on the cheek. "I'm afraid so."

He still held my arm. "We're doing a show tonight at Belladonna. It's a big deal. I'd really like you to be there."

I mentally calculated how many busts Narcotics and Vice had made at the Belladonna club and decided that for Trevor, it *was* a big deal. The people at Belladonna didn't posture—they were real badmen. Poor Trevor.

"I'll try," I promised, still grinding away at the whole "Be a decent girlfriend" thing. "Now I really gotta go."

I got my gun, badge, and jacket and escaped to the Fairlane, happier to be away from my house and my boyfriend than any sane woman should be.

CHAPTER 4

I floored the Fairlane along the Appleby Expressway, taking a downtown exit rather than my usual so I could avoid work for a few minutes longer. My cell phone rang while I was sitting at the light on Devere and Branch. The caller ID said the medical examiner's office wanted to speak with me, so I answered even though driving and talking were worth a $200 fine within the Nocturne City limits.

"Luna, it's Dr. Kronen."

I managed to shift and make a left turn with one hand, and jockeyed the phone to my other ear. "What's up, Bart?"

"I have the results of the tox screen on your overdose case, if you'd like to stop by."

Visiting the Nocturne City morgue was right up there with taking a relaxing vacation to the Middle East, but I cut across two lanes and turned back into the maze of downtown. "I can be there in ten."

The morgue, one floor of the subbasements beneath the main laboratories for the department, stank of old formaldehyde and the barely contained waves of decay that emanated from the autopsy bays and the set of wall freezers I had to pass to make it to Kronen's office.

He looked up as I came in, glasses dropping down his nose. "Ah, Detective." He fished around in a pile that, to my eyes, appeared to be a chaos of folders, lab reports, and receipts for meals at the sushi restaurant around the corner. "Here are your results. As you can see"—he flipped open the report and gestured me over—"nothing untoward in the blood and fluids, for a drug user."

"Heroin?" I guessed.

"Actually, no," said Kronen, tracing a wiggly line with his finger. "This represents trace elements of a drug that I have not identified. It does share several bases with heroin, so I assume it is a street mix that has not made it into wide use."

"Yeah, maybe because everyone who shoots it dies a horrible death," I said.

"Could be," Kronen agreed. "I'll do further analysis and fit the autopsy in when I have a spare moment to make an official ruling of accidental death, but I feel safe to say you can shove this one to the bottom of your pile."

"What pile?" I muttered, taking the report. Thanks to Matilda Freaking Morgan I had no cases.

"Detective," said Kronen as I turned to leave. "I hope that . . . at the scene . . ." He sighed and brushed a grain of rice from the front of his shirt. "No offense was meant. Although you being were does explain why you can't stand the smell in the autopsy bay and how you . . . you are a fine investigator. I'm glad to work with you anytime." He gave a small smile and picked up a thick medical journal with dog-eared pages.

Unprepared for such a statement from Kronen, I

managed to murmur, "Thanks, Doc," and make my exit before I blushed redder than arterial spray. Now if only the department at large felt the way Kronen did, my life might not be quite so hellish.

I sighed as I drove back up Highlands toward the precinct house. Who was I kidding? I was a disaster magnet and had been my entire life. Peace-love-and-hugs from my fellow men and women in blue wouldn't change that. Nothing would, except me magickally not being were, and I doubted that was happening anytime soon.

A typical Friday night at the Twenty-fourth consisted of a passel of drunks, a few tweakers certain we were the bug-daemons come to suck out their souls, and a tough guy who decided that no, he didn't want a DUI arrest for going fifty-five in a twenty-five in his Porsche and was currently screaming at Rick.

"Sir," Rick said as the arresting officer wrestled with the suit. "If I knew who you were, do you think I'd be any less inclined to book you?"

"Fuck you, pencil neck!" the suit bellowed. "I want a lawyer! Where's my phone? I'll call him myself, since I doubt a lower life form like you can operate one!"

I came up behind him and felt in the pockets of his tweed greatcoat until I found his sleek little flip-phone. I snapped the earpiece off the base and dropped it on Rick's desk. The suit turned, mouth open, and I clamped a hand on his shoulder and growled, "Settle down." My eyes stung as I let them flicker to gold for a second and then fade back to gray. It's a nice trick to use on drunks, one I'd had to conceal very carefully before the Duncan debacle to avoid one of my coworkers grabbing a clip of silver bullets and shooting to kill.

He gaped like a wide-mouthed bass for a second. "I'll sue?" It came out very small. I winked at Rick and went through the metal detector while he asked the drunk, "One more time, sir . . . address? And if you give me any more lip I'll get the lady detective back out here to break something else."

I felt almost happy as I came into the squad room. Maybe this whole not-hiding thing would work out after all. I had always used my were instincts and the heightened senses that came with the bite, but keeping the strength and the uncontrollable temper under wraps was a struggle. If I didn't have to be so damn careful all the time, who knew what could happen? Maybe if I cleared enough small-time crap fast enough, Morgan would let me off the leash.

A woman was sitting on the edge of my desk, examining the family photo of me, Sunny, and our grandmother I kept there. I froze a few feet away and cleared my throat loudly. "What the Hex do you think you're doing?"

She turned to face me and a perky smile blossomed. "Detective Wilder?"

Somehow I knew I'd regret this later, but I said, "That's me."

She slinked up from her perch and extended a hand wearing expensive lotion and perfect French tips. "Shelby O'Halloran. I just transferred in, from Vice at the Nineteenth."

"Okay . . ." I said, doing what every cop does when they meet someone new—composing a mental arrest sheet. "Mind telling me why your butt is on my desk, Shelby?" Five-six or -seven, hundred and fifteen pounds, blond hair, ice-blue eyes. No marks or scars.

Tattoos—that would have to be left to speculation, although her low-cut white knit top didn't show me any—

"I've been assigned as your new partner."

Wait, what?

"You're my what?" I repeated out loud, blinking stupidly. She smiled, wide glossy lips stretching over a row of little white Chiclets that some dentist must be having wet dreams about right this second.

"Your partner. I understand you've been without one ever since you were promoted to detective."

"Yeah, and I like it that way," I growled. Shelby picked up a black tote and slung it over her shoulder. "Lieutenant McAllister said they'll have a desk for me by tomorrow, but for tonight would it be okay if I stored my things here? You don't have anything in your bottom drawer."

Heat leaped in my chest, and my jaw ground in what laymen refer to as homicidal rage. "You looked through my drawers?"

"You were late," said Shelby with a shrug. "I was bored."

I pointed my own raggedy-nailed finger at her cute button face. "Don't move." Spinning on my heel, I banged into Mac's office.

"Don't even start with me, Wilder." He held up a hand at the sight of me. "Wasn't my idea. Morgan requested her transfer before you came back on duty."

"And no one *told* me?" I sputtered. "Mac, I cannot be partnered with the living, breathing incarnation of Barbie. All she needs is a pink convertible and a giant hairbrush!"

He reached into his right-hand drawer and pulled out a crumpled pack of Camels. "I haven't had one of these since you went on leave, but suddenly I have a feeling this night can only degenerate."

"Mac, you can't . . ." I started.

"Wilder, it is *out of my hands*!" he snapped. "Now if you want to screech at somebody, go find Morgan. Otherwise, take your new partner and go do your job."

Hah, right. I slammed his door behind me hard enough to shake glass and barreled down the hall to Morgan's office, where I rapped and didn't wait for her clipped "Enter" before barging in.

"What the Hex are you doing assigning me some Vice bimbo?" Very subtle, Wilder. Way to get her on your side.

Morgan removed her glasses and bored into me with a glare that would have reduced a lesser woman to a puddle. Good thing Morgan only came *close* to being the scariest thing I'd encountered in my life. "Detective Wilder, if I wished for the officers under my command to question my judgment I would put a suggestion box outside my office."

"But I've never had a partner!" I said desperately. "I've been solo ever since I came to Homicide!"

"Detective." Morgan rapped her knuckles on her desk to punctuate the word. "I don't know what kind of house Wil Roenberg was running, but the fact that he allowed someone at your level of instability to careen around the city without backup is sufficient comment. Every detective in every precinct I am assigned to will have a partner. Including you."

Since I was on a roll with the bad impulses for the evening, I opened my mouth to object again.

"You are not a special case because you are were, Ms. Wilder!" Morgan hissed, standing. She only came to my shoulder, but she was wide-bodied and had an expression on her face that Ghengis Khan might have envied. "I will not tiptoe around your condition! Follow orders or get out—those are your choices. Which do you choose?"

My palms tingled and the were slid to the forefront of my consciousness as it felt my dominance being tested. I ground my teeth, and worked the tendons in my neck with a pop, and managed a tone that was verging on normal. "Thank you for your time, ma'am."

Morgan strode back to her seat and picked up the papers she had been reading. "The next time you disrespect me will be your last as a member of this department, Detective Wilder. Clear?"

"Clear, ma'am," I whispered, looking at my shoes because if I looked at Morgan, I was going to rip the bitch's head off.

"Then we're done here." She motioned me out, and I left, shutting the door carefully behind me.

CHAPTER 5

Shelby was looking over the lab results Kronen had given me when I got back to my desk. I snatched the folder from her hands and slammed it onto my desk with a bang. "Let's get one thing straight, miniskirt. I don't want you, and I'm not inclined to like you, so don't expect some sisterly bonding experience while we catch bad guys and make the world safe for justice and puppies, all right?"

She didn't react to the slur except to shake her head slowly and smile. "Whatever you say, Luna. I'm here to do my job. If you have some sort of issue about partners that's your thing."

Hex her. What gave her the right to be so laid-back?

"I see that you're working a possible OD case," Shelby said, picking up the folder again. "What's our next move?"

I wondered if tearing her throat out would be classed as justifiable homicide once a jury heard her talk?

"Don't tell me you don't have any leads," said Shelby in a snippy tone. "Have you talked to his dealers, his shooting partners?"

"It's an accidental death," I said. "The ME is going

to rule it that way as soon as the autopsy goes through."
And then, I had the perfect way to get rid of Shelby for
the night. "All that's left for us is family notification."

No cop in their right mind wants to be the one to
ring the bell and tell a mother or husband or child that
their loved one is dead. Especially when that loved one
had more tracks than a railroad yard and showed up dead
in a sleazy part of town. I figured Shelby would remember a pressing manicure appointment or have a
waxing emergency as soon as I brought the subject up.

Instead she shrugged and said, "Okay. We can grab
some dinner on the way back."

Hex it, I was really starting to hate her.

In the car Shelby said, "You haven't mentioned my
last name yet."

I kicked the Fairlane up to fifth as we merged onto
the expressway and heaved a sigh. "Am I supposed to
be impressed by the great O'Halloran moniker? Quiver
in awe, perhaps? Genuflect?"

The O'Halloran family is Nocturne City's fairy
tale—poor Irish immigrants who started as servants and
laundresses and grew to be a worldwide banking con-
glomerate. There was also the business of Siobahn
O'Halloran, a member of the original family, stabbing
the wife of a prominent society man to death back in the
1880s. And the rumor that the O'Hallorans were caster
witches, every one of them.

"You *have* heard of us?" said Shelby in the same
tone her rich relatives probably used on the maid.

"I've heard of you, and I've heard all the rumors too,"
I said. "If you're expecting me to be afraid, forget it.
My cousin's a caster witch."

Shelby laughed, brushing her honey-streaked hair

behind her ears. "If we're trading rumors, Luna, should I mention the ones I've heard about you?"

My fingers tightened on the wheel and the Fairlane slipped slightly to one side. "What have you heard?"

"Just that you're a were," said Shelby with a sly grin. "And that you were phased when you killed Alistair Duncan. Under the law, that makes it murder."

I turned my eyes on her, and the dry sting told me they were blazing gold. "You want to see the truth first-hand, Shelby?"

"Oh, relax." She flapped a hand at me. "I'm just getting under your skin. Fair play for that 'miniskirt' remark."

"Word of advice, Shelby. You don't want to find out what's under my skin."

"I apologize." She sounded sincere. "I didn't know you had so little . . . control. I've never spent any time around weres."

I reminded myself that she wasn't insensitive, just dumb as a bag of hammers, and that thought helped me succeed in not killing her until I got to our exit just outside the city.

The dead junkie's name had been Bryan Howard. The address listed on his DMV record was in the Bottomlands, the swampy former landfill west of downtown along the bay, where the city smoothed out to scrub trees and strip malls. Occasionally a sinkhole opened and swallowed one of the cheap wood-frame houses whole, and a sobbing welfare mother sued the city, and there was a scandal until a story that didn't involve putting poor people on the evening news came along.

The Bottomlands reeked of tidal flats and that

ever-present scent of decay that makes the air heavy and the people hopeless. Howard's address led us to a shingled duplex rife with damp rot and a yard containing a rusty swing set and an abandoned doghouse. The porch light was shot out but in the dusk no one appeared to be home.

I picked my way between discarded plastic toys and stifled a chuckle when Shelby stumbled and cursed. Night vision came with the were package. I pulled the rusty storm door aside and pounded on the inner. "Police!"

"We shouldn't be here," Shelby told me, casting a look up and down the silent street.

"I couldn't agree more. I'm going to have to burn these clothes when I get home."

"No," said Shelby urgently, pointing to a gang sign sprayed on a street-lamp pole. "We really shouldn't be here."

I pounded again. "Mrs. Howard? Anyone? Open the door!"

"Hex me," Shelby muttered. I took another look at the gang sign and felt a familiar twist in the pit of my stomach. It wasn't a gang tag, it was a sigil—a blood witch marker indicating ownership of the territory.

"Shit," I muttered, too low for Shelby to catch. Shelby was a caster witch, their natural rival. The bloods would see her as an invader, badge or no.

"So how does a caster witch become a cop?" I asked her to take my mind off the fact that we might die horrible sacrificial deaths before the night was over.

Shelby looked at her feet and kicked a rusty toy fire engine away. "When she's not a witch."

I raised an eyebrow. "You didn't get the blood?"

"No one in my family can figure it out," she said. "My father practically disowned me—said it must be my mother's fault."

How well could I relate to that? The only were in a family of witches. The only child of the drunk father. The only woman in the academy.

"I can't believe I just told you that," Shelby muttered. "Forget it, okay? Suffice to say I don't enjoy my family's financial favor and I have to make my own way."

Figuring it was a lost cause, I knocked on the door once more and then let the screen slap shut. "Why Vice? That's a rough assignment for a woman."

"Imbalances of power bother me," said Shelby simply.

"Let's go," I said, and saw her shoulders relax. I hadn't seen anyone else on the street, but she was really fearful. I could smell it rolling off her underneath her deodorant and perfume, like fumes of molten copper. I suppose if I had been raised in a family of witches I might be paranoid too, but with my grandmother, I was more afraid of the magick that she'd showed me existed than of what *might* be lurking out there in the unknown.

The door behind me swung open and Shelby jumped a mile. I turned fast, hand going inside my jacket to touch my gun.

The stringy-haired woman staring at us through the screen blinked once. "What do you want?"

"Are you Mrs. Howard?" I asked, flashing my shield at her. She looked at it for a few seconds and then back at my face.

"I called in."

Shelby fidgeted next to me, casting looks back at the

street every few heartbeats. I shot her a glare as I said, "Called who, ma'am?"

"Dirk Bukowski, my parole officer. He sent you, right? 'Cause he said I didn't call in?"

I didn't know anything about Bukowski, but it didn't surprise me that the dirty, skinny woman peering through the rusty door had a record. Her forearms were bruised with circular clusters from large-bore needles, and her fingers quivered where she held onto the door handle.

"Mrs. Howard, we're not here to violate your parole. I need to talk to you about Bryan."

"Then stop calling me Mrs. Howard," she sniffed. "He's my brother."

"Can we get this over with, please?" Shelby hissed at me.

"Excuse me," I said to Not-Mrs.-Howard, turning on my unwanted partner. "What the Hex is the matter with you?"

"I can't be here!" she said frantically. "This is blood witch territory and *she* is a blood donor!" Whatever that meant.

"I don't have room in my job for your bullshit," I murmured to Shelby, pitching my voice low and dangerous so she got the message. "Either you can handle Homicide or you can't. And if this bothers you that much, you can go wait in the car."

She stiffened at that, and crossed her arms defiantly. "Just hurry it up, Detective."

"I'll do the best I can, Detective," I told her with a wide fake smile. Flighty wench. As soon as I got the notification over with, Shelby O'Halloran and I were due for serious words.

"What happened to Bryan?" said the Howard woman from the door. "He get picked up again?"

"I'm afraid . . ." I started, but a man's voice bellowed from inside the rotting house.

"Stella! Close the fuckin' door, it's freezing!"

"Cops are here, Dusty!" she screeched back. Dusty appeared a few seconds later, a lanky wastoid with a ponytail and yellowed skin that looked like moldy paper.

"What the Hex are you doing here?" he demanded. He saw Shelby and I were both of the female persuasion and curled his lip. "I forget to pay a parking ticket? This the meter-maid patrol?"

I focused back on Stella Howard. "Ma'am, I'm sorry to have to inform you that your brother Bryan was found dead last night."

Stella folded at the knees, sinking down onto the linoleum floor with a wail. Dusty stepped back as if she might contaminate him.

"Not Bry!" Stella howled. "Oh, Bry . . ." She crumpled in a ball, shoulders heaving. I opened the screen door and reached out to touch her.

"Hey!" Dusty exclaimed. "You can't come on private property! Get the fuck out! Stella, shut up!"

I pointed a finger at him. "One more word and I will put my foot where your few remaining teeth currently reside."

"I warned him," Stella sobbed. "I told him that junk would kill him." She raised her face to me as I rubbed her back. She was bony and cold through her thin shirt.

Shelby stepped up to Dusty and asked, "Are you also aware that Mr. Howard died of a heroin overdose, sir?"

Stella looked at me with a glassy gaze. "That true?"

"It appears so," I murmured. "He was dead on the scene." I left out the part about the unidentified drug and the petichial hemorrhages.

"Figures," Dusty muttered. "I told him that stuff would bring his dumb ass to bad ends."

"Stop talking about him like that!" Stella screamed. "It wasn't his fault!"

"Woman, I am gonna smack your mouth if you don't shut it!" Dusty shouted.

"Shelby, get him out of here," I snapped. "And if he slips and falls I'll be inclined to look the other way."

She put a hand on Dusty's elbow and escorted him into the next room with an iron grip.

"Do you need somewhere to stay the night?" I asked Stella gently. She shook her head.

"I gotta go to the free clinic tomorrow . . . have to be there by six A.M. to stand in line."

"Methadone?" I said. She blinked rapidly and shook her head so hard her greasy hair flew.

"I never touched that crap!" she said fiercely. "Not after what it did to Bryan."

I pointed at the circular track marks on her arms. "Stella, I'm not going to bust you. If you need help, better tell me now." I didn't know where this alternate-reality kindhearted me had come from, but I think it had something to do with the desperate, trapped-animal look in Stella Howard's eyes. She reminded me of something in myself, at a younger, more terrified age. A million roads spread out before you, all of them bad, and no map to navigate.

"I'm anemic," said Stella. "Not on smack." She pulled a pill bottle bearing the logo of the public health service out of her pocket and handed it to me. Sure enough, it contained large white pills and was purportedly to treat severe anemia.

"How . . ." I started, and then Shelby's blood donor comment made sense. I could smell nothing but plain human from Stella and Dusty, but the gang sign outside and the big needle marks in Stella's arm filled in the blanks. "You sell it to them," I said, understanding. She nodded once.

"And it's not illegal, so you can go now."

Maybe not in the sense that cooking meth and stealing Ferraris was illegal, but selling human blood to witches definitely walked in the gray zone. And if the blood witch Stella was associated with allowed her to participate in workings as a reward for a ready supply of blood . . . that was just bad all around.

I helped Stella up and brushed my knees off. "Think very hard about what you're doing here, Stella. You may not be a junkie, but you're feeding addicts just like the dealer who sold Bryan his last shot." If Bryan Howard had really died of an overdose at all.

"I know what I'm doing," said Stella, her lips compressed. "We don't push it to the gangs on the street. Dusty and I are respectable commodities."

I couldn't formulate a response to that one, so I murmured, "I'm very sorry for your loss," and called to Shelby that it was time to go.

"She called herself a commodity," I fumed to Shelby as we drove back to the precinct. "Like . . . like she was a freaking slave! And liked it!"

"She is a slave," said Shelby in a tone that let me know she was entirely unbothered by Stella Howard's plight. "Blood donors are like prostitutes, only worse, because they let blood magick happen as a result of their trafficking."

I took my eyes off the road to study her. She was picking something out of one of her nails, then blew on them and examined the tips in the flickering road lights.

"You don't care," I said, not a question. Shelby crinkled her brow.

"Why should I? People like that deserve whatever comes to them. They debase themselves willingly."

"I can see all that time in Vice did wonders for your outlook on the world," I muttered.

"I'm a realist, Luna. I never would have pegged you as an idealist." Her tone was lightly derisive, and I wanted to slam the brakes so her pert little nose bopped against the dashboard.

"I'm not a Hexed idealist," I growled, and just to be difficult I continued, "I think Bryan Howard may not have died from an OD."

"Of course he did," said Shelby dismissively. "Once you dilute your blood with hard drugs you're of no use to blood witches. He probably killed himself because he couldn't be someone's donor bitch any longer."

She was one to talk about bitches. I had heard the cold academic tone Shelby used before, usually in talk directed at weres. It ran prickles of anger up and down my back, and I pressed the accelerator a little harder.

"A suicide still isn't an accident," I persisted. "I think we should look into it."

"And I think we should close it so I can do some actual casework," said Shelby. "Just because Morgan has you on a choke collar doesn't mean I can't make my bones on a real murder."

The Twenty-fourth came up on my right and I popped the emergency brake, squealing the Fairlane to a stop at the curb. I reached over a jostled-looking Shelby and shoved her door open. "Out."

She cocked her head. "Why should I get out here?"

"Because that's the precinct house," I said, "and if you don't get your smug little buns out of my car I am going to slap you."

"You take things way too personally," Shelby told me as she collected her coat and climbed out. I took the brake off and revved the engine.

"What am I going to tell Morgan about you leaving?" Shelby demanded over the noise.

"Tell her to bite me," I said, popping the clutch and roaring away.

CHAPTER 6

The Belladonna club hunkered behind Nocturne University, a ramshackle ex-brothel that had been outfitted with a stage, a bar, and questionable restrooms. On weeknights it was mostly scenester college kids, but weekends brought out some of the less wholesome crowd.

Still, a booking there meant local celebrity and Trevor's band was doing a sound check when I walked in. I had left my shield and gun locked in the glove compartment of my car, since I was off duty, and my black jeans, combat boots, and scuffed jacket blended me right in with the rest of the clubgoers.

I ordered a whiskey on the rocks from the bartender for show, because I didn't want to embarrass Trevor with my usual club soda with a twist. Whiskey had been my choice poison before I'd largely stopped drinking.

"Hey." Trevor's smooth voice washed over the crowd via a crackly PA. "Thanks for coming out. I'm Wicked, and we're the Exorcists."

Someone flung a bottle that shattered at Trevor's feet, but he ignored it and strapped on his black Fender to play the opening chords of "Deadly Sin." I sighed.

"Deadly Sin" was an ode to Trevor's ex-girlfriend, the one who ran off with the Exorcists' former drummer.

"Something wrong with your drink?" the bartender hollered as the rest of the band joined Trevor for the industrial-heavy chorus.

The bartender was big and heavily pierced, so I shook my head. "Don't blame you!" he shouted. "This shitty music would put me off booze too!"

I dropped my forehead onto my folded hands. Sure, the Exorcists were a goth band in a post-industrial world, and they had a stupid name, but they weren't *that* bad.

"Deadly Sin" died away with a moan from Trevor— Wicked was his stage name, another thing I'd tried to talk him out of—and he grabbed the mic stand, leaning on it and breathing heavily.

"That was for Sherrine," he whispered. "The dark goddess who broke my heart. Sherrine, mistress of my soul . . ."

I looked back at my glass. Suddenly, the whiskey seemed mightily appealing.

"This next one is new material." Trevor abruptly straightened up and handed his Fender to his roadie. "It's about being delivered from the darkness."

He started to sing. *"Black like the face of a brand-new moon, Never seen eyes hold a love so true."*

I froze, certain that every head in the place was turned to me.

"Luna, my Luna, I'm mood-mad for you."

Oh, Hex me. This could not really be happening. Dating for a couple of weeks and he was writing songs in my name? Could an offer to join him forever in the dark pit of his bleeding soul be far behind? And gods, couldn't I have inspired something other than a power ballad?

The bartender noticed me hunched in abject humiliation. "You Luna? He singing about you?"

I threw back the whiskey and jumped off my stool. "Not anymore, he's not." I took off at a run for the ladies' room, shoving my way through leather-and-spike-clad patrons, all of whom were transfixed by Trevor's earnest shriek.

"*Luna, my Luna*— Luna, where are you going?"

I managed to slam the door and slip the bolt lock, face heated past boiling. What in the seven hells did Trevor think I was? His dark goddess, 2.0? And why did he have to *sing* about it? In front of *people*?

I banged my forehead against the door. It just figured—I attracted one man who ran off never to be seen again, and one so clingy that he wrote poetic songs in my honor after knowing me for less time than it takes to obtain a new driver's license.

Breathing deeply slowed my pounding heart and I stayed leaning against the door for a few ticks of the clock, trying to convince all of my were parts that Trevor was just a plain human, foolishly in love, and didn't mean to turn me into a laughingstock in front of the entire club.

That, and I owned the deed to the Siren Bay Bridge.

If I stayed in here long enough, I could slip out during "Devils in My Mind," which involved a strobe light. And then I could move to an obscure third-world country, dye my hair, and forget this ever happened.

Opening my eyes and moving toward the sink, I caught sight of a crumpled male figure on the tile floor.

He was in a pool of vomit and blood, body curled rigid like a seashell.

"Aw, shit." I dropped to my knees and half-slid over to him, rolling him onto his side and moving his head to clear the airway. I felt for a pulse in his neck, but nothing beat under my fingers.

I examined his open, bloodshot eyes and clawed fingers, nails digging into the palms so hard they rent flesh. Hex it. He was dead. I let the body fall back to its original position, and my eyes drifted upward to the dingy wall above his head. In the low light the words could have been stained in purple ink, but I could smell the fresh blood mixed with bile.

save me

My first order of business was to grab the bartender. "Do you have a key to the women's bathroom?"

"Who the Hex knows. What of it?"

"I need a key!" I demanded, hitting the bar with the flat of my hand. He fished in the cash register and handed it to me, along with a sour look.

"Better bring it back . . . and no shooting up in there!" he warned. I ran back to the ladies' room and locked it, preserving the crime scene as best I could, which amounted to practically nothing. Public bathrooms are the absolute worst place you can drop dead, for everyone concerned.

Then I went to the Fairlane, got my badge and gun, and called Mac.

"Get CSU on the wire," he said after I'd given him the ten-second version of finding the body. I left out

Trevor's musical styling and the fact that I wasn't, at the present moment, on duty like I should be.

"And call your partner," McAllister added.

"Mac, no," I moaned. "I can't deal with her right now. Can't you come instead?"

"You know what I had planned for this evening, Wilder? Drinks with a nice girl from the clerical staff at the Thirty-third. You know what I'm going to be doing now?"

"What?" I asked, knowing that I had him.

"Having drinks with the nice girl from the Thirty-third. Morgan gave you a partner, Wilder. You're a grown-up; you don't need me there to referee. Go fly free and all that."

I squeezed the phone and it gave a pathetic chirp.

"I'm late," said Mac. "Have you finished thinking evil thoughts about me so I can hang up?"

"Yeah, go. Have a good time," I muttered, ending the call. I dialed dispatch and had them put me through to Dr. Kronen's private number. Then, after Bart had the address of Belladonna, I pulled up Shelby's contact number and called.

"O'Halloran," she answered, sounding perky as a cheerleader for Dallas.

I pushed down the urge to break things and said, "Shelby, it's Luna."

"That's what my caller ID says. I thought you were off duty."

"Well, the dead guy in the bathroom of my boyfriend's club changed my mind. How fast can you get over to the university?"

I could practically see her composing her speech for her promotion to lieutenant. Witch.

"I'll be right over!"

"Take Devere and loop around behind the campus. Belladonna bar, you can't miss it."

She had already hung up.

I went back to the bathroom and stood by the door, tapping my foot as I waited for Bart and Shelby to arrive. Trevor was still onstage and people were milling and drinking without a care in the world.

Scenting the crowd yielded me nothing except the overwhelming urge to force deodorant on every person in the place. A sensitive nose is rarely a blessing, in practice. There are a lot of smelly things and people in this world. But tonight, none of them scented of blood, which left me at a dead body and a dead end.

I caught a flash of khaki and blond at the doorway and saw Shelby flash the bouncer her shield and then shove him out of the way. "This is a mess!" she shouted at me over the heavy synth of Trevor's music. "We need uniforms in here to secure the scene!"

"Nobody's leaving until the set is over!" I shouted back. "And I'm thinking causing a scene in a place like this is the last thing that will help the investigation!"

Shelby took out her phone and spoke quietly into it, turning back to me with a self-satisfied expression. "The head dispatcher is a friend of the family. She'll have every available uniform here within ten minutes."

"How fabulous," I snarled, turning the key in the bathroom door. "Shelby, if I didn't want anybody to listen to me I'd take a goddamn vow of silence."

"I'm not following," she said, pushing past me and pulling on gloves next to the body. I slammed the door after us and bolted it, drowning out the club noises except for the heavy heartbeat of bass.

"Partners respect each other," I told her, pulling on gloves of my own. "Partners don't go over each other's heads."

Shelby bent over the body, examined his hands and face and began to search through the pockets of his black jeans. The man's black button-down was open almost to the navel, leaving little to the imagination. He was skinny and powder-pale with a small tufting of black hair on his chest.

"That's true," Shelby said. "But you don't seem to want me for a partner, so as far as I'm concerned our proximity is an unfortunate stumbling block to my career goals."

"You know, miniskirt," I said loudly, "I haven't done anything to offend you. I think you're just worried that getting stuck with the were detective is going to sink your precious career." She didn't look up from her examination. I added, "That, or you're just a class-A rich bitch who can't even succeed at slumming a blue-collar job." I adopted Morgan's snotty tone almost without realizing it, and felt appalled when I heard myself say, "Maybe you'd be better suited to marrying another trust-fund waste of space and pumping out a few brats, because you don't have any skills that I can see." Her head snapped up and she glared at me.

"You crossed a line there."

"If you want to swing on me, you might as well," I said. "Then we'll both have it out of our systems and we can get some work done."

I held her gaze steadily, letting her know I wasn't afraid, that I was dominant. Or trying to be.

"Luna, you're probably the most unpleasant woman I've ever been around." Shelby sighed. She came up with a wallet in the dead man's back pocket and tossed it to me. "But we're both good cops. You're right, I am a bitch. Get used to it or quit and go pump out some kids yourself."

I realized I had been holding myself on the balls of my feet, ready for Shelby to take a punch at me. A deserved punch. What I had said was unforgivably nasty. I relaxed and shrugged instead. "I can live with it if you can."

"Finally, something we agree on," Shelby said. There was a pounding on the bathroom door and she hollered, "It's closed!"

"CSU!" the knocker responded. Shelby unbolted the door and let them in. I opened the black canvas wallet and pulled out the usual—credit cards, bus pass, receipts. No driver's license, but there was an ID from the Liquor Control Board. The sharp-boned face hiding under black hair matched the rictus grin of the dead man at my feet. I read the name off.

"Oh crap."

Shelby left CSU to photograph the body and scan it with a portable ultraviolet light and peered over my shoulder in the dim light. "What's wrong?"

I handed her the liquor ID. "The dead guy is Vincent Blackburn."

Outside, Trevor's music cut off abruptly and I saw patrol officers in their blues corralling the crowd. I turned my back on the chaos and tucked Vincent's ID back into his wallet.

"This is so not good . . ." Shelby muttered. She had a gift for understatement. If the O'Hallorans were the squeaky-clean face of caster witches, the Blackburns were the things that went bump in the night, blood witches whose incredible family fortune had been pissed away after the death of their scion's wife.

Nocturne University was built on the grounds of the old Blackburn estate. The family itself was scattered to the four winds. And now one of them was here, dead at my feet, and I was going to be responsible for finding out how it happened.

Freakin' fantastic.

"Detective, we have some marks here," said a CSU tech, lifting Vincent's arm. Ugly black tracks marched in a row to his elbow, the most recent one still oozing blood droplets.

"That figures," said Shelby. "That just figures. Junkie freaks, living in filth. Every one of them is bad."

"Could we set aside personal and socioeconomic issues for one tiny minute here?" I asked her, crouching next to the tech. The bathroom's lighting was weaker than a guttering candle, but I borrowed the tech's flashlight and examined the tracks. They were stark under my light, deeply bruised from regular use. I flashed over his wrist, hands, the other arm. It was free of marks, but both wrists had circular stains of bruises on the inside.

"Luna, he obviously OD'd," said Shelby. "Maybe he got a shot of the same stuff as our other guy. Probably a new mix that some jackass dealer is making in his bathtub. I'll check with my guy in Narcotics. Let's bag him and get out of here."

I pulled Vincent's shirt open and noticed similar oblong bruises on his clavicle, as well as nipple rings and diagonal red welts across his pectorals. The welts were healing, but the bruises were fresh and dark.

"Come on," said Shelby, who was standing as far away from Vincent's body as she could get and still be in the room. "My shift is almost over. We can take another look at the morgue tomorrow."

"No," I said, seeing another rising bruise on Vincent's jawline. "No, we're waiting for the medical examiner."

"He's here," said Kronen, coming through the door and positioning himself next to me. "What's so important?"

I showed him the bruises, the tracks, and the welts. Imprints of violence are hard to erase. Vincent would be buried with his bruises. They would never fade. Over Shelby's irritated sigh I said, "I think he was restrained."

Kronen swabbed blood from the fresh track in Vincent's arm and nodded. "By a person. These marks were made by fingers, I believe."

Shelby blew out a puff of air behind me. "So he was in a fight. So what?"

I stripped off my gloves and stood. "So maybe the fight ended with him getting a hot dose shoved in his arm. That's a murder. We're homicide detectives."

Shelby flipped her hair over her shoulder, gathering it into a nervous ponytail and then letting it fall again. I looked into her eyes. Panic was rising from their depths and it got worse every time she looked at the body. "I don't think this merits an investigation," she said desperately.

"Well, I do," I said. "And partners listen to each other. We're working the case."

I touched Kronen lightly on the arm. "How soon can you have him bagged and autopsied?"

"For you, I'll push him through in the express lane," said Kronen. "Ten gunshots or less."

"Hilarious," I assured him when he mistook my silence for disapproval. No matter how long I work in the department, I'll never get used to morgue humor.

"Can we *please* go file a report now?" Shelby demanded. On the other hand, cop humor was something I could use a little more of lately.

"Yeah, yeah, we're going," I assured her. Behind her, Trevor pushed through the crowd to the uniforms guarding the door.

"Luna!"

I went over to him, taking his hand and guiding him away from the scene. He stopped me, gripping my shoulders. "What happened in there? Why did you run out on me?"

I bit my lip. "Someone died, Trevor."

He sagged, and then gathered me into his arms, which turned me into a human-sized wooden board. I forced myself to relax and return his embrace.

"Are you okay?"

"I'm fine," I muttered against his shoulder. "It's not my first dead guy in a bathroom."

He let me go and peered at the barricade. "Who was it?"

"I can't discuss the details of an open case," I repeated perfunctorily, and then it hit me that Trevor and Blackburn might have run in the same circles. Vincent certainly dressed the part. "It's Vincent Blackburn. Looks like he might have had an accident." If the accident was being held down and injected with poison, that is.

"Hex me." Trevor passed a hand over his face. "That sucks, man. That's really messed up."

I took his hands in mine. "Do you know *anything* about Vincent? Could you help me?"

"He bartended at some fringe place downtown . . . one of those shitty basement venues, whips and chains, you know."

"Fetish club?" I wasn't surprised. The Blackburn family had a reputation for being into anything that involved blood and pain, preferably a willing victim's.

"Luna," said Trevor suddenly. "Did you like my song?"

Shelby came out of the bathroom and motioned toward the door. I waved her ahead and faced Trevor.

"I have to know," he said. "I put my heart into it." And dammitall, he meant it. His eyes searched my face and I forced myself to soften. He was a good guy. He thought he loved me. The song was something totally normal. Sweet, even. I would not think about how it could never, ever close the hole in my heart. Would not, would not, would not.

"It was a very sweet thing, Trevor," I said, kissing him on the cheek. "You're sweet."

"Don't talk like that." He grinned. "You'll ruin my reputation." He kissed me on the lips, for a lot longer than I'd planned on, and then released me. "Go to work, babe. I'll call you soon."

CHAPTER 7

Shelby was leaning against a sporty white Nissan in the parking lot, tapping one stiletto-heeled foot. I made her footwear as brand-new Jimmy Choos and had a brief flash of envy before I said, "Blackburn was a fetish club bartender, but my boy—source—didn't know which place."

"Well, if you're determined to work this to death, it shouldn't be too hard to figure out which one," said Shelby. "They're a specialized industry, very insular. We could pay his employers a visit."

"And here I was just thinking I hadn't seen enough middle-aged men being spanked recently," I said, unlocking the Fairlane.

"That's only the surface," Shelby told me with what I'm almost certain was glee. "Good fetish bars have dom/sub, flogging, footplay . . . and a lot of other options."

"Great," I said. "Can't wait to get my toes licked by some guy in a collar and a leather bikini."

"You were the one who wanted to pursue this," said Shelby. "Meet you back at the house to file our report?"

I bit my lip. "We need to notify Vincent's family. The sooner, the better." With two notifications in as many days, I was not on the winning square at the cosmic roulette table. But the Blackburns were a clannish bunch, and I had a feeling they wouldn't be too specific about where their fury landed if they found out Vincent was dead from someone other than the cops.

"If he even has a family; the Blackburns are strictly underground," said Shelby. "Nobody knows where they live."

I got in the Fairlane and opened the passenger door. "I do."

Ghosttown is the creeping rot on the underside of Nocturne City, a place where no one goes unless they're desperate and where plain humans disappear faster than the ash on the end of a burned-down cigarette.

Shelby grabbed my arm as I pulled off the expressway at Exit 43. "You cannot be serious."

I glared at her hand until she moved it. "Do I look like I think this is at all amusing, Shelby?"

The Fairlane ground over desiccated pavement and broken glass, and I pointed it down the wide boulevard that had once been the heart of the federal housing project burned in the Hex Riots of 1969.

"I thought no one lived here," Shelby murmured, face pasted to the glass as we passed blackened cement boxes that had once been homes and shops. My headlights picked up a few skinny, hunched figures on the edges of the road, and my hands tightened on the wheel.

"Don't let the name fool you. There's a lot more than ghosts here." Including most of the blood witches in

Nocturne City. My cousin Sunny, a caster witch herself, had told me all the juicy rumors of the Blackburn compound, guarded by blood wardings and full of depravity beyond imagination. Probably an orgy or two to round it out. Then again, Sunny was prone to exaggeration. The one concrete fact I'd gathered was that the Blackburn manse was somewhere near the center of the projects.

"Unbelievable," Shelby murmured. "It's like Wonderland."

"Like Hell, you mean." Being in this strange shadow-world made me break out in a nervous sweat, because weres lived in Ghosttown too. Were packs, all of whom defended their territory jealously. And here I was, an Insoli were, strolling in just as cocky as you please. Insoli are cast out by their pack after receiving the bite. Or, in my case, they run away as fast as their legs will carry them. The lowest of the low, untouchable. That's me.

Most days, I was fine with being Insoli. I had never had a pack and didn't want one. Someone, or thing, jumped in front of the Fairlane, hooting. I jammed on the brakes and the scent of dirty were invaded the car. A ragged teenage boy beat his fists on my hood once and then took off across the boulevard.

Today was not one of those days.

"Do you know where you're going?" Shelby asked, watching the retreating were. I was just hoping that his fifteen testosterone-fueled buddies weren't right behind him, looking to mate. Ford Fairlanes weren't built to keep out horny were men.

"Not really," I said, "but I have a feeling we'll know it when we see it." I drove forward again, keeping an eye out for sigils and ward marks, or anyone who looked vaguely anemic.

I had hoped never to come back to Ghosttown, but I always did, like a sailor to a siren call. A few miles away, in the section of the projects hit worst by the Riots, I had killed Alistair Duncan. Not in time to stop him from sacrificing Dmitri's sister Olya to his working, but he was dead all the same. Murdered by my were.

"Stop it," I muttered out loud.

"Stop what?" Shelby asked, and I waved her off. If I had shot Alistair Duncan in the head, I wouldn't have this tempest of guilt and blood inside me. He needed to be killed. I had done the job. Whether by a bullet in the brain or teeth to the throat, I had done what was right and demanded of me.

And I had let the phase take me willingly, and once again someone had ended up dead because of it.

I was actually happy to see a brick apartment house marked with a blood sigil on the door. You know things are bad when you're looking forward to meeting the head of a black-magic-using, human-sacrificing clan more than to being alone with your own thoughts.

"This is so not the place I want to be," Shelby said. She got out of the car and adjusted her shirt so her gun showed.

"You and me both," I told her, locking the Fairlane, not that it would do any good.

"Do you have any idea of the stories I've heard about these people?" Shelby demanded as I advanced on the door and knocked. The sigil was real blood— old and dried to crackling, but real, human blood.

"I can probably guess," I muttered, brushing my

hands on my jeans. "Look, just try to not be . . . yourself, and we'll keep it short and sweet."

"Sure." Shelby snorted. "And after this, we'll all go ice-skating at the rink in the ninth circle of Hell."

The door swung open and a hollow-cheeked face peered through the crack. "What?"

I presented my shield and a smile, which produced no discernable result.

"Cops aren't welcome at this address," the face said. "Piss off."

My foot kept the door from slamming shut, and I vowed if he'd hurt my boots I'd kick him. "We're not here to harass you. I need to see whoever's in charge."

"Blackburn doesn't traffic with plain humans," said the doorman. He cast a look of contempt at Shelby and then focused back on me. "Get a warrant if your panties are in a bunch. Otherwise leave us alone."

"Hey, genius," I said, reaching through the crack and grabbing him by the front of his mesh shirt. "If I really wanted to come in, do you think your pasty ass would stop me? I'm being polite, and you've got about five more seconds of that before I kick the door down and walk over you."

"She'll do it," Shelby confirmed. The doorman's mouth crimped in disgust.

"Give the meat puppets a little power and they breed a world of fascists," he sniffed.

"Whatever," I said, shoving the door open wide. "Go be a good little houseboy and tell Blackburn we need to see him."

In full view he was tall and painfully skinny, shocking pale skin against black clothes. "And what may I tell him this is regarding?" he asked, sniffing down his nose at us.

I said, "Tell him it's about Vincent."

After disappearing and reappearing with a summons, the doorman led us up a flight of narrow stairs with questionable integrity, and down a hallway lined with small efficiency apartments, most missing their doors. The dour décor was mid-century industrial, dingy gray carpet under my feet and acoustical tiles leaking black mold above us. My nose rebelled and I coughed discreetly, covering the lower half of my face.

"How many people are in here?" Shelby asked quietly as we passed an apartment where a woman holding a baby was cooking.

"Enough to make our lives unpleasant if we misbehave, I'd guess," I whispered back.

We traveled up two more flights to the top floor of the building, which had been half-gutted to create a series of larger rooms.

The doorman left us in a parlor furnished with threadbare Persians and ravaged leather chairs that spat stuffing at me when I tried to sit in them. He mumbled that Mr. Blackburn would be with us shortly and shuffled out.

Along one wall, the building's mailboxes had been installed minus their doors, showcasing a variety of bottles, knives, and even a caster or two. Shelby picked up one of the flat oval discs caster witches used to channel magick, made of a mellow blood-colored wood. "This is purpleheart. Got to be at least a hundred years old. And the tree it comes from is extinct."

"Put that down," someone rumbled from the door-way. I jumped reflexively and found myself face-to-face with a short man with iridescent white hair, a black open-collar shirt, and a mightily pissed-off look on his face.

"Mr. Blackburn, I'm sorry," I said, snatching the caster out of Shelby's hands and placing it back in its spot. It prickled my palms where I touched it and I brushed them together. Getting too close to magick always has a bad effect on me. "I and Detective O'Halloran apologize for her rudeness."

Blackburn grunted. "Never mind." He stared at both of us for a long minute. His eyes were almost all black with only the barest rim of lighter color, and he scented of char. Blackburn had been touching darkness for a long time, and it was stripping his humanity away as surely as acid strips skin. "Neither of you could put it to use," he said. His wrinkled mouth puckered into a smile. "Might as well be red water beating in your veins," he told Shelby. "It's sad, all the inbreeding the O'Hallorans do and they can't even produce magickal children. Or maybe it's *because* of the inbreeding."

"You bastard!" Shelby hissed, taking a step toward him. I put out my arm like a turnstile bar and caught her.

"Mr. Blackburn," I said, "we need to talk to you about Vincent."

His lips puckered in annoyance, a grimace that slid into a rueful smile. "What has my worthless son done now? He's in trouble?"

"I'm afraid so," I said. "Mr. Blackburn—"

"Victor," he corrected me, still smiling.

"Victor," I amended. "Your son is dead."

Nothing was apparent in his face immediately, but then the smile dropped and Blackburn swayed like someone had smacked him with a brick. His sallow cheeks grew spots of color and he reached out a ragged-nailed hand to grip the edge of the postboxes.

"Victor?" I said, reaching out to catch him if he passed out. His body didn't look like it could take much more than a light breeze.

"How?" he whispered, knuckles white.

"We don't have a cause of death . . ." I started, but he cut me off with a slashing gesture.

"Was he murdered?"

"Mr. Blackburn, I really can't—"

"Was he murdered?" Victor bellowed. He grabbed the nearest jar and flung it across the room. Sticky liquid dripped down the wall where it shattered.

Footsteps clattered and a petite, teenage, and female version of Vincent Blackburn stuck her head in the door. "Daddy? Is everything okay?" She caught sight of us and drew back, eyes wide.

At the sight of her, Blackburn drew himself up and pressed his lips together, the picture of contained fury. "Detectives, this is my daughter, Valerie. Valerie, these are Detectives O'Halloran and . . . ?"

"Wilder," I said quietly, holding out my hand. "How do you do?"

Valerie didn't take it, just flicked her gaze between the three of us. "Daddy, what's wrong?" she demanded.

Blackburn buried his head in his hands, sitting heavily in one of the armchairs.

"Ms. Blackburn, I'm sorry to have to tell you this," I said, "but your brother Vincent was found dead earlier this evening of an apparent drug overdose." It wouldn't matter to these people how Vincent had died, just that he was gone.

"No!" she wailed, running to her father and putting her arms around him. "That's not possible."

"I'm afraid that's how it happened," Shelby said, speaking up for the first time. She pulled out her notebook and pen and scratched a date at the top of the page. "Now we need some information. How long had your brother been using illegal drugs?"

Victor's head snapped up and he fixated on Shelby like an angry predator. "What? What in seven hells is that supposed to mean?"

I grabbed Shelby by the arm and led her to the corner of the room, our backs to the Blackburns. "What the Hex are you doing?"

"Getting statements from the victim's associates," she said, shrugging me off.

"Shelby, this is his *family*. They just found out their son and brother is dead. Give them a gods-damned break."

"Why, so they can get their stories straight?" she asked. My jaw-dropped expression obviously didn't telegraph that this was a bad idea, because she went back to Vincent and Valerie and asked, "Was Mr. Blackburn's lifestyle one that would put him at high risk for this sort of incident?"

"You've got some nerve, you bitch," Valerie said, twin tears working down her face. "Just because we don't use shiny little circles like you, you think you're better than us? Or is it that you're afraid?" She left her father and came close to Shelby, jabbing her finger into Shelby's chest. "Afraid of what the big, bad blood witches might do to you? By your reasoning, my brother deserved to die. Am I right so far, circle-scribbler?"

"Back off me, Ms. Blackburn," said Shelby, her hand dropping to her gun.

"Burn yourself!" Valerie shot back. Shelby drew.

I crossed the fifteen feet of space in under a second, using my were speed without even thinking. I grabbed the barrel of Shelby's department-issue Glock and twisted it sideways, bending her wrist and trigger finger along with it. I disarmed her with a quick shake and pinned one arm behind her back while she thrashed, body heaving with rage.

"Settle the hell down!" I snarled, and felt my eyes phase and my teeth fang out when she didn't obey.

"Hex me," Victor murmured, staring. "I'd do as she says, Ms. O'Halloran."

Shelby twisted to look at me and immediately went limp. "Oh, shit."

Oh, shit, indeed. The were raked its claws at the back of my mind, demanding release and reign of my body for the fight it had not started, but ached to finish.

"Luna, let me go," said Shelby.

"Do us both a favor and don't move," I growled, heart pounding. I could feel my fingers tensing and the claws stabbing just beneath the surface. It was still two weeks to the phase, but some of the were's less lovely traits came out whenever they felt like it.

"Luna . . ." Shelby said again. The were snarled and I released her, stepping back with my hands raised as she stumbled away from me. She didn't cower, like prey, just stood on the opposite side of the room disheveled and angry.

I breathed in, out, and finally felt my hands relax and my eyes phase to their normal color.

"Well, that's something different," said Valerie Blackburn finally. "Never seen two cops go at it before."

Victor stood and pointed toward the door. "Get out, both of you."

I picked up Shelby's gun and put it in my waistband. "I'm very sorry, Mr. Blackburn."

"I believe *you* are." He nodded to me. "You are an honorable creature. However, if you don't get that thin-blooded little bitch out of my home . . ." He flicked a curved silver knife from somewhere hidden and held it loosely at his side.

"We're leaving," I promised, dragging Shelby by the wrist when she started to open her mouth. Blackburn and Valerie watched us go, and the doorman glowered as he followed us to the entrance to make sure we were really gone.

CHAPTER 8

"What the Hex were you doing in there?" I exploded at Shelby as soon as we were on the sidewalk. "You do *not* draw your weapon on unarmed suspects!"

"Her *blood* is her weapon!" Shelby screamed. "Those people would have bled me dry without a second thought, Luna! And you too! Do you have any idea how much were blood goes for on the black-magick market?"

"The Blackburns are not enemies in your holy war!" I shouted at her, hitting the side of the Fairlane for emphasis. "I don't have time to keep a handle on your issues, Shelby! Either get a grip or get out of my way!"

"Get a grip?" she said incredulously. "Coming from the woman who almost snapped me in half, that's really ironic."

I growled, and this time it had nothing to do with the were. Shelby O'Halloran pushed my buttons, plain and simple.

"I'm sorry," she said. "I'm sorry. That was unfair."

"Bet your ass it was," I muttered. "Rude too."

Valerie Blackburn broke our discomfited silence, finally. She slipped out the front door of the apartment building and waved us down. "Not you," she said when Shelby followed me. "I'll only talk to Detective Wilder."

In what may have been the first smart decision of her young life, Shelby backed away and let us have our privacy. Valerie favored her back with a glare. "Sanctimonious witch. How do you put up with that?"

"Heavy drinking seems to work pretty well," I said, and earned a tiny smile. Valerie had the same black hair as her brother, but hers curled past her shoulders and her eyes were a molten brown. In another few years, she'd be stunningly beautiful, but right now her round cheeks lent her an air of cherubic mischief.

"My father would never tell you any of this," she said. "He's been shamed."

"I promise he won't find out any information came from you," I said. Valerie bit her lip.

"I hope Henri isn't watching us."

"If you mean the scarecrow dressed for a Cure concert, he's not," I assured her. "I'd smell him."

"That's cool. I've never met a were." Valerie appraised me up and down. "You look pretty normal."

"Twenty-eight days of the month, I am," I said. "Or twenty-seven, if it's one of the short ones."

"Vincent's shacked up with a guy he met at his club," Valerie blurted. "Was, I mean. Sorry." She looked at her feet and I knew from experience she was hiding tears.

"Your brother was gay?" Somehow, on the list of offenses that would embarrass the head of the Blackburn clan, a fondness for the un-fair sex seemed relatively minor. Still, maybe Vincent the elder was one of those traditional, family-values sort of black magicians—America, apple pie, and blood rituals.

"He's—was—bisexual," said Valerie. "He had girl-friends before, but then him and my dad started fight-ing and he moved out."

"What did they fight about?" I asked.

Valerie blushed. "My brother wasn't very good at magick, Detective. He wanted to leave and go do a show, like a band gig, or work on his art. He painted and did these really cool ink drawings. Daddy freaked out and said that he might as well slash his wrists and trans-fuse himself with plain human blood."

"That sounds like something your father would say," I agreed. "So Vincent felt the pressure and got a boyfriend as a Hex-you to Senior?"

"Yeah," said Valerie. "Except the guy is total sleaze. Vincent used to be really sweet. He was good, with the painting. After he got the job at Bete Noire he totally changed. Last time I came to the club looking for him he yelled at me and called the bouncers. I know I'm un-derage, but talk about Jekyll and Hyde."

I'd be willing to bet my entire shoe rack that the job at the club coincided with Vincent's drug use. All I said out loud was, "What's his boyfriend's name?"

"Samael," said Valerie, rolling her eyes. "Like Samuel, only goth and pretentious? Star tweaker freak of Bete Noire. You can't miss him."

I touched Valerie's shoulder lightly and she flinched. "I'm going to do the best I can to make sure your brother doesn't slip away without someone answering for his death." There I went again, making crazy promises to dead people. I really needed a new hobby.

"Thank you," Valerie said. "That's nice, but I guar-antee you're the only one who cares."

"If someone killed Vincent, it's my job to care," I said. "Have a little faith in me."

She didn't; I could tell from the hard expression in her eyes. Valerie was probably the same age I'd been when I'd gotten the bite and had to leave my admittedly shitty life behind. You never get over a loss like that. The least I could do was bring in the person who'd caused it.

"Thanks for your help," I said finally. "We'll be in touch."

Valerie turned without speaking and went back inside, a small sad shadow against the dark face of Ghosttown.

"What did she want?" asked Shelby when we were moving.

"We have the name of the club and the name of Vincent's unsavory boyfriend," I said, omitting the rest. If Shelby handed out any more sarcasm and snobbery tonight I'd lose it.

"Good," she said. "We'll hit it first thing tomorrow."

I turned a corner and caught sight of the Crown Theater, an old movie house. A row of road bikes sat at the curb, just like the last time I'd come.

The Fairlane's tires squealed as I gunned the engine and sped back toward the expressway, suspension be damned. The Redbacks were still in their old pack house, minus Dmitri. For a second I thought about turning around, but what would I say? Would anyone there even know me? Most of the Redbacks close to Dmitri had been killed by Duncan's cronies when he got involved with me.

Gods be damned, why did the wound have to keep

opening? I needed to shut him out of my mind. Dmitri Sandovsky was not coming back. He wasn't my white knight.

He was just gone.

CHAPTER 9

You feel like glass on the tail end of a long shift, rigid and breakable. When I finally got back to the cottage, all I wanted was to make it to bed without allowing myself to have a psychotic break.

A small red convertible was parked in my driveway and my throat closed up a little. I left the Fairlane crooked on the crushed shells and ran to the door, finding it unlocked.

Sunny was curled on the sofa with a teacup and yesterday's paper. She looked up when I entered and cocked an eyebrow. "You're late."

The wall clock said six A.M. No wonder I felt shattered. "What are you doing here?" I said in a carefully neutral tone as I stowed my gun, conspicuously not locking the desk.

"Am I not allowed to visit my cousin anymore?" Sunny said, setting the paper aside.

"I don't know," I said. "Are you? What do Rhoda Swann's Rules of Life say this week?"

Sunny's mouth curled down on one side. "You're never going to get over Grandma Rhoda letting me move back in, are you?"

I slammed the drawer shut and said, "*Letting* you? That's a great twist. She *let* me bargain you back when I needed her help most. Actually, no. That makes perfect sense in her bizzaro version of the world."

"Luna." Sunny sighed. "This may come as a shock, but I'm a person, and I do occasionally make my own decisions." She went into the kitchen and I heard the water start. I followed out of habit. Sunny set the clean mug in the rack and faced me. "It's easier for you to believe that Grandma manipulated me away than to admit this was partially your fault."

"Wow, are you and Dr. Merriman sharing the same Psychobabble Bullshit handbook?" I asked with my eyes wide.

Sunny flipped a hand at me. "Don't start. Displace your anger onto a punching bag or something."

I burned. I'd forgotten how immune she was to my inherent bitchiness. Still, it felt good so I kept it up. "And how *is* life in Grandma's gingerbread cottage?"

"No one's broken in and tried to kill me yet," said Sunny quietly.

That one, I didn't have a snotty comeback for. I sat down and examined my hands so Sunny wouldn't notice she'd scored a point.

"You've kept the cottage in good shape," Sunny said. "No new damage. How's your moonphase?"

"Fine," I said. It was pleasantries now, and I hated the way Sunny swept things under the rug by reverting to small talk, but I was too tired to poke at her anymore. "I'm fine. The restraints have been enough for the past few months."

Sunny nodded. "Glad to hear it. You know you can call me if you ever need anything."

"Not on the warpath to cure me anymore?" I asked with a thin smile. Sunny shook her head.

"You made that choice when you killed Duncan. I saw how trying to control the phase was killing you. I'm sorry I pushed so hard."

Well, I'm sorry you ran out on me was the first thing that came to mind. "Forget it." I stood up. "I need to get some sleep. Me and my new partner are going to some fetish place tonight, and I'm exhausted."

"Partner?" said Sunny. "That's new. Who is he?"

"She," I said. "Shelby O'Halloran, the little witch that couldn't."

"O'Halloran?" Sunny's eyes lit up. "Of *the* O'Hallorans? Luna, that's amazing!"

"Not the adjective I would have chosen, but yeah. She's something."

"Can I meet her?" Sunny demanded. "I'd like that so much. The O'Hallorans are the Kennedys of magick."

"Complete with booze and whores?" I asked. She rolled her eyes at me.

"You just don't like her because you have that thing about magick."

"It's not a 'thing,'" I said. "It's a well-honed instinct to avoid something that tries to kill me every time I get close to it." And the fact that magick was like gods-damned Kryptonite when it came to me. I couldn't use it, didn't like it, and it made me nauseous. This was the first in a long line of disappointments for my mother and grandmother, right up there with the time I'd done that admittedly ill-advised home nose piercing.

"What's an O'Halloran doing as a cop?" Sunny wondered. "Does she use magick on the job?"

"She's a dud, magickally speaking," I said. "Didn't

get the blood. Doesn't have much of a gift for police work either."

"I'd still like to meet her," said Sunny. "It would be nice to hear her insights on workings."

"Come by the Twenty-fourth some night and follow the screaming," I said. "She's pretty obnoxious."

"Well, you can be too," said Sunny with her damned logic, "so you two must be very alike." She checked her watch. "I have to go. Grandma needs my help with a sun ceremony."

"Wouldn't do to keep Grandma waiting," I said with a saccharine smile.

"Before I leave . . ." Sunny hesitated and then offered, "If you're going into a rough place tonight at work, I could give you a protection rune. I'm still learning but my technique on basics is good."

I started to brush her off and then realized that once she was gone, I'd be alone in the silent house again. I got a marker from the junk drawer and offered her my right wrist. "Scribble away." Never mind that I didn't believe anything, including cold hard bullets, protected you from something really evil.

"I noticed a new toothbrush and shampoo in the bathroom," Sunny said casually as she started to draw something that looked like either a Celtic knot or snakes in a mosh pit. "Has Trevor been staying here?"

"Sometimes," I said, fighting not to jerk my wrist. The marker tickled the thin skin and I felt it spread as the magick came to bear on the rune Sunny was working.

"I said it when you hooked up with him—you can do better." Sunny finished the design and began to trace over it again, adding flourishes around the perimeter.

My entire arm felt like it had fallen asleep, rife with pinpricks.

"Well, I don't care, because right now I like him," I growled. "And since when are you my social director?"

Sunny jabbed me with the marker and I flinched. "He's a broke musician who calls you 'babe' constantly, wears clothes that make him look like a reject from a Nine Inch Nails video, and his songs are ridiculous," she said.

"Gee, Sunny, tell the audience how you really feel."

She finished and I whipped my arm back to my side, glaring. "I'm not ditching Trevor just because you've got some sort of artistic snobbery going on. You hate all of my boyfriends. You didn't like Dmitri either."

"I liked Dmitri very much," said Sunny, picking up her bag and finding her car keys. "At least he was honest."

The pain from Ghosttown magnified until it threatened to break my chest. "So honest that he ran off and never spoke to me again," I whispered. "A real winner."

"I'm sorry," said Sunny. "It's not my business anymore. Be careful tonight, Luna."

She opened the back door and stepped out. A moment later I heard the convertible crunch out of the driveway. I stayed at the kitchen table for a long time, watching the sun come up to start another bleak day.

CHAPTER 10

Bete Noire occupied a basement level beneath a used-clothing store in downtown Nocturne City, one of those little pockets of grunge on an otherwise spotless façade. A small pink neon sign was the only indication there was anything going on behind the black steel security door.

I spotted Shelby's Nissan and pulled in behind her, flashing my headlights once. She got out and we both looked at the club's entrance, imagining what must be occurring within. "Have you ever been here before?" I asked.

"Not to this one," said Shelby. "I did an underage sting at Top Hat, and that was enough to last me a very, very long time."

"Top Hat?" I was only half sure I wanted to know.

"Dom/sub specialty," said Shelby. "Along with the kiddie porn being filmed in the back room, of course."

I adjusted the straps of my lace tank, skin prickling at the thought. I'd worn a black and pink bustier underneath my biker jacket and black jeans that had fit me properly sometime during a past presidential administration. Still, tight was tight, and who needed to sit down, anyway? I'd swapped my usual motorcycle boots for the patent leather stiletto version with steel heels and a liquid shine, three inches and counting, putting me over six feet. I felt a bit like a slutty Godzilla next to Shelby's petite frame.

She'd managed to find an all-black outfit, but it still screamed upper-tax-bracket soccer mom. Maybe the patrons of Bete Noire would think she was part of the fantasy show. Her one nod was a pair of do-me red spike-heeled Manolos.

"Nice shoes," I said.

"Thanks. Are we going in or shall we move on to complimenting each other's hair and makeup?"

I snarled inwardly and stomped across the sidewalk and down the short flight of stairs to the club door, raising my fist to knock. Shelby stood behind me fidgeting.

"How many stings did you do in Vice?" I asked to make conversation.

"I don't know or care," said Shelby. "The slime like my look. That's all that mattered."

When I cocked an eyebrow at her defensiveness, she spread her hands. "What? Do you know exactly how many dead bodies you've found?"

"Actually found myself, or been called in on? Because those are two different numbers."

"It doesn't really matter," said Shelby. "Just stop talking shop and turn off your copdar. If I can feel it, the people inside will eat you alive. People in our profession aren't welcome unless we're up on stage, being spanked in our dress uniforms, so chill unless you want to experience it firsthand."

The door swung open before I could muster a reply,

and an innocuous bouncer in a black T-shirt and jeans asked for our IDs. I gave him my driver's license, which he swiped under a black light, and then he stepped aside, motioning us into the club.

"Could I have my license back?" I asked, holding out my hand. He shook his head, a gray ponytail wagging.

"You get it back when you leave. Have a good time, ladies."

Shelby pushed me from behind and I moved inside, washing myself in the throbbing noise and light and smell of Bete Noire.

Nothing—not mutilated bodies, living, bleeding victims or my own attack by Joshua, the were who bit and turned me fifteen years earlier—could have prepared me for the inside of Bete Noire.

An octagonal cage was the central focus of the room, and raised platforms rested at each of the four corners. The rest of the tiny space was painted matte black and crammed with tables, a deejay, and a bar that was of the nailed-together-plywood variety.

Pink light saturated everything, along with throbbing house music and the beehive chatter of close to a hundred people shoehorned into a space that would comfortably hold forty.

"Hex me," Shelby swore as a man in a torn mesh shirt and a conspicuous lack of pants jostled her. Her face was stark white under the lights and her expression was one of realizing that the bright light at the end of the tunnel was a freight train.

I followed her gaze to the cage. A corseted woman was shackled to one of the chain-link walls, ball-gagged and blindfolded as a steady stream of men and women entered the cage, some selecting a flogger or a toy from the card table near the woman, some using their bare hands. The line stretched nearly to the bathrooms.

Shelby was still staring with a goggling expression of disgust, and I gripped her upper arm. "Why don't you go get us some drinks?"

She nodded slowly and finally managed to tear her eyes away from the chained woman. I let out a breath as she disappeared into the roiling crowd. One more stareapalooza like that and she'd have us blown.

I manhandled a skinny girl in a body stocking out of the way and secured a tiny table with two chairs for when Shelby came back. It still held empty drink glasses from the last occupants, and I moved them aside. My fingers came away gritty. I sniffed and touched them to my tongue, which immediately lost feeling on the tip. A smell of bleach undercut with sweetness invaded my nose.

Nothing like a little high-grade cocaine to liven up your evening of bondage and humiliation. But I wasn't Narcotics, and no one in my sightline was putting anything up their nose. All I could do was watch and wait for Samael to show up. Samael. His real name was probably Herbert.

"May I clean your boots?"

I jerked my head up to see a normal-looking— good-looking, in fact—guy in a red button-down and black slacks cut fashionably loose. He smiled and let his tongue flick out, revealing a silver bar through the flesh.

"Excuse me?"

He knelt down and grasped my left foot. "May I

clean your boots?" His free hand proffered what looked like a whiskey and Coke. "I'd be willing to buy you as many of these as it takes."

I've heard a lot of strange things from men, particularly in the days when I wasn't too concerned about their criminal records or level of sobriety. My first instinct was more a "What?" than outright disgust, but my potential boot-cleaner had an adorable anxious expression on his face, plus he'd already bought me a drink. And if I shrieked and flailed like a Christian coed, that would Hex the whole point of the night.

"These cost three hundred dollars," I warned boot guy. "And I'm very attached to them, so be careful."

"Thank you!" he exclaimed, dipping his head in a courtly gesture. "So many first-timers are afraid to experience."

"It was that obvious, huh?" I said as he raised my foot gently, gripping my ankle like Prince Charming laying the glass slipper on Cinderella. He was almost familiar when he smiled, a generic beauty like soap stars possess.

"No offense meant, miss. You're very beautiful."

"Thanks . . ." I started, when he opened his mouth and started licking my foot, right over the instep. Only the fact that this was *not* the weirdest thing I'd ever been a part of, sad as that was, kept me from jerking. To boot guy's credit, he didn't make any noises, just licked in an efficient manner until he'd covered every visible millimeter of my foot.

"May I move your pant leg to finish?" he asked sweetly. It took me two heartbeats to muster anything other than a squeak.

"Um. Sure."

"What the hell?" said a voice from behind me, loudly. I twisted, careful not to dislodge boot guy, to see Shelby holding two club sodas in glasses etched with naked pinup silhouettes.

"Shelby, this is . . ."

"Mark," said boot guy without missing a beat.

"Mark," I repeated. "And we were just engaging in a little friendly boot cleaning. Thanks for getting the drinks. Such as they are." I begged her with my eyes to be cool, because her posture was telegraphing that she wanted to run the hell out of the club, get back in her Nissan, and keep driving until she hit Mexico.

"Well, that's . . . that's great." Shelby sank into the other chair, defeated. I'd never seen anyone look as miserable, and I'd be a liar if I didn't admit I sort of enjoyed it.

Mark finished with both of my boots and sat back on his heels. "Thank you, miss. It was a pleasure. Would your friend care to participate?"

"No, she would not!" Shelby shouted, drawing looks from nearby tables. I jabbed her on the arm.

"Mark, maybe you can help us."

He stood up and brushed off his pants. "Anything at all, miss."

"We're looking for Samael. He works here?"

A shadow flickered over Mark's face and then he blinked, smile back in full force. "You do like to live dangerously, for a first-timer." Whatever *that* meant. "Samael only works private VIP appointments. He's booked months in advance. But if you ladies want personal attention, you can always choose from the wall." He pointed at the wall over the bar, which was lined with black-and-white photographs.

"Thanks, Mark."

He bowed again and disappeared into the crowd. Shelby grabbed me by the arm. "Are you insane?" she hissed.

I jerked away from her. "Are you? You're acting like a virgin on her first date. I thought you'd been to these places before!"

"Top Hat wasn't anything like this," said Shelby, looking at the nearest platform. Two men were engaged in a slave-and-master display.

"I'm going to take a look at this wall," I said. "If you don't want to have someone offer to tongue-bathe you, I suggest you stick with me."

Shelby leaped up and followed me so closely I felt like I was back in preschool, playing Choo-Choo. The noise and the stench of closely packed, sweaty people were starting to make my head throb, but I'd never admit it. It almost smelled like a pack house, the overwhelming assault of pheromones jolting my senses repeatedly.

The wall had about twenty photographs on it, some of them not of people's faces. I guess there was something to be said for getting to the point.

"This whole night is a loss," said Shelby at my elbow. "If this Samael guy doesn't come out in public, what's the point?"

I was starting to agree with her until a peaked, prematurely aged face in one of the photos leaped out at me. He had looked a little different trying to stab me in the eye, but throw on a leather dog collar and some makeup and it was him.

"Edward," I said. Shelby looked where I was pointing.

"Who the Hex is Edward?"

"The junkie who tried to kill me the night I found Bryan Howard." I grabbed the bartender's elbow as he was passing and he favored me with a look that would have withered Napoleon. "What do you know about Edward?"

"That he wouldn't be into you," the bartender said, jerking his arm away. "Men only, strictly femme."

"It's not for personal reasons," I said. "I just need to know how long he's worked here and who his associates are."

The bartender's lip curled. "Listen, little miss newbie, if you're looking for a story to tell your suburban friends about your night in the big bad city, go get drunk and raped in Waterfront. What we do here is private and we don't need your business."

Charming. Obviously my feminine wiles were powerless. I dug in my wallet and found five twenties, slapping them on the painted plywood. "A hundred bucks if you get me an appointment with Samael, tonight."

He reconsidered Shelby and me, eyes narrowing. "Who are you people?"

"People who know what we want," I said. "Samael. Tonight. Can you do it, or are you really just pushing booze?"

His hand snaked out and snapped up the cash, and he opened the folding section of the bar. "Come into the back room. We'll negotiate. You." He pointed at Shelby. "Wait out here. I can't be seen with someone in that square an outfit."

I gave Shelby the nod to let her know it was okay and she backed off reluctantly, looking genuinely worried. "I'll be right here."

The bartender led me into what turned out to be a

storage room and locked the door behind us, pocketing the key.

Or maybe it wasn't so okay. He took out a Baggie of something not confectioner's sugar from his back pocket and offered it to me. "Want a little snort to relax you?"

"No. I want Samael."

He rolled his eyes. "You could try being nice to me, sweetie. Ever think of that?"

"Sorry," I said. "Walking, talking rodents tend to bring out the worst in me."

He laughed, rubbing the coke along his gums. "Doesn't matter. You're not getting in to see Samael anytime soon, anyway." The Baggie disappeared and he advanced on me, fast, pinning my shoulders to the wall. "I think you'll find that this experience will broaden your horizons plenty. And you *did* pay me." He licked up the side of my neck and laughed again. "Gods, I love a stupid straight."

One hand dropped to tug at my bustier and waistband. My shock that this was actually happening, that a plain human was about to assault me, finally sank in. He had no idea what I was. To his eyes, I was a dumb career woman who had gotten herself in over her head and was currently paying the price.

The were exploded into my consciousness and I snarled. The bartender stopped his fumbling with my zipper and stared, eyes wide.

I latched a hand onto the back of his neck, so hard I could feel the twin tendons curl under my fingers. Then I drove my knee into his crotch and held it there, crushing him in a vise until he screamed, which was almost immediately.

"Gods damn it!"

I kneed him again, with all of my were strength. "The gods have very little to do with this, you son of a bitch."

He howled and folded like a hastily erected tent, limp on the floor, shaking so hard I thought he might have a convulsion. I can't say I would have stepped in if he did.

I hauled him up, his right arm in a textbook restraining hold, and pointed him to the door. "Unlock it."

"The . . . the key's in my pocket," he whimpered, tears streaming from his eyes. "You bitch, you killed me . . ."

"You've still got one working arm, so I suggest you use it."

"It hurts!" he moaned.

"Of course it hurts," I agreed. "Testicles are fragile, aren't they? Now open this door with that key, or I open it with your head."

He managed to fumble out the key and throw open the door, exposing us to the noise and crush of people once again. Shelby rushed over to us. "What the Hex happened?"

"She assaulted me!" the bartender howled. "I want the police!"

"You tried to assault me first," I said, "and we are the police."

"Jesus," Shelby said. "And you got on my case for calling attention!"

"Sorry that getting mauled wasn't on my agenda for the evening," I snapped. "Hey, spitwad, where's Samael?"

"In the back room," he moaned. "He'll be with clients."

I twisted his arm to give him a little impetus. "Take us back there."

He complied, staggering but managing to stay upright. He was just damn lucky it wasn't close to the phase, or he'd be wearing his crotch as a hat.

The back room was an innocuous door located behind the cage that simply read PRIVATE. The chained woman had been replaced by another, a redhead, and the line was still just as long.

The bartender knocked at the private door. "Not a word," I warned him, ratcheting up the pressure on his wrist. He cringed and nodded.

After a long moment the door swung open and a topless woman with electrical tape crossing out her nipples peered at us.

"Robbie, you've got to stop letting the pretty ones use you so," she said with a smile quirking her lips. "Samael is going to be most displeased to be disturbed."

"We're sorry, really," I said before Robbie could open his mouth. "Please. We just want to talk to him."

She looked me over, tongue protruding slightly between her lips, and I felt dirtier than if I'd just won a wet T-shirt contest judged by longshoremen.

"Come in then, you beautiful hot thing," she told me. I shoved Robbie back into the crowd and went through the door, Shelby following. If being a beautiful hot thing to a Wendy O. Williams clone was what it took to finally have some answers, then a beautiful hot thing I was.

"I'm hot too," Shelby groused as Wendy led us through a small foyer into what had, at one time, been a walk-in freezer and was now draped with velvet and lit with the same smoky pink as the rest of the club.

"Shelby? Really not the time," I told her.

"Some ladies to see you, dearest," said the woman, and she ushered us in.

My first look at Samael was sort of a letdown—he was average height, muscled but nothing special, wearing leather rock-star pants sans shirt and a dainty leather Lone Ranger–style mask. There were no tattoos, no scars, not even an earring.

Then he faced me, and I found myself looking into eyes as cold as a winter ocean. His mouth was just slightly too large for his face, which made him look obscene and mad all at once. Beside me, Shelby's scent spiked from nerves to pure fear in a jet of copper.

"Ah," he purred, setting down the flogger he held and extending a hand. "To what do I owe the pleasure?"

Pick the last thing on earth I would do willingly right at that moment, and touch Samael was it. He had the sinuous, slightly oily quality to his movements that reminded me of a were on the hunt, a creature wearing human skin.

I kept my hands at my sides and said, "We heard that you and Vincent Blackburn sometimes worked as a team. Is he here?" Innocent and guileless, that's me.

A smile flickered and died on Samael's face. "Vincent is dead, pretty."

How the hell had he known that? "He is? How awful."

There was a moan from behind Samael and I peered around him to see a girl strapped to a padded massage table, bloody red marks defining her ribs and breasts. Samael's assistant walked over and casually began to fondle her, making soothing noises.

"Is she okay?" Shelby asked. She was still twitchy and I willed her not to make a scene.

"She is experiencing the greatest pleasure of her life," said Samael with a smile. "She will learn the rituals of pain and come to expect it as a reward. A very fortunate young lady."

"Sorry to take up your time," I said. I had been about to identify myself and question Samael properly, but I became aware of the soundproofed, closed-in room and thought better of it. Right now, I just wanted to teleport out of the Creep Dimension and go home.

"I know you, young lady," said Samael to Shelby, fixing his glacial eyes on her.

"Oh, I don't think so," said Shelby. "I've never been here before." She tugged at me. "We can't get that two-on-one team-up we wanted, er . . . Hester. Let's go."

Hester? Well, Shelby won the prize for worst undercover improv ever.

"No," said Samael and we both reflexively stopped. "No, I remember you now." He stripped off his mask and crossed the space to Shelby, squeezing her arm so hard she cried out. "Top Hat," he said. "You're the little bitch who arrested me in front of half a dozen colleagues. Do you have any idea the humiliation I suffered?" His formal accent was gone, replaced with an edge born somewhere in New York or Jersey.

"I do, and I also remember pulling you off a thirteen-year-old girl," Shelby spat. "Get your hands off me!"

Samael threw her across the room and Shelby hit the metal wall, crumpling. He turned on me, but I already had my gun out. "Police," I said. "Show me your hands."

Rage flaming like blue fire in his eyes, he slowly raised them.

"On the ground," I said. "Slowly and calmly. Clasp your hands behind your head."

He didn't move, just shifted his eyes over my shoulder a split second before I felt something heavy smash into my skull. Stars spun and I went to my knees. I lost my grip on my gun and felt hard hands pull me up by my arms and hair.

I lashed out, growling and fighting as a were, not a homicide detective. My jaw twinged as I fanged out and I dimly heard the girl's shout as she and Samael struggled to contain me. Someone hit me again, and everything went black and soft as cotton as I spiraled into darkness.

CHAPTER 11

I came to with mesh pressing into my cheek and the rhythmic chanting of a crowd in my ears. My head vibrated like a guitar string and I felt sick when I tried to raise it. I touched the back of my skull and a little blood came away on my fingers.

"Luna!" That voice I recognized. Shelby swam into view, arms pinned by two bouncers and nearly engulfed by the crowd pressing in. Mesh separated us. I was in the cage.

A hand lifted my head by my hair and I swatted weakly. "Now, none of that," said Samael, squirting my face with a water bottle. It was cold and stung at the small cuts the mesh had left across my skin, but it did wake me up.

"I'm a cop," I said. "So is Shelby. You can't do this to us."

Samael leaned close to my ear, his breath caressing it. "Do you really think anyone in this place will care *what* you are, cop?"

He had a point there.

The floor of the cage vibrated as Samael crossed it and opened the door, admitting two scrawny men in jeans, torsos bare. Maybe that was Bete Noire's dress code—shirtless, scrawny, servicing.

The men milled behind Samael, bringing with them an overdrive version of the hormone-laden stink that permeated the place. Again I was reminded of the pack house and then realized with a start that the two men were weres. Crap. This was nine shades of not good.

"You want to see fear?" Samael asked the chanting crowd. "You want to see the primal urges that drive us all?"

The crowd cheered like Led Zeppelin was about to come on stage. Samael made a quick exit and as soon as the door slammed shut the two were men advanced on me. They reached out and propped me up against the wall of the cage, staring. I glared up at them.

"Don't touch me."

"Insoli have no rights," said one. "Shut up."

"Yeah," said the other. "No pack leader for you to run back to and tattle once we're through." He thrust his groin at me suggestively.

Oh, Hex it. They were in rut, and wanted to mate. With me. The first one leaned down and sniffed behind my ear. "You're ripe, baby. We're gonna give the people a good show."

"No!" Shelby was screaming. "No, let me *go*! She's my partner!" She ground her foot into one of the bouncer's insteps and he released her. Shelby took off through the crowd, a few of whom made a halfhearted attempt to stop her. More were interested in my imminent violation.

"Oh no, that's fine," I muttered after Shelby. "I'll just stay here and clean up. You run along."

"Hold still," said the second were. "Don't want you

to struggle. But if you wanna scream, that's okay." He nosed against my neck to give me a domination bite, the kind that mates use to show claim of each other. I whipped my head sideways and smashed my forehead into his nose. It gave a satisfactory snap, even with all the noise.

I forced myself to get to my feet, slipping off my boots and wincing as the cold bare mesh cut into the balls of my feet, trying to balance and prepared to fight without any luck at all. My concussion was already wearing off, but even with my were speed-healing, I was in bad shape to take on two males.

The first one roared at seeing his dominance challenged and hit me on the side of the head, sending me staggering. I stood upright again and locked his eyes, backing him up toward the opposite wall. If I could pull a dominate, I could get out of this alive and reasonably intact. If, and it was a very big If. Were men in rut tended to be single-minded, to say the least.

He came at me again and I kicked him in the gut, sending him backward to rattle the mesh. Dominate or no, I wouldn't lie down and die. I'd fight like my ancestor wolves of the Dark Ages and beyond, tooth and nail until someone beat the last breath out of me.

The male with the broken nose jumped on my back, his weight almost felling me. I aimed an elbow over my shoulder and, when he let go, pivoted and slammed a right into his face. His jaw skewed sideways and he yelped, cowering.

I felt pain across my palm and looked down to see long black nails extending from both hands. My field of vision was shifting to black-and-white. Hex it all, I was phasing. The blood and sex had called the were, and it was nosing outside its cave whether I liked it or not.

The first male tried to get to his feet and I snarled, the dominate holding this time. He moved, cautiously and with his head ducked so as not to challenge me, but still moving. Sneaky bastard. I decided to put him down before he got the chance to be a smart bastard.

The obvious flaw in that plan showed up the second I moved into his range. Something stinging hot cracked me across the face, exploding white lights of pain onto my vision. One of the floggers from the display, sharp-edged and tipped with steel points.

I hissed as blood went into my eyes and I was half-blind. The second male hit me in the lower back and I went down, every part of me shrieking. No. No, this couldn't be it. One—I didn't know which one—hit me in the face and I felt blood start from a cut lip. I swiped back with my claws and heard a yell as I met flesh. I wouldn't stop, wouldn't . . .

They held me down, hands on my clothes, and I still fought, if you could call the feeble twitching a fight. I just wanted to pass out, to not know what they were doing to me, but I fought to keep my eyes open through the blood.

Then one set of hands was lifted off, and I heard a crash as a flying body hit the side of the cage. The second male let go of me and scrambled away, shouting, "Hey, man, what the Hex are you doing?" before an ugly fist-induced thud cut off his cries.

I got to my knees, using my forearm to wipe the blood off my face. I really, really wanted to curl in a ball and be sick, but the mystery of who had saved me took precedence. I struggled up to stand, hands on knees, and saw a tall male form slamming the second were's head rhythmically into the mesh, his face becoming pulpier and less recognizable with each hit.

"Hey," I rasped, inaudible above the crowd, just as happy to root for the stranger as they were the males. "Hey!" I shouted again. The man stopped his beating and turned to face me.

"What? Don't tell me you're gonna complain about me saving your lady-cop ass, darlin'."

I swayed, catching myself on the cage. He was gone. I was dead, and this was a cruel hallucination on my journey to Hell. "Dmitri?"

"One and only," he said, holding up the other were and hitting him in the gut. The male fell to the cage floor and got sick. "Fuckin' flea-bitten piece of shit," Dmitri said, stepping back in disgust.

The other male looked at the two of us, eyes flicking between Dmitri and me as he calculated his odds of remaining alive. I snarled at him. "Take a hike, and pray I don't decide to come find you."

He ran. Smart guy, considering the night I'd had so far. Dmitri shook his head, something that may have been a grin flirting with his mouth. "Still the same tough bitch. Can't say I didn't miss that."

My first reaction on seeing Dmitri Sandovsky had been utter shock. My second was righteous fury. I hit him, closed fist. A girly-girl slap would not do justice in the present situation. He stumbled, putting a hand to his jaw.

"Hex it, Luna! What the hell's the matter with you?"

"You!" I hissed furiously. "You're what's the matter! How long have you been back in the city and not told me?"

The club music cut off with a screech and normal fluorescent lights came up. The door to the outside filled with Nocturne City police officers in riot gear. Someone with a bullhorn announced that this was a raid.

Relieved as I was that Shelby had chosen now as the time to actually do something right, it wasn't enough to stop me from noticing Dmitri trying to sneak out of the cage. I grabbed his arm. "You think we're finished here, buster?"

His mouth quirked as he turned back to me. "Do you really want to have this conversation in the middle of a sex club, Luna?"

Had a point there—I'd seen enough of Bete Noire to last me several consecutive lifetimes. I got my shoes back on and led him by the arm down the steps and into the hall by the bathrooms as police herded patrons up against the club's four walls. Samael smiled blandly as a uniformed officer put real handcuffs on him.

Dmitri jerked his arm away once I stopped walking. "Manhandling is decidedly not the way I wanted to be welcomed back."

"Really!" I snapped, eyes and mouth wide with pretend shock. "Because I was wondering if you wanted my welcome at all. How long have you been back in Nocturne? And don't lie!" I added as an afterthought.

"Don't worry, I'm not looking to get punched again," Dmitri grumbled. "I just got back last night."

"And of course, the first logical spot you'd go to is a fetish bar," I agreed. "Why didn't I think of that?"

"Hex me, Luna, will you shut your mouth and let me explain?" Dmitri snarled. His deep emerald eyes flared to gold and I was unpleasantly reminded that Dmitri didn't need a moon to phase—his pack magick let him do it whenever he damn well pleased.

"You'd better explain, and don't tell me to shut up."

"It's a fifteen-hour flight from St. Petersburg. I was jet-lagged, and the apartments above the club are a Redback safe house. *So* sorry I didn't immediately inform you of my social calendar."

His Eastern European accent was stronger, I noticed, more rolling *r*'s and soft sounds than I'd remembered. He'd lost the gravelly edge during his stay in the Ukraine, but the accent wasn't *all* bad . . .

"Were you ever going to call me?" I asked, kicking the dirty linoleum with the toe of my very clean boot.

Dmitri touched my face briefly with his fingertips. "Of course I was. Once I had a minute to myself, and it was safe." He shook his head. "What were you *doing* here, woman? This place is rough even for you."

"Working," I said. "And getting the crap beaten out of me, although that wasn't in the plan."

He chuckled. "I only saw the tail end, but I think those stains are gonna feel you come morning. And then they'll have to explain to their pack leader how they managed to get so beat up, and he'll probably just kill them."

My face was already healed over, but it still stung, and the bruises I'd incurred weren't going away anytime soon. Whenever I breathed, stabbing pain in my side was the reward. Dmitri's forehead crinkled. "You okay?"

"Fine," I said quickly. "Listen, is there someplace we can talk?" Someplace where I could ask him the five million questions that had accumulated since he left me. And maybe hit him again, if his answers weren't satisfactory.

"Come outside," Dmitri said, opening the fire door and leading me into the alley behind the club.

Dmitri let the door click shut behind us and fished in his denim jacket for a clove. He'd given up his leathers with the Redback pack insignia, and wore a plaid shirt over a black tee as a nod to the cold. And it was more than cold, it was freezing and prickling my skin painfully.

"Hex it!" I exclaimed. Dmitri paused mid-puff.

"What?"

"Those bastards stole my jacket while I was unconscious!" I shivered and crossed my bare arms over my torso. That jacket had been my favorite too—something I'd taken from an ex-boyfriend, Ted or Jed or something. We'd had a fight and I had stormed out into the rain and never gone back. The jacket had fit me better anyway.

Dmitri draped his denim over my shoulders as my teeth started to chatter. "Much as I enjoy the view . . ." He nodded at my now-pert bustier.

"You're such a male."

He grinned around the cigarette. "There's no help for it."

"Why didn't you ever call me?" I asked softly. "Or even write to me? I've been going insane dreaming up stuff that could have happened to you." Didn't mean for the last part to slip out, but Dmitri had the effect of making me babble to counteract his overwhelmingly silent presence.

"I told you in that e-mail I couldn't," Dmitri said, flicking the clove into a puddle. "Luna, things have gotten complicated."

"Then explain them to me," I snapped. "Try to make up a good excuse for why you ran off and never spoke to me again."

"I'm talking to you now, aren't I?" he said, infuriatingly calm.

"You know that's not what I mean," I muttered. "I thought I could trust you."

Dmitri closed the space between us and raised my chin with one finger to meet his eyes. "You can trust me," he whispered. "You will always be able to trust me. But I . . . I can't do this. Please try to understand."

His proximity was too much. Everything around me washed away and I stood on tiptoes to press our lips together. A sense of rightness filled me, something that I'd been missing since Dmitri left sliding back into place.

"Luna, I said I can't." As quickly as the kiss started, Dmitri took me by the shoulders and firmly pushed me away.

Embarrassment and anger fought a quick battle over which would be first and anger won out. Hot humiliation washed over me and I swung at him again. He caught my fist, pinning it to my side.

"What the Hex do you mean?" I hissed. "Why did you even come back?"

"Dmitri." The voice was female, heavily accented, and accompanied by a cloud of perfume that suffocated my senses. It could not disguise the heavy musk of were.

Dmitri looked over my shoulder, eyes narrowing. "I told you to wait upstairs, Irina."

"I heard shouts," Irina said, stepping under a streetlight. She was just a little shorter than where I stood at five-ten, broad-shouldered with Viking cheekbones and a thin straight nose. Her brown hair, streaked with gold, shone under the lamp.

"It's under control," said Dmitri. "Go back inside."

Irina planted a hand on one nonexistent hip and glared at me. "Who the hell is this?"

"Who the hell are you?" I countered, giving my own glare to Dmitri. "Who the hell is she?"

"I asked first," she snarled, stalking over and physically yanking Dmitri's hand away from mine. "Why do you let this trash touch you, darling?" she demanded of him.

Darling? I looked at their linked arms, at the proprietary way she touched him, and all of the blood in my body made fast tracks for my feet. "You bastard," I managed.

"Luna, don't," said Dmitri. "I told you it was complicated. Irina is—"

"I don't give a fuck what Irina is!" I growled. "You son of a bitch, you told me you were coming back for me!"

Irina tugged on Dmitri's hand. "Make the Insoli stop shouting. She causes my head to ache."

"Bitch, my foot will cause your ass to ache in another second," I told her.

"Enough!" Dmitri roared. "Luna, it's not your place to talk like that. I'm sorry, but Irina is a member of the pack. I couldn't tell you, but I'm sorry." He ran his free hand through his dark red hair. "Gods, I'm sorry."

"You should be," I said. "How could you? How *could* you?"

I heard twin footsteps at the mouth of the alley and

two figures who smelled of were approached us. Their scent was usual but different from Irina and Dmitri—aged, like they'd been locked away for a long time.

The man spoke to Dmitri in what I assumed was Ukrainian, and he snapped something back. There was a macho display of fang-showing between them, which Irina seemed to enjoy. Witch.

The woman, who looked like someone's nice old granny, complete with a severe white bun, looked me over. "You are not what we expected," she said.

"Who *are* you people?" I asked helplessly.

"I am Yelena Krievko," she inclined her head. "And my partner is Sergei Peskevitch."

"Okay," I said, "no offense, Grandma, but this is sort of a personal thing between Dmitri and me, so would you mind hobbling back to the bingo hall until we're through?"

She slapped me across the face, so hard my ears rang. I fell against the wall of the club, totally blind-sided. I couldn't believe anyone so petite and *old* could be that strong.

"Yelena! Gods!" Dmitri shouted, coming to help me up. I batted him off with a growl. I didn't want the same hands that had been holding Irina for the past three months touching me.

"She would do well to learn a little respect for her betters," Yelena hissed, and her face partially phased, all fangs and wide yellow eyes. She reminded me of Baba Yaga from the old fairy tale.

"Would everyone *stop* with that Insoli crap!" I snapped. "Dmitri, tell me what is happening. Tell me right now or someone is going to get hurt."

"Sergei and Yelena are two of the pack elders of the Redbacks," Dmitri said. "They brought me back to the city."

All the fury ran out of me. So he hadn't come back on his own, to see me. Irina caught my eye and smirked, stroking Dmitri's arm. I gave her a token snarl, but inwardly I just felt broken. Why *would* he come back, if this was what he had waiting for him with his pack?

"You are in serious trouble, young woman," said Sergei. He was small and brown, like a walnut topped by a thatch of black hair. "Dmitri, show her."

Dmitri rolled back the shirtsleeve on his right arm, and even before he exposed the crescent-shaped black scar, I knew why he'd really come back.

The daemon bite had healed, smoothed over with scar tissue that looked like lava glass. The rippled edges of the crescent, where a daemon-called werewolf had sunk his teeth into Dmitri, were as clear and precise as ever, more like a tattoo than a memory.

"It hasn't gone away," said Dmitri. "The pack elders don't know why."

"I'm sorry," I whispered. "Does it hurt?"

"Not most of the time," said Dmitri uncomfortably. "But it . . . affects me—adversely." He looked at Sergei and Yelena and bit off whatever he'd been going to say. Hex the were packs and their secret-society bullshit.

"As long as Dmitri is infected, he is a danger to everyone," said Yelena. "We do not know what he is capable of. He has been stripped of his pack leader status and will return to our primary den in Kiev until a solution can be found."

"Then why come back at all?" I asked wearily, focusing on Dmitri.

"He agreed to lead us to you," said Sergei. "So that punishment could be metered."

My head snapped up. "What punishment?"

Sergei and Yelena exchanged glances, unspoken knowledge passing between them. I stared at Dmitri. "What punishment?"

He wouldn't look at me.

"You are an Insoli and you seduced a high-ranked pack member," said Irina with a toss of her head. "You are no better than a whore. What do you think will happen?"

I may have been an Insoli, but that didn't mean I had to take abuse from whoever decided to give it, especially not a furry mail-order bride drooling on the man I had considered a mate. I went for Irina and she yelped, stepping behind Dmitri. My swing glanced off his chest. "Move!" I panted. "If she has something to say she can say it to my face!"

"I already did," Irina sneered from her hiding place. "Whore."

I lunged again and Dmitri caught me, giving me a shake that snapped my teeth together. "Cut it out, Luna!"

"Spirited," Yelena muttered to Sergei. He grunted.

"I'm sorry this happened," said Dmitri. "But this is a pack matter, and I'm bound by pack law. The elders have decided."

Oh, I couldn't *wait* to hear what the old fogies had decided about me. Almost as exciting as finding out you needed to get a cavity drilled.

"You are not welcome in our pack house," said Yelena. "A new mate—a proper mate—has been chosen for Dmitri, and if you attempt to contact him again, you will be dealt with. It is only through his mercy that you are not hunted tonight. Go, and have no further dealings with the Redbacks on pain of your life."

Involuntarily, my entire body started to shake. "You can't do this to me. This isn't the Dark Ages."

"It is our law," said Sergei. "Leave now or be killed." He took Yelena's arm. "Come, darling. You'll catch a chill."

They retreated down the alley and I heard a door slam. I turned on Dmitri. "You let them do this."

He looked at his feet, Irina still holding his hand. "If I don't let pack justice take its course, I'll suffer just as harshly, Luna."

"This isn't justice," I told him. "This is you, being a gods-damned coward." I turned my back on him, in deliberate disrespect for his pack dominance. I was numb, not really hearing or seeing or feeling anything except the pavement under my feet.

"Luna."

I stopped, not turning around.

"Please don't hate me."

"Too late," I whispered, and walked away.

CHAPTER 12

Shelby found me sitting on the Fairlane's hood, hands pressed over my face. I was tired, so tired that I was numb. I could curl up and sleep right here, if only to forget Dmitri's betrayal.

She touched my shoulder and I started.

"You okay?"

"No," I said. "I'm not." I left it at that and she didn't pry. How could Dmitri do this, allow his *pack* to do it? Blindly following pack law was for simpletons, followers who, if plain human, probably would have ended up in a cult that made you shave your head and wear really unflattering robes. It was the main reason I chose to remain Insoli, even with the slurs and the headaches over dominance and the constant knowledge that any pack leader could forcibly claim me for mating. Better hunted than subservient.

"We're finding a lot of controlled narcotics on people," said Shelby. "So the night wasn't a total waste."

"Was for our case," I muttered, rubbing my gritty eyes with the back of my hands. They came away smeared with makeup and blood.

"Detective!" a uniform hollered. Shelby touched my shoulder again.

"You sit tight. I'll deal with this." She walked over to the uniform, who had a cuffed suspect by the arm. I recognized my errant boot-cleaner. Too bad. He had seemed like a decent guy.

Shelby conversed with him for a moment and he flashed her that grin, and again I got the tingling sensation of familiarity from his face. He allowed Shelby to take his wallet and examine his ID. Her face shifted to a point between shock and embarrassment, and she quickly gave the wallet back, gesturing at the officer to uncuff boot guy. They shook hands and Shelby sent him off with what looked like a sincere smile and an apology.

"What was that?" I asked when she came back, brushing her hands together like she'd dirtied them.

"That was a mistake," she said shortly.

"This whole night was a mistake," I said. It's not every evening that I get beaten up inside a giant cage and find out the only person I've cared about in quite some time is shacked up with an Eastern European Were-Playmate. Yeah, this was definitely in the top ten of Luna's Worst Nights Ever.

"I may have something to cheer you up," said Shelby tentatively. I twisted my sweaty, tangled hair into a bun and gestured for her to talk. If she was talking I wouldn't be thinking of eighteen creative ways to kill Dmitri and Irina with my bare hands.

"This club only has one owner of record," said Shelby. "But if the Blackburn kid worked here and drugs are flowing in and out, maybe we can track the money."

"Nice thought," I said, "but somehow I don't think Narcotics will welcome us onto their turf with open arms." The guys in Narcotics were a squirrelly bunch. They had access to more federal databases than Homicide, but they were stingy and always acted like they were doing you a favor by letting you peek. And half of them were wannabe DEA agents who screamed if you so much as breathed on something they considered their case.

Shelby flipped a hand. "Who said anything about Narcotics? My uncle Patrick will help us. My family's corporation can access anything the department can."

I knew that, as did anyone who occasionally glanced at a newspaper. Patrick O'Halloran was the public face of the O'Halloran Group. He was always showing up on CNN to babble about the stock market. On television, I found him smarmy.

"He'd be happy to do it," said Shelby. "I'm his favorite niece."

I just bet she was. Another witch that I'd have to pretend to be polite to and end up owing something.

Then again, he was definitely a notch above a sweaty Narcotics detective wearing too much cologne. "I don't think he'd be able to do much good without relevant details," I said. "We can't tell him we're investigating drug money. We can't tell him we're investigating a drug-related death. Hell, we can't even tell him it's a death, period. You know what McAllister would say about leaking details to civilians." More like, what Mac would yell and throw across the room if he found out.

"He'll keep it in strictest confidence," said Shelby, and when I opened my mouth to argue, she continued,

"It's too late—I already called him and made an appointment for us tomorrow."

I glared at her. "This may not matter to the star of the Vice squad, but I don't have a lot of room to bend rules lately."

"You worry too much," said Shelby. "Go home and get a decent night's sleep. You look like Courtney Love after a three-night bender."

"You look like June Cleaver on speed."

She flashed me an irritatingly perky smile and went to her car. "Eleven o'clock sharp tomorrow! Meet me at the O'Halloran Building."

I watched her taillights disappear around the corner. A van loaded with patrons arrested inside the club followed her a few minutes later, bound for the Las Rojas County jail. These dead junkies were turning into a full-blown investigation. I could just imagine Matilda Morgan's eye twitching as she read Shelby's and my reports.

A cold mist was blowing, stinging my face with tiny droplets of chill, but I didn't get in the Fairlane and go home like good sense dictated.

I thought if I just waited long enough he'd come out of the alley and wrap his arms around me and explain that it had all been a terrible misunderstanding. But he didn't, and I was sitting there alone letting the cold sink into me and numb my wounds long after everyone else had left the scene.

Bete Noire's pink neon sign blinked off as the last patrol officers strung tape over the door and padlocked it. A few lights still gleamed in the apartments above, and I watched them wink out one by one before I finally drove away.

Halfway across the Siren Bay Bridge I realized I was beyond the point where I could sleep. My hands were shaking and the lights strung across the steel span seemed overly bright, my were night vision haloed in gold.

I changed lanes and took the exit for the port of Nocturne City, driving between stacked crates and cranes that threw crazy shadows across the pavement, like a giant's hand had marked the earth.

Light spilled out of a converted warehouse ahead, the only structure still bearing any signs of life at this late hour. Plain black letters advertising KICKBOXING— SHOTOKAN KARATE—SELF DEFENSE paraded across the cinderblock front. The dojo was open twenty-four hours and catered to cops, bodyguards, and insomniacs.

I parked in the gravel lot and got my gym bag out of the Fairlane's trunk. My muscles were stiff from just the short car ride and I winced, anticipating the punishment that too many delayed workouts would bring.

Mort, the owner of the dojo, looked up from his desk as I jingled the bell over the door. "Wilder. Thought you might be dead."

"No such luck," I told him. "Although that might change after I practice."

He grunted. Mort looked like he should be working the corner in a *Rocky* movie. He was bald, squat, and very white, and you'd never guess he held a fifth-degree black belt in Shotokan, or that he'd been a bare-knuckle boxer in Thailand after he blew out his knee fighting competitively. He was one of the toughest people— human or were—that I'd ever known.

"You owe me for last month," he said, picking up his paperback romance novel, something called *Unbridled*

Desires. The cover featured a big-bosomed woman riding a horse, caught in the embrace of a muscular and mostly shirtless alpha male. *True love knows no boundaries,* said the teaser line.

"What a crock," I muttered.

"Pardon?" said Mort.

"Nothing," I assured him quickly, digging seventy-five dollars in bills out of my wallet to bring my membership current. He whistled.

"Lotta cash. You on the take, Wilder?"

"Mort, if I was, I wouldn't be working out in this craphole."

"Very true," he said.

I went into the women's locker room and changed into loose black running shorts and a sports bra, taping my hands but eschewing the twelve-ounce practice gloves I usually wore. I needed to hurt, to beat the anger and humiliation out of my system.

Start forgetting Dmitri all over again.

Thai boxing is good for one thing, and that's inflicting damage. It's an unholy cross between martial arts and western boxing, blows hammered in with fists and feet with the sole purpose of hurting your opponent so badly he never gets up again.

At least, that was the theory I operated under when I used the techniques I'd learned from Mort on the job.

I started with a series of straight jabs, barely touching the bag, getting a feel for my feet and hands again after a long week away from the gym. My balance was off because I was so tired, but I managed a few combinations and a series of straight kicks before my breathing turned harsh.

Dmitri was welcome to Irina. What man wouldn't want a slutty pack groupie to do his every bidding? He was slime and I was well rid of him.

Even my inner voice sounded unconvincing. I sped up my combinations, the bag swinging to mimic a real opponent.

Fine. He cheated, he lied, and I still wanted him. That made me the sick one, but he was still the bastard. The best thing to do would be to move on.

Right. Forget his eyes and his smile and his scent and his hands, which caressed Irina instead of me. Wipe that rightness I felt when we had been together out of my mind.

I became aware I was kicking the bag sloppily, dropping my hands, attacking blindly. I'd already be horribly disfigured in a real fight.

A chirping sounded from the locker room. Mort didn't look up, but my ears recognized my cell phone. I debated answering for a good second—I was off duty, totally justified in taking a sick day, and in a really bad mood.

But it could be important. It could be Sunny. Or Dmitri.

I jogged out of the main gym and grabbed the phone just as it was about to go to voice mail. "Hello?"

"Why didn't you call me?"

I slumped on the bench next to my gym bag, sweaty back and butt sticking to the wood. "Trevor."

"Where have you been?"

Standing so that I didn't get a cramp, I paced back and forth, swinging my free arm. "I was working."

"You said you'd call me after my set was over."

"I'm sorry. I don't remember saying that. Although I did incur blunt-force trauma to my head a few hours ago . . ."

Trevor heaved a sigh on the other end of the line. I could hear a quiet burble of conversation in the background and knew he was probably in the Poe Bar, a hipster drinking joint he and the rest of the Exorcists used to unwind after their gigs. "Babe, this isn't like you. Is there something you need to tell me?"

Just that my old boyfriend is back with his large-breasted new woman and I'm harboring homicidal desires toward them both. "No. Look, I'm sorry I forgot but I'm really tired. I had a bad night."

"Yeah, listen," he said. "The band got an invite to play a two-nighter in San Romita. It'll be kinda dead because tourist season is almost over but the club owner has major connections on the East Coast." He paused and I heard him sip something. "I'd like you to be there."

My already-thumping heart went to warp speed at the mention of San Romita. I hadn't set foot in my hometown for fifteen years, not since I'd gotten the bite. I still wasn't sure if I was lucky or unlucky to have escaped a dead-end, off-season life with my nutso family and non-existent future.

"Babe?" Trevor sounded impatient.

"I'm sorry," I whispered. "I can't."

Trevor gave a sharp sigh. "What do you mean? You never take any vacation time. You work twenty-four/seven. For forty-eight hours, you can't take time out and support me for a change?"

The teeny logical part of my brain that hung on tenuously, no matter how damaged I got, pointed out that a few weeks of dating was hardly enough time to have the "You don't support me" talk. The rest of it was screaming, *No no NO!*

"It's not that. Honey."

"Then what is it?" Trevor snapped.

The only way to tell him the truth would also tell him that I was a were. "I don't expect you to understand, Trevor, but please believe that I just can't."

"Yeah, I believe that," he said, the acid in his tone cutting through my panic to land on the wound Dmitri had opened. "You know what? You're selfish. You take from me and you never manage to give anything back. You wonder why everyone in your life holds you at arm's length? That's why, Luna—because you never stop and consider anyone except yourself."

I opened my mouth to start yelling, then snapped it shut again when unexpected tears brimmed in my eyes. He was so right it hurt me physically. I'd alienated Sunny because I didn't think about her safety. I'd driven Dmitri to Irina because I demanded a sacrifice he couldn't make.

"Listen . . . this is too intense for me right now. I'll call you later," said Trevor.

"Don't bother," I whispered, but he'd already hung up. I deliberately set the phone back in my gym bag and walked back to the main room, flexing my hands. The were filled my mind with cloying rage and frustration, always demanding a release. Always, every time I got angry or hurt or scared, that would come. The thing that hid in the dark places that were mine would always drive the people I loved away, if it didn't drive me insane first.

And right now, it was hungry for satisfaction.

I walked in a straight line, picking up the pace as I angled for the heavy bag I'd been working, setting my arm and letting my momentum carry me through the left cross. A sound like a shotgun blast filled the gym and the bag snapped free of its hook, flying a good ten feet away from me under the impact of my full were strength.

Mort's head snapped up from his paperback. "Jesus Christ, Wilder. A little decorum." He took in the dismembered bag, insides oozing from where I'd hit it. "Jesus," he said again.

"I'm so sorry!" I said reflexively, coming down from my rage-induced hit. The buzzing in my ears subsided, the were crawling back into the hole of my subconscious.

"Don't be, don't be," Mort muttered, probably more worried about potential litigation than about damage to his gym. "Goddamn shoddy bolts," he said, looking at the hook that I'd torn clean out of the crossbeam it was attached to.

"Yeah," I agreed, relieved he wasn't holding up a cross and screaming "Begone, daemon!" after my display. "Yeah, you should get those looked at."

My hand stung and I looked down to see blood trickling between my fingers. I'd punched clean through the tape and skinned all four knuckles on my left hand. "I'll be going," I told Mort, cradling my hand to my chest. I didn't want to hurt Dmitri or Trevor anymore. I just wanted to curl in a ball and sob.

"Sure," he said distractedly, still shaking his head at the broken bag. "Have a good night."

I pulled on a sweatshirt over my bra and didn't bother with the rest, practically running out of the gym.

In the Fairlane I took three deep breaths and forced myself to stop focusing on the deep ache that had started in my abdomen. Whether it was overexertion or Dmitri's hurt, I didn't know and didn't care.

I had to put him behind me, accept that he was gone. Otherwise, all the thin threads that kept my humanity together would snap.

If that happened, I knew exactly what I was capable of, and it was enough to keep me shivering a long time after the Fairlane's heater had started to work.

CHAPTER 13

"Why are you crying, Insoli?"

Standing at my bathroom mirror brushing my teeth, I was reasonably sure I wasn't dreaming, but the dulcet voice inside my head begged to differ.

I spun, and my toothbrush clattered to the floor as I beheld Asmodeus, daemon, abandoned, a fugitive from the realm where the evil and powerful citizens of the netherworld resided. He was tinged in gold, as always, and his lion's feet scraped at my bathroom tiles.

"Not crying," I muttered, spitting into the sink.

"Who wounds you?"

"Why do you care? Are you going to go beat them up?" If I was flippant, then I wouldn't have to process that the number-one star of my recent nightmares had just manifested in my bathroom.

Asmodeus breathed out a cloud of gold and dark magick, and every hair I possessed stood on end. He shook his head, his crocodile eyes flicking over and around me, like he could perceive my spirit. Hells, *like* nothing. Asmodeus saw everything and he wasn't slow on the uptake.

"You do not see, Insoli, but threads are gathering around you like a spider spins down to an insect. You are pulling yourself hand over hand into a pit from which there is no egress. Do not follow your impulses."

"Here's an idea," I said loudly. "I'll go to bed and try to forget how much things suck, and you can go Hex yourself."

Asmodeus laughed. *"You suddenly hate me, after I saved your life?"*

Saved at the price of Dmitri. Saved just so everyone could find out my deep dark secret. Thanks, jackass. "What do you want from me?" I muttered. "You were all . . . released, and crap. Can't you be free somewhere else?"

"I am drawn here, now. Later I will be elsewhere. I am a free agent, as you said. Warnings you may ignore, Insoli, but do not ignore what is in front of your eyes."

I started to tell him that if I wanted prophecy, I'd go take in *Stigmata*, but there was the stench of char and Asmodeus was gone. I may have blinked and missed his leaving, but I didn't think so.

Was Asmodeus just bored, and playing with the humans and near-humans? Or had the gods determined that I needed a faithful daemon to spring up when things got rough?

"Thanks a lot," I muttered before I fell asleep. It was the closest I'd gotten to a prayer in a long time.

How long my alarm clock had been screeching, I didn't know, but when I was finally able to move my arm and slap it to off, the little blue display read 10:30. As in A.M., not P.M.

"Crap!" I shouted, jumping out of bed and catching my foot on a pile of dirty jeans. "Crap crap crap!"

I had less than thirty minutes to make it downtown for our meeting with Patrick O'Halloran. Somehow I didn't think one of the richest men on the West Coast would take kindly to being stood up. Plus, I'd have to endure more whining from Shelby.

Five minutes later, I was dressed enough not to get arrested for indecent exposure and my Joan Jett–esque hair had been tamed down to something resembling normal. Anyway, the tousled bed-head look was sexy. Or at least that's what I told myself as I controlled my tangled mid-back mass into a hair clip.

I took the longer route via the expressway rather than get stuck in lunchtime traffic on the bridge, broke several laws governing moving vehicles, and screeched into the garage of the O'Halloran Group building with two minutes to spare—literally.

"Miss!"

I turned from locking the Fairlane to see a pimply-faced youth in a blue uniform and cap running toward me, waving his arms.

"Miss, you can't park there!"

I checked the Fairlane—between two white lines, no bodies trapped under the wheels. "This isn't a parking space?"

"That space is reserved for clients who have business with the O'Hallorans," he said, with the kind of arrogance only nineteen-year-old boys can muster. As someone who was turning thirty in less than two weeks, I wasn't inclined to put up with his power trip.

"I have a meeting with Patrick O'Halloran at eleven," I said. "And you're making me late."

"I doubt that, miss." He sniffed, looking me point-edly up and down. I followed his gaze and knew how my torn Diesels and Dead Kennedys T-shirt must look. Hey, at least my outfit was free of crime-scene blood. He should consider himself lucky.

"Let me put it this way," I said, pulling my shield out of my jacket—my black canvas jacket, Hex that rat bastard thief—and shoving it under his nose. "This is a police matter and you're interfering. Stop doing that."

"That might not be real for all I know," he said. I wondered how much trouble I'd get in to for locking him in my trunk until the meeting was over.

"Luna!" someone shouted from the garage entrance into the tower. Shelby came barreling over to us, dressed in a gray wool skirt and power blazer.

"Spreading the good word of the Watchtower on the side?" I asked her in greeting.

"Vaughn, Detective Wilder is here to meet my un-cle," Shelby chastised the garage attendant. "Shame on you for delaying us."

Vaughn swallowed. "Your—your uncle?" I swear to the gods he went stark white under the fluorescent lights, like one of those cartoon characters.

"Uncle Patrick, not Uncle Seamus," said Shelby, rolling her eyes. "Make sure nothing happens to the detective's car, Vaughn."

Vaughn started breathing again and nodded so hard I was amazed his head didn't pop off and roll away down the garage aisle. "Yes, ma'am, Miss O'Halloran! Sorry, Detective! I thought you'd look more like Miss Shelby here."

I took his ridiculous peaked cap off his head and

threw it in the opposite direction. "You know what they say about assumptions. Go fetch."

He went scrambling after it and Shelby yanked me into the elevator. She punched the button for the forty-second floor and said, "Be glad it's Patrick we're meeting, and not Uncle Seamus."

"Why, does Seamus have a trapdoor in his office that he uses to send late appointments to the shark tank?"

Shelby cast me a dead-serious look. I spread my hands. "Sorry. I overslept. Concussion will do that to you." That and a cheating rat bastard ex . . .

Stop it. Forget it.

"So if Seamus and Patrick are your uncles, who's your father?" I asked, changing the subject for the sake of my sanity.

"He was Thomas O'Halloran," said Shelby shortly. "He and my mother are both deceased."

Hex me. Everyone knew about Tommy O'Halloran and the dramatic, drunken plunge off the Siren Bay Bridge that killed him. "I'm sorry," I said aloud. Shelby shrugged.

"I was only ten. How well do you know your parents at that age?"

The elevator slowed, blinking down the floors. I noticed a ward mark carved into the wood wall of the car above the indicator light, and another over the door. My skin crawled reflexively. It took powerful magick to permanently ward something, the magick of a caster witch with decades of practice and no little amount of innate skill.

"Are you cold?" asked Shelby. "You're shaking."

"I don't like workings," I said, gesturing to the ward marks.

"Get used to it," said Shelby as the elevator dinged and the door rolled back. "They're everywhere."

She didn't lie. The crown molding in Patrick's lobby was carved with a repeating alphabet that spelled out a protection working, managing to look decorative and sinister all at once.

A receptionist, cool and pretty as a glacier, looked me up and down while Shelby asked, "Is Patrick ready for us, Vera?"

"He'll just be a moment," said Vera with a perfunctory smile. I sensed the air thicken between her and Shelby and wondered what was going on there.

Behind Vera's head, the huge O'Halloran Group logo dominated the wall. I couldn't stare at it for too long without blinking and I figured out why—the logo itself, the symbol emblazoned on the checks at my bank, was a ward mark.

Maybe a civil-service salary wasn't the only reason I was always broke.

"Impressive, isn't it?" said Shelby at my elbow. Vera had returned to poking at her sleek silver computer.

"It's opulent," I said. "I imagine if I was a certain type of person I'd be pissing myself in fear."

Vera's head snapped up at the comment. "What?" I demanded. She flared her surgically perfected nostrils and looked away from us.

"Don't worry about her," Shelby whispered. "She's some second niece twice removed of my uncle Seamus. Nepotism at its finest."

"She seems a little high-strung," I remarked. "Like one of those yippy dogs."

"She's a bitch," said Shelby bluntly. I blinked. Shelby

bit her lip and looked at her sensible shoes. I was surprised she didn't shove a bar of soap in her perfect mouth after that comment.

I mimicked Vera and breathed deeply. Shelby smelled like tea tree oil and high-end soap mingled with that nonsmell plain humans give off. Vera smelled distinctly prickly, her blood foreign.

"I get it," I told Shelby. "She's a witch, you're not. Friendly rivalry going on there?"

Vera slammed her hands down on her desk. "Must you speak? I'm trying to concentrate."

"Vera, shut up," said Shelby. "If you're so bugged, go tell Patrick we're here." She flushed pink. It was the most emotion I'd ever seen her display.

Vera rolled her eyes and pushed a button on her elaborate desk phone. A moment later a smooth male voice instructed, "Send my favorite niece in, will you, Vera?"

The opaque glass doors to the inner workings of Patrick O'Halloran's office slid back and Shelby marched ahead, not giving Vera a glance.

"It fits that Shelby would surround herself with your type," she murmured as I followed. I did an about-face on the heel of my Cochran boot.

"What do you mean by 'your type'?"

Her mouth quirked. "Merely that Shelby seems to content herself by consorting with the lower ranks of creatures to make up for her, hmm, shortcomings."

A few years ago—hell, six months ago—I would have slapped the superior smirk off her face so hard she'd be a Picasso. But I was tired, I was Shelby's guest, and somehow I didn't think Patrick would be inclined to help us if I beat the snot out of his racist secretary.

Instead I indicated her pointy-shod feet and said, "Friendly word of advice: real Manolo Blahniks don't have plastic heels that have been painted. Hope you didn't pay full price. People might think you were, hmm, less than bright."

She gaped, and I walked after Shelby, smiling. Shelby rubbed her hands over her face before knocking on a sleek wood door with inlaid steel. "Sorry about that. Vera—my whole family—they're a little bit lacking with outsiders." She looked genuinely upset, like I might suddenly decide not to sit with her at lunch.

"It really bothers you, doesn't it?" I said. Shelby grimaced.

"Let's say I know what it's like to be a black sheep."

"You and me both, partner," I muttered as the door swung open.

Patrick O'Halloran was behind his desk, one foot propped up. He was in shirtsleeves and his salt-and-pepper hair was strategically tousled. He stood and embraced Shelby, kissing her on the cheek before extending his hand to me. "Patrick O'Halloran. Please, just call me Patrick. Any friend of Shelby's is one of mine."

I let my hand be pumped in a carefully calculated not-too-hard grip. Patrick exuded more wattage than a spotlight, although up close I could see the lines of his tan and crow's feet gathering around his eyes and mouth. He wasn't as perfect as the cameras would have us all believe.

"We couldn't be more proud of Shelby," he said. "And she's told us some impressive things about you."

"Uncle Patrick, you can stop selling," said Shelby. "Luna's not gonna buy it."

Patrick laughed, his teeth so white they could have been used as a beacon for small aircraft. "No, I guess you're right, sweetheart," he said. To me, "She's sharp, isn't she?"

"Oh yes," I said politely. "Shelby's been a fine partner." If *fine* stood here for *irritating* and *prissy as hell*.

"We need you to look at the financial history of a nightclub," said Shelby. "I can't tell you why, I'm afraid."

Patrick held up his hand. "Say no more. Anything you need, kiddo—you know that."

Shelby shifted uncomfortably standing in front of his desk. I was playing very hard at being relaxed, hands in my jacket pockets, hip cocked. If I had been any cooler I would have whipped out a comb and said "Eeyyyy!"

It was decent cover for the fact that I found Patrick O'Halloran really creepy. He was like a Ken doll, saying the right things at the right time, with the well-cut suits and the silk tie and the gentle handshake.

"The name of the place is Bete Noire," said Shelby, giving him the address. Patrick pulled up an FTC database window and typed quickly, generating a number. He pressed the intercom button on his phone.

"Vera, can you generate a report for this tax ID, please?"

She burbled something back and he clicked off, lacing his hands behind his head. "It'll just be a minute. Sit, please. Tell me how things are going at your new assignment."

"Very well," said Shelby, subdued. The more Patrick turned up his voltage, the more Shelby retreated. Not that I wasn't enjoying the quiet.

"How about you, Luna?" said Patrick. "I remember seeing your name in the papers last spring. How are you holding up after having to kill that man?"

I felt a violent twist inside me, and searched Patrick's eyes for any hint of malicious intent. His plastic sincerity never slipped.

"Well, Patrick," I said. "I still have nightmares more often than not of seeing a friend get her throat cut and someone I loved nearly die. I wake up screaming, soaked in sweat, tasting Alistair Duncan's blood. How does it sound like I'm holding up?" I held his pale blue eyes and, just for a second, something flickered there— a short-circuit of the smile and the pat banter that came with being the public face of his family.

"It sounds like you were lucky to get my little niece here to watch your back," he said finally, the walking-talking-wets-his-pants Ken doll again.

"*Lucky* isn't the word I'd use," I muttered, ignoring Shelby's mildly horrified expression. The witch had given us what we needed—I didn't have to pretend to be on my best behavior anymore.

Vera swished through the door, long black pencil skirt and see-through blouse hugging her skeletal frame in all the right places. If I had been a necrophiliac I might have found her quite sexy.

"Thank you, dear," said Patrick as he took the report, paged through it, and then handed the top sheet to Shelby. I leaned over to face tightly packed columns of information, mostly useless to us, unless we were going to pull an Elliot Ness and bust the owners of Bete Noire for delinquent taxes, of which there were many.

"Primary name on the deed to the property and the business records is the guy we already knew about," she said. "He didn't provide any of the personal information that the state requires, so that's a wash. But here, someone else co-signed a loan five years ago from my uncle's bank."

The name was Benny Joubert. The loan officer at the bank had attached a copy of a driver's license and the face that stared back was brick-jawed and aggressive, with a crew cut that would make a drill sergeant weep, and hostile little eyes.

"Gotcha," I muttered, folding the photocopy and shoving it into my jacket pocket.

"You can't—" Shelby started, but Patrick waved his hand.

"It's fine. Take it, if it helps."

"Thank you so much, Uncle Patrick," said Shelby, standing up. "We've taken up too much of your time."

"Don't be silly," he exclaimed. "After this, I'm taking you two ladies to lunch. I don't get to see you often enough, Shel."

"Oh, darn it, I'm meeting Muffy and Jody at the country club to play badminton in an hour," I said, snapping my fingers. "Maybe another time for me."

Shelby latched onto my arm with a strength that was impressive, for a human. "We're really swamped with this case, Uncle Patrick. Sorry."

He stood up, grabbing his suit jacket off a hanger behind his desk. "I won't hear it. Meet me downstairs at my car in ten minutes. I know a great little fish-and-chip bar down on the bay where we can all relax."

Shelby slumped. "Okay. We'll meet you downstairs."

CHAPTER 14

In the elevator, she stripped off her blazer and crumpled it in a ball under her arm, looking like a deranged gun-toting librarian in her conservative blouse and waist rig. "Believe me, we're lucky to be getting off with lunch," she said. "The last time I introduced a boyfriend to Patrick, he took the guy duck hunting and plugged him in the shin with birdshot."

"Accidentally?" I asked.

"No one ever figured that out for sure," said Shelby. We rode the slow descent in silence for a few ticks and then she said, "I'm sorry."

"For what?" I asked. "Trust me, I'm used to people being jerkoffs about the were thing. And sure, your uncle is a little overbearing, but I've seen worse. Much worse."

"I'm not sorry for that," said Shelby. "I just . . . forget it."

I didn't know what to say back to her. Shelby was trying to say she was embarrassed I'd seen her like this, the meek little good girl that hid inside the bossy detective. I knew it, because when I'd lived at home I'd been the same way. I was sorry for my father being a functioning alcoholic. I was sorry for my mother living deep within the mystical Land of Denial. Ashamed that I couldn't mold my life to normal, no matter how hard I tried.

The elevator stopped on the twenty-fifth floor and a man so tall and wide he made me feel delicate stepped in. The car creaked softly.

"Shelby!" the giant exclaimed when he saw her. "My girl, why didn't you tell me you were comin' down today?"

A split second of animal panic passed across Shelby's face and then she smiled back. "I thought you were traveling, Uncle Seamus."

"No such luck for you, girl." He chuckled. "What brings you around? And I'm terribly rude," he said to me, extending his hand. "Seamus O'Halloran. They let me pretend I run this place."

"Luna Wilder, Shelby's partner at the Twenty-fourth." I shook his hand, expecting another politician's grip, and found my fingers nearly pulped in his enormous palm. I winced and tried to pull away, but he kept grinning and squeezing so I pressed back, letting him feel the were.

"Quite a grip!" he said, letting go of me. "Pleasure to meet one so lovely. You're quite an improvement over the average flatfoot, my dear."

I smiled, not meaning it at all, as I studied Seamus. I could see where Shelby got her almost Slavic looks from—Seamus had a shock of white-blond hair topping a powerful, florid face and blazing blue eyes. He was paunchy in the middle but still enormous, the kind of man that you wouldn't screw with physically or any other way.

"Patrick is taking Luna and me out to lunch," Shelby was explaining. Seamus laughed, a booming sound in the small space.

"You watch your ring finger, missy," he told me. "Patrick's the only O'Halloran never to take the plunge, and someone as beautiful as you is like dangling a steak in front of a starvin' Doberman."

"I never get tired of being compared to meat," I said pleasantly. "Please, if you value your health, don't ever do it again."

Dead silence clamped down around us. Shelby looked like she might vomit on her ugly shoes. Seamus stared at me, color rising in his neck and face, those hard, hard eyes boring like drills.

I glared back. My head was hurting from being around so many witches and workings, I needed caffeine, and I'd had it with smart remarks directed at me. I figured if Seamus hauled off and smacked me, at least I'd get some paid time off and the satisfaction of handcuffing him.

A grin split Seamus's face, like a thunderstorm rolling back to admit a jolly sun. "My lords," he boomed, clapping me on the shoulder. "My lords, girl, you've got moxie. Good for you."

The elevator reached the lobby and opened to reveal a huddle of corporate drones waiting for a car. They all shrank back when they saw Seamus.

"Thank the gods," Shelby muttered, making a beeline for the stairs to the parking garage.

"No offense meant, Miss Wilder," said Seamus. "You're obviously a woman with her head on straight who would never be interested in my idiot little brother."

He whipped out a business card and scribbled on the back with a gold pen. "If you ever need assistance—anything within my power—please call that private number."

"Yeah. Thanks," I said, and backed out of the car just before the doors rolled shut again. My skin prickled with raw magick where he had touched my shoulder. Seamus O'Halloran was the most powerful caster I'd ever encountered, and he scared me. I so needed to get out of this damned office building.

A lobby café saccharinely named Koffe Kart caught my eye and I bought a large latte without my customary shot of hazelnut. I just wanted to wake up, shake the heavy feeling that being inside of so many workings and wardings gave my body and my mind.

My phone trilled. "Where are you?" Shelby demanded. "We're waiting in bay forty on the first level."

"Gods, I'm coming," I said. "Blame your uncle. He gave me his number." I snapped the phone shut on Shelby's enraged squeak and grinned to myself. Maybe this day could be salvaged.

I pulled out Benny Joubert's photo again as I walked and called McAllister. "Mac, I need you to look at a guy named Benny Joubert—that's J-o-u-b-e-r-t."

"Do I wear a short skirt? Do I look like your secretary?" Mac asked.

"No, but thanks for the mental image all the same."

"Luna, you're not still working that junkie case, are you?" he said. "Morgan's all over my ass to close it and move you on to other things."

"Such as what, the exciting world of collating and filing?" I grumbled.

"It beats losing your job, and costing me my best detective," said Mac shortly. "Here it is—Benny Joubert has had two arrests and one conviction for possession with intent. Charges were reduced from distribution of controlled substances. Must have rolled on someone . . . He looks like a mid-level dealer to me. You on to something?"

"Maybe," I murmured, looking at Joubert's face again. "I'm more interested in what he is than what he does."

"What in the seven hells does that mean?" Mac demanded.

"It means I know a were when I see one," I said. My phone hissed as I descended into the garage. "Forward the file to my in-box. I'll see you later, Mac."

He said something that might have been "be careful" before the call cut out.

"*There* you are!" Shelby called before I could ponder Benny Joubert's nonhuman status. Behind her, Patrick sat in a shiny Jaguar that didn't even pretend not to be compensating for something.

Shelby walked a couple of steps toward me and squinted. "Is that coffee? Couldn't you have waited?"

"No!" I snapped, taking a large sip for emphasis.

Shelby paced closer. "Just hurry it up!"

"Let's go, ladies!" Patrick called. "This train's leaving the station!" He turned the key in the Jaguar's ignition.

A roar filled my ears, and for a ridiculous half-second I thought it was the car's engine, but a hot hand made of air grabbed me and slammed me to the floor and a blinding white-orange flash filled my eyes as the Jaguar was engulfed in flames.

I hit the cement on my back, concrete and glass raining down. My jacket and jeans mostly protected my limbs, although I touched a stinging spot on my cheek and saw blood.

Ringing—no, screaming—was the only thing I heard as I managed to raise my head. I was deaf from the blast, totally incapacitated. The Jaguar was on fire, a twisted frame already turning black all that was left. In the driver's seat, I could see a charred shape that I didn't want to look too closely at. Shelby's uncle was toasted.

Shelby.

My legs worked when I tried to stand on them, although I could feel deep bruising starting everywhere from being hit by debris. "Shelby!" I screamed. I couldn't hear myself, but I sucked in toxic smoke, so screaming seemed like a good guess.

She had been so close to the car, so much closer to the blast radius than me . . .

If she was dead, I didn't know what I'd do. Five minutes ago I hadn't even liked Shelby. Now, suddenly, the thought that she might be dead was almost too much to bear.

No one else got to leave me.

"Shelby!" That time, I could hear myself a little, but all of my senses were still overwhelmed by fire and smoke and debris.

Close to the car, the bomb had blown a huge chunk out of the garage wall and ceiling, rebar and concrete tiles lying in a rockslide around the car. Half under the biggest piece of ceiling, Shelby was lying unconscious.

She *had* to be unconscious.

I crouched and felt for a pulse, which was steady but faint. She had a bad cut on her temple that was steadily pumping blood, and there was the matter of the five-hundred-pound piece of concrete trapping the lower half of her body.

"Shelby!" I slapped her cheek. "Wake up!"

After the longest wait of my life, she choked and opened her eyes. "Oh gods."

"Stay still," I said, reading her expression and her lips more than hearing. "How hurt are you?"

"My leg." Tears sprouted in her eyes and she let out a mewl as the pain hit. "My left leg. It really hurts . . ."

"That's good," I said.

"How in *hell* is this good?" Shelby screamed at me.

"Pain means you're not going to spend the rest of your life blowing into a tube to move your wheelchair," I said. Black smoke began to billow from under the Jaguar's hood. The fire was getting hotter and smellier and louder. "We have to get out of here," I said. "The other cars are going to catch and then we'll have fifteen bombs instead of one."

"Oh gods," said Shelby, eyes dilating until they were almost black. Her breathing went shallow.

Crap. Of all the times for a person to go into shock. "Listen!" I snapped my fingers in her face. "I'm going to try to lift this block but you're gonna have to move fast because I can't hold it. Got that?"

"My fucking leg is crushed!" Shelby howled. "How am I supposed to move *fast*?"

"Figure it out, unless you want to get extra crispy," I snapped, grabbing the concrete by the smoothest edge and getting to my feet. I bent my knees and braced myself.

I didn't know how strong I really was. I had never tested the were strength—most of the time I was more interested in hiding it. I was fairly certain I couldn't go around tossing Volkswagens, but who knew for sure?

Bright lady, if we get out of this, I promise I'll stop being mean to Sunny and Shelby and that I'll really make an effort to make things work with Trevor. But I can't do that if I'm dead, and charred corpses are really unattractive, so please—don't fry me.

"Get ready!" I told Shelby, and then shoved at the block with every ounce of muscle in me. There was a rock-smashing screech as rebar tore free of masonry, and I felt the block start to slip no matter how hard I braced it. "Shelby, go!" I gasped as I pushed even harder, pulse screaming in my ears. I felt something give in my shoulder at the same time the block moved, and I fell back as it crashed to earth.

Shelby sat a few feet away, bleeding from a torn hole in her calf. "Hex me," I said reflexively. Rebar had punched right through muscle and bone.

The car next to the Jaguar was burning now, the upholstery giving off an acrid chemical smoke. Genuine all-leather interior, my ass.

"We gotta go," I told Shelby, pulling her up and draping her right arm over my shoulder. My other arm wasn't working too well, hanging limply by my side and sending fierce jolts of pain through me if I jostled it.

Later. I could hurt later. Now we had to run.

Outside we were nearly flattened by a ladder truck and an ambulance, sirens screaming. Vaughn the parking attendant stood outside his booth, watching the whole sideshow with a fish-eyed expression.

Two EMTs came running to take Shelby off my hands and my body decided it would be a good time to collapse on the sidewalk. I can't say I disagreed with it.

CHAPTER 15

Years later, or so it seemed, an EMT crouched next to me, shining a light in my eyes. "Were you inside, miss?"

"Ow! Turn off that damn flashlight! Yes."

He took it away and strapped a portable pressure cuff on me, nodding at the gauge. He felt my pulse and said, "Your vitals are stable. Can you walk over to the ambulance with me?"

I nodded and attempted to stand. My vision swam and my knees buckled. The EMT caught me by the arm and I screeched at the resulting pain, having forgotten temporarily that I had damaged myself. *Only you, Luna, could hurt yourself worse than a car bomb.*

"Whoa!" said the EMT. His name badge said "Chen." "Let's take a look at that." He switched sides and guided me to the ambulance, making me sit on the rear bumper while he rummaged in one of the lockers. "Did you fall or get knocked into something during the blast?"

I only dimly heard him, my concentration fading out as I watched the fire. Black smoke was roiling out of the O'Halloran's garage, and three ladder trucks were parked at the entrance, firefighters running in and out with axes and hoses and oxygen tanks. Down the block, another squad was evacuating the tower, workers clustered on the sidewalk staring in our direction, watching the flames slowly die as the firefighters got the blaze under control.

"Miss?" Chen crouched in front of me again, holding an ice pack and a roll of Ace bandage.

"My partner," I murmured. "I lifted a block of concrete off her and hurt my shoulder."

Chen whistled. "You're Detective O'Halloran's partner? That took some balls."

"Too bad I don't have any." I smiled weakly. "But thanks anyway. Is Shelby going to be okay?" My survival-driven panic was fading and I was aware of hurting all over, ears ringing, mouth dry as ash. Shelby had to be okay . . . I had gotten her out of the fire, hadn't I?

"She's on her way to Nocturne City General," he said. "She lost some blood, and her leg needs surgery."

Knowing Shelby was all right compelled my mental grip to relax and the were burst forth, thrashing and howling at the pain and the adrenaline I'd expended saving Shelby and myself. My jaw started to ache, and my lower back spasmed, the telltale warning that my body wanted to phase.

I *couldn't* at this time of the month, but I could fang out and sprout claws, and then I had the distinct feeling Chen would be a lot less enthusiastic to play doctor.

"Fix my shoulder," I growled.

"You should go to the emergency room . . ." Chen started.

"Is it broken?" I asked, struggling to stay normal. All of my instincts wanted to bolt and find a safe place to hole up and heal, far from prying eyes.

"No, it's dislocated, but . . ." Chen started.

"Then fix it, please. Now."

He sighed, but gripped my wrist firmly. "Brace yourself. This is going to really hurt."

I gripped the frame of the ambulance and choked on a scream when Chen jerked my arm violently and my shoulder snapped back into place with a soft *thop*! A split second of violent, mind-bending pain and I was left with a dull ache and a functional arm.

"Thank you," I said tightly to Chen. The fire was out, just stinking smoke boiling from underneath the skyscraper now. Police cruisers had arrived, and I saw two unmarked sedans in colors I'd describe as "lightly toasted" and "well done" pull up behind them. McAllister emerged from the first, Matilda Morgan from the second.

Hex me.

Mac waited for Morgan and they walked together, a bad sign. If my lieutenant and my captain were in concert, heads were going to roll.

Morgan looked at me, looked at the fire, and back at me again. She tapped one finger against her teeth. "Detective Wilder, is this your idea of keeping a low profile?" Her tone was light and pleasant, but the rage burning in her eyes was hotter than any bomb blast.

"No, ma'am," I muttered, looking at my feet.

"Lieutenant, I must say I'm disappointed," she told Mac, facing him. She barely topped his collarbone, but Mac looked like a rabid pit bull was chasing him and he'd just realized his shoelaces were untied. "Your record is exemplary, but having seen the way you run your detectives I'm beginning to wonder just how accurate that is."

Mac's rangy face turned tomato-colored, although his expression never altered. Mac is like a dormant volcano—it takes a hell of a lot of pressure to make him blow.

Morgan continued, "Property damage, officers under your command willfully disobeying orders, other officers grievously injured because of these oversights—you might as well have sent Detective O'Halloran to the hospital yourself." She drew herself up, her blocky body reminding me of nothing so much as one of those fantasy-novel dwarves who seem cute until you notice they're swinging an axe at your shins. "Rest assured that all of this will be reported to the disciplinary committee, and I very much doubt you will have your shield much longer."

"Stop it," I said. Morgan turned on me and had I not already been in pain I would have felt it from the sheer force of her glare.

"Excuse me?"

"Leave Mac alone." I met her gaze. "You want to blame somebody for all of this, blame me. But have the guts to do it *to me*. Don't punish Mac because you like to play mind games."

"Luna, this is a really bad time for speeches." Mac sighed. Morgan held up a hand and he reluctantly shut his mouth.

"I think this is the perfect time," she purred, a grin that I can only describe as triumphant on her face. "Do go on with your impassioned outburst, Detective."

"I know you don't like me," I said. "I can't figure out if it's because I'm a were or because I just rub you the wrong way, but in any event, I'm a good cop, and I am doing the best damn job I can, and if you can't get past this animosity and see that, then Hex you."

I stood, looking down at Morgan. "My partner almost died, so if you'll excuse me I'm going to go find the person that almost made it happen."

Morgan narrowed her eyes, daring me to step past her, to be the one to break contact, but she didn't explode like I'd thought she would. Mac remained carefully bland next to her, but I could smell his sweat under the well-worn suit.

"Carry on, then," said Morgan finally, as if coming to a decision. "I think we're done here, Lieutenant McAllister." She spun and went to her car, weaving past a CSU team that was approaching with cameras and field cases.

Mac gripped my arm. "Don't get the wrong idea, here—I appreciate what you said, but don't you ever do that again. You're *my* detective and if you buck protocol I'm going to suspend you."

I blinked. "Hex, Mac. You're welcome."

He pressed his lips together, giving me a look that was all too fatherly. "You're not all right, Wilder, and this whole mess just proves it. I can't give you special treatment. I need you to be on your game, or off my squad."

What was it with all the men in my life telling me what was best lately?

"Luna?" Mac crossed his arms, waiting. I was saved when one of the CSU techs broke off and touched my shoulder.

"Detective Wilder? We need you."

"I have a crime scene to secure," I told Mac coldly.

He looked like he wanted to say something else, then turned and went back to his car.

"Thought you could use an assist," said the tech.

"Thanks, he—" I began, and then registered the tech's handsome dark face from my memory. "Pete!"

Pete Anderson grinned at me and shook my hand. "Good to see you, Detective."

I'd met Pete during the Duncan case, when he'd been working in the identification bureau as a lab tech. Poor Pete had endured a lot from me on that case—hostile were packs, being held at gunpoint, and my general bitchiness about the whole situation.

"You got promoted," I noticed. He was carrying a gun and wearing a blue field-investigator's jacket.

"Damn right, I did," he said. "The department figured it was the easiest way to keep me from suing their asses off after that Roenberg mess."

"I'm glad you're here," I told him, and meant it. Pete was one of those steady humans, the kind who radiated stillness and competence. They were the only kind I could be around for extended periods of time.

"Me too. Let's see what we've got."

The garage was still hot and made my eyes water from the noxious smoke, but the fire department pronounced it safe to enter. Pete's team members swarmed around the smoking hulk of the Jaguar, taking pictures and bagging debris that had been thrown everywhere by the blast.

I saw a piece of car embedded in the concrete wall of the garage and flexed my shoulder. I really had been damn lucky.

Pete flashed his light over the Jaguar's interior and the charred corpse of Patrick O'Halloran, wincing at the barely recognizable shape. "Someone knew what they were doing," he murmured. "Hot and fast. No chance of survival. Get a picture of that," he instructed the tech with the camera, pointing at the wall behind the car. Aside from the surface concrete being blown off, it was intact.

"Something there?" I asked, examining the scene as best I could in the smoky half-light.

"Not there," said Pete. "The garage is still intact, which means the tower above it is still intact."

"So?"

"So this bomb wasn't meant to bring down the structure. It was meant to kill."

I coughed, trying to clear my parched throat. "Who'd want to kill Patrick O'Halloran? He's a figurehead. Wouldn't it be smarter to go after Seamus?"

"That's your area," said Pete. "I'm here to find out how they managed it." He touched the frame of the car experimentally and then climbed through the mangled passenger door and examined the interior. "Huh," he said.

"See something?" I asked.

"That's the problem," said Pete. "All that's here is car." He clambered back out and illustrated with his penlight. "Fire follows the path of least resistance, right? It blew through the windows and the vents to the engine compartment, which caused the gas line and the tank to blow as secondary charges."

"Where's this going?" I asked, knowing I wouldn't like the answer by the grim expression on Pete's face.

"For the explosion to follow that path, the bomb would have to be planted under the front seat." He offered me his flashlight and I leaned in, trying to ignore the obscenely sweet smell coming from the cooked body in the driver's seat.

The seats and dashboard were intact, charred and melted but still retaining their shape. I pulled my head back and gave Pete a puzzled look.

"Shouldn't there be more, I dunno, exploded parts?"

"There shouldn't be anything left of the inside of that car," said Pete. "For all intents and purposes, this could have been a freak accident. If it wasn't for the point of origin, I'd say his gas tank ignited."

"But it didn't . . ." I murmured. Something tickled at my consciousness, the birth of a theory that wouldn't quite come clear. "Pete, how do you kill a witch?"

He goggled at me. "I haven't the faintest idea."

"You can't," I said. "Because any witch worth his blood won't let you close enough to do the job."

"Something come to mind?" Pete asked carefully, because I was pacing back and forth like a caged beast. How would you kill a powerful caster witch on his home territory, surrounded by workings and ward marks and protected by his own power?

You wait until he's in the one spot with no wards, I answered myself. *And you blow his face off.*

"Detective?" Pete said anxiously.

I dug in my jacket pocket and found my car keys. "I'll be back. Don't let anyone in here except the CSU team— not firemen, not the medical examiner—no one."

Running for the Fairlane, I belatedly realized that this was a bad idea and that also my car was probably totally trashed. I'd only parked about fifty feet away from the explosion.

The thought made me jog faster, because in the ten years I'd owned the car I'd never managed to so much as dent the fender. The Fairlane was trusty and sexy and mine, and if the SOB who set the nonbomb had blown it up too, then the gods help them.

I skidded to a stop, seeing a huge starburst crack in my windshield from where debris had rained down, but no obvious fatal injuries. The Fairlane started, a little more grumbly than usual, but it purred as I pulled out of the garage using the alternate exit, flashing my shield at the uniformed officer guarding it. As I accelerated into the street the Fairlane shuddered once and then slipped smoothly into gear. I sighed with relief. It's a long drive to Battery Beach.

CHAPTER 16

Grandma Rhoda's cottage looked duller in the light of day, no longer a spooky Carpenter Gothic house of horrors, just a ramshackle old Victorian that was slowly but surely sliding down the dune.

Sunny's convertible was in the driveway, alone. That didn't mean anything, though—Grandma Rhoda didn't drive. In my less charitable moments I speculated about pointy hats and brooms as modes of transportation.

"Sunny?" I called, knocking cautiously on the frame of the screen door. I didn't know what kind of wards Rhoda had put up since I'd visited last. I'd had Dmitri with me, and hadn't exactly endeared myself.

Footsteps sounded and an eye covered the peephole momentarily before the door opened. "Luna." Sunny frowned, in confusion or surprise I couldn't tell.

"I need your help," I said, cutting to the point.

"Oh gods, what's happened to you?" Sunny said immediately. She has this habit of assuming that I'm always on the verge of dire peril. We'll ignore for the moment that most of the time she's right.

"Nothing's wrong with me," I said, more snappishly

than I intended. "I have a crime scene that I want you to take a look at."

Sunny blinked. "Me? Why me? I'm not good around blood, Luna."

"Oh, don't worry. I'm fairly sure all of the dead guy's blood got burned up."

She blanched and I made a heroic effort to curb the ingrained instinct that all siblings and close relatives of the same age have to mess with each other. We weren't fifteen anymore. "Please, Sunny?"

"I don't see what good I'd be," she said. "And Grandma is going to be home soon . . ."

"They used magick," I said. "They killed Patrick O'Halloran."

Sunny's eyes went wide. I knew that would get her.

"How?" she whispered.

"I was hoping you could tell me."

She nodded slowly. "Of . . . of course. I'll get my bag and meet you at your car."

The minute we pulled into the garage Sunny started to shiver. "Cold?" I asked.

"No . . ." Sunny murmured. "Just power . . . a lot of power . . . all around us."

"That would be the magickal electric fence the O'Hallorans erected around this entire tower," I said. I could feel it too, if I let myself—the dull pinpoint between my eyes, like a disembodied whisper you can't quite make out.

"Incredible," said Sunny. "Just incredible. I can't believe I'm actually here."

"Well, I can't believe they were stupid enough to leave their parking garage unwarded," I said. "Let's go."

Yellow tape had gone up around the scene in the time I'd been gone, and Pete was scribbling a field report on his clipboard while his team packed up. He greeted me with a nod. "Detective. Ms. Wilder."

"Swann," Sunny corrected him. "I'm her cousin on the mother's side."

"Whatever brightens your aura," said Pete. "Why are you here, exactly?"

I took Pete aside. "You know Sunny's a witch, right? And O'Halloran too?"

"I've heard all the same rumors you have," said Pete in his unflappable way.

"Pete, would you consider for a minute that maybe magick was used here?" I said. He rubbed his chin.

"Detective, I haven't forgotten those weres. I haven't forgotten what happened with the DA. Magick makes a helluva lot more sense than an invisible bomb or a CIA conspiracy."

"Sunny can tell us how they used it," I said. "If you don't mind her taking a look around."

Pete thought about that for a second, and then nodded. "I'm thinking I'll just leave this part out of my scene report."

"Smart man," I said. Crumpled in my back pocket was a bandanna stained with sweet-and-sour sauce, and also doused in the nastiest, stinkiest floral perfume I could find at Nocturnal, the snooty department store where Shelby probably spent most of her free time. "Sunny, take this." I lifted the tape and we walked forward, but Sunny froze when she saw Patrick's body.

"I'm going to be sick."

"No," I assured her. "No, you won't. Just breathe."

"Gods," said Sunny, clapping the bandanna over her mouth and nose. "Does it always smell this bad?"

"Not always," said Pete. "Although last month there was this guy we dragged out of the bay, must have been floating for a good two weeks, and when we pulled him out of the water his stomach—"

"Pete," I warned in the voice I use to stop fleeing suspects in their tracks and make reticent ex-boyfriends squirm. "Let's let Sunny work in peace."

My cousin was as green as a soccer field, but she took a breath and walked closer to the car, kneeling down to trace the ground a few feet from the driver's side door. "Did you see this?"

I looked at the charred concrete, feeling dumb. "Burn marks?"

"It's a circle," said Sunny, and the niggling thing just under my consciousness snapped into place. What I had mistaken for the blast radius *was* a circle, surrounding the Jaguar far too neatly to have been caused by a bomb.

"Simple," Sunny said. "Set your circle for an incendiary working but don't close it. When anyone else crosses your working, poof." She gestured at the car. "He never had a chance. Can I please get away from this body now?"

Pete helped her up, then stopped. "There's something shiny under the car."

I crouched next to him, seeing a small tube about the size of a cheap lipstick or an expensive cigar. Pete slipped on a glove and snagged the object, while I slipped on a glove of my own to receive it.

The tube was unmarred except for some soot and

had a twist-off top. "What is it?" Sunny called from outside the tape.

"No clue," I muttered, unscrewing the two halves. A piece of rolled paper, thick linen or parchment, fell into my palm. I unrolled it to reveal spidery ink cursive: *We see with empty eyes.*

"Crap," I said.

Nocturne City General is not the hospital you want to be in if you're sick or maimed. It looks more like the setting for a Stephen King novel than a real hospital, low asbestos tiles and green linoleum circa the early 1970s, all capped off by flickering fluorescent tubes that fill the air with a constant buzz.

It's also not the place you want to be if you're a were—the smell alone will make you faint. Bleach fumes trying to cover up thirty years of sweat and blood and dying, and not doing the job.

Shelby's room was a semiprivate on the second floor, which some overambitious contractor had tried to cheer up with hot pink paint and a wallpaper border featuring playful kittens.

"Hey," she said weakly, raising a hand trailing IV lines. "Long time no see."

I didn't respond, just tossed the note in its evidence baggie on the blankets next to her and crossed my arms. Shelby read it, her already drawn face going pale. "Where did you get this?"

"The bomber left it for us," I said. "Thoughtful of him, or her."

Shelby swallowed and I saw her eyes dart to the call button resting on her nightstand. I reached across her bed, jerked the thing out of the wall in a shower of sparks and tossed it in the trash. "You and I are going to talk, and no one is going to interrupt us."

The fear in Shelby's eyes told me everything I needed—the message meant something to her, and that meant she'd lied to me. "Luna, you've got the wrong idea."

And the hits just keep on coming. "No, see, I think I've got it exactly right. Vincent Blackburn turns up dead, and a car bomb obliterates your uncle. The bomber leaves a message for us—the same phrase that I've heard other blood witches use. 'An eye for an eye' comes to mind, Shelby." I leaned in, so close I could smell the old blood from her wound, and said evenly, "There's a gang war going on between the blood witches and the casters. How long do you think it will be before the Blackburns start in on your generation?"

Shelby passed a hand over her eyes. Her shoulders were shaking and she turned her head away, ostensibly so I wouldn't see her tears. For a cop, she cracked awfully easy. I've had purse snatchers who held out longer. "I'm waiting," I said. "Tell me the truth now or I go straight to Morgan and get you suspended."

She let out a harsh sound that could have been a laugh. "The truth? This war isn't about Vincent Blackburn. It's always been there. Blood witches and caster witches. We've always fought them, and they've always hated us. It never ends, so what's the point of even trying?"

"The *point*," I said, "is that I don't appreciate almost getting turned into a chicken-fried steak because of some idiotic feud between a couple of bored old men. It stops here."

Shelby flipped a hand at me, as if I were hopeless.

"No, it doesn't. Now Seamus will retaliate and they'll scuttle back under their rock until the next stupid junkie turns up dead." She levered herself up on her elbows. "You can't stand in my uncle's way. He'll do what he has to do to protect my family. He always has."

"People are dying," I said. "Real people. They may be junkies and whores and the bottom scrapings of this city, but they're *people*. Not blood witches or caster witches." I sighed. My head hurt and I wanted to go home and wash the smoke smell off me. "Don't you want to figure out who killed Vincent, bring it out into the open? Don't you want to make this end?"

"It's beyond my control," said Shelby coldly. "I'm just the mutt of the family. They've always hated the Blackburns and they always will. I don't know anything beyond that. I was never *privy* to the magickal secrets. Unworthy, you know."

The bitterness in her voice could have been mine, when I talked about the were packs and the Insoli. I thought of my grandmother shaking her head and asking, *Why couldn't you have the same blood as your cousin?* I too knew the stigma of being normal among the witches.

In spite of her lying to me, I felt my resolve to be hard-assed soften. "And why do the Blackburns hate your family, Shelby? I've seen enough relationships go wrong to know that loathing so deep doesn't happen because of a few bar fights or stray spells."

I sat next to her and straightened out her blankets, a gesture that Sunny would often perform after I'd woken from a nightmare when we were children, living with our grandmother. Shelby sighed and rubbed at her tears with the back of her hand.

"I'm sorry."

I passed her a tissue without comment.

"All I know," said Shelby, blowing her nose, "is that a long time ago, my family stole something from the Blackburns, and they'd kill—have killed—to get it back."

" 'It' being . . . ?"

Shelby's mouth quirked without any humor. "You think they'd tell me?"

I had to agree with her there. For all I complained about my dysfunction, Shelby must have had it ten times worse. I couldn't imagine being so shut off from your own blood. Must be the were in me, that irresistible urge to form a pack.

Shelby's breathing leveled off and her eyes fluttered. "Sorry," she said again, yawning. "They're giving me a bunch of painkillers."

"Any idea when you'll be out?" I asked.

"The doctor said less than a week. The rebar missed all of my major veins or vessels or whatever."

I would never vocalize that I'd sort of gotten used to having her around, but still—it beat the hell out of the lone-wolf act, even if she never shut up. "Good," I said aloud. "I'll let Mac know you're out of surgery."

"Luna?" she called as I headed for the door. "I really am sorry."

"I know." I waved a hand. "Forget it." If she hadn't been sorry before the bomb went off, she was now, sure as there were seven hells.

My phone went off and I waved to Shelby, pantomiming I'd come back later. She was already asleep. I went into the stairwell so I didn't fry someone's pacemaker and answered.

"Luna, it's Bart Kronen."

Dr. Kronen calling was odd, but not totally unfounded. "You autopsying the bomb victim? I thought for sure I'd have to deal with that prick from day shift, the one who looks like Eli Wallach if he was really old."

"Bomb?" said Dr. Kronen, then, "Never mind. I don't care to know. The reason I'm calling is I've turned up some unusual results from your overdose murder."

I sat down on the steps, biting my lip. "The Blackburn kid."

"His tox screen came back with some . . . interesting markers," said Kronen. A door slamming sounded in the background and Kronen lowered his voice. "Could you please stop by my office? I feel these results need to be discussed in person."

The back of my neck prickled at his secretive tone. "Something wrong, Bart?"

He was silent for a long time. "Perhaps," he said finally. "I'll know better when I can show you what I've found."

CHAPTER 17

Kronen's office door was shut when I arrived, and I knocked softly after checking to make sure I was alone in the hallway. His head poked out a moment later.

"Come in, Detective." His office was the same, softly lit with crackling jazz coming from his computer speakers. "Shut the door," he said.

"What's going on, Bart?" I asked. "Don't tell me you found alien DNA."

He didn't smile, which I took as a bad sign. "Before I share these results, Detective, I want you to know that I pride myself and my lab on our competency. I have no doubt these results are accurate."

"Bart," I said, "I've never called your results into question." One of the first lessons I'd learned on the job was that you can teach a cop to be a human lie detector, but you'll never teach them to quantify evidence as well as a medical examiner. The MEs live for the minute and the obscure, and they're our best weapons, sort of like Batman and his utility belt.

"I just want to establish that before I share this report with you," said Bart. "Because it's odd. Very odd." He flipped open one of his ubiquitous plain brown folders and handed me a toxicology report labeled with Vincent Blackburn's name and case number. I pretended to make sense of the squiggly lines on the chart and the periodic abbreviations showing what chemicals had been in Vincent when he died.

"This," said Kronen, pointing to one line, "is the victim's blood type—A positive, as you can see. This"—he slid his finger to the next line—"is a second blood type found around the puncture mark and in trace amounts throughout his circulatory system."

"I thought they only doled out one blood type per body," I murmured.

"They do," said Kronen. "Someone injected this into him."

I felt a warning brush of sickness in my gut. "Gods, what would that do?"

"For someone with A-positive blood, injecting him with another type in sufficient amounts would cause anaphylactic shock," Kronen said.

I closed my eyes and imagined Vincent Blackburn suffocating as his airway closed off and his heart went into overdrive to expel the poison. You only killed someone that way if you truly wanted them to suffer.

"There are some other trace elements," said Kronen. I turned the page and saw his neat, cramped handwriting next to the chemical signatures. *Charcoal. Lead. Copper.* The throbbing between my eyes returned with a vengeance. I'd seen the list before, in my grandmother's slanted script.

"Any of this hold significance, Detective?" asked Kronen. "Because frankly, when I screen a man's blood expecting to find heroin and turn up trace metals instead, I become a bit puzzled."

"They're ingredients." I sighed. "Ingredients for a caster witch brewing a spell."

Kronen's eyebrow crooked. "What does this mean?"

"It means we're right," I said, blood pumping in my ears a little too loudly. "The Blackburn case is a murder, someone planned this out carefully, and he sure as hell wasn't a random OD." Damn Shelby to hell. She could have prevented this by telling me the truth about the feud after we found Vincent. She could have saved her uncle's life.

"These results are also consistent with the OD case you brought to me," said Kronen. "Although in lesser amounts, and a slightly different composition."

Trying to grasp at the threads was like being blind in a roomful of cat's cradles. But then, the switch flipped, and I saw it. "Son of a bitch!" I said, louder than Kronen was comfortable with, because he shushed me.

"Bryan Howard was a fucking test," I muttered. "They dosed him to perfect their working. Edward, that fucking jerk, they must have paid him off . . ."

"Do I want to be privy to what you're theorizing, Detective?" said Kronen.

I was angry, so angry I could have kicked a hole in a steel wall. A man died for nothing—a fucking academic experiment. An innocent man, for all intents and purposes. A sacrifice. "No," I said finally. "No, you don't, Doc."

I thrust the report back at him. "For now, keep this under your hat. Can you rule Vincent's death as a murder without the report?"

Kronen stroked his chin. "I have a feeling showing this to anyone else will merely prove unwise. Am I correct?"

I thought of the mass of officers who had responded to Patrick O'Halloran's bombing, versus the dozen or so who had shown up when I'd found Vincent's body. Would Matilda Morgan believe for one second that a pillar of the community had offed a drug dealer because of a magickal rivalry?

Of course not. She'd have me fired. Or committed.

"You're absolutely correct. Thanks, Bart," I said. He gave me a nod and shuffled the report to the bottom of the listing pile on his desk. I figured it was as safe there as anywhere else.

"Be careful," I told him in parting. Not that I could do anything against the financial pull and good name of the O'Hallorans. When I tangle with magickal entities like Alistair Duncan, I at least know I'm on reasonably equal ground. When it came to attacking people so powerful in both the shadow and light aspects of the world, I was as helpless as the next pavement-pounder with a badge.

I didn't like that, not one bit. People who kill because they think they *can* fire my rage like no other. I decided then and there that the O'Hallorans were going to answer for starting this domino-fall of deaths. How I'd do it would be another issue altogether. But then again, I never let the little things bother me. That's probably why I spend so much of my life in trouble.

When you have a break in a case, the truth is it usually births more questions than it answers. Sure, a caster witch had killed Vincent Blackburn, but any lawyer would point out it didn't *have* to be one of the O'Hallorans.

Besides, if the O'Hallorans had instigated this war, what could they possibly have to gain? The Blackburns were dying out, and Vincent hadn't been hurting anyone. Shelby would explain it away with "live by the sword, die by the sword" but I knew it wasn't that simple. The Blackburns were the wronged party here.

Something was missing from this pat little scenario, a thread of connection between Vincent and his killer that I was betting the O'Hallorans hoped I wouldn't find. They could preach wrongs and counterwrongs all they wanted, but the fact remained that restarting a war that had been dormant for as long as I'd been alive was bad business, as well as just plain stupid.

I had one solid lead in this increasingly weird case—Benny Joubert, the other principal in Bete Noire, the were privy to Vincent's dealing.

I got in my car and thought about that for a few minutes. Joubert was a male were, a pack member if he was pushing drugs on the streets of Nocturne City. Weres controlled most of the drug and skin trade, and the gods help you if you forgot that fact. He was also a violent, repeat offender and I was one lone Insoli female.

Only one person sprang to mind as a potential partner in this venture, and it made my chest tighten so much I thought all the breath would be forced out of me. The idea of seeing Dmitri again, with Irina, happy? I couldn't stomach it.

On the other hand, if I wanted to keep working the case and not end up raped and mutilated in Joubert's Dumpster, he was the only person I could ask to help me. I vowed that I wouldn't kill or maim him, no matter how maddening he got, and headed for downtown.

Irina opened the apartment door, the skin between her eyes creasing when she saw me. She was going to need

Botox in a few years. "What are you doing here? You trespass."

"Not much good to call the police," I quipped with a hopeful smile. "I need to talk to Dmitri."

"No." She started to shut the door. I stuck an arm out and caught it with a bang.

"I don't think you understand. I *need* to talk to Dmitri and I am *going* to talk to Dmitri and I am sick of having doors slammed in my face."

She pushed against me, grunting with the effort, but I held firm, staring into those gold-brown eyes and not bothering to hide my contempt. "You're just wasting my time, Irina. I'm coming inside either way."

"When I get you alone . . ." Irina hissed.

"Oh, don't flatter yourself, princess. I'd tear you up and use what's left for bacon bits." Bravado will carry you a long way, and I hoped it disguised the ugly twist of fear inside me. I had no idea how strong Irina was, and you'd better believe I hadn't forgotten she could phase at will. Still, the amount of rage her pale pretty face stirred in me had to be good for something.

"Irina?" Dmitri appeared from what I could only assume was the bedroom, shirtless, in faded jeans and a studded belt. I felt the surge of territorial instinct, a snarl rising to the surface as my imagination leaped to an image of what they must have been doing when I knocked.

"Ah!" Irina went backward, on her butt, and the door flew back to smash the wall, coming off the top hinge and hanging crookedly. Dmitri watched the whole thing dispassionately, his eyes flicking to gold when he saw me.

"Luna." He came over and helped Irina up. She held onto him with a whimper.

"She wants to kill me."

Seven hells, if I had to see one more second of her Scarlett O'Hara act I was going to turn green and start smashing things.

"I don't think she's going to do that." Dmitri's mouth quirked. He gave Irina a squeeze and released her. "Go back into the bedroom, darlin'. I'll just be a minute."

"You can't talk to her!" Irina said with alarm. "The elders—"

"Are not going to find out about this, are they, Irina?" He gave her that look, the one that was all dark green eyes and shadowy promises of pain, the one he'd used on his pack when he was their leader. Irina dipped her head in a gesture of submission, exposing the back of her neck, then disappeared into the bedroom and shut the door.

"You've got her well trained," I drawled, covering up the gut punch of loss that hit when I saw them together with a cruel tone. "Does she wear a little collar with a bell?"

"Hex it, Luna." Dmitri sighed, sinking into a ratty red armchair. "Did you come here just to bust my balls?" The apartment wasn't much better furnished than his old pack house in Ghosttown—it looked like someone's foreign grandparents had lived there for about forty years and never cleaned anything.

"No," I said. "Surprisingly not. I came because . . ." The end of the sentence stuck in my throat. How could I ask him for favors after the way we'd parted? After he'd chosen his Hexed pack over me?

Because I needed to prove that he still wanted me, of course. I'd been surviving without a breakdown on the hope of this very moment ever since the horrible scene at Bete Noire.

"Dmitri, I need your help," I said firmly, loudly enough for Irina to hear. "I have to do something danger-ous, with some dangerous people, and you were the only person I could think of who would go with me."

Composing his face into careful lines, Dmitri steepled his fingers. "I can't help you anymore, Luna."

"Hear me out," I said, holding up a hand. "There's a were named Benny Joubert that I need to question in a murder. If I go alone, I'll just be an Insoli, and a cop be-sides, and he'll hurt me badly, but I'll still go. So think about it for a second before you say no."

I can be pretty damn manipulative when the occa-sion calls for it. It worked too, because Dmitri dropped his act and passed a hand over his eyes, messing up his copper hair even more than the undoubtedly fabulous sex with Irina already had.

"Do you have any idea what you do to me?" he mut-tered, so softly I had to move closer to hear.

"Apparently, nothing like what Irina can do," I fired back, feeling like crap the moment the words came out. Dmitri dropped his hand and looked at me, unabashed hurt on his face.

"Dammit, Luna. You should have let me bring you into the pack when I had the chance. All of this—the elders, my mating with Irina—this all could have been you." He sighed and dropped his elbows on his knees, supporting his chin. "I think about you all the time. I smell you. You're in me just like the daemon."

I touched his bare shoulder with the very tips of my fingers, a gesture I'd used when we were together to gauge his mood. He let out a small shuddering breath.

"I need your help," I said again. "I'm asking you. Please." *Please say yes. Please prove to me that this is all a terrible misunderstanding.*

"How can I not?" Dmitri sighed. "You're going to do it anyway. I know you."

Not exactly what I'd hoped for, but I'd take it. "Thank you," I said, all the tension trickling from me. "Really. Thank you." I didn't realize just how much I'd been dreading confronting Benny Joubert alone. From hard experience, I know I can't stand up against an adult male were unless I'm phased, and it would be one hell of a trick for that to happen on this particular day.

Dmitri stood and opened the door to the bedroom. Irina jumped back, looking embarrassed. "I am coming with you."

"No," said Dmitri automatically. "You stay here with Sergei and Yelena, where it's safe."

I searched his voice for any hint of love and the concern a were would hold for his mate, but there was just cold practicality. My inner vindictive bitch did a little dance.

"Dmitri . . ." Irina started and flowed into a rapid-fire scolding in Ukrainian. I could tell it was a scolding because she was shaking her finger. Dmitri growled and brushed her off, putting on a T-shirt advertising Jack Daniels and a leather jacket. He snapped something else at Irina and after a few seconds of pouting she brought him his boots and slipped them on his feet.

"Gods, you get any more mail-order bride and I'm going to puke up hearts and flowers," I said. Irina and Dmitri both glared at me.

"Be quiet, Insoli," said Irina. "You got what you wanted, now there will be silence."

"There will be one hell of a smack in the mouth for you, you keep that up," I said, mimicking her throaty accent. "Let's get this over with. The sooner I don't have to look at your cheap highlights, the better off we'll be."

Irina opened her mouth to reply but Dmitri stood and held up his hands. "Enough, from both of you. Irina, stop baiting Luna. Luna, stop making it so easy."

Irina shut her mouth, plump red lips pressed so tightly they almost disappeared. Guess there were a *few* advantages to no longer being Dmitri's mate. Dominates are ugly things when they're used to control someone lower in the pack than you.

"Fine," Irina finally sniffed, her eyes bright with fury. "I can only hope you get your throat torn out by this man we are going to see."

I rolled my eyes as she left the room. Dmitri gripped my arm. "Who *is* this Joubert guy? What's his pack?"

"I don't know," I said honestly. "I just know that he's hairy and not very pretty." Your pack and pack magick determines pecking order in the greater scope of weres. Redbacks were near the top, from what I could tell. I should have been a Serpent Eye, the pack with no pack magick, but in a way being Insoli was better than being a Serpent Eye. They scared the hell out of most other weres, for good reason.

"Hope Joubert's not a biter," Dmitri muttered as we left the apartment.

"You and me both," I said.

CHAPTER 18

The dispatcher gave me Benny Joubert's address of record, a three-story stately home in Needle Park. Needle Park was actually the Bowers, once upon a time, a small bedroom community in the lull between Cedar Hill and the city outskirts that had been built by the sailors who came through Nocturne in the nineteenth century. Since then, fewer families and more drugs had moved in, and now Needle Park was as sad and dangerous, in its own way, as Waterfront or Ghosttown.

I parked at the curb, tucking the Fairlane between overflowing trash cans and what I assumed was Joubert's car, a late-model black Mercedes. No one had touched it, and that made me nervous. Joubert would be a major player in the neighborhood to command that sort of respect.

"Okay," I said as we paused in a row on the sidewalk. "You two just hang back here unless I get into trouble. No sense in spooking him."

Irina sniffed. I lasered her with a glare. "You didn't have to come, princess."

"Who else will watch over Dmitri?" she snapped.

"It is your fault he was infected in the first place. We cannot trust you."

Sometimes, no comeback works as well as an extended middle finger.

Irina pursed her lips sourly and deliberately turned away, pretending to examine the decaying wood-frame houses and cracked pavement with great interest.

"One more time," I said. "You wait here unless something bad goes down. Got it?"

"Don't piss him off any more than you have to," said Dmitri.

I hated that he knew me so well. Writing him off as a fling would be worlds easier than feeling the twinge that our past mating caused between his were and mine. That's why weres only give the bite, in theory, to men or women they plan to stay with for the rest of their lives. Dmitri was 0 for 2 with his mates, as was I. Although I didn't count a predatory Serpent Eye forcing himself on a fifteen-year-old girl, really. It sure as hell wasn't my fault Joshua had lost his mate, but I was the one left with that burning need to replace him with a pack leader or another male—hell, female. Any were would do, in an Insoli's more instinctual moments.

Life as a packless were woman sure was a laugh and a half, most days.

I reached Joubert's front door, which was covered with a heavy steel security grate, and rang the bell. When that produced no discernable sound from inside, I kicked at the grate and shouted, "Joubert! Open up!"

After a long two minutes I heard shuffling and the clacking of at least three dead bolts being thrown, and then the inner door swung open. Benny Joubert smelled almost as bad as he looked. His skin had a yellowish cast and the wild brown hair in his photo was longer and greasy. Up close, his face was bisected with scars—knife or claw, I couldn't tell.

"What the fuck do you want?" he said by way of a greeting.

I tried to breathe through my mouth and said, "I need to ask you about Vincent Blackburn."

His small dark eyes squinted at me, almost disappearing into their close-set sockets. "You a cop?"

"Yes," I said, deciding that playing it straight was probably the quickest way to get what I wanted.

"Let's see some ID."

I let him examine my shield until he nodded slowly and unlocked the grate, shoving it to the side. "Vincent Blackburn. I heard that queer turned up dead."

For a were, whom most plain humans on earth hated and feared with a passion usually reserved for IRS audits and Freddy Kreuger, Joubert had a charmingly backward outlook.

"*Mr. Blackburn* was murdered," I said. "I'm the detective in charge of the inquiry. I understand you're a partner in the club where he bartended."

Joubert shrugged. "I don't do the hiring. If I did we wouldnt've had so many goddamn fairies in the place."

"Well, Tinkerbell," I said, "I'm not interested in your employee procurement. I'm interested in the drugs you and Vincent were funneling through Bete Noire."

He snapped from his sagging posture to rigid attention and I could tell my status had been upgraded from "minor annoyance" to "dangerous nuisance."

"What the fuck did you just say?" he demanded hoarsely, pig-eyes taking on a light. He was scenting prey, just as I would if our situation were reversed. Why couldn't it be reversed?

I stepped into his personal space, one foot resting on the threshold. "I said you're a fucking drug pusher, and while we're on the subject of personal failings, are you aware of the wonderful invention called deodorant?"

Joubert should have gotten mad and started calling me names and given me a reason to arrest him, but his nostrils flared and then he laughed. "You think you scare me, coming around my place and flashing a badge?" His hand snaked out and grabbed me by the hair, exposing my throat in one deft movement that I never would have thought possible from his pudgy, scarred frame. "You don't know what scared *is,* you In-soli bitch."

Crap.

I had just enough time to process the single thought before Joubert slammed my head into the security grate so hard I saw fireworks. He whipped me into his house by the hair, tossing me halfway across his foyer, where I landed in a heap. The door slammed shut and Joubert advanced on me, already loosening the fly on his filthy khaki pants. "Now you and me are going to have a real chat, bitch—one that involves you scream-ing my name."

Gods, my head. It was bleeding, a lot, worse than when I'd hit the mesh in the cage. And it hurt, so much so that my ears were still ringing. *He's killed you,* the logical part of my brain whispered. *These are your last moments of coherent thought. Get ready to be a turnip for the rest of your life.*

My logic has a tendency to turn pessimist at the worst times.

Joubert grabbed my hair again and pulled me eye-level with his fly. "Sometimes, you have to show 'em how to put their mouths to good use, but they usually catch on."

What was he doing, conducting a seminar? I was oddly detached, not panicking at all, and I knew it was from blood loss. Head wounds bleed fast and thick, and they don't stop until they're good and ready.

"Understand, bitch?" Joubert asked me. He wasn't using the word *bitch* in the sense that a plain human would—he meant it to indicate he was going to breed with me and I didn't have a say in the matter.

I muttered under my breath.

"What's that?" Joubert demanded.

I raised my head and blinked away the blood, which stung horribly. "I said, a Tootsie Roll would be more satisfying."

Never knowing when to shut the hell up *can* come in handy, under the right circumstances. Joubert snarled and raised a stubby hand full of ragged nails to hit me, but his door splintered inward and he spun instead, yanking my hair painfully.

Dmitri crossed the foyer in one long stride and grabbed Joubert's free arm, twisting it like a piece of spaghetti. I winced at the crack. "Get your fucking hands off her," Dmitri said, "or I'll amputate this arm here and now and then start in on your balls."

"Hex you!" Joubert snarled back. He and Dmitri showed their fangs, trying to establish dominance over one another. In the meantime, Joubert was still tangled in my hair, so I bit him on the wrist, hard. He shrieked and let go of me. "Is this your bitch?" he asked Dmitri. "I understand a man has needs, but you should have trained her better." His lips parted in a salacious expression. "Or better yet, let me."

You know that expression, *cold fury*? I thought it was just a saying until I saw the expression on Dmitri's face. It was blank except for anger, and not the hot passionate kind that ends in stabbings and double suicides. This was merciless hunter's rage, all of it focused on Joubert.

"That," he said in an even tone more terrifying than any snarl, "was a royally bad fucking idea."

Dmitri growled, showing his full fangs, and his eyes went black, as if someone had spilled ink across the pupils. I recoiled against the bottom of the stairs instinctively. His eyes weren't supposed to be black. No living thing's eyes were supposed to look like that . . .

Joubert gave an animal yelp as Dmitri threw him across the room to hit a wall, landing in a rain of plaster. I saw long, curved razor claws blossom from Dmitri's fingers and he walked after Joubert in that same measured, even pace.

My bleeding head was slowing, and although my skull still throbbed I thought I might live. How many concussions did that make for the week? Never mind, my head was clear enough to realize we needed Joubert alive. I opened my mouth to say so, but Irina came bolting through the door and threw herself at Dmitri, screaming, "Stop! Don't kill him!"

Dmitri shook her off like one kicks away an annoying terrier, and Irina landed on her ass for the second time that day. "Stay out of my way," he told her, swiveling his head slowly to lock her eyes. Irina wilted like a cheap bouquet, real fear coming alive in her expression.

I was feeling it too, seeing the Dmitri I knew replaced by this icy façade with the dead man's eyes. Joubert was whimpering in the corner, his dominance well and truly gone. Dmitri paused over him, hands hanging loosely at his sides, then he reached out and lifted Joubert up, the hairy were's feet dangling a good foot off the ground.

Never in my life have I wanted to walk away from a fight as much. But I got up instead, swaying badly but conscious and reasonably functional, which was all I could hope for these days, and went to Dmitri. "Don't."

Dmitri purred in his chest, the small expression I knew to be his prelude to an explosion of temper. "He hurt you. He tried to claim you. You're *mine*." His hand tightened on Joubert's throat, the black talons digging in.

Well, halle-freaking-lujah. At least the daemonic Dmitri realized he still cared about me. Overjoyed as I was, I still had his mating instincts to contend with.

"I know," I said. "He's a piece of shit and he deserves to die. But not now. Now I need you to let him go."

Dmitri shook his head. "I want to kill him for you. I'd like it."

As would I, truth be told. Nothing like hacking up the competition to show a girl how much you care. I ignored the frisson of heat Dmitri's planned action sent through me and touched his arm, firmly, pressing down to make him release Joubert. "We need him alive if he's going to talk. After that, you can do whatever you want."

He met my eyes and his black gaze burned like an oil fire on a winter sea. "Whatever I want?" he rasped.

"Anything." I nodded, my mouth dry. Hex it, why did he have to be so gods-damned attractive when he was homicidal?

Dmitri blinked and released Joubert, who tumbled to the floor. He glared up at us and massaged his throat. I pointed a finger in his face and said, "Don't you twitch."

"What the Hex happened?" Dmitri demanded. His voice was back to normal, dusty and irritable. He blinked and his eyes were green again.

"You don't remember?" I said cautiously.

"Not really," Dmitri admitted. "Just remember smelling blood, and busting in." He looked at Joubert. "What's his problem?"

All the primal lust that had been generated as I stood there trying to convince him not to kill Joubert disappeared on the cold wind of reality. "Get him up," I said, gesturing at Joubert. "After I question him, you and I need to have a talk."

Dmitri looked uncomfortable, hitching at his jeans like a teenager on a date. "Problem?" I snapped. I was embarrassed, and I react to most bad situations by getting bitchy.

"No," Dmitri muttered, his face coloring slightly. "I'm just . . . er . . ." He adjusted his fly and folded his arms across his chest. "I'm fine."

Irina hauled herself to her feet before I could fully parse that the near-bloodshed had gotten both Dmitri and me hot, and what exactly that would mean to my next therapy session. "Dmitri, let me take you outside. You are not well."

"I'm fine! Hex it, Irina, stop hovering!" he snapped. She pulled back like he'd slapped her.

I grabbed Joubert by the collar and hauled him into his dining room, sitting him in a chair. He growled when I touched him, but it was halfhearted. "The Loup will kill you for this if they ever find out."

"And I'm supposed to believe you'd tell your pack that you got your ass kicked by an Insoli and a Redback?" My turn to laugh. "Buddy, you are so lucky your windpipe isn't lying halfway across the room right now."

He glowered. "What do you want, cop?"

"Vincent Blackburn," I said. "I know his death was murder. I know the O'Hallorans set it up, for whatever reasons they have." Still working on that one. "Who did the dirty work?" I asked Joubert. "You? He screws you over and you decide to get in bed with the caster witches' revenge?"

Joubert snorted. "Hell no. Vincent wasn't smart enough to screw me. That kid was such a junkie, he would've worn a dress and humped a goat if it'd get him dope. Always broke, always a waste of space."

"Listen," I said. "If you don't tell me who killed this kid—and I know you know, or have a reasonably good idea—the city is going to burn down and the next time you move a kilo of coke will be in six months, after everyone is done cleaning up from the fucking riots."

Unmoved, Joubert sighed and stared up at the ceiling. "Why Vincent?" I murmured. "He was out of the family. What could he possibly have done to deserve a death like that?" Remembering Vincent's curled-up body, I had an unwelcome flash of what his last minutes had been like—senseless pain and agonizing death. I'm violent by blood and instinct, but the casual, calculated causing of pain to another living thing is foreign to me.

"I said he was always broke," said Joubert, patting his pockets and bringing out a squashed pack of cigarettes. He lit one up and exhaled. "The club gets a lot of high-profile clientele. Vincent, the dumbshit, decided that selling coke to 'em wasn't enough. He was gonna make a buck on the back end with dirty videotapes and stained panties."

And like a wave breaking on shore, I saw in the clean light of logic why Vincent had been murdered. Not for a magickal war. Not for revenge, or honor or anything lofty like that. "Blackmail."

"Yup," Joubert nodded. "The dumbshit," he said again. "We had a decent sideline going. Just like that fairy to go fuck everything up."

"Who was he squeezing?" I asked. "Give me the names and we'll leave you alone." Or I would, at least. I couldn't vouch for Dmitri, who was skulking in the doorway to the dining room like a surly shadow.

Joubert stood nervously and paced away from me, scattering ash on his antique rug. "I can't do that. It'd be bad for business."

"I don't have all freaking day," I said. "If it makes you feel better you can just write them discreetly on a pad and I'll pretend I found it among all my love letters from Dmitri here." Someone close to the O'Hallorans. It could be anyone in the city—anyone respected, or rich, or whose face showed up in the *Inquirer* often enough to get embarrassed about their penchant for adult-sized diapers and baby bonnets.

Joubert took a long drag on his smoke, killing it down to the butt, and exhaled. He looked at himself in the full-length mirror on the opposite wall and heaved a sigh.

"I'm not going away," I said. "Get cracking."

I'll never know how fast it really happened, but one instant Joubert was staring morosely at his unattractive reflection and the next his fist had flashed out, shattering the mirror and raining glass shards all over the dining room.

"Hex it!" Dmitri said. "What the hell are you doing, Joubert?"

Joubert didn't answer him. His body was rigid and his throat was working like he was trying to speak. He turned like a toy soldier doing an about-face, jaw still twitching, and I smelled his blood before I saw the jagged piece of mirror clutched in his hand.

"No," I said. "No . . ."

Mechanically, Joubert raised the glass shard, every inch of his stubby body straining against the motion. He gave a strangled groan and I saw a blood vessel burst in one of his eyes, the red stain spreading across the pupil.

I looked to Dmitri.

"Do something!" he yelled at me, always the helpful one.

"Joubert, don't do this." I started for him, palms up so he wouldn't feel threatened. I considered telling him he had a lot to live for, but he was a middle-aged drug dealer who had back hair and lived in a house that looked like it had been decorated by Bizarro Martha Stewart. Somehow I figured that would just make things worse.

As soon as I was within grabbing range, Joubert lashed out at me with the piece of glass.

"Hex me!" I jumped backward and felt the ragged mirror shard catch on my coat. Another jacket ruined. "Joubert," I pleaded. "Just put it down."

He looked right at me, with his bloodstained eyes, locking me in with a gaze so terrifying I will carry it with me until the day I die. His eyes were trapped, terror-stricken, begging someone to help him even as he raised the mirror shard and cut his own throat.

Someone screamed, and I saw Irina bury her face against Dmitri's chest as Joubert collapsed, no longer stiff as his life ran out onto the carpet in a brilliant red cloud. I just stood, shocked beyond movement for two or three seconds, and then my training took over and I ripped the stained cloth off the dining room table and fell beside Joubert, pressing against the deep half-moon wound in his neck with all my strength.

Too late, of course. He'd severed his artery and he only twitched once as he bled out, heartbeat becoming thready and then nonexistent under my now-crimson hands.

I rocked back on my heels. "Shit."

Dmitri pulled me up and away from the body, giving Irina a terse, "Wait for us in the car." He guided me out of the dining room and held my shoulders, forcing me to look up at him. "What the Hex was that?"

Under his touch, I realized I was shaking. "I think we both know what that was, Dmitri."

He tilted his head back and closed his eyes. I didn't want to deal with the truth any more than he did—that what we'd seen Joubert do to himself could only be dae-mon magick, something human witches weren't sup-posed to be able to use.

Of course, Alistair Duncan had proved that wasn't always the case.

"Has to be a blood witch, right?" said Dmitri, falling into his old role of asking me questions until I an-swered my way to the truth.

"Right," I said. What I didn't say was that the Blackburns killing Joubert didn't make any sense. They could barely afford to buy cup noodles, never mind patronize an exclusive fetish club to the point where they'd be ripe for blackmail. Hex it, what would you blackmail them for? Their jars of blood and black leather pants? Unless Joubert had been the one to dose Vincent—and he struck me as the kind of guy who only went after small, helpless things in a violent manner—they had no motives.

"Let's toss the house," I said, pushing my half-baked collection of bad hunches to the back of my mind. "Try to find out who the other partner in the club is."

"Never thought I'd actually be saying this, but shouldn't we call the cops?" Dmitri asked.

I turned my back on Joubert's body and the sick stink of were blood, and went into what turned out to be the kitchen. It smelled bad in there too, but it was bearable. "Not yet," I said. "I don't want my captain busting in just now." Under stress, I have this unfortunate tendency to get rude and hostile and sometimes kick people in the shins, none of which I thought Morgan would appreciate.

"Fair enough," said Dmitri. He opened the fridge and winced, his nose wrinkling. "Hex me. Somebody needs to deal with the science experiments in here."

"At least it's not heads. Or fingers. Or—"

Dmitri held up a hand. "I get it."

"Why did you take Irina as a mate?" I blurted. "How could you not know what it would do to me?"

Dmitri sighed, his back to me, leaning against the closed door of the fridge. "We've been over this, Luna."

"I know, I know." My voice took on a bitter edge I hadn't known I was capable of. "You have to do what your pack says. Wouldn't want to get put on a choke chain."

He hit the fridge hard, with a closed fist, and I jumped. "You think I *like* this?" he snarled, turning around. His eyes were ink-stained again, black overtaking the green in the space of a heartbeat. "You think I woke up one day after a night of wrestling with this thing and said 'Gee, I wonder how badly I can hurt Luna today?' Is that what you think I did?"

"I don't know," I said, sticking my chin out. "But I think getting to screw Irina out of screwing me must have been a definite perk."

I was pissed off, and I didn't care anymore what Dmitri thought. He'd stomped on me just like any other pack were, and like any plain human asshole guy, he'd traded up for a newer, sluttier model.

Dmitri growled and came at me around the kitchen table, backing me up against the sink.

"Get off me," I snapped, pushing at his chest with the flat of my hands. "Go wait in the car with your whore."

He roared and pinned my arms down at my sides, squeezing my wrists so tightly I felt the bones shiver.

"Don't call her a whore," he whispered.

"Then what should I call her?" I struggled against him, refusing to allow the dominate I could feel rolling off his smoky gaze to take hold. "What is she to you, Dmitri? Your one true love?" I bit off the last three words and spat them.

Dmitri slammed his hips into mine, my wriggling having aroused his attention. His face was an inch away, his scent seeping into my every pore. I wanted to rage at him and I wanted to sob. I wanted Dmitri, no matter how crappily our last time together had ended. I hadn't ached this badly for Trevor or any of my plain human boyfriends.

I hadn't even needed Joshua this badly.

"What is she?" I whispered again, tears working down my cheeks.

Dmitri dipped his head into the curve of my neck just behind my ear, and scented me with a deep shuddering breath that mimicked my heartbeat. "She's not you," he said.

He looked like he wanted to say more, but I grabbed the back of his neck and pulled our mouths together, kissing him so hard I cut my lip on my bottom teeth. Dmitri licked up my blood, his hands sliding around my waist and pulling me flush with his whole length. I moaned as he broke off and trailed down my neck, nipping at the skin in ways I never imagined could feel so spectacular.

"What in seven *hells* is going on?" Irina demanded from the doorway.

Dmitri stepped back abruptly, putting an arm's length between us. "I told you to wait in the car."

"You took a long time," said Irina, her bottom lip trembling. "And now, I tell you that you can walk back to our fucking apartment." She turned on her heel and strode out, the fury on her face compounded when she slammed the front door hard enough to knock objects off the kitchen shelves.

I straightened my shirt and smoothed out my hair. Nothing to be done about the flush on my face. Dmitri hung his head, scuffing the linoleum with his boot. "I think she forgot we came in your car."

"Sorry," I said, even though I didn't really mean it. The small, nasty part of me was gratified to see the same hurt I'd felt written on Irina's face. That part whispered the bitch had it coming. More of me just felt foolish for falling into the trap of my instincts yet again. Way to go, Luna. Way to stay professional and keep your cool.

"Don't worry about it," said Dmitri. "My fault as much as yours."

"I'm almost done here," I said neutrally. *Don't look at Dmitri. Don't think about what almost happened. Don't you* dare *think this changes anything.*

While lecturing myself, I quickly glanced into each of Joubert's myriad drawers. Most held oddments of flatware or food. I found a snub-nosed .38 revolver in the drawer nearest the sink. An old rotary-style phone sat on the counter above it, and an address book was open to the *C*'s.

"Finally," I muttered. In reality, suspects rarely hide their good secrets inside clever cubbyholes or a box of Cap'n Crunch from 1986. Most of the time, they're just as dumb and obvious as the rest of us and leave things lying around in plain sight. The page held only two entries—a place called Cat's that I assumed was a strip club or a brothel and a smudged number where Joubert had scribbled *Carrie—Koffe Kart #* next to it in handwriting that would make a nun weep.

The Koffe Kart was the lobby restaurant in the O'Halloran Building. Coincidence, I might have believed before I got Vincent's autopsy results. Now this was something incriminating. Besides, it was fun to imagine one of those prissy caster witches cozying up to Joubert.

I tore the page out of the book and shoved it in my pocket, nudging Dmitri. "Let's go."

Once we'd gotten out of the hushed house, I called in the suicide and then turned to Dmitri. "Need a ride back to downtown?" I was hoping he'd say no, because being in a car with him would be the most awkward thing in the world right now.

"Can you just drop me in Waterfront?" he asked. Waterfront was his old pack territory, and belonged to whoever the new pack leader of the Redbacks was now. Going there was practically begging for an ass-beating.

I started to say no, then thought of Irina and the way Dmitri had shoved me away when she came in. "Sure," I said. "Hop in."

CHAPTER 19

I left Dmitri standing on the sidewalk on Cannery Street and I can't say I felt bad about it. Traffic was bad, so I parked at the precinct and walked down Highlands, letting myself stare at the skyscrapers of downtown and think about the O'Hallorans.

No caster witch I knew of was capable of using black magick, no matter how much they wanted it. They couldn't use their own blood as a focus, and by its very nature their magick focused toward positive outcomes. Sure, they were as bitchy and insular as the next group of magick users, but as sure as I was that an O'Halloran had killed Vincent and Joubert, I couldn't for the life of me glean how, and it was giving me a headache.

Seeing the snarled knot of honking cabs and pissed-off civilians on foot ahead, I turned onto Devere. Nocturne University loomed at me, black bricks gloomy even in the sun. A hobo with a shopping cart shoved it toward me. "Got any change? Anything at all?"

I handed him a dollar and he snatched it away, tucking it into his coat pocket. I shivered. Cold wind always seemed to whip down Devere, an east-west street lined with narrow old buildings. "Thanks," said the bum. "Wouldn't need no money, 'cept Wylie ripped off my bottle earlier today. Said he needed it more on account of fall bringin' out his arthritis. Damn fool."

I left him muttering about Wylie's many character flaws and kept walking toward the university. Shelby had said her relatives stole something from the Blackburns a long time ago. A spellbook, the written workings that are supposed to be memorized and burned? Some sort of blood focuser that would allow a caster access to daemon magick? Whatever it was, the O'Hallorans were using it, which meant they were no longer playing fair. If I figured out exactly what had been stolen, I'd bet my yearly salary we'd break Vincent's case.

Not that betting *my* salary is any kind of grand gesture. I turned up my collar against the September wind, and headed for the university grounds.

The faculty offices at the university were nearly as cold as the outside air. Somewhere far away a radiator clanked and groaned, doing little good. I climbed to the third floor on foot, figuring it would warm me up, and rapped on the door marked JACOB HOSKINS—MYTHOLOGY.

"Who is it?" Hoskins's voice was nervous, with no inflection. He's one of the twitchiest people I've ever met, but also one of the most honest. In my line of work that's about as rare as a chaste call girl, so it might explain why I like him so much.

"It's Detective Wilder, Professor." I knew better than to just walk into his office—such a trespass would send Hoskins into cardiac arrest. Plus, there was that promise

I'd made last time we talked to never darken his doorway again, or something equally dramatic.

"Ah." I heard brisk footsteps and the door opened exactly an inch. I put a game smile on my face.

"Hi, there."

Hoskins pursed his lips and opened the door all the way. "If you were going to disappear for an entire summer, you might have written me a postcard. Even something via that dreadful e-mail would have sufficed."

"Why, Professor, I had no idea that you cared."

He snorted. "You are at least compelling, Detective, which is more than I can say for this year's crop of freshmen. Come in, please."

Having been given passage to the inner sanctum, I stepped over the threshold and into Hoskins's painfully sterile and organized space. All of his books lined up exactly one inch from the edge of the shelf. His tribal masks and paintings were displayed in rows along the wall. The large desk held no papers, no evidence that anyone even worked there except for a flat-screen computer monitor and a gold pen resting precisely next to a blotter.

Hoskins returned to his desk and removed a stack of essays from the middle drawer. He clicked the pen to life and began marking them in handwriting so small it could have been mouse tracks. "What brings you here, Detective? How do you find yourself?"

"Fine," I said, deciding a recounting of exactly how crappy the past week had been would just waste time. "I needed to ask you something about the Blackburn family."

"Well and good," said Hoskins, making a neat slash

through an entire paragraph on the page he held. I felt sorry for the student. "But I am a professor of occult mythology, not history."

"This is in your area, believe me," I said. Hoskins had some experience with the practice as well as the theory of magick. He had taught the Cedar Hill Killer, a blood witch trying to summon the same daemon Alistair Duncan had succeeded with, many years ago. The affair still made the veins on Hoskins's neck bulge if you brought it up.

"Then continue, Detective," he said, writing some scathing remark on the last page of the essay and setting it aside.

"A long time ago—I don't know how long—the O'Halloran caster witches stole something from the Blackburn family. I need to know what it was."

"Ah," said Hoskins. "You are speaking of the murders which resulted in the founding of the university."

"I guess," I said. "Was that why Gertrude Blackburn ended up dead?"

Theodore Blackburn, the first scion to settle in Nocturne City, was a wealthy man, depraved and ruthless by all accounts, who had turned to blood magick to increase his profits. Siobhan O'Halloran, the family's maid, had taken it upon herself to slash Madame Blackburn across the throat and leave her body as a message for Mr. Blackburn, a sort of polite missive that the white witches of the city weren't going to take his crap anymore.

Unfortunately, Gertrude had gotten off a magick shot before Siobhan managed to kill her, and Theodore returned home to find them both dead. He was so devastated that he turned to drink, lost his fortune, and ended up losing his estate to the city, who turned it into the university. Or so the PG-13 version of the story went.

"I will only say this," said Hoskins. "After Gertrude's death, the Blackburn family went into a tailspin, and the O'Hallorans went from immigrants in shacks by the waterfront to powerful bankers in less than a half century. Use your own deductions."

I sighed. "But you have no idea what the object actually *is*."

Hoskins shook his head. "That is a carefully guarded secret, in the Blackburn family as well as with the O'Hallorans."

"Crap," I muttered, seeing my easy closure to Vincent's case dart away, laughing. "Thanks anyway."

"You might try the collection," said Hoskins. The way he emphasized the last word was ominous, the way Doctor Doom might say "the lair."

"What collection?"

"The books the Blackburn family left to the university. Or were seized along with their property, I should say. Quite a phenomenal resource."

"And the collection would be . . . ?"

Hoskins pointed toward the main part of the Blackburn mansion. "The library."

I like libraries. They're orderly, and very human. Unless it's an occult bookstore, the energy running through the place is clear and benign—nothing to give a magiphobe like me prickly skin.

The girl manning the reference desk was very pale, with stringy brown hair falling over big John Lennon–style glasses. She blinked up at me. "Yes?"

"I need to see the Blackburn collection," I said. She frowned.

"I'm sorry, only faculty and thesis students are allowed access to those stacks."

My badge elicited another series of rapid blinks. She licked her lips and said, "You can't just show me that and expect me to give you all of our information."

"Look," I said, trying to remain calm and sisterly. In my jeans and boots and black long-sleeved shirt, I probably looked like the Gestapo to her. "I don't care about anything except the books. They may have information pertaining to a homicide investigation."

She perked up. "Like on *Law and Order*?"

"Yes," I said patiently. "Just like that." I'd sing the theme song from *Cop Rock* if it would make her let me into the stacks.

"Wow. That's new." She took a key ring from her desk drawer and walked around me, leading me into the rows of books. "This way."

The Blackburn books were in a small climate-controlled tomb behind PHILOSOPHY Kafka-Nietzsche. My guide unlocked the glass door and went in, picking a pair of cotton gloves out of a bin and handing them to me. "Put these on to handle the books. Please lay them flat to read. And let me know if you need anything else, Detective. My name is Lauren." She blinked again. "Do you need to take down my information for the case file?"

"Not unless you're a witness to a crime," I said.

She perked up. "Somebody stole a Sumerian translation text from the reference section two weeks ago."

"What's the world coming to?" I commiserated, shutting the glass door. She looked disappointed.

The gloves weren't really cotton, they were some sort of special fiber that I assumed kept my bad nasty skin off the old books. They itched. I resolved to make this quick and scanned the neatly aligned shelves for anything useful.

The Blackburns had been well read, for their time. Most of the books were high quality, covered in leather, Dickens and Verne and one scandalous Stoker. On a low shelf, a series of leather-bound volumes with no titles on the spine caught my eye. The tasteful plaque informed me they were *BLACKBURN FAMILY DIARIES*.

"Scandal," I murmured happily. I pulled the first ledger off the shelf. Some sort of household records, lots of notations about buying soap and flour and killing cows.

The second diary had *Property of Theodore Lucius Blackburn* on the inside flap. I set it down carefully on the table and flipped to the first entry.

June 18, 1886

My wife purchased this journal for me at the market, noting that my previous one had grown full in the admittedly dull recounting of my various endeavors. That she believes my writings will be held for posterity is rather a touching sentiment, though I would never voice such a thought.

The diary spanned more than two years, and in that time Blackburn traveled to Africa, the Caribbean, and China, keeping a meticulously detailed account of his travels. Once or twice, he talked about circles or the phases of the moon, but if an unwary eye had been reading, no one would have ever guessed he was a powerful blood witch. I supposed it would have been bad for him if some nosy servant had read all about blood workings and what they entailed in Theodore's crystal-neat hand-

writing. Who wants to buy dry goods and lumber from a
black magick user?

February 13, 1889

On the foredeck of steamer *Star of Shanghai*,
bound for San Francisco and then home. I am
pained that I will not be with Gertrude for St.
Valentine's Day. None of her letters have reached
me in months due to my rapid exodus from the
Orient.

I must recount something, for this page is my
sole confessional these many months. I purchased
the object from an antiquities dealer in Beijing,
thinking it nothing more than an amusing fake
trinket peddled to foreigners. However, I came to
recognize the writing as some form of ancient
Arabic text, and began to fear, instead of doubt,
the object's authenticity.

Blackburn's handwriting, normally as easy to read as
print, grew shakier with every word. Whether the pitching ship was making him quake, or the subject matter, I
didn't know.

I *feel* it inside my mind, mad as that surely sounds,
and when I look too long at the letters carved into
its surface my head begins to ache. The translator
informed me it was a relic known as the Skull of
Mathias. A human skull, every inch of it covered in
these runic scribblings that hold such a terrible
power I can barely stand to remain inside my cabin.

I conceived to throw it over the side, but the
night I thus decided, a squall hit us and three of

my traveling companions were lost. After that I have simply been making my sleep scarce, although even when I am not below deck I see it, staring at me with empty eyes . . .

I drew my hands away from the page as though they'd been burned. *Empty eyes*. I traced Blackburn's last sentence and muttered, "I found you, you son of a bitch."

Outside, where I was permitted to use my phone, I called Sunny. Rhoda answered. Typical of my luck.

"Luna," she said icily when I identified myself. "What do I owe this call to?"

"You don't owe it to anything," I said, silently adding, *you shriveled old bat*. "I need to talk to Sunny."

"Sunflower is not available," she said in that same tone. I got the feeling I ranked about one notch above a telemarketer.

"What, are her lips sewn shut?" I mentally slapped myself in the head as soon as the comeback was out. Pissing off my grandmother wouldn't get Sunny on the line.

"She's at the grocery store," said Rhoda. "Perhaps I can help you, since I know you only call when you want something?"

"Actually, if I had a choice, I wouldn't call you at all," I said cheerily. "I have better things to do, like poke myself in the eye with a stick." *Suck on that, you hag*.

"Very well," said Rhoda. "I'll refrain from telling Sunflower you called in this state. It would only upset her."

I'd like to say I had a good-cop brainwave at that point, but really I was just angry and looking for a little payback. "Wait a minute," I said. "If you're so smart, then yeah, you can help me. What's the deal with the Skull of Mathias?"

She wouldn't know. Rhoda prided herself on her complete disassociation with dark magick. She was a snob that way, the same way that made her treat her non-witch relatives like shit.

A long silence stretched and I grinned. She'd have to admit she was at a loss, and then my day would get better. I might even go have a cheeseburger for lunch. Gods knew I deserved one.

"The Skull is fiction," said my grandmother. She sounded subdued, almost wary, like I'd just told her I knew she was really a man. Not that she is. That I know of. "It is reputed to be the head of the first blood witch, Mathias, who was given his power from a daemon. His skull was inscribed with every incantation and working he learned. Daemon magick, unrefined."

"That sounds about right," I said.

"But of course it doesn't really exist. A caster witch would have known that." She was back to the arrogance again, and I clicked the phone shut gently. I knew at least one caster witch who believed the Skull was real enough to use it to kill, and another one who would tell me all about it, whether she liked it or not.

CHAPTER 20

Shelby had been moved to a private room on a higher floor of the hospital, one that had been redecorated in this decade. Flowers and balloons filled the place with cloying smells, and I sneezed. She looked up from her magazine and gave me a cautious smile. "To what do I owe the pleasure?"

I slid one of the plastic visitor chairs to the side of her bed and straddled it backward. "You can tell me about the Skull of Mathias."

Shelby shrugged. "I don't know what that is."

"Come on, Shelby." I tapped my fingers on her bedrail, and saw her follow my every move. She was nervous as a virgin bride. "I let you get away with that poor-little-innocent-me crap before, because at the time, you told me what I needed—that your family stole something from the Blackburns. Now I know what, and I need you to tell me the particulars."

"I don't know!" Shelby exploded. "Nobody *tells* me anything, they just expect me to shut up and be a good daughter! You think they *trust* me? Get real, Luna."

She had a point, and my bullshit meter wasn't pinging off the charts like the last conversation we'd had. Besides, I felt sort of sorry for Shelby—we'd had parallel lives, both of them crappy.

"So I take it you have a lead?" she asked me, breathing deeply and getting back under control.

"Yeah," I said. "But you're not going to like it."

"You think someone in my family killed Vincent Blackburn," she said. I tried not to show I was startled. *Poker face, Luna.*

"Well . . . yes. I do. Your family or someone very close to them."

Shelby moved her bed into the sitting position and regarded me with those cold blue eyes, the same expression I'd seen on Seamus on her. "Then you have an obligation to pursue your lead. But don't ever ask me to help you convict a member of my own family, Luna. I won't do it."

"They're killers," I said, getting angry, thinking back to see if I had ever held any such loyalty to my grandmother and my parents. Never had. "How can you protect them?"

"They're my family," said Shelby. "They're my blood. And no offense, but this whole thing is something that you're not part of, and don't fully understand."

"Sure," I said. "Tell yourself that if it makes things easier to mask."

"Please go," said Shelby politely, lifting her magazine again. "I'm tired and in a lot of pain."

"I'm going to figure out who did this," I said. "Whether you help me or not."

Shelby didn't reply.

I left the hospital in a pissed-off state that was rare even for me. So my partner was no help, and probably hated my guts even more than she had at the beginning of our dysfunctional little alliance. Nobody who knew anything would talk to me. Not only was I an outsider, I hated magick to my core and it probably showed.

Of course, I realized almost immediately that I was being stupid. There *was* a witch who would help me, if only out of his own desires for vengeance. It would have to be good enough for now.

In my car he appeared to me, a flare of gold in the rearview mirror. I swerved and almost went off the overpass on the Appleby Expressway. "Hex me!"

"What are you running toward, Insoli?"

"Leave me alone!" I shouted at Asmodeus, pulling over and putting on my blinkers.

"The Skull of Mathias is not your provenance, Insoli. You will bring down exactly what you seek to hide from if you go toward it."

"Cryptic much?" I snapped at him. Where was a good exorcist when you needed one?

"I am drawn to convergences, Insoli, and one is happening as we speak. Dark magick. Magick that kills. You would do well to stay away."

Before I could shout at him to leave again, a tractor-trailer blew by with its horn blaring. Wind rattled the Fairlane and when I looked back into the rear seat Asmodeus was gone.

"Hex me," I muttered again as I tried to stop my hands from shaking. The tight sense in my chest, the sense that Asmodeus had been right, eased after a few minutes and I drove on.

After all, everyone knew you couldn't trust a daemon.

The Blackburns' building didn't look any better in daylight. In fact, I could see the cracked brick and peeling paint and garbage all over the sidewalk, so it was measurably worse.

I pounded on the door and got the same surly guard, in what was probably the same ugly mesh shirt and studded jeans. "I need to see Victor," I said. "It's urgent."

He raised an eyebrow at me, but stepped aside without comment and pointed up the stairs. "Be my guest. Cop," he added as an afterthought. I had the feeling I was supposed to be insulted, but didn't dwell on it.

Scratchy classical music drifted from the top floor of the apartments, and I pushed open the door to see Victor nodding in his armchair. He looked very old, used up and spat out by the power that ran in his blood.

The moment my foot landed inside the door, his eyes snapped open and fixated on me. "Does anyone in your generation knock, Ms. Wilder?"

"Sorry," I said without thinking. Once he was awake, the sheer force of his will animated his face and body with the intensity of a wildfire.

He sighed. "Never mind. Valerie's running wilder by the day. Soon she'll be exactly like you. Tea?"

I took my cue to sit down across from him. "Coffee, if you have it."

Victor picked up an old-fashioned servant's bell and jangled it, then sat back and steepled his fingers. "I take it you're not here socially."

"No," I said. "But I am here asking a favor."

He frowned. "You know, according to magickal law, I can—"

"You can compel a favor in return, I know," I snapped. "What'll it be?" Yet another reason I hated most witches. They're so damn OCD about balance and favors and all that crap.

"I *can,* but I *won't*," said Victor patiently. "You don't have anything I want."

"Well . . . well, fine," I said, blushing. "Don't ask, then."

"You don't like witches very much, do you?" said Victor. I snorted.

"What gave you that idea?"

"I don't blame you," he said. "We're an untrustworthy, self-serving, insular bunch." The creepy servant came in and brought a tray of steaming mugs. Victor added sugar to his tea and sipped. I tried my coffee after a discreet sniff to make sure it wasn't riddled with poison. It wasn't half bad.

"I need to get some information," I said. "And you're the only person I know of that will give me the straight truth."

"Very well," said Victor. "Ask away."

I bit my lip. "What is the Skull of Mathias?"

At first, I thought Victor was having a heart attack. He froze with his cup halfway to his lips and stared at me, absolutely still, his breathing as rapid and shallow as a hummingbird's. "Victor?" I said cautiously. "You okay?"

"How do you know about the Skull?" he whispered, setting his mug back in the saucer. China rattled as his hands shook.

"Doesn't matter," I said. "What does is that you

people yanked me into the middle of your idiot feud over this thing, and I want to know what it is, close my case, and return to a world that has at least a veneer of normality." I set down my coffee and leaned toward Victor, who still looked like the reaper was standing on his grave. "You owe it to your son. He deserves to rest. And Valerie deserves to know who killed her brother and why." I didn't say anything about what Victor deserved—he'd killed Patrick O'Halloran, or ordered it done. Even if I could never prove it, he was guilty as a crooked priest.

Victor was composed again, bright eyes missing nothing. Only a tight jaw and a line of white around his mouth betrayed the shock he'd had. "I can see why you've lasted so long as an Insoli," he said finally. "You never give up."

"Not until I'm dead," I agreed. Victor sighed, pulling out a battered silver flask from his pants pocket and adding the contents to his teacup. The liquid was black and oily. I decided it would be better if I didn't scrutinize the smell too closely.

"How much do you know about daemons?" he asked me finally.

Asmodeus flashed into my mind, the implacable gold eyes searing through my skin and into my thoughts. "More than I want to."

"One time, they walked among men," said Victor. "Gifting the nonmagickal with abilities to kill or destroy. The caster witches did not appreciate the implied challenge, and cast the daemons into their shadow realm."

I knew all of this. I also knew that not *all* the daemons had been cast from ye olde mortal coil. Unfortunately for me. "So what's the twist ending here, Victor?" I said.

He rubbed his chin. "Mathias was the sole human given permanent magick, the power to draw workings from his own body. His descendants diluted and abused the power until they were reduced to using their own blood, or the blood of victims, to focus the terrible gifts the daemon gave their ancestor."

"The first blood witch," I said.

"Yes, but also not a blood witch," said Victor. "Mathias needed no blood, just as a daemon needs no focus or buffer. When he was killed a follower inscribed every working and spell he had conceived onto the master's own skull."

There are those questions that you just don't want to ask, because you know the answer will send you down a path that no sane person would walk. But in my job, you ask them anyway and walk into the dark forest willingly. "What would happen if a modern-day witch got hold of the skull?"

"Nothing," said Victor, "because the means to read the carvings are lost. My family inherited bits and pieces of translations made through the ages, but the key to reading the symbols was destroyed. By the damn caster witches, of course."

"Going hypothetical," I said, even though I wished we weren't, "what can the Skull do?"

"You'd have no need for blood," said Victor with a sigh. "No need to rely on donors or your own frailty. As much magick as you could ever want ripped directly from the ether."

Just like a daemon.

"Thank you," I said. "I'm sorry to take up so much of your time." Amazing how you can be all Miss Manners when your thoughts are whirling and you feel like you might pass out. The compulsion spell used on Joubert was daemon magick, the same kind I'd seen during the Duncan case. If the O'Hallorans had figured that much out, how close were they to unlocking the skull?

What would happen if a human being wielded inhuman magick? My experience led me to conclude nothing pretty.

"No bother," said Victor. "I was waiting for Valerie to come home so she can assist me in a working." He checked a watch on a chain, tarnished like everything else about the Blackburns' home. "Where is she?"

Something ugly twisted in the back of my mind, that instinct for bad that cops develop after any time in the field. "When did she leave? Where did she go?"

Victor tucked the watch away. "She went shopping, I believe. One of the bodyguards, Calvin, was with her."

"Calvin has a cell phone?"

Victor nodded.

"Call him." What kind of father let his daughter wander around in the middle of a gang war? Unbidden, the image of Vincent's body jumped into my mind and I pulped my temples with my fingers to make it go away. Valerie wasn't dead yet. I hoped.

"No answer," said Victor, setting down a rotary phone. "You don't think . . ."

I grabbed him by the elbow and headed for the stairs. "Let's go."

Victor balked against me. He was strong for a man who looked like death's door, but I was stronger. "You don't have to involve yourself, Detective," he said as we speed-walked down the creaky wooden stairwell. "This is between me and the O'Hallorans."

"I'm not doing this for you, you stupid old man," I

said, shouldering open the door to the lobby. "I'm just not in the habit of letting innocent people die."

"How white-knight of you," he murmured. I turned a glare on him.

"Like you'd know anything about that." I was fishing for the Fairlane's keys with my free hand, the sharp air of the outside scratching at my face.

"What did you do, Detective, to inspire this headlong urge to champion the helpless?" Victor asked. I stopped and faced him. My memory, already hyperactive from returning to Ghosttown and seeing Blackburn, exploded with a vision of bloody screams and torn flesh, more sounds and scents than sight, blurry and soaked in red.

Victor hissed and I knew my eyes had gone gold. "Do you really want to know?" I whispered.

He considered for a moment and then shrugged. "At the moment, I am grateful to accept your help in finding my daughter."

"Good," I said shortly, blinking away the were from my vision. No one knew about Joshua and that first full moon except for Sunny and Dmitri. Even they didn't know the whole truth. In a way, killing Alistair Duncan during the phase had been a blessing, because the memory of his blood and screams covered up something older and darker that I tried to bury deep down, where even my dreams couldn't find it.

My key was in the Fairlane's door when I saw the man staggering down the sidewalk toward us, dragging himself like a Romero zombie. I put my right hand on my gun, holding it down at my side in a neutral position. This was Ghosttown, after all—jumping to conclusions about someone's creepiness rarely stood you in good stead.

Victor solved my dilemma for me by rushing forward to catch the man before he fell. "Calvin!" he shouted. It wasn't a shout of concern, more like one a sweatshop owner might give if a worker dropped dead during the height of holiday shopping.

I ran over and got Calvin onto his back. He was shaking and his pupils were pinpoint, bloody spittle around his mouth. "Shit. He's in shock." I dashed back to the Fairlane and popped the trunk, got a blanket and threw it over poor Calvin, who had started to wheeze like a set of defective bagpipes. "Lift his feet," I snapped at Victor. I stuck my fingers down Calvin's gullet to check for airway obstructions, and jerked back when I felt his throat clamp down around the digit.

"What's wrong?" Victor demanded.

"He's dying," I said shortly. Victor shook Calvin's legs.

"Where's Valerie? Where's my daughter?"

Calvin's eyes rolled toward us as his limbs began the tachy twitch of flesh deprived of oxygen. "They . . ." he gasped out. "Have her. Have . . . Valerie."

"You're not dying!" Victor shouted, dropping Calvin's legs and grabbing him by the hair. "You failed! You don't get to escape that easily!"

I sat back on my heels as Calvin's last breath wuffed out. "Too late, Victor."

"Damn him!" He let Calvin's head drop back to the pavement. "He was supposed to be protecting her."

I examined Calvin's body cursorily, and saw the swollen red puncture mark on his neck. "Well, at least we know who took her," I said. The O'Hallorans were getting arrogant.

Victor grabbed my arm, so hard I knew I'd see bruises when I took off my shirt. "Find my daughter, Detective Wilder. Get her back from those bastards or I swear I'll burn this city to the ground."

And of course, I didn't tell Victor Blackburn that he had to follow proper channels, that my hands were tied by the legal system. That Valerie might already be a sacrifice to the O'Hallorans' struggle to unlock the Skull. I just nodded and helped him up. I was a cop, but I was a were too, and this time my were side won the battle between duty and the older blood code between creatures other than humans.

"I'll find her."

Victor watched me grimly as I got into the Fairlane and gunned the engine. "You'd better."

CHAPTER 21

Nocturne City General informed me that Shelby had checked herself out and gone home, against her doctor's advice. Dispatch gave me a swanky apartment tower in Mainline, not fifteen blocks from the family's tower. Seven hells, the O'Hallorans probably owned the apartments too.

I hit the buzzer marked "1023—S. O'Halloran" repeatedly, keeping up a sustained rhythm until Shelby's irritable and sleep-deepened voice demanded, "What do you want?"

"Let me in," I said.

"Luna?"

"No, it's the shoe fairy. I come bearing Prada. Just open the damn door."

The intercom clicked off and there was almost a full minute before the door buzzed at me and I pushed into the marble-and-bland lobby, complete with faux Italian fountain and soft classical music.

A minute is a long time. Shelby could be going over the balcony. She could be loading a shotgun for my knock on her door.

When did you get so paranoid, Luna? I wondered as

the stamped-brass elevator doors closed behind me. I think it was probably right around the time a car bomb went off in my face. I had no reason to trust any of these witches, and even less reason to trust Shelby since she was the only one who had (a) lied to me and (b) could hurt me and (c) would probably do both if I threatened her comfortable blood-money lifestyle.

The elevator opened on the twentieth floor with a ding, and I went down two doors to Shelby's. I pressed the bell and felt ridiculous standing out of the way, pressed sideways against the jamb, but that didn't stop me from doing it.

"Door's open!" Shelby hollered from inside. Her apartment was done in those soft ladylike colors that I imagine all wealthy people use in their homes—a white sofa and a shaggy tan rug, pastel peach countertops in her kitchen and a large brocade chaise that Shelby was propped on, her bandaged leg on a pile of pillows.

"This beats the hospital," I said, hesitating to walk on floors that probably cost more than my entire cottage.

"I couldn't stay in there another day," said Shelby. She had deep blue half-moons under her eyes and looked drawn, the way anorexics and addicts get sallow and lifeless at the end of their cycles.

"Valerie Blackburn went missing a little while ago," I said. That brought a spark back into her eyes, but she pretended to be interested in rearranging her cashmere throw.

"Shame."

"Yeah, it is a shame, especially since I know you know where she is."

Shelby sighed. "We've been over this, Luna—I can't help you." Her tone was flat, like she was shooing away a panhandler. My jangled nerves had been looking for an outlet all day, and I picked up the closest object— some sort of pricey-looking terra-cotta vase—and flung it against the wall with all of my strength.

"*Don't* tell me you can't help, Shelby," I said softly, my voice dropping into the threat register. "And *don't* play this game with me again, because you'll lose."

Calmly, her right hand appeared from under the throw, holding a snub-nosed Smith & Wesson .38 Special. Powerful little guns. Popular with cops. "Leave," Shelby told me.

"You'd really shoot me?" I asked. "You'd gun your partner down in cold blood because of this family you belong to?"

Shelby shook her head, but her gun hand never wavered. "You don't understand, Luna. You can *never* understand. For them, I'd jump off the top of this building. I'd kill for them. It's just what my uncles demand. If you don't do things by their code you're dead anyway."

I swallowed, because my throat was closed with that damned self-preservation-induced fear. Could I disarm Shelby before she killed me? Maybe. Before she shot herself? Hell no.

"You told me right after we met that imbalances of power bother you," I said. "You preach this O'Hallorans Forever crap, but you left. You became a detective because it bothers you, what they do. I saw it in your eyes when we met Patrick. You hate them as much as Victor Blackburn does."

Shelby's nostrils flared and her eyes took on a wet glitter. Good. If she cried, I could disarm her.

"Don't make me kill you, Luna," she hissed.

"Don't make me believe you will, Shelby," I said.

"Listen, put aside what you feel for just a second. Be a cop, not the black sheep. Valerie Blackburn is fifteen. She's a victim, and you know that she's going to be killed." I gambled on one step toward Shelby. The gun jumped up at me, level with my eyes. Crap. Crapcrapcrap. Why was I *always* the one who ended up on the receiving end of bad situations?

Adrenaline junkie, my traitorous inner Luna whispered. *Never satisfied until things are in flames.*

"If I help you they'll know," Shelby sniffed.

"And what will you have lost?" I said. "Trust me, Shelby. I know you can never win back approval that was never given in the first place." And I did know that, which might explain why I was half glad to get the bite as a teenager. It made me brave enough to get the hell out of San Romita and make a real life for myself.

"Gods!" Shelby cursed. She thumbed back the .38's hammer and my heart skipped with it. "Why did you have to run this down? Why couldn't you just let it go as some dumb junkie dying a dumb death?"

"Because I do my job well," I said. "And so do you. You're a good cop, Shelby. Don't become what your family thinks you are."

She shuddered like I'd slapped her, and then dropped the gun on the floor, covering her face with her hands. Her shoulders quivered as she broke down without a sound.

First, I picked up the gun, eased the hammer down, and put it in the waist of my jeans, where no one could get any crazy ideas. Then I went and sat next to Shelby, rubbing her back until she'd emptied herself of sobs.

"Gods," she said again. "I've been so terrible. I'm just a terrible, terrible partner."

"Not that I made it very easy," I conceded. "Listen, if you want some touchy-feely sentiment, make an appointment with Dr. Merriman. Where's Valerie?"

Shelby scrubbed at her eyes with the silk cuff of her pajamas. "Seamus would take her to Basin Lake. We have a private lodge there. It's very isolated, especially in the fall."

Basin Lake was over two hours east of Nocturne City, in the foothills of the Sierra Fuego range. For all I knew, Valerie was dead already.

"Thank you," I told Shelby, and meant it. For someone I'd disliked instantly, our partnership could have turned out worse.

"I hope she's all right," said Shelby.

I was already dialing Mac on my cell phone. "So do I."

"Get over to the precinct house, now," had been Mac's only sentence when I'd called him to request backup at Basin Lake.

"Mac, I don't have time for this! A girl's life is in danger!"

"I don't care if Mary Magdalene and Jesus Christ have returned to earth and are out there in the street doing a cha-cha with Saint Peter," Mac yelled. "Get your ass back here now or I fire you on the spot!"

The phone went dead in my ear. I had never heard Mac sound so angry—but Valerie was still going to die whether I was fired or not.

"Shit," I muttered. If I went to save her without jurisdiction, or authority, nothing against her kidnappers would stick, and anything *I* did, like shooting someone deserving in the head, would.

I darted the Fairlane through traffic like a shark cuts through an oceanful of swimmers, missing bumpers and fenders and mirrors by inches. I didn't have time for this—whatever Mac wanted, it had better be good.

Rick gave me a sympathetic look when I stormed into the precinct house. "She's waiting for you in her office."

Oh, this was the last freaking straw. I was a homicide detective, not a juvenile delinquent to be summoned to the principal's office at her whim. I threw open Morgan's door. "What!"

She looked furious, all pretense of the cool career woman erased from her pink face. "You are a disgrace!" she barked. "You deserted a crime scene and have repeatedly disobeyed my orders! Hand over your badge and gun and get out of my station!"

I blinked. "You're firing me?"

Morgan laughed. Not a pleasant laugh, a coyote laugh. Predatory. "You think I'd give you the satisfaction of collecting unemployment after the hell you've put the department and the O'Hallorans through? I'm suspending you without pay, pending a psych evaluation."

Now the truth came out. "Did Seamus O'Halloran put you up to this?"

Morgan's eyes narrowed. "What are you insinuating, Detective?"

"That Seamus is persuasive," I said. "Rich, and persuasive."

Morgan looked at the ceiling, clenching and unclenching her hands like she wanted to put a fist through something. Probably me. "Give me your shield and weapon, Luna."

"No," I said, surprising both of us. "No, ma'am, I'm sorry. Seamus O'Halloran is a kidnapper and a killer and if you won't let me prove it then I respectfully decline to obey your instructions. You'll just have to suspend me by force. Ma'am."

The flush went out of Morgan's cheeks and she shook her head at me. "Un-freaking-believable," she muttered. We both stood there, she at a loss, until I stepped back into the hall and quickly walked away before Morgan could collect herself. McAllister caught me by the bullpen.

"What the Hex happened?"

"I think I'm suspended," I said, "but that part wasn't real clear."

Mac heaved a sigh. "Again?" Suspending me had been one of former Captain Roenberg's favorite hobbies.

"Looks that way," I said. "Listen, I'm headed up to Basin Lake. Sorry to have caused you all this trouble."

Mac stopped me with a hand. "Why are you going after Seamus O'Halloran, Luna? I know third-world dictators who are afraid of the guy."

"Because he's gotten away with enough," I said. "He's a nasty, evil old man and he thinks just because he can make a little magick shift into this realm we should all cower. There's that and the whole murder thing."

"You know," said Mac, chewing on the end of an unlit cigarette. "You're a lot of things, Luna, but I've never known you to be wrong. Go. I'll call in some backup and notify the Hilltop County sheriff."

Concern flooded me. The last time Mac had gone to bat for one of my cases, he'd wound up nearly jobless and dead. "You could lose your pension over this, Mac."

"Hell, I'm planning to live on a boat in Florida and fish all day." He grinned. "What do I need a Hexed pension for?"

It had been a long case, and my inhibitions were shot to hell, so I hugged Mac hard, whispered, "Thank you," and ran back to the idling Fairlane.

CHAPTER 22

Basin Lake appears in flashes at first, like a ghost you can only glimpse in the corner of your eye. The main highway is a two-lane terror of twists and switchbacks leading up the spine of the mountains, and I never slowed below fifty-five the whole way. Occasionally I could spot the black inkblot shape of the SWAT team's Bell Huey through the evergreens, but otherwise I was alone in the forest.

At last I rounded the final turn into the congealed clump of gas station and general store that passed as a resort town, and saw the lake spread out below me, the relic of a long-ago cataclysm, now ironically serene and bluer than it had a right to be, considering the situation.

In one direction, the road led to a public boat launch. The other was blocked off by a tastefully rustic wooden gate bearing a tastefully rustic sign that read PRIVATE.

The SWAT helicopter swooped overhead and banked. My radio crackled. "Seventy-six, this is Tactical One."

I grabbed the radio as I sized up the gate. It was made out of logs, solid, but the hinges were rusty and the whole thing looked pretty rotten. You'd think the

O'Hallorans could afford decent security. "Tac One, go ahead."

"Received radio confirmation of search warrant from county sheriff," the anonymous SWAT officer told me.

"Roger, Tac One," I said. At least I wouldn't add jail time to Morgan's suspension for busting in on the O'Hallorans. Not that I cared anymore.

"Team will deploy from landing pad at rear of residence," said the radio. The O'Hallorans had a helipad? Figured. "ETA ten minutes."

Too long. The witches had already had a full three hours with Valerie. If she wasn't dead or maimed beyond recognition already, she would be at the first whirr of SWAT rotors over the lodge.

"Roger, Tac One. Ten minutes." I hung my speaker back on the dash and clicked the radio off. Then I put the Fairlane into reverse and backed into the parking area of the general store, across the highway from the gate. I carefully checked both ways for log trucks and drunken fishermen, then depressed the clutch and put the Fairlane in first. "I'm sorry," I apologized to the car, then stomped on the gas pedal.

My six-cylinder block roared like a fighter jet taking off, and the tachometer jumped into the four thousand range. I slipped my foot off the clutch and the Fairlane jumped forward, across the highway and through the O'Hallorans' gate with an impact that ricocheted me off the steering wheel and whipcracked my seat belt against my body.

Ignoring the ringing in my head, I wrestled the car under control as it headed for the ditch at the side of the gravel road. A piece of my undercarriage fell off and I ran over it, wincing at the hellacious grinding sound coming from my engine.

I shifted and gunned up the road, spraying pebbles from my back tires. Belatedly, I dug my flasher out of the glove compartment and stuck it to the Velcro strips on the dashboard, starting it revolving as I raced up the mountain toward the lodge.

The O'Hallorans' lodge, if it could be called that, was one of those new buildings made to look old and not pulling it off very well. The aged patina of the wide porch and the carefully arranged log walls looked like a giant-sized challenge on a miniature golf course.

It was also surprisingly deserted. One black Humvee sat in the driveway, but no sentries sighted me in their crosshairs from any of the gabled windows and the only sounds after I killed the engine were water birds crying over the lake.

The silence creeped me out far more than if I'd faced an armed regiment of Seamus's security people. It was a dead silence, like I imagined you'd find at Chernobyl just after the blast. Bad magick prickled around me like air, and the place just *smelled* wrong, an undertone that made the were snarl and retreat into its cave inside my subconscious mind.

Keeping the Fairlane between me and the lodge, I crawled out the passenger door and around to the trunk, where I pulled out my Kevlar vest and strapped it on over my T-shirt. Not like anyone inside couldn't aim for my head, but it was better than nothing. I checked my Glock to ensure the clip was full and tucked the extras from my shoulder rig into my back pocket.

From the treeline across the lake, I heard the soft *whud-whud-whud* of the SWAT helicopter. All my training dictated I should wait for them to make entry before going in—seven hells, I shouldn't even *be* here—but my imagination served up a mutilated Valerie Blackburn and I eased my shaking body out from behind the Fairlane and moved in a tactical crouch across the open expanse of gravel to land against one of the tree-sized porch posts.

My heart was hammering and sweat trickled underneath the forty pounds of Kevlar piggybacked on my torso. I wasn't scared, any more than I'd been the other times I'd made entry on an armed suspect, but that unidentifiable wrongness was seeping into me, throwing my senses out of whack.

"Police!" I shouted. "Exit the building with your hands up!" That never does any good, but routine reassures me. No sound came from inside the lodge. I listened hard, with my were hearing, and detected a few soft murmurs and shuffles, normal sounds of inhabitation. That was enough—someone was in there.

I moved up to the door, keeping myself out of the lines of sight from the broad picture windows on either side, and hammered against it with the butt of my gun. "Police! We have a warrant!" "We" being me and the approaching SWAT team, which would do all the good of pointing my finger and going "Bang!" until they landed.

The door was solid pine boards as wide as I was, strapped with iron bands. No way I was kicking that thing in Dirty Harry–style, even with were strength. The same ward marks were burned into the frame. I was very glad at that moment not to be a witch.

Out of a sudden bout of logic, I tried the massive iron pull-handle and the door creaked open. I jumped back, aiming into the shadowy interior. Nothing jumped out at me. No bullets flew. As far as tactical operations went, this one was about as hot and heavy as one of Sunny's meditation circles.

"Police. We have a warrant!" I called halfheartedly one more time, then stepped into a tiled foyer with a cathedral ceiling full of rough-hewn crossbeams, sterile and devoid of any sign that people actually lived here.

Every sense I possessed was on edge, and my palms were slicking the Glock's grip with sweat. My instincts were screaming at me, the fight-or-flight ingrained into my blood wanting to get the hell out, away from the crushing quiet and that subtle, rotten scent that cloyed the air heavier and heavier the farther I went into the lodge.

A kitchen appeared, all copper countertops and empty cupboards, and I saw that the hallway after it opened into a gallery facing the lake, solid floor-to-ceiling windows giving a panorama view. In that weirdly detached part of my brain, I thought, *Must be a bitch to heat this place.*

Then I heard voices.

"Write, you stupid whore." The voice wasn't shouting, quite the opposite. It was soft and unconcerned, attached to the type of person who's used to being obeyed without question.

Valerie answered him. "I can't. I don't know how to translate this."

I sagged against the kitchen doorway, never more relieved to hear someone speak. She was alive, and well enough to talk. My city wouldn't go to cinders because of the witches and their pointless war.

The crack of a palm on skin echoed into the kitchen,

and the same male voice said, "Karl!" It was sharp this time, sharp like a combat knife. I was glad I wasn't Karl.

"Why isn't the goddamn working . . . well, working?" Karl demanded. "Can't you tell she's lying to us?"

"The working never failed before," said the voice. If I wasn't so ramped up, I would swear I'd heard it before, but I put it down to being hidden in a creepy kitchen while at least two men held a hostage not twenty feet away.

"We should just kill the kid and go for the old man," Karl muttered. "Did I not say this when the order came down to snatch this skirt in the first place?"

"Are you questioning my judgment?" said the first voice. Silence followed. "Good. Now, Valerie. Please read this page and translate the inscriptions."

"I can't," she said again. "I don't know how to translate this." She sounded awfully cheerful for someone being held by thugs employed by her family's archenemy, but we all have different ways of coping.

The calm man swore. "Valerie, trust me. You have no idea how bad it will be for you if you keep resisting."

Certain things—images, phrases, smells—are keyed into your brain the same as nerve endings. Sense a memory, and it can affect you like a blow to the back of the head.

Still, I wasn't sure it was him until I swung around the kitchen door and screamed, "Freeze! Hands behind your head!"

Joshua turned toward me, a pleasant smile on his face. "I was wondering how long it would take you to get out here." He really saw me, and his features sagged in concert with my knees. "Gods. Luna. Is that you?"

Peripherally, I saw that there were at least six other men, all in badly cut suits, loitering in the gallery. Valerie was sitting at a table with a legal pad and pen in her hands and the insouciant Karl gripping her shoulder.

But all I really saw was Joshua. He was older, lines around his eyes and mouth giving him the dignity he'd lacked fifteen years ago. Same burning dark eyes, same thin-lipped cruelty to his expression. His shaggy brown-blond hair had grown into a ponytail neatly clipped at the back of his neck with a silver band. He wore Armani instead of biker leathers, but it was him, surely as I was Luna Joanne Wilder.

"Luna!" he exclaimed. "Seven hells, life sure is funny, isn't it?" He took a step toward me and I raised my gun directly between his eyes.

"Don't take another fucking step." My human brain may have been shocked beyond cognition, but the were knew his smell.

Joshua raised both palms in mock alarm. "Whoa there, girl. Friends. We're not doing anything wrong here."

Rage cut through the shock and the rush of emotions from seeing my de facto pack leader again after years of nightmares and nameless empty places in my heart. The son of a bitch was patronizing me. "Get your hands behind your head," I snapped. "*All* of you!" I added when one of the security men on the leather sofas went for his gun.

Joshua waved a hand. "Don't worry, boys. She's all bark and no bite." Behind him, the SWAT helicopter came in for a bouncy landing on the O'Hallroans' helipad. About freaking time.

I turned to Valerie. "You okay?"

"I'm fine. Why wouldn't I be?" she said, turning her head slowly to give me a puzzled look. Her eyes were glazed and blank, like someone had taken an eraser to her features.

I swung the gun back to Joshua. "What did you do to her?" It had to be another compulsion—Valerie's blank dreamy-eyed stare wasn't induced by anything human.

"Me? Nothing," Joshua said. "And I resent the implication."

I blinked. The Joshua I'd met at a bonfire in San Romita had struggled with anything over two syllables.

"You know, Luna, I never expected to meet you again," he said, walking toward me again. I caught his eyes and stared, marveling at how they burned with a yellow spark even when he was human. "And now that I have, I'm a little disappointed—actually, a lot disappointed. The girl I knew would never join the pigs, much less burst in and wave a gun at her proper mate."

He stopped a few feet from me, never breaking eye contact. My limbs went heavy and I felt as if my own thoughts were being pushed under to accommodate what Joshua wanted me to think. He was disgusted, and that made me terribly upset. I had to fix this, had to show him I was worthy . . .

The SWAT team flooded into the room, yelling and wrestling security force thugs to the floor. I barely noticed them, locked as I was in Joshua's eyes.

"There's a good girl," he said, in the same way you'd praise a toy poodle. "Now maybe we can finish what we started oh-so-many years ago." He reached for me, and I caught the edge of the rampant snake tattoo on his right wrist. Like a cord had been snapped, Joshua's will was replaced by the flood of memories of his attack, the chest-crushing feeling of panic and trauma.

He had tried to pull a dominate. On *me*. And seven hells, it had almost worked. I aimed just to the left of Joshua's ear and put a bullet into the pine paneling behind his head. The SWAT team shouted and covered, aiming their weapons at us. The handcuffed goons couldn't do much except glare.

I met Joshua's eyes again, my fury burning his dominate out of existence. "The next one is a sucking chest wound," I said.

He smiled again, trying to laugh it off, but his jaw twitched with rage. I gestured tiredly to a SWAT officer, suddenly feeling the weight of my vest and gun and my bones. "Get him out of my sight."

"Some things never change," Joshua said as he was handcuffed and hauled away. "Still an uppity little bitch."

I sank onto a leather footstool with the feet of a hoofed dead animal, and put my face in my hands. Joshua. I had hoped for so long he was dead, or in prison, or *somewhere* I'd never have to see him again. Well, a hope and a buck-fifty will get you on the Nocturne Transit bus.

"Detective, we have a problem," said the SWAT captain.

"What is it, Captain . . ."

"Fuller, ma'am, and I'm a sergeant."

"Sorry. Sergeant Fuller. What's the problem?"

He pointed at Valerie, who was still sitting primly upright like a Valium-fueled prom queen. "The young lady claims she's not being held against her will."

That got me on my feet. "What? She was kidnapped, for the love of all things Hexed and holy!"

"So you say, Detective," said Fuller with a calm that was utterly maddening. I bet he was a hostage negotiator. "But Miss Blackburn says she wasn't taken against her will, nor was she imprisoned at any time."

The compulsion was still in full force. I looked at Fuller, the room full of SWAT officers, literal and red-blooded and reality-based to a man. Trying to explain daemon magick, witches, weres, and a caster witch-blood witch feud over a carved-up skull was beyond my abilities right then.

"We have to let everyone go," said Fuller. "No crime, no arrests. I'm sorry, ma'am." He gave me an awkward shoulder pat and a sympathetic smile. Probably thought I was cracking up. Hell, *I* thought I was cracking up.

Joshua, released from handcuffs, sauntered over. "Better luck next time, Miss Detective."

"Stay away from me, Joshua," I warned. "I doubt anyone in Nocturne City would blame me for putting a couple of slugs in your smarmy face."

"Except Seamus O'Halloran," he said, still in that infuriating calm tone. "I'm head of security for his holdings."

"Bend over and I'll show you what I think of that," I growled.

"Charming. I'm really starting to wonder what I saw in you. Oh . . . I remember—you were easy." He dipped his head in a bow and walked out, gesturing for his squad to follow.

I'd like to say that the comment enraged me and I smashed something or punched him in the nose, but it hurt. It hurt almost as much as seeing Dmitri with Irina, in that part of myself I try to keep hidden from general view. Joshua was under my skin. His blood was my blood, and he had the ability to tear me apart whenever he wanted. The only way to get rid of his influence was to join another pack, or die.

Since neither of those were an option at the moment, I went out to the Fairlane, stripped off my Kevlar, sat in the driver's seat with the windows rolled up and screamed until my throat was raw.

CHAPTER 23

The sun was setting over Siren Bay when I finally made it back to the city, illuminating the swooping outline of the bridge in black relief. The cottage was that mellow pinkish color it gets at sunset, the denuded climbing roses hiding the peeling paint and missing boards.

I turned off my cell phone and my land line, tossed my gun on the kitchen table, and shed pieces of clothing as I went upstairs, turning the cranky faucet in the old tub hot as far as it would go. I needed Joshua's stink off me.

Thirty minutes later I was clean and smelled of tea tree oil and peach extract, but my thoughts were no less black. I couldn't remember when I'd been this confused, and furious, and tired.

How *dare* Joshua try to use his dominate on me? And how had I fallen for it? I was a proud Insoli. I bowed to no one. *Except the man who made you,* I whispered.

I wrapped a towel around my head and another around my torso and kicked the growing pile of laundry around the basket as I went past. Tidiness had been Sunny's reason for living, not mine.

If Joshua could exert his pack influence over me, it was bad all around. I'd lose my status as a free were, my effectiveness as a detective. My entire life was compromised the second I laid eyes on him.

Hex it.

I was about to dig an old bottle of scotch from some forgotten party out of the cabinet under the sink and drink myself into oblivion when I heard voices downstairs and froze. I smelled three distinct bodies, two female and one male, all musky with the odor of were.

Weres. In my *house*. Whoever they were, they were about to be very freaking sorry.

I padded down the stairs on light bare feet, balling my fists as I came around the corner into the kitchen. "What in hell are you doing coming into my home!"

Irina, Sergei, and Yelena stopped their whispered conversation and favored me with amused glances. I realized I was still wrapped in fluffy bath towels, one white, one pink.

"We have come to visit you," said Irina with a smirk.

I narrowed my eyes and let them flicker to gold. "How did you get in?"

"Door was open," said Sergei brusquely. I hadn't gotten a good look at him in the alley, but in the bright track lighting of my kitchen he was stout and scarred, like a pit fighter or a Russian mafia heavy.

"Irina wishes to speak with you," said Yelena. She was as delicate as Sergei was ungainly, and my bag of Eastern European clichés might have pegged her as an ex-ballet dancer. I saw tattoos on her knuckles and the suggestion of a previous, much harder life in the harsh lines around her mouth. Okay, maybe not a *ballet* dancer.

"Ever hear of picking up the Hexed phone?" I asked Irina. She glared at me and slapped one fist against her palm. The effect was a little bit like a lingerie model auditioning for a tough-girl part in a movie.

"The time for polite talk has passed," she informed me. I shifted into a combat stance, subtly of course. I may have been wearing a towel, but that didn't mean I had to take her crap.

"Do explain."

"You forced Dmitri to phase in part and expose himself to the infection. You have contaminated him further," said Sergei. He took a breath and I thought that was probably the longest phrase he'd spoken in months.

"We made a mistake not dealing with you permanently the first time," said Yelena. "But Dmitri has always been a faithful member of the pack and we granted his request."

"That was a mistake," Irina expounded helpfully.

Belly-dropping fear grabbed me, but I rolled my eyes and acted like they were keeping me from something interesting on television. "So what, it took three of you to deliver the message? Are your ESL skills really that bad?"

Luna, you did it now. Three pissed-off pack weres in your kitchen and you without even a thong to defend yourself.

I commanded myself to cut the sarcasm and think of a way out of this problem, but none presented itself. Irina stayed in my face while Sergei and Yelena moved to either side. I've watched enough nature shows to know they were circling, preparing to attack the lone prey.

Have I mentioned I really, really hate being the prey?

"You can't just kill me," I said lamely. "I'm a cop. We have real police in this country."

Yelena barked a laugh. "Do you think the Redbacks are concerned with plain human police in any country, Insoli?"

She had a valid point there. I couldn't fight. I couldn't run. I couldn't even dazzle the Redbacks with my nakedness and go for my gun, lying enticingly in the center of the kitchen table. I'd tangled with Dmitri. I knew how fast and unforgiving his brethren would be.

"Do you have anything to say?" asked Sergei, letting me know with a raised bushy eyebrow that I wasn't really expected to speak, and in fact it would be better if I just shut up and left them to their dismembering.

If there's one thing I have, it's a survival instinct, which I think must be a Serpent Eye thing, because when I can't see a way out I get the craziest ideas, like the one that sprang to mind right then.

"I'll cure him."

Irina stopped her slow pace back and forth and stared at me. "What?"

I swallowed and spoke in my License-and-Registration Voice. "I'll cure Dmitri of the daemon blood. You just have to give me a little time."

Yelena stopped circling, cocking her head. "Why are you so confident you will do this? We have not been able to. We are his pack. You are just a wolf snarling in the gutter for scraps."

"No offense, lady," I said, not having to fake the steel in my tone. Cracks about being Insoli always make me cranky. "But maybe that's why nothing has worked. You've got your traditions and you can chant and shake sage sticks at him until the cows jump over the moon, but nothing human or were can cure daemon illness."

Sergei regarded me, stroking his chin, and I stared him down, daring him to try something. Not a dominate, just a pure contest of wills between an Insoli and a pack elder. He eventually dropped his gaze and spat on my floor. "Let her try."

Yelena and Irina immediately began whining at him in Ukrainian, but he snarled and they both fell silent.

"Fine." Irina tossed her head in that spoiled-princess way she was so good at. "Try it and fail. I will be amused to watch."

"Hex me, go bite a blood witch," I snapped at her. "Just admit that you lost this time."

"Bitch," she muttered, going out and banging the screen door behind her. Yelena followed with a flounce. Cold air curled around my calves and I shivered. Sergei snorted as if he smelled something burning and then held up a finger. "You have until the next full moon."

"Shut the door, and don't let it hit your ass," I responded. He left quietly, footfalls that should have been heavy making no sound.

Yeah, I was gonna have to watch that one. And I had just promised to cure Dmitri of an infection borne from a daemon-were hybrid who was now dead, all in little more than a week.

What the Hex had I gotten myself into now?

Of course, the first thing I did was call Sunny—well, after I had put real clothes on.

"Not that I'm not glad to hear from you," she said. "But you have that tone. You know that tone? The one you only use when something royally terrible has happened?"

"Uh-huh," I said cautiously.

"So what happened, Luna?"

I sighed. "You'd better come over."

She got to the cottage within fifteen minutes, no mean feat from Battery Beach.

"You know speed kills," I greeted her. "That'd be a two-hundred-dollar ticket if some bored patrol officer tagged you."

"Oh whatever," she responded. "Cop's cousin, remember?"

Pleased as I was that I'd corrupted her so thoroughly since her help with the Duncan case, I had more important things on my mind, like my imminent and unpleasant death if I didn't get this Dmitri thing sorted out.

I made Sunny cocoa, since I'd finally run out of that hideous jasmine-wheatgrass-whatsit tea that she kept around, and told her the short version of my dilemma, leaving out me wanting to beat Irina about the head with a meat tenderizer until she resembled filet mignon more than a prime choice.

Sunny bit her lip. "Luna, why do you do things like this?"

"I was naked and about to be eaten, Sunny. Not a whole lot of choices."

"Well, couldn't you have offered them money, or negotiable commodities instead of some phantom cure? Gold. I hear gold is very big on the Russian black market."

"First of all," I said, "the Redbacks are Ukrainian. Secondly, you're not helping."

"Well, what do you want from me?" she exclaimed. "I can't magick up a potion to cure daemon poison!"

I had sort of been hoping it would be that easy, but knowing it wouldn't be. "Is there *anything* we can do, Sunny?"

She thought for a long time and then shook her head. "I'm sorry." She was nice enough not to point out that there was really no "we" in this mess—if I didn't come up with a cure, Sunny would continue as normal, albeit less one impulsive, angry, Internet–shopping-addicted cousin.

I pressed my hands over my eyes. They burned, reminding me I hadn't slept in at least twenty-four hours. "Hex it. That's all, then. I'm screwed."

"Only daemon magick can reverse daemon contamination," said Sunny. "So unless you can summon one up with a quick blood working . . ."

We weren't going down that road, no matter how many angry weres were on my ass about this. Besides, I got the feeling Asmodeus didn't exactly come when called. Figured, when I needed the guy he was nowhere in sight. Maybe I could get some sort of special daemon whistle.

"Thanks for your help," I muttered to Sunny, laying my head down on the table. I just wanted to sleep, for about a month, and have the world make sense again.

Sunny stood and patted my back. "Don't worry, Luna. We'll think of something. I'll do research."

"I'll burn a card catalog in offering to the research gods," I mumbled from my prone position.

After I heard Sunny's convertible drive away, I

pulled out my cell phone and dialed Dmitri from memory. I'd deleted him from my caller ID and scrubbed the single e-mail from my laptop's hard drive in that fit of post-cheating rage every woman goes through. Unfortunately, my memory wasn't so easy.

The first time, I didn't even let the phone ring before I slapped it shut. Then I took a deep breath, reminded myself that he had to be told what was going on, and redialed. This time I made it to two rings.

"You're not in seventh grade," I muttered as I dialed and listened to the phone ring before Dmitri answered groggily.

" 'Lo?"

I sat there, trying to think of what to say. *Hey, your new fucktoy came by and threatened my life, so now I have to cure you. Hi, there, remember that daemon bite you got from Stephen Duncan? Hello, Dmitri, this is your insane ex Luna calling to tell you that I have to cure you, or I'm werefood.*

"Luna, I know that's you. I have caller ID," said Dmitri. Face flaming, I shut my phone. I couldn't do it. Everything we'd shared and I couldn't think of one solitary word to say to Dmitri right then. There was no way to explain what had happened with Irina, or why I had really made the deal.

I didn't care about my life one way or the other—hell, I prodded dead people and faced down armed psychotics for a living. Self-preservation was not in the equation.

But I did care about Dmitri. Still. Hex it, I was a pathetic excuse for a grown woman. I got the scotch, and a clean glass, and proceeded to get royally hammered, something that hadn't happened since my days in uniform. I had hoped the alcohol would paint me in a better light with myself, but I still held the same opinion when I staggered upstairs and passed out.

In love. In danger of losing my job and my life. Pathetic.

CHAPTER 24

I woke up to a percussive beat, and after a confused second realized it was my heart beating a tattoo against the inside of my aching skull. The sun was down and after a consultation with my alarm clock I discovered I'd slept an entire day away.

Bang-up way to use precious time I could be using to find a cure for Dmitri or collecting any of the many loose threads of Vincent Blackburn's case.

Hangovers disappear fairly quickly with were healing, and I was walking straight by the time I got showered, dressed, and selected my beat-up black Chippewas, ideal footwear for what I had in mind, which was to drive aimlessly around feeling sorry for myself.

I almost missed the blinking message on my land-line phone, but someone had left a voice mail while I was unconscious. Probably someone hideous, like Matilda Morgan or my psychiatrist.

Figuring nothing could be worse than meeting Joshua, I pressed the code to retrieve my messages.

"Detective Wilder, this is Melissa Gordon with the district attorney's office." She sounded like she'd rather be talking to Charles Manson's voice mail. Not news, considering I'd killed her former boss. "I'm calling to inform you of a court date to testify against Arthur Samuelson, aka Samael, in the matter of his assault charges. November twenty-fifth at ten A.M., Nocturne City superior court part forty-three." She slammed the phone down and my machine bleeped, telling me I had no more messages.

Arthur Samuelson. I knew his real name was something geeky. The only person I knew who had concrete ties to Vincent, who may have seen him the night he was killed. Then I hit on the fact that Samael was facing trial for assaulting a police officer. He was a sex club worker. Even in Nocturne City, it was highly unlikely he'd made bail.

I grabbed my gun and badge and ran to the Fairlane, stopping to assess the damage from ramming the O'Hallorans' gate. One headlight dangled out of its socket. The chrome bumper, added by me when I'd been promoted out of uniform, was smashed beyond repair. A remarkably symmetrical V creased the hood. All in all, it looked like the type of vehicle a carjacker would back away from in terror.

Gods-damned O'Hallorans. I'd be sending them a bill. The Fairlane looked like crap, but it started with a louder-than-usual grumble, the gears hitching as I shifted on the beach road. I just prayed it would get me to the Las Rojas county jail.

It was well past normal visiting hours, but at the brandishment of my badge, a disgruntled guard buzzed me in. The county jail was staffed by the Las Rojas Sheriff's Office, not the department of corrections, and I didn't blame them for being surly. The jail sat well outside downtown, on a desolate strip of shale next to the Vortiger River. It had been a brewery owned by the Vortiger family, Germans who followed our founding father Jeremiah Chopin west from St. Louis in the early days of expansion.

The river named after the Vortigers had survived. Their brewery had not, and the city had seized it and decided the logical course would be to turn it into a jail. Maybe they thought the lager-tinged fumes would keep the prisoners calm.

"Who are you here to see, Detective?" said the deputy inside the cage that controlled the ancient iron gates barring the bowels of the jail. Being inside the building always reminded me vaguely of Alcatraz, or Sing-Sing—an old-style sense of punishment, not rehabilitation.

"Arthur Samuelson," I said. She raised a thick black eyebrow. Her face was squashed, like a bright-eyed bulldog's.

"Sir Samael," she intoned sarcastically. "He'll be thrilled. Gun and any metallic objects stay outside the bars."

I put everything that could be used as a shank in the plastic basket she furnished me and accepted the claim chit. A sickly buzzer sounded far off, and the gate creaked open.

"Make sure you wash your hands after," said the deputy, going back to her magazine.

I walked down the brick-lined hall to the steel door of the interrogation room. The jail was arranged in a cellular construction, with civilian hallways on one side, interrogation and meeting rooms in the center, and the main cell block on the other side.

Inside, I took a seat and waited seven minutes, by the ancient wall clock, for Samael to be brought in.

He was thinner than I remembered now that he was wearing a loose shirt, his hair free of gel and hanging in his eyes. His posture sagged as the guard chained his shackles to the ring in the floor, but his eyes were the same twin high beams I remembered.

"How's your head?" he asked me after the deputy had shut the door.

"How's jail?" I met him smirk for smirk. In normal light, and the silence of the interrogation room, he wasn't even close to some of the nightmarish things that showed up behind my eyes after dark. It also helped that he wasn't giving me a concussion and throwing me in a cage.

"Fine," he said smoothly. "People are easy to control when they're already locked up."

"You like control," I stated, and he didn't take it as a question, just smiled like I'd asked if he wanted a candy bar.

"I think you figured that out already, pretty girl," he said. The hypnotic cadence just seemed overblown, matched with his puke-green county jumpsuit.

"Homicide," I said. Samael blinked.

"Beg pardon?"

"I'm a homicide detective," I said. "Call me anything except 'Detective' or 'ma'am' again and I'll put your smug face through this table."

Samael tilted his head back, gauging me. "Not like I have much of a choice, eh?"

"None at all," I agreed. "Tell me about Vincent Blackburn."

"Confused. Lots of teen angst. Lousy lay," he said.

His lips twitched. Despite my threats and his shackles, he still had control and he knew it. Bastard.

Being were never helps in these situations. You can't beat the crap out of someone without lawsuits flying. Enhanced senses wouldn't tell me anything except that Samael really needed a shower.

"We finished? There's this reality program on at seven that I'm really into."

Oh, it was so almost worth the legal entanglements to just hit him. Well, they hadn't given me the detective shield to help me accessorize. And after a former life as a cocktail waitress and a runaway teenager, I at least knew how to read people.

"How about this," I suggested to Samael in a cheery tone. "You cooperate with me, or I'll have you transferred out of this nice, normal jail full of people ripe for domination to Cedar Hill Psychiatric, where they'll pump you full of Haldol and strap you to your bed." I allowed a slow smile to spread across my face, showing Samael that I was relishing the fantasy. "They might even fit you with a catheter so you *never* have to move."

To his credit, Samael never altered his expression, but I saw a fat bead of sweat work its way from his hairline down his temple.

"Oh, shoot." I snapped my fingers. "I forgot. You're not into bondage."

"What do you want?" Samael muttered. He was rigid, like Indiana Jones in that scene with all the snakes.

"Excuse me?" I said, cupping my ear.

"What do you want!" he shouted, hitting the table. I crossed my ankles primly, one over the other.

"I want you to tell me the truth, *Arthur*."

He flinched. "You want me to spill the big secret, that Vincent got some mysterious phone call or letter written in blood or some noir detective shit? Well, it didn't happen that way. Vincent was a dumb kid and he messed with the wrong people and he got himself dead. End of story. Roll credits."

"If you were any vaguer you'd be a copy of *Ulysses*," I told him. "What people? What did Vincent do?"

Samael laughed. "What didn't that kid do? He worked in a sex club. A lot of rich people came in. They all liked Vincent. You fill in the boring bits."

"Where did he keep his stash of photos?"

Samael blinked at me, and I smiled serenely. He'd counted on having the blackmail angle to bargain with. "Oh, and if you could tell me which rich pervert objected to the idea and killed him, so much the better."

"Hells, I don't know," said Samael after a few seconds of recovering his placid, creepy front. "I make enough cash squeezing people who *want* to be in pain."

"I can't tell you how refreshing it is to meet an honest, hardworking independent businessman," I said.

"Come see me when I get out, Detective," he said with a wink as the deputy led him back to the cellblock.

"Only if you come with a biohazard suit," I said.

Never mind that my encounter with Samael had left me feeling like I needed to take about ten showers; he'd confirmed that Vincent had waved his dirty pictures under the wrong nose and given me direction, something that had been sorely lacking in the case. If I could make it through one night without having to kick down a door or jump out of a helicopter, I'd be a happy woman.

I checked my watch. It was after six, and the evidence depot closed at five. I'd have to wait until morning to check Vincent's personal effects. If he had a stash of compromising media on Nocturne City's version of *Lifestyles of the Rich and Famous*, he'd keep the items themselves or the locations close at hand. Blackmailers were squirelly and paranoid like that.

Too bad Vincent hadn't been just a touch more paranoid. He might still be alive.

After a well-publicized scandal involving gun-toting thugs employed as evidence clerks at the behest of Alistair Duncan, the Nocturne City evidence depot, contained inside the courthouse complex, had undergone a major overhaul and was now staffed by perky postgrads who wore pseudo-official uniforms and tags inscribed with names like *CAMMIE* and *ALISSE*.

"Alyse?" I said when she came trotting over to the service window.

"It's pronounced like 'Alice,'" she corrected me. "And how are you today?"

"Fine," I said cautiously, wondering if the city's new plan was to kill their detectives with goodwill.

"What can we do for you, ma'am?"

"Well, don't you need to see some ID?" I asked. She beamed.

"Sure, if you have some. I'm joking! I just need to take a quick peek at your badge."

I presented it and the case number of the Blackburn murder, and she handed me the logbook to sign the stuff out the same way you'd pass the scones at a tea party. I expected to be sat down and offered a cup any second.

"Don't you think it's too creepy how they keep a dead person's clothes?" Alisse asked as she brought me the large brown paper evidence bag holding Vincent's personal effects. "I think we should donate them to the rummage sale. I'm joking!" she added when my eyebrows went up.

"And I'm leaving," I said, beating a hasty retreat to the Fairlane. It had a flat tire.

I sat on the curb and went through the bag while I waited for my road service. I'm not such a girly-girl that I can't change a tire, but after a childhood with a mechanic father, I reserve the right to make someone else do it, just like preacher's kids get to drink and get arrested.

Vincent's clothes were expensive, but they were worn to that gray-blue color that black clothing gets after too many spin cycles, and they smelled like stale vomit and old blood. Thank the gods I was outside.

Dr. Kronen had sealed all of Vincent's piercings in a neat bag, and only one piece of jewelry jangled free in the bottom. I pulled out a plain ball-chain necklace that threaded a small glass vial, a popular accessory with addicts. The inside of the vial hit me with a whiff of heroin—big shock. Vincent had attached a number of small charms to the chain as well. A seven-pointed star, the blood witch's imperfect circle. A photo locket with a picture of Valerie inside. A small steel key that I mistook for a charm at first, and then realized was stamped with a symbol for the First Bank of Nocturne. Vincent Blackburn had rented a safe-deposit box from a bank owned by the O'Hallorans. Irony is a beautiful thing.

CHAPTER 25

The First Bank of Nocturne was doing good business during the lunch hour. Housed in one of the old Greek Revival piles on Main Street, it was the only branch of the First Bank, and considering the number of corporate types who financed Cedar Hill palaces through the place, the only one it needed.

I found a teller and showed my shield and the key. She bit her lip. "I'm sorry. I can't let you into someone's private box. Vincent was a nice guy. I can't imagine he's doing anything wrong."

"Well, somebody thought he was, enough to kill him," I said. Her mouth and eyes formed quarter-sized O's. "So since any rights Mr. Blackburn might have had to his privacy ceased when he died, how about letting me take a look?"

Sure, I probably traumatized the woman for life, but if she thought a drug-pushing, drug-using blackmailer was "nice," she had bigger problems than me.

The safe-deposit box was a big one, with a flat folding lid. The teller set it in front of me on an oak table and left. I was in a small cubicle, about the size of a handicapped bathroom stall, the walls all done in red velvet and the chair upholstered. I felt like I was inside a well-lit coffin.

"You better have something good for me, Vincent," I muttered as I popped the lid. A stack of file folders greeted me, all neatly labeled with names and dates. I picked up the first one, and glossy photos fell out. Nobody outside of Internet perverts probably wants to know the contents, but suffice to say I wasn't aware there were so many uses for a lit candle.

All the folders were like that. At the bottom of the box were two DV cassettes and a bunch of CD backups of the photos. I settled in for the long haul and began going over each folder, making a note in my book of the names.

Halfway through, I found ROGER DAVIDSON BURDOCK, and opened the manila folder to find Boot Guy staring me in the face. Vincent had clipped his *Fortune* article to the top of the glossy of Roger in a dress. It was a nice dress, probably Gucci.

At least now I knew why he looked familiar.

The folder underneath Roger was tagged SEAMUS MALACHY O'HALLORAN. I stopped, fingers just touching the manila. I had guessed someone in the family, but Seamus himself? He was a scary guy, no denying it, but a perv as well? Where did he find the time?

Only a single strip of negatives lay in the folder when I flipped it open. I held them up to the mellow bulb in the ceiling and winced at what I saw. Seamus, like Samael née Arthur, liked control, and he didn't seem too picky about the gender or age of his partners.

I took a breath of stale air and shoved the negatives back into the folder, bending it double and tucking it under my tight black polo shirt. It made an odd bulge, but I zipped up my jacket and managed to come off as mildly pregnant rather than deformed. The rest of the files and photographs went back in the box. I had the key. They were as safe as I could make them.

Then I left the bank and walked two blocks down from Main Street to the O'Halloran Building. My blood was pumping like I'd just done a five-mile run and the were was panting in my ear, feeding on my slow-burn rage.

Seamus was a murderer and a sadist and he was over. Through. Done. When I finished, his life and reputation would be scraps that stray dogs wouldn't pick at. Perversely, I thought of Shelby as I strode through the O'Halloran lobby and punched the button for the highest floor the elevator went to. She'd be horrified at this course of action, but I couldn't help feeling that, were her leg healed, she'd be here next to me.

At least, that's what I told myself to keep my mind off what a bad idea confronting Seamus O'Halloran was, and it worked until the elevator doors dinged open.

Seamus's secretary was a nice-looking girl, with icy eye shadow and couture clothes she probably couldn't afford. She looked up at me and gave an audible squeak. In the slick waiting area I probably stood out like a Hell's Angel in a roomful of priests.

"I need to see Seamus," I informed her, flashing my badge. She squinted at the gold shield like it was covered in Sanskrit.

"*Mr. O'Halloran* is very busy," she finally said, sitting back and folding her hands.

"I have no doubt," I said. "But consider this—would you rather interrupt him or have me kick open his office door?" I cocked my head toward the frosted-glass double doors that concealed the inner office. "I'm sure these are hooked to a central alarm that has a direct line to the Nocturne City PD. You can deal with me or a dozen uniformed officers. And those guys never wipe their feet."

Her lip curled but she reached for the silver phone on her desk, which had enough buttons to control a space station. I put my hand over hers to stop the call. "Just open the door."

She opened her mouth to say something else prissy, and I let my eyes flame to gold. Sometimes the direct approach is best. The secretary swallowed and then pressed a switch on the underside of her desk. The lock on the inner doors clicked open.

"Smart choice," I told the secretary. She just sat frozen with her head in her hands as I pushed open the doors, letting them bang against the wall. Seamus was pacing back and forth with a phone pressed against his ear, holding the base in his other hand like a movie magnate. His head shot up when I came in.

"Hang up the phone," I told him. "We're going to talk."

"Hold on, Herb," he said into the receiver. "Minor glitch on this end."

"Don't make me ask you again," I warned. "Hang up."

"What in seven hells is going on?" Seamus hissed at me. "How dare you bust in here, you little bitch?"

I walked over to where the phone was plugged into the wall and gently unclipped it, laying the cord on the floor. Seamus jiggled the receiver. "Herb? Herb? Shit!" He turned on me. "Do you have any idea who you just hung up on?"

I crossed my arms. "I don't care if it was Lord Ganesh himself. We're going to talk about Vincent Blackburn. Oh, and the poisoned blood you used to kill Vincent, and the car bomb that almost killed your niece."

I'd expected Seamus to deny everything, yell and wave his arms and swear a lot. He was a rich white guy, after all. What I didn't expect was for him to close the distance between us and backhand me across the face.

Had I been a normal woman pushing thirty, the blow would have flattened me. As it was, my teeth clacked together and I tasted blood on my lip. My neck snapped around, and I held there for a second, waiting for the ringing in my head to dissipate.

Seamus watched me, face florid red. He looked like he was bucking for a heart attack. I shook my head once and then met his eyes again.

"You hit like a senior citizen, Seamus." I would be calm. I would not rise up to the challenge the were perceived. I could probably tear Seamus's arms and legs off with my bare hands, but he didn't need to know that.

"Get out," he ordered. "Before I teach you the lesson you so obviously need."

"Since you mention lessons," I said, taking the strip of film out of my pocket, "I've got one for you." I tossed the strip on the carpet between us. "Always make sure you get all the negatives when you pay someone off."

Seamus looked at me, at the film, back at me, then crouched and picked it up. He turned his back on me and went to the broad window behind his desk, holding the film up to the light.

"Good composition," I said. "Well framed. The faces are very clear. Vincent might have had some actual talent. His sister mentioned he was a painter." I put my hands in my jacket pockets to disguise the rubbery fear that was working its way out of my stomach and strolled across the carpet to Seamus. "But I guess we'll never know, since you had him murdered."

He whipped back to me, the film clutched in his fist. "You think this changes anything? You'll never prove I poisoned that queer. I'm a god in this town, little girl." A shadow of ink started at the corners of his eyes and bled across the pupil. The small hairs on my neck prickled and my lower back twinged, the were equivalent of a red flashing light and an alarm klaxon. I blazed on.

"Of course you didn't hold the needle, Seamus. But you ordered someone to." Or he had forced Vincent into killing himself, by using the Skull. "After all this, witches and magickal wars and blood feuds, it's something so pedestrian. I'm kinda disappointed, honestly. Multiple killings over a bunch of dirty pictures. Puts things into perspective."

Seamus laughed, shaking his head like I was a very stupid toddler who had messed my pants. "You are so focused on what's there in black-and-white, little girl. You can't see that an addict would do anything for drugs and cash. He'd snap some compromising photos, and he'd also cut a deal when he got caught."

Before I could apply that to any sort of sense, Seamus's hand flashed out and twisted in my hair, bringing my face close to his. His eyes were pure black now as he pulled down his power, like the daemons I had encountered. In a human face they were terrifying.

"And now I think I've confided enough to you," Seamus said softly. "Don't resist," he added when I struggled against him, snarling. "Or I'll just kill you out-right."

The compulsion slipped over me like plunging into a pool of hot ice—everything was warm and solid and I just didn't care anymore. It wasn't like a dominate, all heavy limbs and clouded senses, like being drunk. I was still perfectly aware that I was standing in Seamus's office, looking into his eyes, but I saw it all from a small spectator box in the back of my mind. My body and my consciousness were no longer under my control.

"Good," Seamus breathed when he saw the compulsion take hold. "Now walk." Still holding my hair, he led me across the office to a small metal plate set in the wall. He pressed the button and a piece of the wall slid back. I had an odd sort of tunnel vision—directly in front was clear but everything else was a swirl of light and sound and overwhelming sensation.

Seamus dragged me into a small compartment and we started to move, downward. After what seemed like a long wait the door opened and he commanded, "Out."

"What's that you've got there?" said a familiar sharp voice. Seamus grunted.

"She burst into my office and started spouting accusations about Vincent Blackburn. Nothing too deep, but enough to be serious." He let go of my hair and I went to my knees because that seemed like a natural thing to do. "Do what you want," Seamus said. "I put her under far enough that even if she snaps out of it, she won't remember a thing."

Joshua, wearing a new dark suit worth more than my car, stepped into my field of view and whistled. "I love the perks of this job, Seamus. I really do."

"I'll need my car at seven," said Seamus. A door clicked somewhere and he was gone.

Joshua stroked his jaw and regarded me. "Well. All alone, eh, Luna? Remind you of anything?"

Alone, on the floor of someone's van while a beach bonfire rages in the distance. No one is going to hear me if I scream. He holds me down, the rampant snake on his arm poised to strike. I scream anyway.

I beat on the walls of the working Seamus had put me under. I knew what was going to happen, but I couldn't move, could only stare blindly ahead while Joshua put a finger under my chin and commanded, "Stay."

At that moment, I wanted to die. Just go to nothing so I wouldn't have to live what Joshua was going to do to me over and over in my mind, like I'd lived with the presence of his bite for fifteen years. But I didn't die; I stood like a department-store dummy while Joshua disarmed me and tossed my badge into the trash.

"Too bad things turned out this way," he muttered. "You would have made one hell of a Serpent Eye. Armed and vicious, just the way I like 'em."

No. No. I had escaped him once before. This wouldn't happen. Someone would come, I'd break Seamus's working . . .

"Unfortunately," Joshua sighed, "I have to exercise pack law instead of what I'd really prefer to do." He looked me over, head to toe, and if I could have screamed, I would have been breaking glass.

Then Joshua reared back and hit me, hard in the face. I went sideways into a wall, falling like a human-sized board.

"You wouldn't know about pack law," said Joshua, cracking his knuckles. "Our pack law, since you *de-*

serted me. But the gist is, you humiliated me. And now I'm allowed to punish you." His foot connected with my midsection and I groaned, curling into a ball.

"No," said Joshua calmly. "No defending yourself. You're going to lie there and you're going to take it. It's a small thing compared to what I had to deal with when you ran off." He kicked me again and then I really wished I was dead. My head was pounding and my body was aflame, but I couldn't move. I stayed limp and unblinking as Joshua straddled me and picked my head up. "Seamus says that you're still aware underneath those glassy eyes. Hope it's true. I hope you feel this."

He bent his head, and he kissed me, not in the way Dmitri kissed me but the way a were would. He scraped my lips with his teeth and violated my mouth with his tongue, snarling. I smelled his arousal, and then everything exploded as he slammed my head backward into the floor, rhythmically, the slightest smile on his face. Black starbursts appeared in my vision as Joshua hauled me to my feet. The back of my head was cold and wet and I smelled blood, which was merely unpleasant in my detached little space.

Joshua pinned me against the wall and examined my face. My head sagged to one side as dizziness took the reins. "No way, you're not passing out," he said. "Not until we're through. As long as I don't kill you, the pack says it's fair play." He stroked my cheek, from jaw to lips. "And I don't want to kill you, Luna. You're so much more useful alive."

He kept beating me, holding me up with one ropy arm while the other delivered were-strength blows to my face, my torso, my stomach. Finally he hit me so hard that my breath wuffed out of me and spattered blood across his face from the cuts his kiss had opened. He reared back, smearing at his eyes. "Seven hells!" He looked down at the fine droplets on his shirt. "Well, that's just fantastic. Six hundred bucks down the drain." He let go of me and disappeared. I heard water running across the room and Joshua muttering curses.

I slid down the wall and welcomed the blackness that closed in. I was dropping fast over the edge of unconsciousness, and I probably wouldn't wake up. The working didn't let me be too bothered about that part. All my brain cared about was that the pain would stop soon. Below, in the deepest part of my unconscious, the were clawed and howled for life as I sank further and further into the black pool.

I slipped over onto my side and landed on something square and sharp. The fact that the pain penetrated my magick-induced state started a tiny flame in my animal brain, the ingrained instinct to live that every creature possesses. The square plastic shape was my cell phone. Using fingers made of numb twigs, I shook it free and slapped buttons at random. The phone squawked at me and I tensed, anticipating the blow when Joshua saw what I was doing.

It didn't come. He was talking on a phone I couldn't see. "Yes, it's Joshua Mackleroy in the O'Halloran Tower. Yes, the security office. Could you send over a change of clothes? I've had an accident." He slammed the receiver down and cursed again.

I rolled so my body covered the cell phone. Everything was still either in agony or nothing at all. I felt like a log, but I had broken through Seamus's working. I remembered how hard it had been to force Benny Joubert to kill himself. Seamus's magick wasn't perfect yet.

"Un-fucking-believable," Joshua said to me. "Half an hour for a freaking dress shirt. Guess that means we've got more quality time together, eh, Luna?" He crouched down and lifted one of my eyelids, checking the pupils with concern. "Don't go into shock, woman. I'd be disappointed if that's all it took. You haven't even seen half of what I can do."

He'd had a big mouth when I'd first met him, and it hadn't changed. Normally, someone rail-skinny and cocky like Joshua wouldn't even register as a challenge to me. I could subdue suspects twice my weight even when it wasn't close to a full moon. But I was bespelled, grievously injured, and trapped.

So as Joshua reached out to feel my pulse, I did what any self-respecting girly-girl would do and poked him, right in the eye.

Joshua howled and went back on his butt, clapping a hand to his face. "You *bitch*! You fucking blinded me!"

Get up, I commanded myself in a dead voice, knowing that if I didn't move now the Coast Guard would be fishing me out of Siren Bay. My legs screamed, stiff and heavy, as I stumbled like a drunken prom queen across the room. Joshua grabbed for me and I went down, clutching the edge of a plain steel table. I levered myself to my knees and saw a neat row of walkie-talkies in chargers on the table, as well as three stun guns plugged into outlets, green indicator lights winking merrily.

Groaning, Joshua got to his feet and came for me. I snatched up the closest stun gun and depressed the firing button, lashing out blindly as Joshua's hand closed on the back of my neck. There was a zap, and a fizzle of smoke, and the room filled with the scent of burning hair. Joshua screamed, a high animal sound of pain, and crumpled in a ball, unconscious. The stun gun gave off a last spark and fizzled out.

I hauled myself up, using the table and then the wall. Joshua lay on his side, the zipper on his suit pants fused into one strip of silver from the shock. I'd nailed him right in the balls, and that was as it should be.

"Fucker," I muttered thickly, too feeble to offer a kick to go with the epithet. I knew I should check and see if he was dead, but right at that moment, with my face bleeding and my ribs spasming every time I took a breath, I not only did not care if Joshua was shuffled from the mortal coil, but I would have helped him along by shoving him in front of an express bus.

A door stood to my left, steel-reinforced. I stumbled over and jiggled the handle. Locked. A keypad glowed at my hand and I cursed, which came out as a grunt. Needed the code. I cast a glance back at Joshua. He wasn't moving, but who knew how long that would last? I couldn't be here when he woke up.

Seamus had dragged me into a hidden elevator to get me into the room—I just had to find the panel to call it. My vision was still somewhere in the region of Piss Drunk, blurry and vertiginous. I ran my hands over the wall, cheek pressed against the cool plaster, until my fingers brushed a button. Not really caring if was an alarm or to call the elevator, I pressed it and let my aching body sag.

After a few seconds the elevator door slid open. I scooped up my badge and gun and phone and half fell through the sliding door. The crap would certainly hit an industrial-sized fan if someone found those in here with Joshua's zapped body.

Inside the elevator I hit the down button and went to the floor, my legs finally saying "Enough" and giving out. The elevator stopped after a long ride down and opened into some sort of executive washroom. A bald man in shirtsleeves was washing his hands. He saw me and sprayed water all over himself. "Christ!"

He came running over, catching the door before it could close and bending toward me. A red silk tie dangled in my face. "Are you okay, miss? I'm Marty, from corporate accounting. Do you work here?"

I tried to talk. My tongue was sticky and coated with blood, and it was a few tries before I managed, "Help me up?"

Marty and I struggled to our feet and he regarded me like I was the climax of a horror movie. "Geez. This is just awful. Do you want to stay here while I call the police?"

"No police," I muttered, bracing myself on the wall.

"Look, if you're worried about pressing charges or filing a suit . . ." Marty started. Hah. Good one. If anything, Seamus O'Halloran would be suing my ass for trespassing when this got out. That would be my luck.

"Just let me leave," I told Marty. The words hurt. My jaw was throbbing and I had that sharp sprinter's pain that told me some ribs were broken.

He stepped aside, helpless in his thousand-dollar suit and handmade tie, and let me stagger out of the washroom and into a hallway where I saw an EXIT sign glowing like Promethean fire. Centuries and a thousand gray stairwells later, I exited a side door and almost walked into the traffic on Yager Way.

"Thank the bright lady," I muttered. Now I could collapse on the sidewalk and wait for a beat cop to find me. They'd call Mac, and I could explain, and *someone* would go after Seamus O'Halloran.

I didn't like the feeling of having lost, not at all, but there was precious little I could do in this state except sit on a pile of recycled newspapers and tally up the number of my body parts that hurt.

"Luna?"

My head snapped up. Joshua. No, couldn't be. Who was I kidding, of course it could. Well, this time I would kill him. I decided then and there that if I saw Joshua again I was going to rid the world of his carcass and call it finished.

Someone grabbed my shoulders and I lashed out. "Seven hells!" Dmitri shouted, catching my wrists. "Luna! Calm down!"

I stared into Dmitri's face and couldn't help it. Tears started, making bloody rivulets down my ruined face. A thin pale line formed around Dmitri's mouth when he got a good look at me.

"Hex me. Who did this to you?"

"How—how are you here?" I asked stupidly. Dmitri checked my pupils and touched a spot on my cheek that stung.

"You called me. Well, my phone rang with your number and I heard someone talking about the O'Halloran Tower, and then a bunch of noise. Figured I'd better haul ass. Are you all right?"

"No," I said, pleased to have a question I could answer with one word. And Dmitri had been the last person I'd called the night before. One of the buttons I'd punched on my phone must have been send. "No, I'm as far from all fucking right as one can get. And I think I might get sick . . ."

"Might" became a moot point as I bent double and vomited into the gutter. Dmitri steadied me and held my hair out of the way. "Shit. You need a hospital."

"No. No hospital," I said vehemently. Seamus could easily track me there, and I'd have nowhere to go.

To Dmitri's credit, he just nodded in that unflappable way of his and looped one of my arms over his shoulder, taking baby steps while half dragging me. "Bike's this way. I parked it. Wasn't sure if I'd have to go in after you."

"I don't think Irina would like that," I grumbled. Anything I said now would be put down to pain-induced rambling, and I was going to make the most of it. "Fake bitch. Bleaches her hair."

"You make it real difficult for people to help you sometimes," Dmitri said. "And Irina's not like that. She's a good girl."

"I hate her," I muttered. "Her and her big fake chest. Smuggling water balloons . . . do people believe they're real? And her teeth . . ."

"How about we just not talk?" said Dmitri. "Save your strength and all that."

"You know what I hate more?" I slurred. "I hate that she gets to touch you and be with you when I don't. I hate it that you love her." *And that I couldn't make you want me enough to not leave*. Even a severe beating wouldn't get that last part out of me.

Dmitri stopped us at his black road bike. "Luna . . ." He sighed, fishing for his keys. "I don't love Irina. She's my mate. It's my duty to my pack. That's why you can't understand."

Any other day, in any other place, what Dmitri said would have made me jubilant. But with the clarity of trauma, I knew he was right. I *didn't* understand why duty came before desire. I never had. And that was why a woman like Irina would always be chosen over someone like me.

"Ready?" Dmitri said, sticking the key into the ignition.

I whimpered, digging my fingers into the leather of his jacket as he set me gently on the bike, sidesaddle, and then swung my left leg over. He mistook my sounds for pain, which was fine by me. "Okay. Almost there."

He got on in front of me and kicked the starter. "Hang on to me. I'll take you home."

CHAPTER 26

"Home" turned out to be the Redbacks' flophouse. Dmitri carried me up the stairs and laid me gently on a bed that stank of Irina. He rattled around in the bathroom and eventually emerged with gauze, peroxide, and sans his shirt. He saw me staring and shrugged. "You smeared blood all over it."

"Wouldn't it make more sense to take me to the cottage?" I croaked. "I'm not exactly welcome around your pack."

Dmitri shook his head. "They'd know to look for you there. What kind of white knight would I be if I dumped you off?"

"Crappy," I said. He poured peroxide onto a wad of gauze and dabbed at my forehead. It stung like I'd walked into an electric fence. "Hex it!" I shrieked, knocking his hand away. "Just let me heal up on my own!"

Dmitri's mouth pressed into a thin line, then he grabbed a hand mirror from the bedside table and thrust it in front of me. "Look at yourself. You're not healing from that any time soon."

In the mirror, I barely recognized my own face. My

cheeks had swelled, I had an oozing cut on my forehead from hitting the wall, and my right eye was swollen almost shut, blue-black deep-tissue bruising kohling the skin around the socket. Joshua was good at what he did.

"Gods," I said, pushing it away. "How can you even stand to look at me?"

"Please." Dmitri snorted. "If I can get past your attitude, a little swelling ain't gonna stop me." He put peroxide on fresh gauze and handed it to me. "Clean yourself up. The blood smell is driving me crazy."

"Making you crave virgin necks and fear garlic?" I said in a flippant tone as I dabbed at my cut lip. It stung even worse than my forehead and I hissed.

"No," said Dmitri, pacing to the far side of the bedroom. "No, necks aren't what I'm craving."

I stopped dabbing at my face and met his eyes. They were cloudy and inscrutable. I took a breath, automatically scenting Dmitri like he was prey. His forehead creased. "Don't do that."

Arousal slammed into me, the mingled adrenaline from my escape and Dmitri's pheromones colliding in midair. He groaned. "Look, this was a bad idea. I'm going to leave."

"Don't," I said. Sometimes you just know when your life pivots on the next tick of the clock, and this was one of those times. If Dmitri still cared, he'd stay. If not, I'd well and truly lost him and anything we'd shared.

Simple. Animal. A lot less complicated than couples therapy.

"Don't go, Dmitri," I said again. "It's okay."

He hit the doorframe with the side of his closed fist. "Gods-damn it, Luna. If I stay, I'm not responsible for what happens."

I set down the peroxide and sat up, drawing my legs under me. Daring him to come closer. "Fine. Neither am I." My heart was beating loudly in my ears, and blood was rushing to all the tips of my body as the were reacted to Dmitri's scent and the endorphins my body was pumping to cope with my injuries.

This was a lousy idea, but my animal brain didn't care. It wanted what it wanted. Dmitri crossed the room in a few strides and pinned me back against the headboard, purring as he scented deeply of the blood on my face and neck.

"Stay with me," I whispered. Dmitri growled then, and I saw the ink spill across his eyes. Too late, I realized that this might have been an extremely ill-advised method of making up.

Dmitri kissed me, with the same straight-ahead passion he put into everything, tongue licking my blood from my lips. He held my shoulder against the wall with one hand and with the other guided my fingers to his zipper. He was insistent, sure of his absolute control. I opened my eyes and saw that his own eyes were pure black, but oddly I wasn't afraid. *This time will be different.* But it was still Dmitri, daemon blood or no.

He was here. And he was mine.

I stopped resisting. I kissed Dmitri back, ripping his jeans down and pulling him to me. He didn't make a sound, just pulled at my clothes until they tore or the buttons popped off. His urgency was new—before, he'd savored the time our skin touched, teased me to the point of exploding. Now, he seemed scared he might lose me.

"You won't," I whispered in his ear. "I'm not leaving."

Still making no sounds, Dmitri gripped my shoulders,

his nails leaving blood-colored half-moons, and moved into me. I whimpered, because it was rough and hurt, but I met him with my hips. Each motion caused me to gouge furrows down his back, but he just locked eyes with me and I with him. Our breathing meshed for time out of mind, Dmitri's hands on my breasts, almost pulping them as he pushed against me harder and harder. Our twin breaths crested as the climax came. I shut my eyes, closing around Dmitri as my heart thudded and felt him climax in turn.

Wetness dusted my cheeks and I opened my eyes to see the black retreat and Dmitri's green eyes reappear. In the corners, droplets welled. I reached up and kissed them away. I didn't ask why he was crying. I knew it was for the same reason I wanted to.

Afterward I drifted in and out, hearing doors slamming and people shouting in the apartments around us, mingled with dream fragments that I would wake from abruptly, sure that Dmitri would be gone.

His mouth quirked when I rolled over to look at him. "Still here."

I flushed. "I wasn't assuming you'd be gone."

Dmitri got up and pulled his jeans on, rolling his shoulders and the muscles in his back. I saw fading scratches along his shoulder blades, inflicted by my fingers. "Those hurt?"

"Yeah," he said, "but only in the good way. Want some water? Beer? Jack? Those are your choices, I'm afraid." Anything he might be thinking about what happened subsumed, he stood with one hip outthrust, in total control.

I found my bra and put it on, deciding not to push it. My panties were shredded, so I struggled painfully into my jeans and zipped them up. A lot of places still hurt from Joshua's beating, plus a few new spots had become sore. "Actually, Dmitri, I think I should leave before Irina comes back. I'm really not up for that scene."

He waved that off. "She won't be back until tomorrow. I think she went somewhere with the elders."

"She did," I said, wishing I could snatch the words back from midair as soon as I spoke them. "They paid me a visit."

Dmitri froze in the doorway to the bathroom. "What?"

Crap. Crap crap crap. *When* was I going to learn to shut the Hex up?

"Tell me what happened," said Dmitri in that deadly cold voice he used on lower-ranked pack members or people about to be in some serious shit.

"Irina, and Sergei and Yelena," I said. "They came to my cottage and . . . well, they threatened to do unspeakable things to me if I ever so much as thought about you again."

"And?" said Dmitri. Dammit, why couldn't he just be satisfied with the abridged version?

"And," I said slowly, staring at my bare toes. The polish had chipped off my left foot but not my right. "I, um, I sort of made a deal with them."

Dmitri's face went blacker than a dark and stormy night. "What deal, Luna?"

Maybe, I thought, maybe it won't be so bad. Dmitri might actually be grateful that someone was on his side. Yeah, and the Fairlane was going to sprout wings and fly off into the sunset.

"I told them that I'd cure you of the daemon-blood infection by the next full moon," I blurted.

The longest seconds of my life passed by before I could summon the willpower to actually look at Dmitri. I immediately wished I'd just kept examining my feet. His expression was fury, tightly controlled and directed like a laser straight through me.

After a long time he said, "I can't fucking believe you did this."

"What was I supposed to do!" I exploded, defensiveness replacing my regret like a steel security door clamping down over a vault. "Would you have preferred I let them tear me to cold cuts and deliver me in a lunchbox?"

Dmitri crossed the room so fast he was only a blur of copper hair and infuriated green eyes, grabbed me by the shoulders and lifted me practically off my feet. "You think I need to be *cured,* like I've got some Hexed virus? And you think you're going to be a little hero and make sure everyone is perfect and normal?" He shook me and my teeth rattled.

"Let go," I warned him, the were coming to the surface. "I won't play in this scene any day, never mind now."

"You think I'm a dumb beast," Dmitri hissed. His eyes shifted from green to black so quickly it was like oil splashing into a clear pond. "You think I'm some monster skulking in the shadows. That I need *you* to pick up my problems and smooth them over."

"Dmitri, I'm thinking this might be the daemon talking . . ." I started.

"Well, here's a tip, sweetheart," he snarled, sounding more like a were than I'd ever heard him. "Next time, don't fuck the monster's brains out before you offer up your miracle cure. And don't assume the monster *wants* to stop."

"I wanted to help you," I whispered. "Sergei and Yelena were going to kill us both."

"Not everything in the world is your problem, Luna. In fact, most of your grand crusades would work out much better if you kept them to yourself."

Heat rushed into my face. This time, it had nothing to do with arousal. I grabbed Dmitri's wrists and shoved him away from me with all my strength. He fell back and then circled, snarling and black-eyed.

"Hex you," I said, not even caring anymore if he turned me into kibble. "I'm trying to help you. I'm the *only* one trying to help you. But you know what? Forget it. You don't deserve help, you bastard. You deserve to rot, to turn into this . . . thing and spend the rest of your life locked in some bunker in Kiev."

In that moment, I really meant it, and Dmitri knew it. His pupils showed a tiny ringlet of green as I gathered up the rest of my clothes.

"Luna . . ."

"Go roast in all seven hells," I said, walking out and slamming the door behind me.

I made it back to my cottage, shivering inside a taxi, before I curled into a ball and sobbed. I'd thought the debacle with Irina and the pack was the worst I could ever feel, but I'd been wrong.

Then, I hadn't truly believed Dmitri was gone. I'd become convinced that if I were just strong and patient enough, he'd be back.

My phone rang, and I slapped it off the hook and

went back to hugging my pillow and crying like a high school cheerleader who gets dumped the day before homecoming.

Now, Dmitri was really gone, and I hadn't lost him to the Redbacks or to Irina. The man I cared for had been consumed by what was inside him, and there wasn't a damned thing I could do.

It hurt, so much so that I wasn't sure I'd be able to get up again. I just stayed curled in the fetal position, trying to will back what I'd lost and doing a lousy fucking job.

After a while I must have fallen asleep, because when I snapped awake it was dark outside and someone was pounding on my door. The pounding cut off and a key scraped in the lock. Sunny shouted, "Luna? You home? Do you know your phone's disconnected?"

My eyes were gritty and swollen, and my throat was sore from crying. Sunny's footsteps mounted the stairs and my bedroom light snapped on. I heard her suck in a breath. "Oh, my dear gods."

"You should see the other were," I muttered, putting a hand over my eyes to shield them.

Sunny moved it and stared down at me, her expression somewhere between horror and righteous anger. "Who did this?" she demanded. "I'll fry their Hexed balls off."

"Already taken care of," I said, and dissolved into giggles. This day had been too long and terrible to do anything but laugh.

Sunny helped me sit up, pulled a blanket over my legs, and ordered, "Don't move. I'll make you tea." The Rhoda Sunflower Swann All-purpose Cure. She rushed downstairs and I let my eyes fall closed. I could have sworn I smelled beef lo mein. That did it—I was cracking up.

Sunny reappeared after a minute with a tray bearing a steaming mug of tea and a plate of rice and the afore-scented lo mein. Well. At least I wasn't going to add a trip to the padded room to my resume.

"I thought you might be hungry when I came over," she said, tucking a napkin under my chin and plumping my pillows.

"Thanks." I sighed, taking a token bite. It was delicious, and I realized I was starving.

"Why is your phone off the hook?" Sunny asked. I answered around a towering forkful of rice and noodles.

"I sorta had a fight with Dmitri."

"Dmitri?" Sunny blinked. "What happened to Trevor?"

I thought back to our last phone call, and his subsequent silence. "Um, I guess I had a fight with him too."

"Can't say I didn't see that coming," said Sunny. "What happened with Dmitri?"

I set down my fork. "I made a promise I couldn't keep. He let the daemon bite have a little too much lead. It got ugly. That, and it happened right after one of Seamus O'Halloran's thugs beat me half to death, so I wasn't thinking very clearly." I prayed she'd buy the ed-ited version and not interrogate me. I wasn't a very good liar where Sunny was concerned.

Sunny bit her lip. "So, now I must seem like a total idiot with all my esteem for the family."

"Forget it," I told her, hiding my relief behind a toss of my head. "How were you supposed to know?" I filled her in on the rest, the short story of the Skull and my all-around idiocy.

Sunny picked a noodle off my plate and chewed on it. "So they stole the Skull of Mathias from the Blackburns?"

I nodded. Sunny rubbed her temples. "That's really bad."

"You don't know the half," I told her. "They're close to being able to figure out how to use it." I shook my head. "Funny how the Blackburns held onto it for thirty-seven generations or something, and not once did anything bad happen, and now the good guys have the bad guys' ultimate superweapon and all hell is breaking loose."

"People don't always do what you think they should," said Sunny quietly. "You, for instance."

"Ouch," I told her. But as usual, Sunny was absolutely right. It was an annoying habit of hers.

No one would be able to stop Seamus O'Halloran if he gained access to daemon magick. Hell, I wasn't sure if I could stop him now. I was sick of daemons, sick of Asmodeus and Dmitri and the stupid Skull.

I choked on a piece of beef. Sunny whacked me on the back. "What is it?"

"Gods," I said. Like the sun had finally broken through polluted clouds, I grinned. Seamus couldn't be allowed to read the daemon workings, and Dmitri needed daemon magick.

"Luna?" said Sunny with concern. "Is something the matter?"

"Sunny," I said, grabbing her hand. "You have to help me steal the Skull of Mathias."

CHAPTER 27

Sunny thought I was patently insane, of course, and went home after making me promise not to do anything stupid. I duly promised, because stealing the Skull wasn't stupid. It was the solution to all of my problems.

It was why I was driving recklessly into the city, dodging taxis and pedestrians who probably had the right of way. I parked the Fairlane in the valet slot in front of Shelby's building. The valet glared at me when I got out, and then at the Fairlane with its poor dangling headlight. The glare said I'd better come up with one hell of a big tip if he was going to drive this undignified piece of crap around the block.

Shelby answered the door herself this time, and I was relieved to see that her leg was encased in one of those cloth walking casts instead of the Frankensteinian swath of bandages she'd gotten at the hospital.

"Did you come back to give me a hard time again?" she asked morosely. I noticed that most of the art I'd seen on her walls was gone and her apartment was dark except for a single light next to her chaise.

"No," I said, stepping in. "I wanted to ask you

something, and—wasn't there a lot more furniture in here before?"

Shelby blinked. "You came to ask me about my furniture?"

"No, no, something else," I said. Her apartment wasn't just sparse, it was damn near empty.

"Uncle Seamus cut me off," said Shelby. "I'm losing my lease at the end of the month. Sold off some things for a deposit on a new place."

Oh gods. If I had ever felt worse about a decision I'd made, I was hard-pressed to find it. She was sitting here in the dark like the little match girl and I was about to ask her to participate in something even more egregious.

"I'm sorry," I said lamely. "If there's anything—"

"Forget it." Shelby tilted her chin up. "You make the same salary I do, so please don't try to salve your guilt by offering to help me." She hobbled back to the chaise and flopped down. "This was a long time coming, anyway. Ever since my father died. Seamus was devastated, did you know that? He loved Daddy. Big brother watching out for littlest brother and all that."

"Shelby, Seamus is not who you think he is," I said carefully, trying not to let any of what had happened to me at Seamus's behest creep into my voice.

"He never got over me letting him down," Shelby mused. "Figured it was my mother's fault. Did you know I spent a month in a hospital when I was fifteen? I tried to swallow a bunch of Percodans. Seamus made me so miserable."

"My father was an alcoholic auto mechanic," I offered. "And not even a good one either."

Shelby laughed, once. "I'm named after a car. The 1967 Shelby Mustang. Hardtop. Baby blue. My father was driving it the night he died."

I stayed silent, and Shelby sighed, braiding and un-braiding the end of her long blond waterfall of hair. She looked up at me and stared, as if she'd just woken up. "What happened to your face?"

"Seamus," I said. "And his hired pit bull, Joshua."

"What did you do?" said Shelby, with no surprise. "Must have been something that shook him pretty badly, if he risked beating on a cop that way."

I took a breath. I didn't want to, had no right to ask Shelby what I was about to ask, but if I didn't the deaths would keep piling up. The blood of O'Hallorans and Blackburns, blood witches and caster witches, would run in the streets if I didn't put the Skull back where it belonged.

"I went to him and told him I knew that he'd killed Vincent Blackburn. And I know about the Skull too, Shelby. Everything your uncle has been . . ." I left out the part about the evidence being in a crumpled little ball on Seamus's floor last time I'd seen it.

Shelby nodded. "That'd do it." She rubbed her leg. "You got away though. He won't like that."

"Well, he'll like this even less," I said. "I'm going back to the tower, and I'm going to steal the Skull." I fixed Shelby with my most severe stare. "And I need you to help me."

She sat in silence for a long time, still as a store man-nequin. "I should hate him," she said finally. "He doesn't love me. He's made my life hell. He lied to the whole family, about keeping that filthy blood witch relic under our roof." Shelby sighed. "You realize that trying to swim with Seamus is like dousing yourself in blood and jumping in a pool with Jaws."

"He's not the worst thing I've ever come across," I said honestly. Definitely second worst. A close second. But she didn't need to know that.

"I wish everything were so black and white for me," said Shelby. "You have it really easy, Luna, you know that? Good, bad, and no in between."

If only she knew just how in between I was. I'd kill to have Shelby's clean conscience.

"What do you need from me?" she asked. I breathed out a quick thank-you to the bright lady.

"I need to know where Seamus keeps the Skull," I said. "How to get into the tower after hours, and I can handle whatever else crops up." I hoped it was Joshua. One electric shock to the testicles wasn't enough for that jerkoff.

Shelby nodded slowly. "Okay," she said. "Okay," a little stronger. She had a new light to her face, drawn and shaken as it was. I thought that she might just come out of this whole thing all right, if any of us lived that long. If I got the Skull from Seamus. If I didn't, I had the feeling that as soon as he translated the inscriptions, my credit card fees and Shelby's bare apartment wouldn't matter much at all.

"It'll be dark in a few hours," said Shelby. "Hand me that pad and pen?"

I saw the set on her one remaining side table and passed it to her. "It will be dark," she said again. "You can stay here until the sun goes down, if you want."

"As long as you don't expect me to braid your hair

and talk about boys," I said. One side of her mouth curved up.

"I'll draw you a map of the building with the cameras and security routes," she said. "At least the ones I know of. The Skull is probably in Seamus's private safe, in the apartment he keeps adjacent to his offices."

"Thank you," I said, meaning it. Never mind that I didn't know how to crack a safe, despite that idiotic rumor about cops being the best criminals. If I could open vaults and get away with it, I'd be living on my own private island, with a yacht and a helicopter to land on it. That, and a closet the size of Fenway Park to hold all of my designer shoes.

"Don't thank me," said Shelby, "because aside from the map, all I can offer you is luck."

The sun was a thin smear of orange over the bay. I got my car keys and jacket. "I'll be going," I told Shelby, tucking her hand-drawn diagram of Seamus's apartment into my pocket.

"Don't bother calling if you get it," said Shelby in her oh-so-encouraging way. "I have a feeling I'll find out soon enough." She had the grace not to add that if I didn't get it, I wouldn't have to call either, because I'd be dead or beyond the point where talking was strictly possible.

I let my mind wander as I drove the few blocks to the O'Halloran Tower. I should have called Sunny. Too late now. If she knew what I was up to she'd call Mac and he'd raise all kinds of hell and screw the whole thing up. I should have been nicer to Trevor the last time we talked. I should have never let Dmitri Sandovsky into my life. He was the only one I didn't have any regrets over.

"Stop talking like you're going to die," I told myself, in my rearview mirror. "It's depressing as hell."

The tower was quiet at seven P.M., one lonely security guard stationed by the camera bank in the lobby and one receptionist who'd pulled the short straw at the information desk. I scanned the list of brass plates posted just to the right of the door and picked out a name on a high floor. I ignored the guard, because a normal civilian would, and went to the receptionist.

"Maybe you can help me?"

He looked up, bored. "What do you need, miss?"

"Could you tell me which office Gerard Mansfield is in?"

The receptionist clicked at his computer. He was wearing a cheap polyblend vest that was supposed to make him look professional and his nametag said EMMANUEL. I felt bad for Emmanuel, because I was probably going to get him fired.

"Suite seventy-six, on the thirty-eighth floor," he said.

"And the elevators are still running?" I asked with a perky smile. "Mr. Mansfield's expecting me."

Emmanuel gave me a look well beyond his years, that said he was wise to my line of BS and wasn't inclined to go for it. "If he were expecting you, he would have told you that the elevators stop running without a keycard at six o'clock."

Dammit, I had factored in cameras and Joshua's force of thugs, but I hadn't counted on a smart minimum-wage slave blocking my path.

"It's a very *personal* appointment," I purred, placing

one hand on his arm. I should have unbuttoned the top button of my shirt, or worn tighter jeans, or something. Emmanuel wasn't going for it.

"Lady, if you don't have business in the tower, you're going to have to leave," he said primly.

"Okay, fine," I said. "I'll level with you. I'm Jess McMillan with the SEC. Mr. Mansfield contacted us confidentially some time ago with information about inappropriate activities within the O'Halloran Group."

"SEC?" Emmanuel frowned. "Like whistle-blowers and stuff?"

"Exactly like that," I agreed. "We're very concerned about certain transactions Seamus O'Halloran has been involved in."

"That guy's a scumbag," said Emmanuel. "You know he cut health benefits for hourly workers last year?"

"That's why it's so important I get to see Mr. Mansfield right now," I said. Emmanuel shot a look at the security guard, who was reading something with a bikini-clad woman on the cover, and then handed me a white plastic square.

"Keycard," he said. "It'll get you all the way to floor forty. After that it's all private codes anyway."

"Thank you for all your help," I said sincerely.

"Hey, if I get to see the execs led out of here in handcuffs with news cameras flashing in their faces, it'll be enough," Emmanuel said.

I didn't tell him that in Seamus's case, I really hoped he got his wish.

The upper floors of the tower were all dark. Gerard Mansfield had long since gone home, but a cleaning cart sat at the end of the hall with a radio perched on top, playing that song about being all out of love.

I pilfered the key ring off the cart and found that they were neatly labeled masters with floor numbers on the face. Number 38 unlocked Mansfield's door and I slipped inside, leaving the lights off.

A quick search of Mansfield's desk uncovered a fondness for organization, chewing on the ends of pencils, and chocolate-covered cherries. What a saint. I almost felt bad about using him this way.

I found Mansfield's keycard under the candy box, slightly sticky but usable. I had almost made it back into the elevator when the cleaning woman came around the corner and saw me.

"Who are you?" she demanded. "This floor is closed for the evening."

Crap. Somehow I didn't think an unscheduled visit from the Junior League would fly, so I smiled sweetly and said, *"No hablo inglés, señora."*

"You stay put," she said, loudly and slowly. Like that ever helped. "I'm calling security. You stay!" she barked at me when I reached for the elevator call button.

If she alerted Joshua's men, I'd be screwed. I took a quick step, shifted my weight, and came in with a right jab just under her cheekbone. Her head snapped around and she folded before she even felt any pain.

This was a piss-poor heist, I reflected as I dragged her into the elevator with me and swiped Mansfield's keycard for the top floor. James Bond never had to punch out a cleaning lady.

The elevator door opened into blackness at the top of the tower. Seamus's office was ghostly in the lights from the city below, but I could make out the desk and chair and bar, and even the crack in the plaster where

I'd fallen into the wall. Behind the crack I saw the gleam of a metal door.

I turned on some lights, sent the elevator to the basement with the cleaning lady, and carefully pulled away the broken section of the wall. The steel door leading to Seamus's private apartment space was small and scarred, like it had survived a few previous assaults. There was no alarm pad, no high-tech laser grid, but even from here I could feel the prickle of the ward marks that sat like invisible barbs on the surface of the door.

Brute force would not get me through the door. If I touched it, I'd end up extra crispy for Seamus to find tomorrow morning.

"Thanks a lot, Shelby," I muttered. As much as I had convinced myself that this break-in was a bad idea, I felt irrationally disappointed to be foiled by something as simple as a fire door. I slumped in Seamus's high-backed chair with a sigh.

His phone caught my eye, neat prelabeled buttons for LOBBY, GARAGE and SECURITY.

The idea that popped into my head was terrible and dangerous, along the lines of sailing across the Pacific in a garbage scow or buying up real estate in Pompeii. But bad ideas always appeal to me, so I picked up the phone and punched the button.

The voice that answered was gravelly, like it had been catnapping and was trying very hard to disguise the fact. "Security."

"You've got to help me!" I said, putting just enough teenage scream queen in my voice to sound breathy and terrified. "There's someone trying to get in!"

The voice perked up. "Where are you, miss?"

"Floor sixty!" I squeaked, and slammed the phone down. That would get their blood pumping. No one was supposed to be in here except Seamus, I was sure.

Now I had probably sixty seconds before Joshua's thugs burst in. I ran to the switch panel on the wall, slapping them in turn until one rolled heavy black shades down over the wall of windows. I switched off the few ambient lights and waited by the hidden elevator door with my back against the wall.

It was total soft blackness. A plain human would be hard-pressed to locate their own hand in front of their face. With my night vision, I could see the darker-than-dark shapes of furniture and the soft glow of light around the edges of the curtains. It wasn't much, but it would be enough.

The elevator whirred and I heard the soft ding from the interior just before the door rolled back.

I lashed out at the first person out of the car, a squat man with his gun and flashlight both poised in a text-book military stance. The gun, I noticed as I rotated his wrist and slammed the butt backward into his face, was a high-end Sig-Sauer P226. Nothing but the best for Seamus's own private army.

The second guy in the elevator let out a yell as his bleeding partner fell back into him, and got off a wild shot into the darkness. I waited for him to emerge from the car, the light he held quivering like a dying Tinkerbell.

"Who the Hex is out there?" he demanded. "I've got a gun."

The elevator door closed, plunging us into blackness

again except for the thin beam of the flashlight. I
stepped in behind the thug and grabbed his gun arm,
yanking it backward into a submission hold before he
could react. Speed is everything in a fight. The security
thug struggled with me and I kneed him in the kidneys.
He grunted and went to the ground.

"You'll never get away with this!" he promised, although in the dark I could have been a poltergeist for
all he knew.

"Keys," I demanded, putting pressure on his wrist
joint. A few more millimeters and I'd be breaking it. I
didn't want to do that if I could help it, even though the
guy probably deserved it.

"Keys to—ah! Keys to what?"

"O'Halloran's apartment," I snarled in his ear. "Give
them to me."

"I don't know what you're talking about!" he cried,
in a not-very-convincing display of innocence. I leaned
over his shoulder so he could see me and let my eyes
luminesce to gold. The thug's breathing stopped with a
short, sharp intake and he started to shake underneath me.

"Oh, Jesus."

"He won't help you now," I said. The thug swung at
me with his flashlight, free arm swinging in a crazy
cross-motion that only succeeded in clobbering the
thug on his own shoulder. At least the guy had a survival instinct. He wasn't totally hopeless.

I grabbed the flashlight out of his sweating hand and
rapped it against the elevator door. The bulb shattered
and the fractured shadows crept back and blended into
one velvet expanse of night.

The thug was whimpering now. "Please don't kill me."

"Dude, if I wanted to kill you, don't you think you'd be in pieces no bigger than a chicken nugget by now?" I demanded. He gave a shuddering sigh.

"Keys are on my belt. P-please . . ."

I felt around—carefully, wouldn't want him getting the wrong idea—and found a fat key ring clipped to a utility belt. Nifty.

"Please . . ." he said again.

"What?" I demanded.

"Knock me out?" asked the thug. "If you just tie me up, they'll know I got overpowered and I'll lose my job. Just one clip right behind the ear. I can say I never saw you."

Un-freaking-believable. "Joshua's got himself some real quality people, doesn't he?" I muttered, hefting the flashlight. It was a good solid police model. I reared back and aimed low on the blue-black blob of the thug's head. His skull and the flashlight gave a clack, and he stilled without a sound.

Hopefully, he'd thank me later.

CHAPTER 28

I must have tried twenty keys before I found the set that unlocked the dead bolts on Seamus's door. I pushed it open and saw soft lights. My heart momentarily seized as I imagined meeting Seamus face to smirking face, me with no gun and no authorization to be anywhere near him.

But the lights were automatic, brass-plated sconces recessed into satin-hung walls. Seamus had a taste I would classify as Early Caesar's Palace. Doric columns and opulently stuffed sofas overwhelmed the compact space, which was tall and narrow and could have been a utility room in its past.

And at the end of the room, staring at me with twin dead sockets, was the Skull of Mathias. It was set behind glass, mounted on yet another fake plaster column.

I walked slowly toward it, scarcely able to believe I was setting eyes on something so ancient. I felt almost humbled, like I was in the presence of an offering to a dead god.

Closer, I saw that the safe was just behind the Skull, the three-sided glass case built as an extension of the vault. It spoke to Seamus's ego that he kept the thing in the open, for anyone to gawk at.

I stopped, a few feet from the case. From here I could see the carvings, the tiny runic letters that marched across every facet of the Skull. They appeared to move and whorl before my eyes, not in the sickening fashion of daemon magick but the sensuous movement of an object so imbued with power that it was nearly alive. It radiated from the Skull, from the grinning tattooed teeth and pockmarked cheekbones to the bottomless empty eyes.

A card table had been set up along one side of the case, and yellow pads were scattered across it, along with an old clothbound ledger that was as out of place in the tacky room as I'd be at a podiatrist's convention.

Trying to ignore the palpable magick that radiated from the Skull, I glanced at the papers and saw they held repeated lines of cipher, many translated to English. The ledger was more of the same, in handwriting that changed every few dozen pages. The latest was dated and signed. _Victor Blackburn, 1946._

Seamus's words echoed: _You don't realize that a junkie will do anything—take dirty pictures, and strike a deal when he's caught._

Vincent had given the meager translations of the Skull's workings to Seamus. In exchange for his life? Drugs? Did it matter?

But Seamus wouldn't just need the ledger, he'd need Vincent to decrypt the key for him. And when Vincent finally drew the line, he died.

I located a small bifold door at floor level marked TRASH, gathered up the ledger and the notes Valerie had made, and dumped them down the chute. They wouldn't make any sense to me. And no one else needed to unlock the writing on the Skull of Mathias in my lifetime. Not Seamus, and not Victor Blackburn. Sunny would hate me for destroying something of such magickal significance, but she'd get over it.

The Skull stared ahead, seeing into nothingness, while I stared back. Something so small—it really was small, almost child-sized. No one can predict where power will lie, I guess.

The glass case was solid when I pressed on it experimentally, three-quarter-inch bulletproof Plexiglas, resistant to everything short of a cutting laser. A switch was set into the wall just to my right, and I reached for it.

Seamus was arrogant and vain. He'd want to touch the Skull, show it off, reassure himself. I flicked the switch and the top of the case receded with a whir, exposing the Skull to the open air.

"You bastard," I said, but in a triumphant tone. I took out the cloth tote tucked inside my back pocket and slipped it open, wrapping it upside down around the Skull, which felt hard and preserved, like knotty wood.

I held my breath as I lifted the Skull out of the case. This wouldn't end well. It couldn't.

Nothing. No alarm klaxons or spinning red lights or boulders falling on my head. Seamus O'Halloran's ego had done him in. Well, he wasn't the first person to make that mistake around me, although truthfully it stung a little to be so underestimated. At least Alistair Duncan had made a reasonable effort to kill me.

Now there was just the sticky problem of getting back out of the tower. I'd alerted security—sooner or later they'd figure out that their team wasn't responding and send up the cavalry, which would include

Joshua. Since I wasn't looking to get beaten senseless twice in one week, I opted to go through the door marked ROOF.

Wind lashed at me as soon as I stepped out of the bulkhead. This high up there would always be wind, and the air sliced into me through my jacket. No idling helicopters stocked with pilots were waiting on the top of the tower, just an empty gravel expanse dotted with HVAC boxes and exhaust vents.

I'm a creature of earth. I don't generally like to be that far above it. I expected the cast of *Die Hard* to come rushing by at any moment.

Far below me, a searchlight swept the sky over Waterfront, and a police helicopter chattered over Cedar Hill. I could hear car horns and shouts from the street as if they were right next to me, bounced off the walls of the urban canyon I was on the precipice of.

The only exit that presented itself to me was a small, terrifying ladder disappearing over the lip of the roof. I peered down the slick side of the tower, the windows darkened except for a patchwork of bright ones. There was a thin bar next to the ladder and a ledge barely wide enough for my foot about ten yards down. Some sort of harness clip system, for workers navigating the outside of the tower.

A prefabricated shed was set up a few hundred feet away, marked EMPLOYEES ONLY, and I rattled the door, finding it padlocked. I kicked the padlock off its hinges and swung open the door, finding three neon-orange harnesses and hardhats hanging inside.

I secured myself as best I could, lashing the bag holding the Skull to myself underneath the nylon straps of the safety rig. I eschewed the hardhat—who were we kidding here, anyway?

Without looking at the ledge, I clipped the safety rig's lead onto the bar and then swung one leg over the roof. I offered a quick prayer to whatever gods might be watching over foolish were women tonight, and started the long climb down.

I don't know how long I clung to the side of the tower, maneuvering step by step against gusts that seemed determined to peel me off the glass and send me downward like the stray pieces of trash caught in the wind. When I finally touched concrete in the loading area behind the tower, I collapsed and pulled my knees up to my chest, shivering uncontrollably.

The Skull was with me. I had made it out. The next thing I hadn't thought of was where to hide it—I couldn't take it home, or to the precinct unless I wanted a fast track to early retirement for psychiatric reasons.

She was going to kill me for this, but it was the only place I knew that I could be absolutely safe—at least until Seamus found out what I'd done.

CHAPTER 29

Soft light beamed from the cottage windows, and I could hear classical music burbling inside. It was only eight-thirty, ninety minutes since I'd entered O'Halloran Tower. Ninety minutes can seem like a long damn time when you're carting around a priceless artifact, I'll tell you.

I knocked on the door hard, not caring if I roused the neighbors. Nothing like standing alone on the dead-end beach road with nothing except the moon to illuminate the surroundings to make you paranoid. I swore I could feel eyes behind every bush and telephone pole, just waiting to leap and fall on me.

Sunny opened the door. She was in sweatpants and a stained Pretenders T-shirt. Come to think of it, I'd lost that same shirt a few months before I ran away.

"Sunny, you have *got* to stop stealing my clothes."

She cocked her head. "I don't know what you're talking about. What are you doing here?"

I stepped inside and shut the door. "Is Rhoda asleep?"

"No, she is not," said my grandmother from the door-way. I rolled my eyes heavenward before turning to face her. Freaking fantastic.

"Nice to see you again, Grandma."

"It's late," she said sharply. "We're busy." Grandma Rhoda looks like those old wrinkled pictures you find in junk shops of someone's pioneer ancestor—a squat body and a stubborn outthrust jaw, topped by humorless Puritan eyes. You got the feeling that she'd be totally at home shooting buffalo or building a sod house, and if anyone complained, she'd take a strap to their rear end. She's about as far from the stereotype of the wise old witch-woman as you can find.

"Well, don't trouble yourself," I said sweetly. "I'm just here to see Sunny."

"Come back later," said Rhoda, taking a step to open the door. "Or better yet, don't come back at all. Sunflower has enough to do without your burdens."

"Grandma!" Sunny stamped her foot. "We just talked about this! I'm not six years old, okay? I make my own decisions."

But I had locked eyes with my grandmother, and we were engaged in another round of our perpetual wrestling match to see who was more ornery and stubborn. "That's fine," I said. "The gods know, I didn't mean to disturb your oh-so-important workings, Grandma. I just thought you might like to see this." I jerked the canvas bag off the knobby shape of the Skull and held it in my palm. With no small measure of satisfaction, I watched color drain out of Rhoda's face. She braced herself on the doorjamb like I'd slapped her.

"Mathias . . ." she breathed.

"Holy shit!" Sunny exclaimed, then slapped a hand over her mouth.

"So I'll just be going and not coming back, then," I said, starting to put the skull back in the bag.

"Come here," Rhoda commanded in that glass-cutting tone she'd perfected over the years of raising me. I did as I was told, extending the Skull toward her. She took an imperceptible step backward, like a hiker would if faced with a particularly pissed-off rattlesnake.

"It's the real thing," I said, fighting the urge to wipe my hand on my jeans. The oily energy the Skull extruded was making my vision distorted, my head pounding like I'd just woken up from a lost weekend.

"I believe that," said Rhoda crisply, hiding how much I'd freaked her out under contempt. "What I don't believe is that someone handed this . . . *thing* . . . willingly to the likes of you."

"Believe whatever you want," I said, matching her, bitchy tone for bitchy tone. "I need to stay here for the night and I'd like a pad and pen, please." I looked at Sunny. "I have something I need to do."

What would happen to the Skull, I didn't know, but somewhere on its browned and scarred surface was the spell that would reverse Dmitri's daemon poison.

"Okay. Sure." Sunny nodded, eyes approaching half-dollar size.

"You can't stay here," my grandmother offered half-heartedly. "I won't have that thing under my roof."

"Grandma," I said, "in the last week I've had to deal with dead bodies, poisonings, car bombs, and being beaten almost to death. Tonight, I broke into a building and then climbed down the outside to get this thing. Do you *really* want to argue with me right now?"

Rhoda is a lot of uncomplimentary things, but stupid isn't one of them. Her eyes went glassy and hard, and she turned on her heel and strode back into the kitchen. Great, yet another entanglement she'd never forgive me for.

"Got you a pad and pen," Sunny said, appearing from the sitting room. "You can, er, do what you need to do in here." She never took her eyes off the Skull, as if it might come to life and latch onto her fingers.

"Thanks," I said, favoring her with my first smile in what felt like decades. Sunny bit her lip.

"I'm not going to ask how you got that away from Seamus O'Halloran," she said. "I *never* want to know. But this is going to be bad for you, isn't it?"

I set the Skull on the coffee table in Rhoda's living room and slumped down onto one of her overstuffed blue denim sofas. I didn't realize how close to passing out I was until my head sank into the cushions. Gods, I was tired. Tired to the bone.

"Luna?" Sunny pressed softly.

"Yes," I said. "Probably it will be."

"Seamus will kill you." This time it wasn't a question.

"He'll try," I said, forcing myself to pick up the pen and pad, rotating the Skull so I could see the ostensible starting point of the inscriptions, on the crown. "He'll certainly try."

"There was a time I'd have cursed you out for being so foolish," Sunny said with a sigh. "But at the very least, I've learned that you're usually doing what's necessary. Let me know if you need help."

I didn't answer, absorbed in the intricate, tiny carvings, carvings that must have taken years with a steady hand to immortalize on the Skull.

Sunny was so sure that I was doing the right thing. All I heard were the whispers—*overconfident. Thrill seeker. Suicidal.*

They were both right, my inner doubts and Sunny, but I really hoped that when it came to me dying horribly, they were both wrong. I stared back at the Skull. "Just you and me now," I told the blank face. Mathias didn't reply.

The symbols were definitely an alphabet, squiggly and menacing, a psychedelic cross between runic and Sanskrit. My hand cramped before the first line on the pad ended.

Then it started to shake. Then the rest of my body did, entirely against my will. The pen scratched crazily across the pad, leaving a long line like a river on a map.

Flashbulbs exploded in my eyes and I felt the world abruptly shift under my feet. My entire universe was pain, the strongest I had ever known. Worse than being shot. Worse than the phase. Every nerve ending and subatomic particle in my body screamed in concordance. Through it all I felt my forehead impact on the low table as I collapsed on the floor and my tongue swelled to a thousand times its normal size, blocking my throat.

I was way beyond screaming for help. All I could do was curl up and let my consciousness be seared away by the pain. This was dying, I knew more certainly than I'd realized anything before. The end, roll credits, houselights come up, and the audience goes home.

Someone was shaking me, hard, by the shoulders. Their touch was like a branding iron and I wanted them to stop more than anything. I couldn't speak or raise a hand, so I just prayed to die quickly.

And as abruptly as the fit had come over me, the pain stopped.

"Luna!" Sunny screamed, shaking me hard enough

to rattle teeth loose. Her round pale face was verging on hysteria. I saw it, translucent and glowing, filling my entire field of vision. I blinked. When had Sunny's eyes been a thousand shades of blue, like tiny ice chips floating in an arctic sea? And veins the same blue appeared just under the porcelain skin we'd both inherited.

I breathed in, trying to tell her everything was fine, and choked instead. Scents of pine cleaner and dust and also garlic, tomatoes, and ground tofu assaulted me.

"Who's making Aunt Delia's lasagna?" I croaked.

Sunny sputtered. "I . . . we had it for dinner last night. What *happened*? I heard a horrible racket and ran in here and you were convulsing!"

I didn't *think* Sunny was yelling but my ears were ringing. I could hear the rustle of something chewing on the insulation under the floor. I could hear as well as see the blood beating in Sunny's veins. I smelled everything, from the musty old plaster of the cottage's walls to a faint hint of incense from a working, food and soap and sea air borne from the outside. I felt that if I closed my eyes I could navigate through the cottage just as easily—perhaps more so. The last stray pain from my beating eased and disappeared as my were DNA kicked into overdrive.

"I don't say this a lot, but you're really freaking me out," said Sunny. "I'm getting Grandma."

I wanted to object, but it was kind of hard to talk, and I was thinking—gods help me—that maybe getting Rhoda wasn't such a bad idea.

The scent most overwhelming me as Sunny rushed out became smoke. Burned-paper smoke to be exact. The legal pad I'd been copying on lay next to my head, edges curled and blackened, the ink from the rune transcription seared right off the page.

Crap. That couldn't be normal.

"I don't see what the fuss is all—" Rhoda stopped when she saw me and the pile of ashes that used to be the pad. "Oh."

"What's going on?" Sunny demanded. "What's wrong with Luna?"

"More than I can enumerate on," Rhoda said. The old bat. I practically die and she still keeps up with the barbs. She'd probably crack jokes at my funeral.

"Here," said Sunny, crouching next to me. "Let's get you onto the couch." She's strong, my petite little witch cousin, stronger than she looks in a lot of ways, and she hefted me onto the sofa handily. I couldn't do much more except slump there with a blank look on my face, but it beat writhing in agony on Rhoda's throw rug. I sneezed. She really needed to vacuum that damn thing.

Rhoda picked up the pad and frowned at it. "You were attempting to copy the workings," she said, not bothering to hide the accusation in her voice. "Why did you do that?"

"It's a very long story." I sighed. The scents and sounds and vision so vivid they hurt were fading, and now I just felt like I'd gone a few rounds with Batman and lost.

"Tell me what you did," said Rhoda. Hex it if I wasn't ten years old again, having to explain why one of her favorite glasses was broken.

I closed my eyes, massaging my forehead with my index fingers. "I was just . . . writing out the lettering," I muttered. "And all of a sudden I couldn't see. The pain . . . it was like getting hit by a truck and I felt this . . . sort of . . . like my mind was being pushed out, by my senses. Everything went up to eleven." The best way I could describe what had happened, truly.

When I opened my eyes, Rhoda's lips were pressed into a thin line. I had never seen her face exactly like this—her eyes were sharp and wide, and she was breathing through her nose. I was shocked when i realized that my grandmother was scared.

"This can't be happening," she muttered, putting her hands over her face. "Luna, tell me *exactly* what you did."

"I just copied the symbols," I said, puzzled. "That's all."

"Grandma, are you okay?" Sunny said anxiously. "Do you need to lie down or take your pills?"

"You copied the working in your own hand. When a witch copies workings in her own hand, energy is transferred into the spell," Rhoda continued as if she hadn't heard Sunny. "*Into* a spell. The working absorbs the witch's latent magick and that's what makes a working possible, how it manifests." She fixed her panicked gaze on me. "*You* absorbed it. All that magick . . ."

"Okay, a plain-English translation would be good at some point," I said, giving Sunny the she's-crazy look. Sunny was nibbling on her lip like it was nutritious, eyes flicking between Rhoda and me.

"A Path, is what they're called," said Rhoda slowly. "Witches who absorb magick rather than expend it. They store it in themselves and are a human focus for a working. They're very rare." She took a breath and blinked, and she was back to the familiar scary-fairy grandmother I knew. "But Paths are always witches, never weres, so this must have just been something you did to yourself with that filthy blood relic. I'm glad you're all right." She stood up, brushing herself off like close contact with me had soiled her, and went into the kitchen.

Sunny stared at me. "What the Hex is going on?"

"You tell me!" I hissed. "One minute I'm sitting here minding my own business and the next she's babbling on about Paths and storing magickal energy and witches!"

"I hate to tell you she's right," said Sunny. "But Paths *are* those of the blood. Not weres. It doesn't make sense."

I curled up, hugging one of the big throw pillows to me. "Actually, it makes a lot of sense to me. Unfortunately."

"Oh gods," Sunny muttered. "Luna, it *can't* happen. You're *not* a witch—trust me."

"Just because it's *never* happened doesn't mean it *can't* happen," I muttered. "And how do you know for sure, anyway? Serpent Eye pack magick is different for everyone who gets the bite. I may not be the first were to have Path magick." Up until now, I'd always assumed I was defective, devoid of magicks because I had chosen to be Insoli. But the more I talked and the more Sunny shook her head, the surer I became.

It made sense now, the sinuous prickle I felt every time I was close to powerful magick. My aversion to workings and circles and all the other trappings of being a witch. And here I had thought it was just psychological baggage from my childhood.

I voiced this to Sunny, and she slowly nodded.

"I'd believe that at least, Luna. Paths are extremely sensitive to shifting energies."

"Yeah, that's me," I said. "Sensitive as hell to the shifting energies."

"If this is true . . . and I'll admit, you may not be the first. There were reports right around the Inquisition of witches who—"

"Sunny," I said. "Less history. More helping me figure out a way not to explode whenever I brush up against magick."

"I'll help you as much as I can," said Sunny. "But I'm not a Path, or a were. Just the standard-issue caster witch . . . I don't know anything about this branch of magick."

"Thanks anyway." I sighed. She worried her hands together.

"Do you still want to spend the night?"

"No," I said, standing and putting the Skull back into the tote bag. "Right now I think I just want to go home." I shouldn't, of course, but after what had happened to me I wanted to be at home, in my own bed, alone. Screw whatever Seamus would try to do to me. I was beyond caring.

The cottage was dark and desolate, just the way I'd left it. No shadowy security men waiting in the bushes in full tac gear. No trip wires in front of my door.

I put the Skull on the high shelf of the downstairs closet, with boxes of old shoes that I kept meaning to sell online, and went to my bedroom to find my backup gun. Morgan would probably chew me a new ass for losing the Glock, but right now all I cared about was firepower, so I loaded my father's .38 revolver with hollowpoint slugs and set it on my nightstand. I flopped onto the bed, intending to rest for just a minute before taking a shower, and when I woke up again it was morning, and my alarm clock was pinging at me.

Not my alarm clock, I realized after a second. Something from downstairs, an insistent *ding ding ding* that no one with normal ears would even notice from this far away.

I followed the noise into my office and saw that my e-mail in-box was blinking with a new message.

No sender, the address line informed me. Sent from an anonymous box. The message was one word. *Look.*

A video attachment blinked at the top of the message.

Shit. I already knew I wasn't going to like this.

The image jumped into focus, a grainy handheld digital camera. Three plain black chairs against a blank white wall. In the chairs sat three bodies, tied down and slumped over, their heads covered in hoods. One of the anonymous suited security thugs came into the frame and snatched the hoods off. My stomach lurched, even though I'd half known what I'd see.

Victor Blackburn was tied in one chair, his face bleeding from a recent beating. He was gallows-pale, his eyes unfocused. The other figures were Shelby and Valerie. Shelby looked scared, but she wasn't panicking, and her expression was enraged. If I were the security thug, I wouldn't get too close.

Seamus stepped in front of the camera, bending down to look directly into it. "You have two hours to bring the Skull to me. Since I know you won't just give it back, I propose this: participate in the *Certamen Letum,* werewolf. If you best me, I'll release my hostages. If you don't . . . well, you can figure out the rest." He smiled thinly, and I dug my nails into my palm. The son of a bitch was enjoying this. "The O'Halloran Tower. I think you know where that is. Two hours."

The screen went dark.

To my credit, I only sat frozen with disbelief for about thirty seconds before I grabbed up the phone and dialed Sunny. She answered groggily. "Luna, it's six-thirty in the morning."

"What's the *Certamen Letum?*"

Silence. "Where did you hear that?"

"Seamus O'Halloran," I said grimly, "of course. He has Shelby. I have two hours to bring him the Skull and participate in whatever-it-is."

"It's a contest," said Sunny, and I heard shifting as she sat up in bed. "A witch's contest. Literally, 'contest to the death.'"

I had figured it was something melodramatic like that. "So what, we get in a big ring and poke each other with sticks while alien lizard-men look on?"

"It's not funny," said Sunny. "Two caster witches face each other inside a working circle and they raise their energy until one of them burns themselves out. Or dies."

She was right, that didn't sound terribly amusing. "What does he want from me, then? I'm not a witch."

Sunny sighed. "No, you're not. But it doesn't sound like you've got many options here."

Exactly one option, really, because I had absolutely no doubt that Seamus would kill Victor, Shelby, and Valerie if I didn't show up within the two hours—less than two, now.

"Thanks, Sunny," I said slowly. "Thanks for everything."

"Luna . . ." she started, but I hung up the phone and

unplugged it from the wall. Knowing Sunny, she'd keep calling until I answered out of pure irritation. And now I needed to concentrate.

I went into the sitting room, and rummaged in the drawer of the entry table until I found one of Sunny's old pieces of chalk. I kicked the rug aside and drew a double circle, closing myself inside it. I sat cross-legged, trying to ignore the sensation that I was slowly sinking into deep water as the circle closed.

"Asmodeus," I spoke aloud, clearly and sharply. Only once. All that chanting in dead languages that blood witches went through during a summoning was over-rated. All you *really* needed to do was think about them. They always listened, and watched. Waited.

"You called me, Insoli. I was not wrong about your impending trouble."

Asmodeus appeared as if he were shielded by a column of gold smoke, flickering and half translucent. I swallowed. Even half there, the daemon set every nerve and instinct in me on end, screaming to get away. He was Other, dangerous.

"I'm facing Seamus O'Halloran in the *Certamen Letum*," I said. "And I'm calling on your promise to me."

"Ah, but I have already delivered your desire to you." Asmodeus's face was obscured, but I swear he smirked. *"I restored the other creature, the man, when you wished it."*

"You poisoned him," I spat. "It was *not* what I wanted."

"And it is not, often."

"Seamus O'Halloran is trying to use the Skull of Mathias for his own ends," I said desperately. "And I'm trying to stop him. Isn't that worth something?"

"What would you *use the Skull for, Insoli? Can you answer truthfully?"*

"I'd sink that thing to the bottom of Siren Bay," I answered. "I never want to see it again. I hate this, all of this idiotic warring over something that was never meant to be used by people in the first place. It's a perversion."

Asmodeus considered, his gold skin emitting a soft, pulsating glow that was brighter than the early morning sun.

"Go to your witch's contest. I will strike a bargain with you one more time." His form became corporeal, and he reached into the circle and placed a hand on top of my head. A single massive chill racked me, as if my body had been encased in ice. *"Make no mistake, Insoli. One day, I will ask you to repay my terms. And you will have no more recourse. You accept?"*

"Yes," I whispered, shaking. "I accept."

"Face O'Halloran knowing that I have aided you. And do not call me again."

"Then don't keep showing up!" I snapped. Too late. He was gone, leaving behind that charred smell of broken barriers and foreign magick.

CHAPTER 30

I waited the full two hours to go to O'Halloran Tower, and I brought my gun, for all the good it would do me. I really considered leaving the Skull behind, trying to bluff Shelby, Victor, and Valerie free, but in the end I carried it inside using the same canvas bag I'd carried it out in.

The lobby of the tower was deserted when it should have been the fullest, just at the start of the workday. One elevator was operational, standing open, deceptively bright and calm.

I rode it to Seamus's office, and I took out the revolver, sliding my finger along the trigger guard, ready. I didn't expect to use it, but it was familiar, and secure. I'd planned to die fighting ever since I'd gotten the bite, and I hadn't changed my mind.

Two security thugs derailed my grand plans as soon as the elevator reached Seamus's office. They patted me down and took away the revolver. "What did you think you were gonna do with that?" one snorted.

"Put your head up your ass and I'll show you," I snarled. He pulled a mock-scared expression and then pointed at the bag.

"That the object Mr. O'Halloran asked for?"

"Do you have any more stupid questions for me?" I snapped. "Want to know if I come here often, perhaps?"

He jerked his head at the second thug, who led me into the private room behind the desk. "She's here, Mr. O'Halloran," he murmured, and got the hell out.

Not that I blamed him in the least. Seamus glided forward, clad in black slacks and a crew-neck sweater. It was no robe with a pentagram topped with a headdress of antlers, but it was intimidating enough.

"Thank you for being on time, Detective," he said, inclining his head. "And for not attempting anything stupid."

I swallowed and thrust my chin out. "You don't know that."

He smiled. Not an evil smile by any stretch. No moustache-twirling or sardonic smirking. Just a small, satisfied expression that assured everyone he was in complete control.

Bastard.

"I'm sure we don't want unpleasantness at this late date, Detective Wilder. Show me the Skull."

"Show me Shelby and Valerie and Victor," I countered, holding the canvas bag closer.

"They're not here," said Seamus. "Trust me, I've seen all the same spy movies you have, Detective. They're in the secure room in the basement. I think it was a bomb shelter at some point. Very quiet and secluded, to avoid any questions about screaming. But they're alive. I am a worthy witch. I keep my promises."

I looked into Seamus's eyes, trying to see the lie there. He betrayed nothing. But he *was* a worthy witch.

Evil, ambitious, depraved, but still a witch. And they were all OCD about the honor-and-promises crap.

"Fine," I said, pulling the Skull out of the bag. "Let's get this stupid *Centamen* or whatever over with."

Seamus held out his palm and I slapped the Skull into it. "Very good," he said. He went and set it back on its pedestal, and then bowed to me, gesturing to a circle worked into the gaudy floor tiles I hadn't noticed before. "Please."

I made sure we both stepped into the circle at the same time, and Seamus brought his hands together and muttered a few words to close the circle and bring up the energy.

It snapped shut around us like the jaws of a trap, and I almost staggered under the weight of Seamus's power. He was stronger than Sunny by a thousand times, even stronger than my grandmother. Even Alistair Duncan hadn't been this bad.

"By the laws laid down at Rouen in 1597, we battle for honor and for prestige on the even field of a working circle," Seamus said, muttering quickly like you say grace when you're really, really hungry and don't mean it anyway. "Do you stand as a combatant of your own free will, so bound until the contest is ended?"

"Um," I said. "Sure. Yes. I do."

Seamus nodded. "Very good. Unfortunately, I do not."

And as his power hit me, blue flames that burned my clothes and skin and seared me body and soul, I saw just how foolish I'd been. I'd let my worries for Shelby blind me to the fact that once Seamus had the Skull, he didn't need to be honorable anymore. And he didn't need me alive.

You'd better believe I fought, though. I tried to draw the power into me like when I'd copied the runes. I tried to feel the strength Asmodeus had imbued me with and just as quickly screamed as I felt the cold certainty of the daemon's gift burned away by Seamus's magick.

"Whatever little tricks you might have picked up," said Seamus, "won't do you a damn bit of good inside that circle. I'm as safe from you as you are from an inmate at the jail."

"Hex . . . you . . ." I moaned, and then I couldn't speak anymore. My heartbeat fluttered, and it was hard to draw a breath. I was angry, at my own arrogance and that I'd made a deal with Asmodeus for no reason and that someone like Seamus O'Halloran had outsmarted me with casual effort.

I lay in the circle with the blue lines of manifested magick crackling over me, watching as Seamus marched back to the Skull, breaking the circle's bonds. It didn't matter. He had what he needed.

"*Tatum lucidium*," Seamus read reverently from the Skull. "*Tatum nocturnum. Infine mortis, lucium est.*" He kept chanting, low and measured, but I was floating. I saw a bright halo of gold surround everything in the room, and felt cold, but not from my skin. *This* was dying, not the horrible pain I'd experienced as when I read the Skull. This cool nothingness was the end, and I knew it as sure as I knew that I'd failed and Seamus had won.

No. No, I hissed to myself. I may be weak but I was a

survivor. I would live. Battered and broken, I would live because the were would not let me die. No matter how much it hurt, this would not kill me. This was not the way everything ended.

"No," I whimpered, because that was all that came out. "No."

Seamus's chanting stopped and he turned around when I spoke. "What in all things Hexed and holy!" he demanded. "That should have killed you!"

Holy crap, I was really talking. I wasn't floating up toward the ceiling, going toward the light and all that nonsense. My body hurt way too much for that.

Know that I have aided you. The cold wasn't dying, it was the daemon in me, the protection he'd afforded me with his own obscene parody of a life force.

"I know," I muttered. "I know."

The last vestiges of Asmodeus's magick sighed in me and then they bled away, and I just hurt, and felt heavy enough to sink through the floor. But I was alive. Burned, but alive.

"You son of a bitch," I ground at Seamus, rolling onto my side and making it to my knees. "That was the last jacket I owned."

The gold aural glow still flickered softly around me and I stood, shaking off the residual flickers of magick and walking toward Seamus. He stared at me, uncomprehending, until I was almost on him. His eyes were pure black now, and his skin was waxy. The carvings on the Skull were the same pulsating black, alive and crawling over Seamus's skin.

Hex it. Even with my Lazarus act, I was too late.

Seamus turned and bolted up the stairs to the roof,

leaving the Skull to rattle on the marble tiles. I guess he didn't need it anymore.

I followed Seamus, heard the shrieking chant from the stairs, and banged open the door to find him with his arms outstretched and roiling clouds in the sky overhead.

"Infinitum obscura!" Seamus bellowed, and as I watched in horror the clouds coalesced in front of the sun, plunging Nocturne City into blue twilight as if a vengeful god had stretched out his hand.

"Seamus!" I screamed over the shrieking wind. He turned and grinned when he saw me.

"Isn't it marvelous, Detective?" he shouted. "Mathias had a vision of the world and we are alive to witness it! He was a god!"

"And what are you?" I screamed. "You're just a rider on a dead man's power! You're nothing!"

"How wrong you are." Seamus wasn't shouting any longer, but I could hear him as if his mouth were next to my ear. "I am the heir apparent. I am the god's new incarnation."

Oh, spare me. If I had a nickel for every time I'd heard some two-bit methhead shrieking the exact same invective, I could go play the tables in Las Vegas until retirement.

"You want to see?" Seamus shouted at me. "Behold!" He spread his arms and stepped up onto the ledge at the edge of the tower, pivoting to face me. Then he spread his arms and flew.

He didn't fly like Superman, more like he was walking on air, floating up and away from me, out toward the bay. His laughter carried on the wind, distorted and childlike.

At that moment I knew two things: if I didn't stop Seamus soon, the city was seriously screwed. Also, the magick of the Skull had driven him positively bat-crap insane.

"Why is it always me dealing with this shit?" I asked no one, before running down the stairs and sprinting for my car.

I followed Seamus as he floated on the raging windstorm that was bending trees double, using my portable light and judicious pressure on the horn to maneuver down Magnolia Boulevard, dodging flying tree limbs, stalled cars, and snowflake-style broken glass from windows that had imploded in the gale.

Mac answered on the first ring of my cell phone, his voice distorted by static. "Wilder! Why do I know you have something to do with this?"

"Never mind that!" I snapped. "There's some serious bad mojo happening, in case you hadn't noticed!"

Seamus arced along Cannery, over the Waterfront district where I'd first met Dmitri, and then went across the salt flats toward the Siren Bay Bridge.

"Get everything we have to the bridge, now!" I told Mac, and threw the phone aside. I gunned the Fairlane up to sixty miles an hour, the fastest *anyone* had ever gone during morning rush hour in Nocturne City, I was sure, and took the bridge ramp on two tires.

Seamus and I met at the apex, between Nocturne City and the peninsula, above a stretch of angry gray water whipped to rolling breakers by the storm.

I fishtailed the Fairlane and blocked the westbound

lane, jerking the emergency brake to stop, and jumping out. Seamus was standing perfectly still, looking toward the city over the waist-high railing that protected the occasional intrepid pedestrian from the two-hundred-foot plunge to the water below.

The bridge was creaking, the steel cables suspending the span almost whipping as the wind whined between them, creating a ghostly wail.

"Do you see it?" Seamus asked me. "A whole city wiped clean, to be created in Mathias's image."

"Don't you mean your image?" I asked, approaching cautiously.

"Of course," he agreed. "And we'll start by improving my view." He stretched out his hand like he was trying to rearrange the cargo ships lined up along the port docks, then yanked it back in frustration. "No! Why do his teachings elude me? I'll have to consult those fucking runes again!" He smiled wryly. "And just when you think you have it all figured out, eh, Detective?"

I silently held up the Skull of Mathias, which I'd retrieved in the mad dash to my car. "But we never really do."

"Give me that!" Seamus demanded, clenching his fist.

"Why?" I taunted. "You're all, 'I'm a god among men' and everything, so I figured you didn't need little old Mathias anymore."

"You have no idea what you're meddling in," Seamus said, quietly this time. I was way more afraid of his calm tones than his shouting.

"Give me the Skull," he said again, and I saw the same blue power manifest around his fist. The first jolt had been before he'd gotten juiced up by the Skull. This one would definitely kill me.

At the base of the bridge I saw flickering blue and red lights as a line of parole cars sped toward us, but there was no time. I had no way to hold Seamus off, since my good looks and charm had obviously failed.

The smell of salt tickled my nostrils, and I looked down at the water. *I'd sink it to the bottom of Siren Bay.*

"Give it to me or you die!" Seamus howled. I backed up to the bridge rail, grabbing a cable and stepping up, balancing on the narrow metal bar. I stretched out my free hand and let the Skull dance above the wind-racked water.

"Take it from me," I told Seamus. I didn't shout. I didn't threaten. Standing there with the storm tearing at me, I knew what needed to be done to finish this whole sorry mess.

Thrill seeker. Adrenaline junkie. Everything in flames.

I held the Skull close to me. Then I let go of the cable, and didn't try to catch myself as I fell.

You'd think two hundred feet straight down would give you plenty of time for your life to flash before your eyes, but all I saw was a blue-gray blur and all I heard was the scream of air ripping past my ears as I gathered velocity.

Then I jolted, as if the hand of an avenging angel had decided that no, I wasn't going to get away that easily.

But it was only Seamus, floating, holding me by my free arm, his face twisted beyond any expression a human is capable of. "Give me the Skull," he snarled. "Or I let you drop."

"You really think that worries me now?" I said, breathless at my ability to spit invectives even on the threshold of my own death

"I'll take it from you and tear you apart, you piece of trash!" Seamus said, reaching for the Skull. I twisted my arm and locked my hand onto his neck, the primitive fight-or-flight instinct clawing for a last moment of life.

Seamus choked, but not because I was attempting to strangle him in midair. I felt the same pain, but far less this time, accompanied by a rush of adrenaline. I felt and smelled and saw so brightly that it almost overtook me, as Seamus's magickal energy rushed from his skin to mine.

"Gods!" he shouted, and we began to waver and dip above the water. "Gods, what are you doing to me?"

The pain was euphoric, a high unlike I'd ever known. We started to fall faster, Seamus screaming in fear now, not rage. The magick flowed, it Pathed and shaped into something that was *mine,* not Seamus's, and I sucked in a breath and held it as we hit the water and plunged into the freezing bay. I lost my grip on everything except my consciousness, and fell through the water until the energy I'd Pathed from Seamus washed away and I was cold and broken and screaming for air as I clawed toward the surface.

I breached the surface of the bay gasping and screaming. My right arm was broken, and it felt like both of my ankles, but I was kicking like hell to keep afloat, so I must be intact.

I was alive, surfaced, floating in the icy water and fighting the current. The Skull of Mathias was not. And that was all that mattered.

While I treaded water and tried not to pass out from the cold, I spotted a black-clad lump floating facedown near me. Seamus. I stroked lamely with one arm, managing to bring him close to me and flip his body over into a lifesaving hold.

It was over now. Seamus was just another pathetic power-hungry witch who had broken himself on his grand ideas.

The zip of a siren and a motor whirring caught my ears, and I kicked around to see a police boat coming up fast. They got out their life vests and hooks and pulled us both into the boat, where I collapsed shivering on the deck. Someone wrapped blankets around me, and one of the crewmen shouted something into his radio. "Hypothermia . . . one DOA . . . have EMS meet us at the dock . . ."

I sighed, letting myself relax for the first time in days. The Skull was gone for good, and its temptation for people like Seamus with it.

The EMTs took custody of me as soon as the boat pulled into their slip at the port authority. I was shivering uncontrollably by then, from shock as much as from the water. That jangly feeling you get when you know, for a fact, that you shouldn't have survived and yet you're there, seeing the same world through the same tired eyes.

McAllister shoved his way through the knot of officers on the docks and came to his knees in front of me, taking my face between his hands. "You have got to stop doing this to me," he declared. "Gods. Thank Them that you're all right."

"Of c-c-course I am," I chattered. "I'm . . . I'm always okay. Never expected anything less."

Mac looked over at the sodden body on the end of the dock. An EMT was giving him CPR, but even from here it looked perfunctory. "Hex me, is that Seamus O'Halloran?"

"Was," I said with a slow smile. "Was, Mac."

"Okay," he said, spreading his hands. "I'm sure I'm going to hear all about this, like it or not, but I don't want to right now." His bony face crinkled, and I think the idea of hugging me crossed his mind. "Just glad you're alive, Wilder. You'd be a bitch to replace at the salary we pay you."

"Mac . . ." I started.

A scream came from the end of the dock, and I saw the EMT working on Seamus lurch backward, a line of red running from his throat. Seamus came upright, a curved silver knife in his hands—Victor's knife, the one he'd showed me the first time we'd met.

"You," Seamus hissed, staggering upright. "I see you!" He lunged for me, and I saw it all—the knife planting itself in my throat, me bleeding out on the scarred wood of the port authority dock, Mac and the EMTs helpless to stop Seamus as he escaped.

This time, though, I didn't hesitate. I grabbed the first thing from the EMT's bag that my fingers closed around, which turned out to be a pair of surgical scissors, and jammed them into Seamus's thigh as he dove for me. He stumbled backward, and I heard a thunderclap from over my head. Three red stars blossomed on Seamus's chest, and he went backward off the pier, splashing into the water

Mac lowered his Glock. "One of these days, Luna, you're going to have to tell me where you learned those people skills of yours."

EPILOGUE

I ended up back in Sharpshin Memorial, where I'd been sent after my run-in with Alistair Duncan. This time it was only hypothermia and a fractured fibula, not massive internal trauma, so I stayed overnight and got sent home with a neon-pink cast. I'm sure my specialist, Dr. Northgate, found that hilarious.

As I was signing myself out, and letting the nurses draw on my cast, someone appeared at my elbow. "Luna."

His scent was unmistakable, one that haunted my memories. I turned around and poked Joshua in the chest. "Get away from me."

"Relax!" He held up his hands. "You're so godsdamned twitchy. Maybe you should see a shrink."

"Maybe you should get out of my face before I electrocute your groin again, you slimy little shit," I growled with more desire to hurt someone than I'd ever felt.

Joshua had the nerve to smirk. "You certainly proved yourself worthy of membership in the Serpent Eye. Take it, Luna. You don't want to be Insoli anymore, trust me. Not in this day and age."

"Stop telling me what I want," I snapped. I turned to

the nurse who had checked me out. "I'm going outside to get a cab. If this jackass follows me, call security."

He did follow me, and when I didn't turn around, he yanked on the arm that wasn't broken. I exploded. "Don't fucking touch me!"

"Will you stop making a scene?" He sighed. "For everything Hexed and holy, Luna. I'm offering you your only shot at a normal life, one where you don't constantly have to look over your shoulder." He stared me down, and I felt the weight of the dominate. "Take it."

"Would I be yours?" I asked, meeting his eyes.

"Of course." He smiled. "As a Serpent Eye, and Nocturne's pack leader, everything I touch belongs to me."

"Then I believe," I said with a quiet smile, "that you can go Hex yourself."

"I could make you," Joshua said, the dominate falling over me.

I snarled at him. "You could try."

He backed away.

Feeling more free than I had in fifteen years, I turned my back on Joshua and stuck out my arm to hail a cab. He grabbed my shoulders and spun me around. "We're not finished, bitch! You don't get to walk away from me again!"

Someone on a motorcycle cut through traffic and came to a stop in the taxi line in front of me, eliciting honks and threats of bodily harm from the hack drivers waiting for fares. Dmitri looked up at me through aviator sunglasses. "Who's this asshole?"

"What are you doing here?" I said. I could deal with Joshua and Dmitri separately, but together, they made me want to go hide under a rock.

"Your cousin told me you were in the hospital," he said. "Although I figured something awful had transpired after you ran out on me. That's always the way with you."

"We're talking here, my man," said Joshua. "Get lost."

"Joshua, shut up," I snapped, jerking my shoulders out of his grasp. "I'm not going with you, and you can tell all of your Serpent Eyes the same thing. Or let me guess—you'll tell them I was too much of an ice bitch and you decided I wasn't worth it, to keep them from finding out you have a tiny little pecker, and that it's always been that way." I cocked my eyebrow and looked at Joshua's fly. "Can't blame yourself, though. Electrical shocks aren't known for their male-enhancement properties."

"This is Joshua?" Dmitri demanded, shutting off his bike and dismounting. He was moving a little stiffly and I prayed that the pack elders hadn't caught up with him after our little assignation. He took off his sunglasses and stared Joshua down. "This is the prick who gave you the bite and then attacked you?"

"Buddy, she wanted it." Joshua leered at me. "You obviously didn't know our girl back in the day. She was a little slut then, and from the look of you, she hasn't changed. Still spreading 'em for anyone with a bike and a good line, eh, Luna?"

Dmitri snarled and lunged for Joshua, but I barred him with my intact arm. "I'll handle this."

"Gonna tell me what a bastard I am and slap my face, little girl?" Joshua said. "Guess what—I know. And I like it. So why don't you just keep slumming it,

Luna, and I'll find a real woman, and everyone will be happy. Well, I'll be happy every time I think of your sorry ass shacked up with *him*." He gave Dmitri a sarcastic bow.

There's a time for sugar, for honeyed words even when you just want to smash something. And then there's Joshua.

"Tempting as that is," I told him, "I'd rather do this." I slammed a left cross into Joshua's face with every ounce of were strength in me, aiming to drive teeth into his brain. He dropped like a sack of rotten vegetables, skull hitting the pavement with an audible impact.

I kicked him once with the toe of my shoe. "Hope a dog pisses on you."

Dmitri wrapped an arm around my waist and kissed my cheek. "Nice shot, babe."

"Whoa, whoa," I said, pushing him away. "What's this 'babe' crap? The last time we talked you hated me."

"Forget that," Dmitri said, trying to embrace me again. I shoved harder this time and he went back a step.

"What are you smoking, dude? You don't get to touch the goods after the scene we played."

Dmitri shrugged, looking adorably sheepish. Hex him. "I made a mistake, Luna. Aren't I allowed to make mistakes?"

"And you expect me to just forget everything else because of that," I said. Dmitri thought for a minute.

"Well . . . yeah."

Were men. Un-freaking-believable.

"Fine," I said, because I really didn't have twenty bucks to spend on cab fare. "You can give me a ride home. But no touching."

"How about after that?" Dmitri's eyes darkened around the edges, a little black slipping in there among the facets of green, like an oil spill, or a slowly bleeding cut.

"After that . . ." I swung my leg over the passenger seat of the bike and decided to be honest. "After that, Dmitri, I have no idea."

Sunny was at my cottage when Dmitri drove me up on his bike, and she threw her arms around me, jostling my cast. "Ow," I said, and hugged her back hard with my good arm.

"Have you seen the paper?" she demanded, thrusting it at me. The lead story on page one of the *Nocturne City Post-Herald* was the shooting death of Seamus O'Halloran by Lieutenant Troy McAllister after a "vicious and unprovoked attack on city personnel."

"Bet your ass," I muttered. Below the fold on the first page was a story about a massive IRS audit of the O'Halloran Group's holdings. Assets had been frozen. Executives had fled the country. Business as usual for the most powerful caster witches in Nocturne City.

"The *Inquirer* is even worse," said Sunny. "They got a photo from the scene, Seamus lying there on the dock all cold and dead . . ."

"Mmm," I muttered, scanning the print page to see if my name showed up anywhere. Maybe I could scrape together enough savings for a new identity and radical plastic surgery . . .

Fortunately, the most unusual thing about the story was that the reporter gave total credence to the witch rumors, stating that Seamus O'Halloran's death had been brought about by an unspecified "malignant force." I was just glad my picture wasn't splashed next to Seamus's. But it would come. No one could deny that weres and witches and Hex-knew-what walked right alongside the plain humans every day, and their brand of chaos was becoming more and more prevalent.

I wondered how long it would be until another disaster like the Hex Riots broke out.

Dmitri took the paper out of my hands and guided me to the sofa, putting my feet up and brushing stray hair out of my eyes. "What did I say about the touching?"

He sat next to me and put his arm around my shoulders. "You honestly telling me you're not enjoying this, at least a little bit? We've got a downright cozy and domestic scene here."

"You keep this up and I'm going to get used to it," I warned.

"Maybe that's not so bad," said Dmitri. I stared at him.

"Don't tell me the black knight has finally decided to pick a castle."

"Maybe," he said again, giving me an utterly cryptic smile.

"Well, all right then," Sunny announced loudly as Dmitri went in for a kiss. I moved my head and waved goodbye as she gathered up her purse.

"We'll talk tomorrow, Sunny. Come over if you like."

"But not too early," said Dmitri, still smiling. It was the longest I'd ever seen him in a good mood and I felt discomfort churn in my stomach, that offbeat nervousness of irons left on or doors not locked.

"There's a really ugly car pulling in," Sunny announced. "Some blond chick driving."

My stomach flip-flopped. "Shit," I said aloud, just before Irina pounded on the door. Sunny opened it before I could tell her not to.

"I thought I would find you here," she said to Dmitri, striking a pose in the center of my braided rug.

"Irina." He sighed. "What the Hex do you want from me?"

"Nothing from you," she snapped. "But from *you*." She pointed one French-tipped finger at me. "You made promise. Have you delivered?"

"No," I said honestly. "The one chance I had to stop the daemon blood is at the bottom of Siren Bay, probably in very small pieces. Hey, there's an idea. You could always dive in and look for it. Without oxygen."

"You have failed," said Irina. "Dmitri, come on. The pack will deal with this Insoli whore."

What was it with people calling me a bitch and a whore today? I was beginning to feel a lot like the former. I started to stand, to tell Irina to get the Hex out of my house and follow it up with force, when Dmitri spoke. "I don't have to go anywhere, Irina."

"What?" She devolved into rapid-fire Ukrainian, and Dmitri sighed.

"Irina, shut up. Just shut your mouth for once in your goddamn life." He grabbed his T-shirt and stripped it off, hissing a little with the same jerky movement from the hospital.

Sunny said, "Hex me," and I couldn't even manage that. Dmitri's right shoulder was one solid bruise, the cloud-colored purple and blue of a stormy sky, with twin weeping red marks at the center. A bite. A were bite.

Irina slapped a hand over her mouth. "Dmitri . . ."

"I'm no pack leader anymore, suspended or active," Dmitri told her quietly. "So leave, Irina. Run on home to Sergei and Yelena."

I recognized the humiliation bite for what it was—a mark not intended to harm, just to scar and let any other were know that the bearer had been demoted, in no uncertain terms. It's the equivalent of pinning a sign on someone who gets fired that says I CAN'T HACK IT.

"Oh seven hells," I groaned. "Dmitri, this wasn't necessary . . ."

Irina's sob cut me off. She *broke,* right there in front of me, and I saw the same wash of deep-seated betrayal that I'm sure had played out on my own face when she snuggled up to Dmitri outside Bete Noire. Hands shaking, her face lily white, she hissed at us, her lips drawing back over rapidly phasing fangs. "You . . . didn't . . . tell . . . me . . ."

"Why would I?" said Dmitri. "You would have just tried to talk me out of it."

"I'm your *mate!*" she screamed at him. I had thought about hurting Irina so often over the past week. So sure I'd be gratified to see her brought down to where I was living in these Dmitri-less days.

But I wasn't. I felt rotten, and embarrassed for her.

"I'm not your mate," said Dmitri. "I'm with Luna, and that's the way it should be."

Sunny, who had watched the entire thing silently but with ever-growing eyes, took Irina by the arm. "I think it would be best if you left now, Irina. For everyone." She took her out to her car and I waited until she'd driven away before I rounded on Dmitri.

"You left, and I realized you'd gone to find a way to cure me," said Dmitri. "And I knew Irina would never, ever do that. So I decided where I had to go, and I went to Sergei and he courted me out of the pack."

"Are you Insoli now?" asked Sunny in a small voice. It was good she could talk because the only thing that would have come out of my mouth was yelling.

"No," said Dmitri. "I'm still Redback, just . . . lower. I can be dominated, so it'll behoove me to stay out of the Nocturne pack's way for a while." He turned to me, took both of my hands in his. "That's where you come in."

"Dmitri," I whispered. "I wasn't asking you to do this."

"No, you weren't," he said. "But I'm willing and able, all the same. If you won't change for me, Luna . . . I guess it's up to me to do so for you."

Part of me said to let him go, release him, tell him I wasn't worth it. The much bigger part was complete again, hungering to have Dmitri back beside me. I hugged him hard, and he squeezed me in return. "I have to get some stuff from the safe house, then I'll be back, okay? I'll be staying as long as you'll have me."

"This will never work," I said, but I couldn't help but smile. "This is going to be so hard."

"Probably," said Dmitri. "But I don't really give a fuck anymore." He kissed me. "Back soon, babe."

I knew that there would be repercussions, that the pack elders of the Redbacks would never let an ex-pack leader and an Insoli live in peace for long. But at that moment, I believed Dmitri, so I let go of his hand

and told him, "Don't be long." And I let myself believe that when he walked out, he'd be back.

It took a month for my arm to heal. Were healing is great for scrapes and cuts but lousy on broken bones. Dr. Northgate didn't notice—he was amazed I was even alive after my plunge off the Siren Bay Bridge. I didn't tell him that I felt much the same way.

And I didn't tell anyone that I no longer felt that gaping presence in my mind, that edge always beckoning to me. Dr. Merriman might think she'd had something to do with my improvement, and I couldn't let that happen.

My first shift back on the job after Seamus had died and my med leave ended, I went through the motions of writing up the paperwork that had accumulated while I recovered, and waited for the inevitable. Forty-five minutes after I'd sat down at my desk, Matilda Morgan appeared in the squad room door. "Detective Wilder, my office. Now."

I went in expecting to get fired. I'd flaunted every protocol the department had laid out, I'd gotten my partner taken hostage, and I'd been nothing but a hostile little bitch where Captain Morgan was concerned. At least, I figured, I'd take it with some dignity. Hell, I wouldn't even scream or break anything.

"Detective," said Morgan, "I just need to say one thing. You are the worst law-enforcement officer I have ever commanded."

Well, that was par for the course. Captain Roenberg had thought the same thing.

"I'm sorry to hear that, ma'am," I murmured, waiting for the speech that ended with *Turn in your badge and gun.*

"You are also the best detective," said Morgan. "And by far the most tenacious. By far."

I blinked at her. I was honestly at a loss for words, and that disconcerted the hell out of me.

"You'll be pleased to know that Shelby survived her ordeal with aplomb," said Morgan. "In fact, there's a former O'Halloran security employee in intensive care right now, thanks to her efforts in freeing herself and the other hostages."

Good for Shelby. She wasn't the ice-princess, shrinking-violet cop I'd first met. Maybe I could allow myself to think I was a bad influence.

"Get back to work," said Morgan, "and please try not to kill anyone for at least a week."

"Ma'am, I . . ." I said. I couldn't think of a single adequate response to Morgan's words. She was letting me back on the job. I think she might have even *complimented* me. Gods, if all I had to do to get administrative approval was dive off a bridge, I'd be doing it twice a week.

"Thank you for your attention, Detective. Dismissed." She waved me out of her office, and I think as I shut the door she may have given me a tiny smile. But then again, I probably imagined that part.

At my desk I stared at my overdue case report, the blinking cursor mirroring my heartbeat. I was a homicide detective again. No one was looking over my shoulder for a reason to get rid of me.

I could do my job.

"You know what this desk needs?" said Shelby,

dropping her bag next to my keyboard and sitting on the edge of my desk. "Plants. Big, leafy, smelly flowering plants. Don't you think that would liven things up?"

I could have hugged Shelby, but I decided that might destroy my reputation as a tough and heartless were, so I just grinned. "Nice to see you not-tied-up."

"Nice to see you not-dead." She grinned back.

I stopped smiling when I realized what had happened to her on that day. "I'm sorry about your uncle."

Shelby's mouth twisted downward. "Don't be. I'm not. He's been a shadow over my entire life and I for one am glad the bastard is dead." She picked at the stitching on her bag, which was probably made somewhere in Italy and cost more than a year's maintenance for the Fairlane. I still hadn't been able to afford to get that damn headlight fixed.

"Then I'm glad you're okay," I said. "I saw that video and I . . . well. I was worried."

Shelby flipped a hand. "That guy Seamus had watching us was a joke. I played that 'Oh, I'm so sick and thirsty' routine, and gave him big eyes. Jerkoff never knew what hit him."

I laughed. It was good to see Shelby as a normal woman and not as a family-oriented robot. I imagined this was what she'd been like before her father had died.

"I owe you an apology too," said Shelby, looking at her hands.

"Why's that?" I asked. "Steal lip gloss out of my bag? Try on my shoes?"

"I've been lying to you," said Shelby, and her expression was so serious I thought someone had died all over again. "I *am* a recent transfer," she said reluctantly. "But not to Homicide."

My heart plummeted to somewhere in the vicinity of my stomach. "To where, then?"

Shelby sighed. "I'm with Internal Affairs."

You know that expression "Knock me over with a feather"? Well, screw the feather because I had just been hit by a Mack truck. "You're IAB?" I whispered. "What the Hex are you doing here?"

"Morgan requested an undercover officer to partner with you," said Shelby. "To assess the viability of kicking you off the force."

That witch. After she had just paid me a backhanded compliment too. I was about to unload my uncensored feelings about Morgan and Shelby when I realized something: I still had a job. Rick wasn't escorting me out the front door with a cardboard box full of my things.

"You gave me a good report," I said to Shelby, gobsmacked all over again.

Shelby smiled. "It's not everyone who will go toe to toe with my uncle for me."

"Hex it," I muttered. "Shelby, I've said so many terrible things about you . . ."

"Never mind that now," she said, picking up her bag. "I really just came by to tell you I'm taking a leave of absence from the department. And that it'll probably be permanent."

"Why?" I demanded, standing up as she did. "You're a great cop! You can't leave just because you feel guilty about spying on me or some ridiculous thing like that."

She laughed once. "Don't take it too personally,

okay, Luna? I still have obligations to my family. They need me. The Nocturne City PD doesn't. It's as simple as that."

I did hug her then, and she embraced me, prim and short, just like the rest of her. "Don't be a total stranger, okay?" I said.

"Will do," said Shelby. "See you around, Luna."

"See you," I said. I watched her leave the squad room, then sat down at my desk and got back to work.

After my shift was over, I drove home and found a single light shining from the kitchen window of the cottage, just like it used to when Sunny lived there.

Dmitri greeted me with a grin instead of a mug of tea, but he was just as welcome. "I've been waiting for you, Ms. Working Woman. Did you bring your handcuffs?"

After a month, having Dmitri around most of the time was still extremely weird. I hadn't seen him during the last phase, and now the moon was waxing again, within three or four nights of full.

"Is that all you think about?" I asked as I put my new gun and shield in the entry table drawer and locked it.

"Pretty much," said Dmitri, pulling me close. "I just want to get some quality time in before I take off for the phase, if you know what I mean."

"Dmitri." I pushed him away and held him at arm's length. "Stay."

"No." He shook his head instantly. "I'm too unpredictable, Luna. With the daemon bite, I just don't know what could happen. I black out totally now when the moonphase comes. I could hurt you."

I took his wrists and looked into his eyes. He wasn't

going to wriggle out of this. "You've never hurt me before."

"I wasn't a monster before," he whispered. Hot sadness flooded through me. *This* was what he thought of himself, of us? I took his face between my hands.

"Dmitri, you are *not* a monster."

"So you say," he muttered.

"I do," I agreed. "Deep down, you know it too. And I say you're going to stay. I'm not afraid of the daemon bite. I'm not afraid of you."

"Maybe you should be," Dmitri murmured.

"Maybe." I shrugged. "But I still want you to stay."

His jaw worked like he wanted to object, but finally he wrapped his arms around me, pressing me against his chest so I could hear his heart beating. "You're the most damn stubborn woman I've ever known, do you realize that?"

"I do," I said, "and I know you wouldn't want me any other way."

Dmitri took me by the wrist and opened the front door. "Come here." He led me out onto the drive and we both basked under the moon, letting it fill us and tantalize us with the promise of the phase. "This is you and me," Dmitri whispered. "No matter what. You and me, Luna. I promise."

It was sweet of him to try and reassure me, really, but as I leaned against Dmitri's solid body, saying a silent prayer to the bright lady for Vincent Blackburn and all the nameless, faceless victims that Seamus had claimed, I knew the only certainty we had was that we didn't know anything the future might hold. No one could promise me a happy ending, not even Dmitri.

But I'd face the unknown as I always had, and with Dmitri's help, I'd be able to do it with my eyes open.

"Luna?" Dmitri said. "You okay?"

"Fine," I murmured, looking out over the ocean. "Let's go inside."

"Something on your mind?" Dmitri asked mischievously.

I kissed him, and let him lead me back to the cottage. "No. I just want to enjoy the time we have."

Turn the page for a sneak peek at the next
NOCTURNE CITY novel, *Second Skin*

My cell phone buzzed against my hip. The Caller ID blinked DMITRI. "Hold on," I instructed Bryson, who was standing obstinately in front of my car with a hang-dog look.

"This bed is awfully big without you in it." Dmitri's voice sounded like dark red wine spilled on pale skin, Eastern Europe blended up with clove smoke.

"Hi, honey," I said flatly. Bryson gave me the eye, like I'd just started speaking in Esperanto.

"Do you know what I wanna do to you right now? I'd start between your thighs . . ."

"Sure, no problem. Gotta go." I slapped the phone shut and jerked open my door. "The answer is still no, Bryson." I turned the Fairlane's engine over with a roar. "Either get out of my way or be my speed bump."

"It's weres!" Bryson yelled at me. "Dead weres! Four of them so far!"

I hit the gas and squealed out of the motor-pool lot before he could finish, leaving him in a trail of my exhaust.

At home, I unlocked the front door of the cottage softly. The sky was still light at the very edges, over the water, pink and frayed like glimpsing silk through a torn skirt. "Dmitri, you awake?" I called. It was a courtesy. Dmitri could scent me as soon as I stepped out of the car in the little circular driveway that pushed up against my broken-down rental cottage on the edge of the dune.

"Up here." He didn't sound husky and pleasant anymore. I kicked off my flip-flops and climbed up the stairs to the bedroom rather more slowly than a woman coming home to her sexier-than-anything were-boyfriend who had given up his pack and his entire life to warm her bed. Not nearly as fast. Not nearly.

"Hey," I said, sticking my head around the door. "Thanks for waiting up for me."

The lights were off, but I didn't have a problem seeing Dmitri wrapped in nothing at all atop my sheets. It was stuffy in the room, stale and unpleasant, and I sneezed.

"If you're sick, do me a favor and don't spread it around."

"Oh, gee. Hex you too." I sat down on the edge of the bed and slipped out of my sweats, rolling over to lie next to Dmitri. He shoved me away. "Get off. It's too hot."

"Oh, *gods*," I hissed at him. "Look, I'm sorry. I was tied up when you called and I came straight home to apologize. I didn't realize that tonight was the night we both acted like twelve-year-olds."

There was silence for a long time, and I listened to Dmitri breathe and smelled his sweat mixed in with beer and a little bit of soap. "I'm sorry too," he said finally. "Just . . . I heard someone else's voice, and I assumed . . ."

"Sweetie." I took his hand in the dark. "My captain is a man. I work with four guys. Hell, even my manicurist has a penis."

He stiffened again. "Was that your manicurist I heard on the call?"

"No," I said, moving my free hand over his stomach, fingers scrubbing in small circles. I stopped, thinking about the desperate way Bryson had followed me.

"Who was it, Luna?" Dmitri sucked in his breath.

"It doesn't matter. It was nobody I want to keep thinking about."

He jerked away from me and sat up with a snarl. "Tell me who was fucking there with you! I can smell him all over your skin!"

I sat up too, rod-straight, and we quivered silently with our backs turned to each other. "It was David Bryson," I said. "He accosted me in the locker room after I was washing the blood spatter from a suicide jumper off of me, and he followed me out to my car and I have had a really *shitty* gods-damned night, by the way, so thanks for asking and you have sweet dreams."

I snatched my pillow and the blanket from the bed and started to storm out, but noticed just before I reached the door that my pillow case was decorated with blood droplets.

Those hadn't been there when I'd left for work. "Dmitri?" I said.

He rolled over with a snarl. "Oh no," I exclaimed, grabbing him by the shoulder and rolling him back toward me. "What on earth . . ."

His face was puffy at the jaw and his left eye was blackened and scraped on the orbital bone. The cuts were already healed over, but the old blood remained. I reached over Dmitri and turned on the bedside lamp, bumping his side as I did so. He hissed in pain when I brushed his ribs.

"Okay," I said, as I surveyed the cut lip, the array of bruises on his torso, and fresh scars on his knuckles. "Don't tell me. You went down to the slaughterhouse and beat up some meat, and the meat won."

"Funny," he muttered. "Real funny."

Guilt sucker-punched me. "I'm sorry. I didn't see . . . What happened? I'm sorry we fought." My words tumbled like gangly things, not sure of their legs. "I'm sorry," I mumbled again.

"No big deal," Dmitri said, throwing a hand over his eyes. "Just a misunderstanding."

I got off the bed and walked around to his side, and stood over him with my hands on my hips, glaring, until he rolled his eyes. "Bleeding all over the house?" I said. "That pretty much defines 'Big Deal.' Who did this to you?"

Dmitri sighed. "I walked down a street I thought was safe, and it wasn't. Territory had shifted. I got jumped."

"By what, a Transformer?" I said. The bruising was bad. Dmitri was tough, and big, and had daemon-powered blood running in him, a bite that turned him from were to something else whenever he got too angry or too . . . anything. The bite made him black out and a host of other unpleasantries, but it also made him damn near invulnerable. This shouldn't have happened.

"Six or seven weres from some pack running things on Cannery Street now," he said. "They came up on me fast, had baseball bats, mostly. I think one had one of

those police batons. Anyway. I knew you'd freak out so
I thought we could discuss it after I healed."

"This shouldn't have happened," I said out loud.
"You weren't doing anything wrong. You don't even
have pack status anymore. What would they gain
from beating you?" I bit my lip. "*How* did they beat
you?"

I was babbling like a cop, trying to work through the
permutations and find the conclusion, close the case.
Dmitri showed his teeth. "I disrespected them." His
fists worked. "They were within their rights, fucked up
as it is. You wouldn't understand."

"*I* wouldn't understand?" I demanded, my old anger
coming back.

"You've never had to deal with pack law," said Dmitri.
"You get off easy whenever you run into territorial bor-
ders because you're so damn willful. I just hope you
never hit on a pack with a better hand at dominating other
weres than you."

"Gee, thanks for the thought," I snapped. Silence
again for a minute, while we both tried to stay calm. Finally, I tamped down my frustration and got myself under control. I was getting good at that, lately. "Do you
need an ice pack?"

"No."

"I still don't understand why you got into a fight in
the first place," I said. "Can't you just back off, accept
that they're dominant?" I knew that you could, from
experience.

"I could," Dmitri said, his eyes swimming with
black. "But I didn't."

Oh, Hex it. My skin was full of thorn-pricks in that

moment, as the air around me grew cold. "Dmitri. What did you do to those weres?"

His eyes were full black now, the daemon blood coming even as we sat there, calm. "Nothing they didn't deserve."

My own were instincts snarled *Get away*, but Dmitri lunged across the bed and grabbed me before I could move. He was so much faster with the daemon bite . . .

One hand held the side of my face. The other traced down my body, rough palm on my bare skin. Over my hips, past the V of my thighs. My body responded to him, but my brain was busy thinking *Oh shit* as I stared into his black eyes.

"Dmitri," I said softly. "Tell me what you did."

His hand stopped moving, just shy of its goal. "I didn't want to," he said, in a voice so small and wounded I wasn't even sure it was his. "I was gonna walk away but one of them said something about my mate . . . about you. They knew who I was, who you were, and I . . ."

I shut my eyes, all of the fear and tension running out, leaving me rubbery.

"I have no standing in the Redbacks," said Dmitri. "If they got through me to you, I could do nothing. So when I felt it, the darkness coming on . . . I let it take me."

He'd let go of me, and I caught him this time, wrapped my arms around him. "I'm sorry," I whispered. "I'm sorry."

"You shouldn't be around me now," Dmitri said roughly. He put us at arm's length. "I just . . . I need to just forget."

"No," I said. "You need to not be alone. And this

city needs not to have were packs running loose. Gods-
damned animals."

"Luna, the packs . . . it's just the way things are."
Dmitri sighed. "Times change. The packs have been
jumpier than ever since that O'Halloran thing, and your
department choking out the drugs and brothels downtown hasn't helped either. You want to do something,
tell Vice to ease off." He found a pair of shorts and put
them on, and crawled under the sheet. "Please. Just go
and let me heal."

"Don't do this," I gritted. "After what you just told
me . . . *please* don't shut down on me."

Dmitri didn't answer, just gave a long shuddering
sigh as his body tried to work through the daemon inside it and the injuries without.

After another long quiet minute, I went downstairs
before I said something bitchy and insensitive.

On the sofa, I lay in high dudgeon for a long time,
making myself be as still as possible except for breathing until the urge to tear and hurt had died down to a
level where I wouldn't rip the neck out of the first person to cross my path.

The were had a lot of trouble staying at bay in me
sometimes, but I had a lot of experience keeping it in.

One thing was as clear as the bruises and the blood on
Dmitri's body—whatever was in him was getting
stronger, and the man I'd met was slipping away. Something cold and black as Dmitri's eyes uncoiled in my gut
at the thought, the whisper that one day I'd wake up next
to a stranger, who killed without a thought and didn't
know the difference between me and prey.

Also clear was the fact that I wasn't going anywhere,

even though the thought of seeing Dmitri change made me sick.

"Shouldn't this be easier by now?" I asked the darkness. Dmitri had tossed away his future with the Redbacks to be here with me, when his pack elders had forbidden us from being together. He'd chosen *me*. That should be enough. Should be, but that awful black thing was still there, laughing at me.

ACKNOWLEDGMENTS

Thanks as always to Rachel Vater, my fabulous agent, and Rose Hilliard, my lovely editor at St. Martin's Press.

To Team Seattle—Richelle, Kat, Cherie, and Mark. Thanks for helping me keep my sanity (mostly).

Thanks, Mom and Hal, for giving me a place to stay while I wrote *Pure Blood* and for being a supportive and understanding family.

Agent Heidi Wallace of the ATF remains a peerless source for firearms knowledge and law enforcement procedure. Any errors are mine, not hers.

Most of all, thanks belong to all of my readers, who love Luna and Nocturne City as much as I do, and interact with me on a daily basis on my blog. Keep reading, and I'll keep writing.

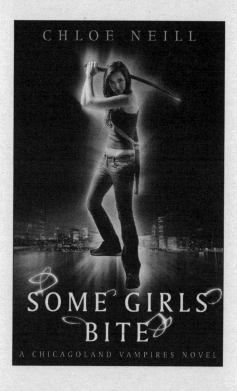

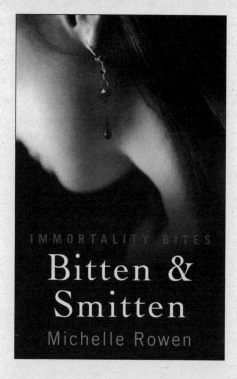

Caitlin Kittredge is an author by night and a mild-mannered game designer by day. She lives in Massachusetts with comic books, cats, and tea. Though somewhat reclusive, she can be lured out of hiding by antique books, cult films, and good music. When not writing, she's most often haunting thrift stores for vintage clothes, reading obscure history books, or plotting world domination.

Learn more about Caitlin Kittredge at:
www.caitlinkittredge.com